September Comes In

by

FRANCES MARGARET McGUIRE

HEINEMANN

LONDON MELBOURNE TORONTO

William Heinemann Ltd

LONDON MELBOURNE TORONTO
CAPE TOWN AUCKLAND
THE HAGUE

First published 1961
© by Margaret McGuire 1961

Printed in Great Britain
by The Windmill Press
Kingswood, Surrey

Contents

BOOK ONE

1 The New House, June 1901   3

2 The Garden   9

3 A Royal Occasion   24

4 Visits   30

5 Spring Weather   46

6 Family Life   56

7 The Dinner Party   63

8 The Cauliflower   90

9 Across the River, 1902   98

10 Lily Lees   108

11 The Moreton Bay Fig Tree   115

12 Come Winter   120

13 The Coach Journey   130

14 The Picnic   144

15 The Storm   157

BOOK TWO

16 Defence of the Weak, 1904   173

17 The Goddess of Fortune   184

18 The Continental   192

19 The Ogre, 1910   201

20 The Ball, 1913   223

21 The Return of the Goddess, 1914   241

22 The Goddess Looks On   252

23 Ebb-Tide   265

24 High-Tide, 1915   273

25 Shadow of the Goddess   281

26 September Comes In   292

Grey Winter hath gone, like a wearisome guest,
    And, behold, for repayment,
September comes in, with the wind of the West
    And the Spring in her raiment!

HENRY KENDALL

Book One

I

The New House, June 1901

ELIZABETH had never before seen the sea. It stretched in front of her now, like a silver tray on the dining-room table, polished and flat; and the sun stood upright on its edge. Elizabeth had never seen the sun that way up before either. At home it was always high over your head like an umbrella and much too bright and hot to look at unless someone gave you a piece of glass with smoke on it. The smoke generally came off on your nose and made black streaks on your hands and clothes. But no one seemed to mind because when you were allowed to do that it was a special occasion called an 'eclipse' and the sun looked like a half-sovereign. But this sun was bigger – as big as half-a-crown or as big as a soup-plate. It made Elizabeth think of the soldier and the tinder-box and the dog with eyes as big as saucers, and the dog with eyes as big as cartwheels, and the dog with eyes as big as windmills, guarding the piles of gold.

All the sand was gold and it went for miles and miles down that way to the purple cliffs, and miles and miles down that way to nothing at all. From Elizabeth to the sun was a golden path. Whenever Elizabeth moved the path moved too, up and down the sand, always stretching between her and the sun: a golden path, quite solid and real, across the silver tea-tray of the sea.

Along the sand Elizabeth moved, trying to dodge the path, pretending to go one way and suddenly going the opposite

3

way; but the path was always too quick for her; she could never surprise it.

Where the dry sand joined the wet sand were myriads of shells, jostled into piles and swept fan-wise into curves by the tide. Elizabeth discovered that in spite of their almost microscopic size each shell was of distinctive colour and design: trumpets of coral and Chinaman's hats of chrome and henna; pearl-white fans and purple buttons and black cups lined with turquoise and rimmed with ivory. She picked up handfuls of them and put them in her handkerchief, but Miss Una said, 'Throw them down again, dear, they're that dirty and smelly! You'll be able to play with them every day. You'll soon be tired of them.'

Elizabeth found that the shells, so clean and exquisite on the beach, became dull and rank as soon as she picked them up. But in the rest of her prophecy Miss Una was wrong, for Elizabeth never grew tired of looking at them and always wondered how anyone could create something at once so small and so perfect in design.

The sun had ceased to be round like a soup-plate and was getting hotter and hotter and melting on to the edge of the sea; and the golden path was spreading wider and wider, trembling and breaking at the edges.

'Come back to the house,' said Miss Una. 'It's getting late.'

They plodded through the thick white sand, up on to the sandhills covered with grey grass. It was not like ordinary grass. It had blades nearly as tall as Elizabeth, made of satin on one side and velvet on the other. It had a sweet, salty perfume, rather like the shells. Elizabeth tried to pick some, but it was too tough and cut her fingers.

On the top of the hill Elizabeth turned round to look at the sun once more and found, to her surprise, that it had almost disappeared. The golden path was quite gone, and the sea was as dark as the silver tray when it hadn't been cleaned for a

long time. There were clouds in the sky which had not been
anywhere about a few minutes before. They were covered with
blood-red down and lined with purple. Far away were the hills,
not the little sandhills of the beach, but the true hills which lay
between the coast and the great plains of the north and east.
That was where they had all come from, Miss Una said, when
the train brought them to the seaside. Far away in the north
lay the plains of Undaboo where all her life had been and
where she had known no horizons but those of salt bush and
the opalescent crags of the Flinders Range.

'Hurry,' said Miss Una, 'we'll be late for tea.'

They ran down the last slope and the metal of the road was
firm under their feet.

It was nearly dark when they reached the new house. Elizabeth had not had time to look at the house, for she had been
sent out to the beach with Miss Una soon after they arrived
from the train. They had been driven from the train in a four-
wheeled cab with two horses, by a man with a limp moustache
and melancholy eyes. He kept whipping up the horses with a
long-handled whip, not at all like the whips Elizabeth was
accustomed to, which had very short handles and yards and
yards of lash. This whip seemed to her all handle and no lash
at all, and the horses ignored it, neither jerking their heads nor
increasing their pace. The driver whipped them every minute
or so, but always carefully replaced the whip in an iron socket
which held it upright. Elizabeth watched the ritual several
times and came to the conclusion that it was an empty formal-
ism, except perhaps in the summer when the whip might
serve to disturb the more nervous of the flies that settled on
the horses' rumps.

The cab, piled high with luggage, trundled along the white-
metalled road and turned in at a driveway guarded by a pair
of rather dilapidated iron gates. The drive was hardly more
than a semi-circular sweep of gravel to skirt an enormous

monkey-puzzle tree which over-topped even the second storey of the house.

Elizabeth had only a glimpse of shrubberies and paddocks before she was following her mother and Miss Una into the house, and Elsa was bringing Eleanor and Marian up the front steps. Elsa was one of their own aborigines of the Undaboo tribe. She had been baptised by a zealous Lutheran missionary who had given her a name more suited to a Gretchen of his native Bavaria than to a plum-hued maiden of the Australian bush. Elsa would stay with the children till they were settled and in some measure reconciled to their new home. To leave her behind had been more than the ties of affection could support.

Inside the house Father was telling the men where to put the cases. There were sounds of hammering and the heavy tramp of boots on the ceilings. Mother was asking: 'Are all the carpets laid yet?' And Aunt Emma Woodstock was answering: 'Yes, we got them down yesterday. And if Elsa will just take those children down to the beach for a couple of hours it will give us a chance to get the beds made. They can have their tea when they get back.'

But Mother had not been inclined to send Elsa with the three children, for none of them had ever seen the sea and they might be capable of any folly in the first excitement of so stupendous a novelty. In the end it had been Elizabeth alone who was taken by Miss Una, while eight-year-old Eleanor had volunteered to 'unpack' and six-year-old Marian 'to help'. By the time tea was set in the little room under the stars Eleanor and Marian were quite familiar with the new house and Eleanor in her grown-up manner undertook to show Elizabeth the way and to take her hand in the shadows of the passage.

To Elizabeth the house seemed enormous. Of course, home at Undaboo was big. It took you quite a long time to go from the front hall to the kitchen. But at Undaboo the house was bigger outside than in, spread out flat on one level, with sprawling verandas on three sides. This house was bigger inside than out. It was all piled up on itself with ceilings that lay in the shadow of distance above your head and a staircase that curved up into the uttermost darkness. Elizabeth had never seen a staircase before, except today at the railway station. This house was rather like a railway station, she thought, as she ate her egg, except that the bread and butter was nicer and the smell was different. But all the smells here were different.

'Mother says that Eleanor and me are going to school to-morrow,' said Marian, cutting her bread and butter into very elegant small pieces.

'You should say, "Eleanor and I", corrected Eleanor. ' "Me" isn't grammar.'

'But it's me who's going,' protested Marian; 'Mother said so.'

'I know it's you, silly. But you should say, "I am going", not, "Me is going" '.

'I don't see why.'

'Because it isn't grammar.'

'What's grammar?'

'Now then, you children,' said Miss Una, 'don't argue.'

Elizabeth had taken very little interest in this discussion. The word 'school' meant nothing to her, and she was used to Eleanor and Marian planning to do things beyond her comprehension. But Miss Una's injunction at once challenged her attention.

'Why?' she demanded.

'Because it isn't manners,' said Miss Una. Elizabeth knew that was final. Manners were one of the absolutes. When you grew up you acquired Manners, and till then the significance of life was wrapt in the mystery and effort of that attainment. She churned the yellow part of her egg with the spoon till it oozed out in viscid globules on to the rim of the egg-cup. Grammar was, apparently, another absolute. When you grew up you had Manners and Grammar. Grammar was a nice word like the thick toffee they bought at Mr Henderson's store which

7

stuck to your teeth and made your jaws tired when you chewed it. Manners and Grammar: rather like each other, but Grammar was thicker than Manners; twin sisters, one thin and one fat, walking along the road and just turning the corner when you chased them. Elizabeth could see them; she wanted very much to catch them so that she could grow up. She ran harder and harder, but the two little girls were always just as far away, though they did not seem to move; and the road was all gold. At the bottom of the road the sun stood up on end. The sun grew redder and redder and ran out on to the sea like the yolk of egg spilling out of the shell on to the rim of the egg-cup . . .

'Well, this is a nice mess!' exclaimed Miss Una. 'You've spilt egg all down your bib. Bless me, the child's asleep!'

2

The Garden

T H E camels were ploughing the sand. The canvas-covered packs swayed and sish-swished to the rhythm of the squelching sand. The north wind sang through the telegraph wires, blowing the sand in horizontal lines against the galvanised iron. Sish-swish, went the sand under the doors, trickling in red rivulets through the crevices and meshes of the wire screens. Sish-swish-swoosh, went the train, racing the north winds across the plains of Undaboo and leaving the Flinders far behind. Sish-swish, sish-swish-swoosh.

'I do wish Beth would wake up,' said Marian.

'I am awake,' said Elizabeth, opening her eyes.

Marian was standing half dressed beside the bed. She turned herself round.

'These are my new bloomers,' she said.

'What for?' said Elizabeth.

'Because I'm going to school, of course,' said Marian.

'What do you have to have bloomers for going to school for?' said Elizabeth. Marian was at a loss and not for the first time wondered why Elizabeth had to know the reason for everything. She herself never asked questions. The effort of pulling on long, new stockings of black cashmere required Eleanor's tongue to protrude and be firmly held by her front teeth, but she withdrew it for a moment to clinch the discussion.

'No one wears drawers at school,' she pronounced and snapped a garter into place.

Feeling that Jove had spoken, Elizabeth pushed back the bedclothes, turned over on her front and slid out of bed. Her own clothes, neatly folded by Miss Una the previous night, were on a chair beside the bed. She picked up her white calico drawers and looked at them with new interest. Just then Elsa came in.

'My word, lil' Miss Marian, you a fine big grown-up girl now in them fine blooms. Come on, 'lil Miss Beth, time for wash.'

'You haven't brought my water,' said Elizabeth.

'No bring-um water now, lil' Miss Beth. Fine new bathroom in this house. Plenty water alonga fine new pipes. More bigger dams in this place than Undaboo. Plenty big water.'

Elizabeth suffered herself to be led into the bathroom where she was at once infected with Elsa's enthusiasm. The room had a leaden floor, the soft metal rolled into a ridge round the walls; one corner was occupied by an enormous built-in bath of grey cement, presided over by a gas-fed water-heater that towered to the ceiling. It was polished like gold except where little green lines showed the joins of pipes and taps. Elizabeth had never seen anything so grand in her life. She tried to read the raised-up lettering in gold on the front but could only recognise 'bath'. She knew that because Marian had taught her to read it on the mat. If you turned it one way it read BATH MAT, but if you turned it over the words became TAM HTAB, with the B the wrong way round. It was TAM HTAB at present because Eleanor and Marian had had their baths and had made it wet, so Elsa turned it over to the dry side.

Like Elsa, Elizabeth was chiefly delighted with the number and intricacy of the water-pipes. At home there had been only one, which, it was evident to even the four-year-old intelligence, was fed by the tank outside. Here there were taps galore, two for the basin, two for one end of the bath and two near the heater, as well as the shower; and pipes that travelled in a bewildering network across floor, walls and ceiling. Certainly the people who built this house could have had little fear of drought.

Elsa and Elizabeth turned on all the taps. The shower came down in a rain of arrows and all the pipes gurgled at once. Elizabeth put in the plug of the basin which rapidly filled and overflowed on to the floor. Her night-gown was saturated and clung to her with soggy affection. She pulled out the plug and the water ran away again. Miss Una came in.

'Oh, my gracious goodness! Elsa, turn off those taps. Well, I never did! You're nothing but naughty children, the pair of you.'

Elsa's grin disappeared. She rubbed her woolly head with a damp and rueful hand. She looked at the brimming basin and the pools of water on the floor and the grin returned.

'My word, Miss Una,' she said. 'Plenty fine water!'

'Well, you get Miss Beth bathed and dressed quick and lively and bring her down to breakfast. Or else there'll be ructions.'

As ructions were to be avoided at all cost, these commands were obeyed without further delay and Elizabeth was conducted to the stairs landing. She had no recollection of ascending the stairs, for she had been asleep when her father had carried her up the previous night. But looking now at their winding depth, at the precipitance of their steps, she had no desire to go down. She clung to Elsa's hand.

'But, lil' Miss Beth, you won't get hurt. These'm stairs plurry safe, you bet.' Elsa had been forbidden to say 'plurry' in front of the children, but the need for emphasis overcame her discretion.

Elizabeth said nothing. She clung to Elsa's hand and dragged back harder than ever.

'Well, I must say,' said Miss Una bitingly, 'I didn't think a big girl like you would be such a scare-baby,' and she walked firmly and thumpingly down the stairs to demonstrate their stability.

'And how're you going to get breakfast, neither,' went on

Elsa, 'if you don't never go down them stairs no more?'

Elizabeth was conscious that she was now confronted with a problem that she alone could solve. She sat on the top step, and clutching the rungs of the balustrade with one hand and Elsa's skirts with the other, she propelled herself with a jerk from one step to the next on her tail. Miss Una stood at the bottom watching this procedure, her lips drawn into a thin line. When the last step had been negotiated, she said: 'Well, you'll have to get used to coming downstairs in the usual way or you won't have a decent pair of pants left to your name.'

'Then I can have blooms like Marian,' said Elizabeth.

'Sish-swish,' sang the north wind.

'Sish-swish,' sang the sand.

'Sish-swish-swoosh,' hummed the train.

'What's that noise?' asked Elizabeth.

'What noise?'

'That noise like a sand-storm, but it keeps going on all the time.'

'I can't hear any noise.'

'Listen!'

'Oh, you mean that noise? That's the sea, of course, silly.'

'Does it keep on doing it all the time?'

'Yes, of course it does. Sometimes much louder than that – when it's rough.'

'What's rough?'

'Why, when the wind blows the waves up big and makes them tumble about.'

'What happens then?'

'The ships rock up and down like your cradle.'

'As big as that?'

'Much bigger than that.'

'Big enough for me to get in?'

'Big enough for us all to get in.'

'Mummie and Daddy too?'

'Yes, mother and father too.'

'Will I see a ship?'

'I expect so, if you're good.'

'Do the ships have sails?'

'Of course they do. Don't you remember the picture of the ship in your Bible?'

'Will I be able to walk on the sea like Jesus?'

'No, of course not. The very idea!'

'Why not?'

'That's enough questions for now. You'd better eat your breakfast.'

'Can I say: "Forwhatwe'reabouttoreceive"?'

'Very well. Be quick.'

The monkey-puzzle had withdrawn nourishment from the soil so that the grass grew scantily under it and faded into patches of earth beaten hard with neglect. Beyond the area of gravel was a lawn where the grass grew rank, and sour-sops lifted themselves dewily from an undergrowth of dandelions and clover. Rain had fallen in the night. The clover was star-spangled with drops which hung mistily from the threads of cobweb between leaf and leaf. Elizabeth tried to pick up the cobwebs, but they were so fine that there was no tracing their origins and they dissolved into a silky dampness when she touched them.

In the house unpacking was at its height. There was no avoiding the medley of garments and toys and pictures and books and piles of crockery. A continual opening and shutting of drawers and cupboards was punctuated by a continual questioning: 'Where is the lid of this vegetable-dish? Where shall I put the Staffordshire tea-set?' with pauses for breath between unstrappings and unlockings and upliftings.

For a time Elizabeth enjoyed the spectacle of the erstwhile household gods reduced to helplessness and disorder; but being told to 'Run along and ask Mother where we are to put the spare linen,' and 'Beth, dear, take these baskets down to the kitchen,' she began to feel herself involved in the same servitude and was glad to go with her father into the garden.

Mr Inglefell eyed the overgrown lawn and pronounced its doom.

'That will have to be cut,' he said. 'Let's find the man. He's probably somewhere about.'

Where the lawn disappeared into a shrubbery on one side of the house, they found a man hoeing the paths.

'Ah,' said Mr Inglefell, 'you'll be Goldfinch, I take it.'

'That's right, sir,' said the man, lifting his cap not so much in salute as for the purpose of head-scratching. 'Frederick Arthur Goldfinch, but always known as Finch, sir, ever since me schooldays, and that's a fact.'

'Well, Finch,' went on Mr Inglefell, 'it looks as though we have some clearing up to do.'

'You're right there, sir,' said Finch, 'and that's a fact. A downright shame to let the place run back like this. But there, old Mr Burling was never known to spend money on himself, let alone a garden. When I heard you'd bought the place I thought to meself, you'd be just in time to save the fruit trees. But I don't know, sir, it's a bit late, really.' Finch leaned on his hoe and regarded the garden pensively. 'It's a bit late, that is, unless you're thinking of re-planting and starting all afresh-like.'

'That's something we must consider,' said Mr Inglefell. They began to walk slowly along the path, discussing the climate and the soil. Finch clumped up sods with his hoe to display the soil's sandiness, and Mr Inglefell prodded at trees and shrubs with his stick. Elizabeth trudged on behind, revelling in the simple joy of getting wet and knowing that she would not be reprimanded because she was 'with father'. Being 'with father' absolved one from all forms of guilt except 'bad words'.

This wetness was different from anything she had experienced before. At Undaboo the rain swept down in a sudden flood that filled the tanks and dams and hissed in muddy streams sucked down by the sand. The grass, forgotten for a year at a time, sprang into life overnight, and Sturt peas flamed a scarlet carpet over the desert. There were no trees except the she-oaks and gums along the creek, dragging out their drought-stricken lives from one flood to the next. Elizabeth knew about only one rain, which was the thunderstorm last February, because before that there had been a three-year drought, and before that she had been too little to remember. When it rained last February they had all been possessed by rain-madness and had run out to dance and shout under the pouring skies till they came to sufficient sanity to drag every available basin and bucket and bath-tub under the gorged gutterings and spouting pipes. No one was scolded for getting wet; the grown-ups were much too jubilant, counting up the inches in the dam depths and reckoning up the chances of the year's lambing. But, with the instinct of childhood, Elizabeth knew that 'getting wet' would now be one of those things that would make Miss Una click her tongue and Elsa exclaim: 'Oh, my golly, lil' Miss Beth, you'm in one fine mess, all right.'

The shrubbery ran out into a wide orangery. Here the grass was so long that it reached above Beth's knees, and so wet that her frock was stained with it. The orange trees, overgrown and neglected, met each other in their rows amid a density of foliage that obscured the sky. The branches bowed down with fruit and their burden of rain seemed doubly weighted by their own perfume and stood close-pressed upon the atmosphere.

'You'll have to have a citrus-doctor to this lot, sir,' said Finch. 'I'm not a bad hand at the pruning meself, but citrus-pruning is a nart on its own, and these is that far gone it'll take a nexpert to save 'em. If that.' He added with emphasis: 'Look at this 'ere heart wood.' He wrenched away a spray of paler, broader leaves. 'Fair criminal to let good trees run wild like this.'

Elizabeth thought the despised 'heart wood' the prettiest of all, the leaves were so broad and shining and smooth.

'What's the fruit like?' asked her father, and pulled down a branch on which hung six ripe oranges.

'Small but sweet. No quality in it. Can't expect that with a crop this size. Best get one of they tree-doctors, sir. The Aggy-cultural Department will send you one if you ask 'em. If he says prune, we prune, but if he says dig up, well, it'll be out she comes and that's all about it.'

Elizabeth was adding orange juice to her other dampness, but was mentally resolving to ask her father later what a tree-doctor was. It was difficult to imagine that trees could be ill, and how did the doctor manage about their temperatures and making them put out their tongues?

She ate oranges until her own tongue began to burn and her eyes to sting with the pungency of the oily skins. Her hands were yellow with syrup. She tried to shake some raindrops from the grass on to them, but this seemed only to increase their stickiness.

At the end of the orangery farthest from the house was a low wall, half fallen into ruin, which divided garden from paddocks. Beyond the wall stood sheds and sties and milking bales, familiar enough to be of interest to Elizabeth.

'Are there any pigs?' she asked, peering through a gap in the masonry. Finch shook his head. Indeed, the grass was as luxuriant between the flags of the sty floor as it was in the garden.

'I've arranged for a couple of cows to be put in here,' said Mr Inglefell, 'but I didn't know there were pig-sties.' He swung a leg over the wall and rubbed a hand critically along the beams of the sty. 'Looks clean enough, but we'll have it fumi-gated, just to be on the safe side. Then we'll put in a litter of young ones. They'll soon use up the skim milk.'

The orangery and the paddocks beyond were bordered by rows of trees, silhouetted gnarled and gaunt against the wintry sky. Watching them so motionless and stark, Elizabeth felt

herself growing sad and lonely. The exaltation of the morning and her enjoyment of the garden were lost as though in
some limitless space. She had felt this before, on the plains of
the north, especially in the early morning when the dawn wind
moved across a thousand miles of earth to ruffle the curtains
of her window. She had had some intuition of it yesterday on
those golden miles of sand when the sun had touched the rim
of the world and spilled out its gold upon the sea. It was the
ending of all things and the beginning of something beyond
them, and yet in which they were included. It fascinated and
frightened her and she resented it because it was outside her
powers of comprehension and control.

'Why don't you cut down all those ugly old trees?' she said
to her father. 'They are all dead.'

Mr Inglefell laughed. The gardener looked down at her. She
saw some quizzical expression in his blue eyes and felt suddenly
shy of having voiced her opinion.

'Those are almond trees,' said Mr Inglefell. 'They are alive
all right. They'll be covered with leaves as soon as the weather
gets warmer.'

'That's right, sir,' said Finch. 'And in another week or two
they'll be full of blossom and, my word, you'll think they're
real pretty then, little lady – a real marvellous sight they are,
with all of them white flowers and no mistake.'

Elizabeth said nothing. The almond trees were alive, but that
only increased the antagonism she felt to their bareness and
blackness. To be alive and yet so bereft of any sign of vitality –
that was to accentuate the feeling of abandonment and to leave
one suspended from familiar things.

The morning had dimmed and the sighing of the sea became
merged in the sound of the rain as it swept inland. Elizabeth
and her father hurried back to the house.

The room in which the children slept was long and narrow
and had a window looking out over part of the veranda roof.

Elizabeth could stand at this window and see right into the heart of the big pepper tree. The cats walked along the guttering of the roof outside or swayed on the overhanging branches of the pepper tree to jump with a thump on to the galvanised iron. They turned to stare at Elizabeth with round eyes, immovable and antagonistic, till urged by sudden necessity to tail-licking and leg-washing. On fine days they would curl into a furry cushion in an angle of the coping, or lie at full length in the sun in somnolent luxury. One of them, a muscular tabby Tom with yellow eyes and belly and tigerish black stripes round his body, came every morning while the children were dressing. At first he was aloofly contented to sit on the roof outside. One morning he sat on the window-sill and watched the children getting dressed till Miss Una came in and shished him out, banging down the window.

'Gives me the creeps to see that big beast sitting there,' she exclaimed. 'And those eyes! Staring at you while you're dressing. Seems hardly decent, somehow.'

Elizabeth had learnt that oblique tactics were better than direct action with Miss Una. She went into the breakfast-room where her mother was lying on a couch under the window. Her breakfast-tray was still on the little table beside her, but she had finished eating and was already at work on a fragment of fine sewing.

Elizabeth went to her side.

'Hullo, my mummie. Are you very well today?'

'Very well, thank you, darling. Mind the needle.'

'Do you think being at the seaside is going to make you very well every day now?'

'I think it might. Now that the unpacking is all done and we've settled down, I shall get better, I expect.'

'Will you be able to see the sea today?'

'Not today, darling. Next week, perhaps.'

'I've seen the sea. Poor mummie, I wish you could see the sea.'

'But I have. Ever so many times.'

'When, Mummie?'

'Years ago. I used to live by the sea then.'

'Was I born then?'

'Not then.'

'Why not?'

'Well – because you are only four years old, and it was much longer ago than that.'

'Did I only start being alive four years ago?'

'M-m. Mind while I thread this, darling.'

'What makes things start being alive?'

'Well, it's hard to explain, because even grown-up people don't really know.'

'Daddy and Mr Finch know. They said those trees outside would start being alive soon.'

'Trees? Oh, you mean the almond trees. But they are alive now. They only look dead because they haven't any leaves. Like people when they are asleep – they look dead but they are not really dead.'

'Are the arming trees asleep?'

'Yes. They always go to sleep in the winter.'

'Is that why they take off their leaves?'

'Y-yes, perhaps.'

'Pussies don't.'

'No. They have only one suit all the year round.'

'There's a very nice cat on our roof. He came up to the window.'

'Did he, darling? What colour is he?'

'He's got yellow eyes and yellow on his tum underneath. And black stripes on his back and a grey tail. He's very clean.'

Elizabeth looked to see how her mother would greet this recommendation.

'He sounds quite handsome.'

'Yes, and he's a very respecterful cat. Much bigger than Ginger and much cleaner.'

Elizabeth thought wistfully of the beloved but mangy Ginger whom parental authority had forbidden to be brought away from Undaboo.

'He lives on the roof outside our window,' she went on. 'I serspect he gets very lonely and hungry out on the roof by himself, don't you?'

'Perhaps he's used to it, darling. And his fur would keep him warm at night, don't you think so?'

'It would be nice if we could give him just a very small drink of milk.' There followed a short pause during which Elizabeth watched her mother's thin fingers turning down the new hem and inserting the needle. Then she added:

'When the cows come, Daddy says we'll have two gallons a day and be able to make butter. They're Jerseys.' Another pause, then. 'I dare say he wouldn't drink more than a very small saucerful.'

Her mother laughed in that sudden soft undertone which Elizabeth called her 'private laugh'.

'Well, tell Miss Una to give you an old saucer, only for heaven's sake don't lean too far out of the window.'

Miss Una grumbled a good deal about it.

'If you must feed the cats, why can't you do it on the back veranda instead of taking a lot of milk up to your bedroom and slopping it all over your window-sill.' She could not understand that, delightful though feeding cats was at all times, feeding them on a roof was an occupation that had something enchanting about it, like a rite of some mysterious cult full of suppressed excitement and joy. Eleanor was not fond of cats, but Marian was sufficiently caught by the novelty of the thing to lend her help. They put the saucer out on the roof and filled it up every evening from a little jug that Miss Una let them carry up from the tea-table. Elizabeth leaned out of the window as far as she could, with the bar of the window-frame pressing into her stomach and making her rather breathless, while Marian watched from behind and held her legs.

The big tabby Tom drank the milk, but remained aloof and impervious to all blandishments.

'He won't come near suscept when we aren't there,' complained Elizabeth to her mother. She secreted small pieces of meat and fish in her handkerchief to carry upstairs, feeling that stronger bribery was needed. Tabby Tom ate them coldly, but gave no other sign of interest or affection.

'Perhaps he is the cat who walks by himself,' said Mrs Inglefell.

'Who was him?' asked Elizabeth.

'Bring me that big red book, Marian, the one that's called *Just So Stories.*'

They looked at the picture of the Cat walking by his wild lone waving his wild tail and Elizabeth did not like him at all. She had never known a cat like that. Even this Tabby Tom was not thin and black enough to be the Cat That Walked. Though she disliked the Cat That Walked, Elizabeth was glad that the Dog did not catch him and that the Man missed his aim when he threw the boots. The Man wasn't a proper man or he wouldn't have thrown the boots; and only badly trained, disobedient dogs chased cats, not proper dogs. Elizabeth felt that the story was all wrong.

The walls of the children's room were papered with a yellow and grey pattern. On these winter evenings it was always dark when they went to bed, but early in the morning Elizabeth could see the patterns on the ceiling as she lay on her back in bed. Sometimes they looked like rows and rows of soldiers with knapsacks on their backs; sometimes they were flower-beds and the soldiers turned into trees and shrubs. At other times they were quite plainly Noah's Ark and the animals walking in two by two. If she squeezed her eyes the whole ceiling came down and hung in mid-air over her head, and she knew it was transparent because when it did that she could put her hand through it. But as soon as she sat up in bed it popped back into place.

At night when the gas was lit, circular rings of light and shadow were thrown on the ceiling and the pattern of little soldiers and Noah's Ark animals was lost. In the incandescent burner the gas hissed gently in tune with the more distant sea, and far away, one after the other, the cocks crew, cock-a-doodle-doo.

Then Miss Una would come. Elizabeth could hear her breathing while she moved about the room, tidying the children's belongings and talking to Eleanor in a voice subdued because she thought Marian and Elizabeth were asleep. The gas would be turned out. The house would grow quieter and quieter. The cocks would began again. Long after Eleanor and Marian were asleep, Elizabeth would lie and listen. Somewhere dogs were barking, a deep baying and a terrier's irritable yap.

'Hark, hark, the dogs do bark,' recited Elizabeth under the bedclothes.

'The beggars are coming to town.
Some in rags and some in tags
And some in velvet gown.'

Then her mother would light the gas in her dressing-room and a shaft of light would thow a strong shadow across the ceiling of the nursery. This was the sky in a new world. There was a giant who lived in the castle in the corner, with walls and towers and a fairy princess.

'Rapunzel, Rapunzel, let down your hair.'

And the woman let down her hair and made a magic. She made a Still Magic, and by and by the cave grew so still that a little mouse crept out of a corner.

'Pussy-cat, pussy-cat, what did you there? I frightened a little mouse under the chair. But still I am the Cat That Walks by Himself. That very minute and second, Best Beloved, the smoke of the Fire at the back of the cave came down in clouds from the roof.'

'Puff,' said the smoke.

'Sish-swish,' whispered the gas.

'Sish-swish,' sang the sand.

'Sish-sish-swish,' murmured the sea.

And far away the cocks crew, cock-a-doodle-doo, cock-a-doodle-doo.

3

A Royal Occasion

ELIZABETH sat on a stool and watched her mother getting dressed. Mrs Inglefell sat in front of her dressing-table while Miss Una brushed her hair. After it had been brushed into a a swathe, Miss Una coiled its heavy length on to the crown of the head and fastened it with pins and combs whose diamonds glinted in the candle-light.

The brackets of candles on each side of the dressing-table were alight. The gas jets of the chandelier suspended in the centre of the room threw a rosy glow from beneath their frilled china shades, and the dangling crystal drops cast miniature rainbows on the ceiling. The room was full of warmth and colour and a combination of subtle aromas. The cut glass and silver of the toilet appointments were reflected in the mirrors against hangings of velvet and satin. The furniture of rosewood covered with cream brocade was strewn with silks and muslins, kid gloves, slippers with jewelled heels, painted fans and trinkets in gold and enamel.

The hairdressing completed, Mrs Inglefell got up and moved across the room. As she walked the gophered frills of her long taffeta undergown whispered against the carpet. Elizabeth loved the soft noises her mother's clothes made as she moved. She compared them in her mind with the rustlings of leaves when the wind stirred the poplar trees, or the settling of the birds in their nests after the sun had gone down. And she loved being in her mother's room: playing with the tiny box of chased silver which held spirit for heating the curling-irons; rummaging in a drawer full of ribbons and perhaps being allowed to keep one or two; extracting drops of perfume from the crystal bottle with the gold cap; picking things up with the glove tongs; taking sniffs from the smelling-salts bottle which made her eyes water, or from the vinaigrette which had a stopper at each end and a gold lid on a hinge to cover it; and even (occasionally, as a special treat if she were exceptionally good) emptying the silver and satinwood jewel-box of its trays and cushions covered with green velvet, and trying on all the necklaces, bracelets, rings, hair combs, belt buckles and ear-rings which it contained.

Miss Una picked up the dress which was spread out on the bed, and prepared to put it over Mrs Inglefell's head. But first the hip-pads must be put on and fastened with ribands. These would spread the folds of brocade and accentuate the slender-ness of the waist. Then Mrs Inglefell bent her head and re-ceived the gown which fell about her in masses of lace and silk.

'Twenty-eight yards round the hem,' said Miss Una triumphantly, 'not counting the lace on the second flounce. I measured it myself. I'm glad you're going to wear this one. Hold your breath for a minute while I hook this corselet at the back.'

'Mummie?' said Elizabeth.

'Yes, darling,' said her mother in a rather stifled voice.

'Will you dance with the Prince?'

'No, darling. It's not going to be a ball.'

'Why not?'

'Because of the Court mourning for the Queen. They're having a State concert instead.'

This was disappointing. Elizabeth thought princes always had balls.

'What was it for the Queen?'

'Mourning – because of her death. Don't you remember just a short while ago, I told you that the Queen had died. So of course no one wants to dance because they feel sad about it.'

'Why did the Queen die, Mummie?'

'Because she was very old and had worked hard and had a great deal of worry.'

Oh!' Elizabeth was very puzzled. She had never imagined that queens would have to work. She had thought of them as perennially young and beautiful, with robes and gold crowns and wings with spangles on them.

'Will the Prince wear his crown?' she wanted to know.

'N – no, I think not, darling. He only wears a crown on very important State occasions.'

'I hear the poor man's got terrible toothache,' said Miss Una, still struggling with hooks.

'Who? The Prince?' asked Elizabeth, immediately interested in this new development.

'The Duke. Well, of course, he is a prince, if it comes to that. But he's the Duke of Cornwall and York too, and that's what he's mostly called.'

'Will he turn into a King and marry the Princess?'

'He's married already, darling. The Princess is called the Duchess of Cornwall. They'll be King and Queen some day.'

'As a reward for his bravery?'

'I think it quite possible.'

'Did he kill any dragons?'

'Well, his name is George, so he might have some dragons to kill, but perhaps not quite like the ones in your picture-book.'

'What kind of ones would he have, Mummie?'

'Bring me the jewel-box, Beth. You can help me choose which pieces to wear.'

'Oh yes,' breathed Elizabeth, dragons forgotten in an ecstasy of anticipation. Tongue between lips, she lifted the box and clutched it to her chest. With a billowing of her gleaming gown, Mrs Inglefell sat down and Elizabeth put the box in her lap. If she had had her choice her mother would have gone forth like Faust's Marguerite, bedecked with the box's entire contents. After much discussion and tryings-on and takings-off, they decided on a high pearl collar with diamond supports which reached nearly to the lobes of the ears, a pendant set with diamonds and tourmalines ('Just the colour of the brocade,' as Miss Una said), a long chain to fall below the waist and a brooch to match the pendant. Both hands were given rings with diamonds, pearls and emeralds, and a bracelet for each wrist. Elizabeth was sure that not even Cinderella was so gorgeously clad as her mother was, now that she was bejewelled. A doubt suddenly assailed her. 'Mummie, are you going in the train?' she asked. (Or would it be a coach magicked from a pumpkin and drawn by six white mice?)

'No, darling. Captain Ross-Bossingham is taking us all the way in his carriage.'

'What's captain?'

'It means he is a soldier. He has just come back from the war.'

'What's war?

'Where there are guns and fighting and a great many soldiers.'

'Is it in England?'

'No, Beth. It's in South Africa. But a lot of soldiers went there from England. Captain Ross Bossingham went there from England.'

'Is he brave?'

'Very brave, and very handsome. So brave that the Queen gave him a medal.'

There was a knock at the door and Mr Inglefell put his head in.

'How are things in here? Nearly ready?' He was in evening dress and looked young and strange to Beth, who seldom saw him after seven o'clock.

Miss Una was busy putting things away in drawers and tidying up the dressing-table.

'I'll be ready in just one minute to fix your tie,' she said.

Mr Inglefell snatched up his youngest daughter and put her on his shoulder. 'Fancy you growing as tall as that all of a sudden!' he said. Beth clutched at his hair and then at the crystals of the chandelier. Mrs Inglefell laughed softly. She stood up in her glory, very tall and fair and brilliant.

Elizabeth saw the banter die out of her father's face. He lifted her off his shoulder and put her down on a low chair, and stood looking at his wife. He did not speak, but when she picked up the ostrich-feather mantle from the bed, he hastened to take it out of her hands and hold it ready for her. Then followed the bag with the emerald clasp, the ivory and lace fan, the long white gloves and the handkerchief of Brussels lace.

The momentary silence was broken by Miss Una. 'Let me look at that tie,' she demanded. 'Playing with that child hasn't improved it, I'll warrant. And gracious heaven, look at the man's hair! You'll have to brush it again before you leave.'

Mr Inglefell gave himself meekly to her ministrations and said, with his chin in the air: 'Bossingham is here. I put him in the dining-room with some of that sherry wine Uncle Het sent us. It's very good, though Uncle Het was sure it would be ruined by being sent to the colonies.'

Mrs Inglefell laughed again. 'And not only his sherry wine,' she said.

'Oh, I don't know. I fancy the old fellow is somewhat reconciled since your trip home.'

'Yes, perhaps. I think he half expected his niece from Australia to arrive in London wearing emu feathers and a grass skirt.'

Miss Una had gone out with a parting injunction to Elizabeth to come at once and get ready for bed. But Elizabeth lingered.

Mr Inglefell buried his hands in the feathers of his wife's cloak. 'You're very beautiful, my dear,' he said, so low that Elizabeth barely caught the words.

'Fie on you, sir,' said his wife. His arms closed round her. 'You're my sweet love.'

'She's my sweet love, too,' said Elizabeth. 'You are both my sweet loves.'

'Bless me, I'd forgotten the child,' said her father, laughing. He put one arm round her shoulders and drew them both close to him. 'Don't you think you've got a beautiful mother, Beth?'

'The most beautifullest mother in the world,' declared Beth fervently. 'I suspect the Prince will want to dance with her after all, when he sees her.'

'It wouldn't surprise me in the least,' said Mr Inglefell.

4

Visits

O N E afternoon when Elizabeth was playing under the pepper tree she heard Miss Una's voice raised in imperative command: 'Beth, where are you? Come at once.' Elizabeth answered the summons and was bidden to 'come and be dressed. You're going driving with your mother.'

'Oo, in the wagonette? Oo, where to, Miss Oonie?'

'Stand still, child. How can I unfasten these buttons with you wriggling about like an eel? Yes, in the wagonette. It'll be ready soon. Wait while I wash behind your ears. Anyone would think you hadn't had a bath for a year. Half the garden on your hands and the other half on your neck, I do declare.'

'Finch says he doesn't see how he can be expected to chop the wood for the kitchen when he's got *all* the garden on *his* hands.'

'I dare say. Bone-lazy that man is. Your father's too soft with him. Now your dress.'

Elizabeth regarded herself with interest. Her play dress had been hurriedly changed for one of blue wool which reached nearly to her new white socks and strapped black shoes. She wore a blue bonnet edged with fur and tied under her chin with blue satin bands. On her hands were the mittens which Great-aunt Mamie in England had netted for her. She went at a brisk trot through the house to find her mother.

'Let me see you, darling,' said Mrs Inglefell, and she tweaked the ribbon-ends to make them stand out more and put soft finger touches to the hair under the bonnet. She herself was dressed in a gown of dark green serge with a high neck. The train of double taffeta flounces was edged with brush binding. A bonnet of yellow straw posied with flowers and Valenciennes lace rode the uplifted waves of her fair hair and added insouciance to a toilette which might otherwise have seemed a trifle sombre for so bright an afternoon. Her shoulder cape and muff of Russian sable were a protection against the chilly air which in spite of the sunshine was a reminder that winter was not yet past.

'There, now you are my pretty pet. Take my hand. Finch is waiting.'

Mrs Inglefell put out a hand clad in creaseless French kid and led Elizabeth down the stairs. At the bottom of the front steps Finch was standing by the wagonette. He had converted himself from a gardener into a coachman by putting on a coat of dark brown stuff, corduroy breeches and soft leather boots which crinkled round his calves. A brown half-topper gave a decidedly sporting flavour to his appearance. Elizabeth was quite in awe at his splendid apparel, for the wagonette and its two bay cobs had just been bought, and this was the first occasion on which Finch had appeared in his new role. He opened the door at the rear of the vehicle and helped Mrs Inglefell up the steps. With an air of properly diffident respect he gathered up her train and laid the several yards of serge and taffeta about her feet. Beth was preparing to make an entry of like dignity, but was disconcerted to find herself suddenly whisked into the air and deposited on the seat opposite her mother.

'There we are, little lady,' said Finch. 'Now, ma'am, where would you like to go first?'

'To Mrs Robinson's, please, Finch, and after that to Mrs Digby Faulkener's.'

'Very well, 'm. Just a nice distance for the time.' Finch climbed into the wagonette, unwound the reins from the iron railing in front, took the whip out of its socket and clicked his tongue to the two bay cobs who, until this, had been placidly leaning their weight first on one leg and then on another and swishing at the flies with their stumpy tails. Away rumbled the wagonette through the gates and out on to the road. Beth felt quite adventurous.

'Where are we going, Mummie?' she asked.

'To see some ladies who have called on me, darling,' replied Mrs Inglefell.

'Why did they, Mummie?'

'Because Daddy and I have just come to live here and Mrs Robinson and Mrs Digby Faulkener and some other ladies came to see us so that we could get to know them and be friends.'

They drove in silence for some time. The clip-clop of the horses' hooves made echoes against the metal road. The walls and hedges of the neighbouring gardens seemed to Elizabeth's impatience to move past very slowly; but presently the wagonette turned from the broad tree-lined avenue into a narrow street where the houses were set close together, separated only by iron railings.

'Number twenty-nine, please, Finch,' called Mrs Inglefell, and in a few minutes the horses came to a standstill before a flight of stone steps. Mrs Inglefell gathered up the yards of green serge and taffeta, Finch opened the door, and Elizabeth and her mother descended to the footpath.

'About half an hour, please, Finch,' ordered Mrs Inglefell, and went up the steps to a massive door on which an over-enthusiastic decorator had painted in bright ochre a pattern of wood-graining unknown to any tree of nature's designing. In Gothic lettering it bore the legend: 'Sans Souci'. Mrs Inglefell pulled an iron lever which shrieked protestingly. A bell clanged somewhere in the depths of the house. The door was instantly opened by a breathless servant girl in a pink cotton frock. A muslin apron sat slightly askew across her stomach and a stiffly-starched cap perched on her head like a paper frill on a mutton cutlet.

'Mrs Inglefell and Miss Elizabeth Inglefell.' Mrs Inglefell announced herself softly and held out the three cards which she had taken from the tortoise-shell card-case in her hand-bag. The maid received them on a Japanese lacquer tray which she placed on a bamboo table already overladen with a fern growing in a china jardinière.

'This way, please, 'm,' gulped the child, and backed nervously into the narrow hall to indicate a door on the left, from which sounds of lively feminine conversation were issuing. Elizabeth felt very important as she entered the room beside her mother. The hum of voices died away as several ladies turned to look at the newcomers. Mrs Robinson came forward with a jingling of bracelets, a swaying of chains, a swishing of skirts, and many little gasps and exclamations of welcome.

'Dear Mrs Inglefell, how very kind of you to come! And your sweet little girl! What a truly delightful child! So fair! Have you got a kiss for me?' Beth did not feel at all inclined to kiss this effusive stranger, but politely turned her cheeck upwards and suffered it to be pressed by a pair of dry lips.

'That's a good little girl! What pretty manners we have, to be sure!' went on Mrs Robinson when this formality had been observed. 'You are not fatigued? But you came in your carriage, of course. Ah, you have not kept the horses?' Here Elizabeth detected a note almost of disappointment in her hostess's voice. Heads were turned towards the window. But Mrs Robinson was once more taking up her recitative. 'Please be seated. This low chair? No, perhaps the ottoman. Or do you prefer the cosy corner? It would be quite out of the draught. I cannot abide a draught, can you? Quite dangerous and so very uncomfortable.'

While these arrangements were being made Elizabeth had time to look about her. The room seemed to be crowded with ladies. There were indeed only seven, but the room was not large and was so clustered with bamboo tables, wool-worked stools, Japanese screens, potted ferns in china baskets, brackets of fretwork, photographs in silver and needleworked frames, carved ostrich eggs under inverted glass bowls, gilded clocks and mats with beaded fringes; the floor was so much taken up by the voluminous flounces of the ladies' dresses; the furniture was so littered with gloves and beaded bags and lace-edged sunshades; the walls were so covered with water-colour paintings and Chinese fans and ebony brackets and pictures of pink-legged flamingoes and lurid sunsets and playful kittens and storms at sea that Elizabeth had much to occupy her attention. Two other children were present, a girl of about seven and a boy perhaps a year older, whose names, Elizabeth soon learned, were Flora and Albert. She smiled at them in a tentative opening of acquaintanceship, but Flora seemed too much engrossed by the conversation of the grown-ups to take much notice and Albert merely put out his tongue and turned his back.

'Were you in town for the royal procession?' asked Mrs Atkins, who was sitting next to Mrs Inglefell. 'I believe the crowd was the biggest anyone did see. Mr Atkins quite refused to let me go by myself, and as he was prevented from attending by pressure of his affairs, I had to content myself by staying at home. You can't imagine how disappointed I was.'

Mr Atkins was the local plumber and Mrs Inglefell could not help reflecting that his clients' drains might have chosen a more auspicious time for misbehaving than the occasion of a royal visit. She liked his wife, who was a hard-working woman of much good sense and few pretensions.

'My husband hired a cab as our wagonette had not arrived,' she explained. 'We had seats in a window at the Beehive Corner, so we saw their Royal Highnesses drive along King William Street to the Town Hall and afterwards when they returned along Rundle Street and Hindley Street.'

All the ladies turned to listen. 'We were in Victoria Square,' said one. 'There was a "monster toss" of over one thousand pigeons. It was the prettiest sight you ever did see.'

Now all the others chimed in to contribute to the description of the festivities: the archways of laurel and palm, hung with oranges and lemons; the flags and flowers and rosettes; the Venetian masts with their festoons of greenery hung with ribbons of red, white and blue; the marching troops, the cheering crowds, the excited bevies of school-children; the fire brigade's archway of ladders in Wakefield Street; the rifle brigades lining the streets; the ranks of bluejackets from the visiting warships, symbols of that empire on which the sun never sets; the mounted policemen in their black, cream and silver uniforms, with their long pikes and fluttering pennants, their white chargers stepping daintily and patiently among the massing people; the crash of guns as the royal salute was fired from the military parade-ground.

'Was it not a shame?' exclaimed Mrs Addup, the accountant's wife; 'we went on Tuesday to the Port to see the *Ophir* arrive, and after we had stood for hours in the rain we found the big boat wasn't coming up to the wharf at all. The poor Duke and Duchess had to come ashore in a dirty old tug. Mr Addup said it was disgraceful mismanagement. Quite upset, he was. A disgrace to the colony, that's what he called it.'

This was greeted with cries of feminine indignation and exclamations of agreement. 'Though how thankful we should be,' said Mrs Watson, 'that the weather cleared up and gave us a fine afternoon.' This pious sentiment was supported by all the others. Mrs Robinson turned to Mrs Addup and chided her coyly. 'We must remember now that we are no longer a colony. After this we must remember to call ourselves the State of South Australia, now that our country is to be a Dominion of the Motherland.'

Mrs Addup was not impressed by this correction. She did not exactly toss her head, but gave the impression that had the occasion been just a little less genteel and her own social standing not quite so elevated, toss her head she would. She sat a little straighter or rather affected to, for her eighteen-inch corset already gave her the ramrod posture of a guardsman. 'Mr Addup says,' she asserted with firm lips, 'that we never were a colony. We were a freely-settled province and have been self-governing for half a century. Not like those others, with their convicts and their currency lads.' At these words an undeniable wave of self-conscious virtue passed over the assemblage. 'Mr Addup says,' she continued, 'that federation will not solve any of our troubles and will only bring a crop of new ones. What can people living in that place – the federal capital or whatever they are going to call it – possibly know about the political needs of the other colonies such as Western Australia and Queensland, so far away?'

The other ladies had no reply to these views, but felt privately that Mrs Addup was rather too 'advanced' to be quite lady-like, and might even be 'feminist' and have opinions in favour of the 'emancipation of women', of which they did not at all approve. Mrs Inglefell gently threw a pebble into the pool of silence which had formed.

'Did you not think her Royal Highness's gown most becoming?' she asked, and was rewarded by a ripple of conversation. The hostess then ventured to pose the question which all the company longed to hear, but which none had so far had the courage to frame.

'Were you not at one of the receptions, Mrs Inglefell?'

'Why, yes. My husband and I had the honour of being presented to their Royal Highnesses at Government House on Tuesday evening. After the reception the Liedertafel gave a concert in the grounds. It was extremely pleasant. The Duchess is very lovely and most dignified and gracious.'

Little rustlings of interest and sighs of envy ran round the room, and undoubtedly this fascinating subject would have absorbed their attention indefinitely had not the maid appeared clutching an enormous tray laden with tea things. Mrs Robinson hastily cleared a table of bric-à-brac and the tray was set down. Tea was poured and handed round, accompanied by a piece of furniture shaped like the Leaning Tower of Pisa, except that it did not lean. It had six storeys, each bearing a plate of cake or biscuits, and Elizabeth wondered if she were supposed to begin at the bottom and work her way up, or vice versa. She was relieved to notice that her mother helped herself from the third storey without appearing to pay much attention to its contents.

After everyone had taken lumps of sugar with the silver tongs and added to their tea a dash of cream from a Crown Derby jug, little fingers were elegantly curled and tea-cups raised to the lips. Elizabeth did her best, but found this difficult to perform without spilling her tea, the cups were so very shallow and stood so high on their three spindly legs.

Conversation broke out again and only subsided when everyone had been politely urged and had as politely refused to drink a second cup of tea. Then Mrs Robinson looked across at the sulky little boy in the corner whose mouth was still congested with cake. 'Now perhaps Albert will recite to us,' she suggested brightly.

Albert's mother bridled importantly and pushed her unwilling child forward. 'Go on now, Albert, do. Say "The noble six hundred." '

'Doan' know it,' said Albert, swallowing the last of the cake.

'Well, I never! You said it real nice at home. Now be a good boy or I won't bring you out again.' This threat seemed to have singularly little effect on Albert, who merely scowled and repeated: 'I doan' know it, I tell you.'

'Well, I do declare,' exclaimed his mother, giving him a push and jerking his collar with a sudden savage tug, 'what your father will say when I tell him . . .' She left the sentence in mid-air, verdict suspended, as though unwilling to enumerate the punishments in store for her disobedient offspring. With a nice display of social tact, Mrs Robinson turned to the little girl.

'I am sure Flora could sing or recite for us,' she said.

Without hesitation, Flora stepped forward, tossed her long curls over her shoulders, curtsied, and recited in a high falsetto voice:

'O Mary, go and call the cattle home,
And call the cattle home
And call the cattle home
Across the sands of Dee;
The western wind was wild and dank with foam,
And all alone went she.'

Her shrill tones pursued the fate of poor Mary 'to her grave beside the sea' without faltering; and having assured her listeners that 'still the boatman hear her call the cattle home Across the sands of Dee', she curtsied again and sat down. Handclapping and congratulatory murmurs greeted the end of the recitation. Flora curtsied a third time and went back to her seat with an air of conscious rectitude. Their hostess now addressed Mrs Inglefell. 'Does your little girl know something she could sing or recite for us?'

Mrs Inglefell smiled and shook her head. 'She is still rather young for public performances,' she said.

'Oh, I am sure she is talented. Such a charming child! So intelligent! A noble forehead, and so pretty. What about a nursery rhyme, perhaps, or a ring-o'-rosy?'

Elizabeth found herself the centre of attention as all the ladies turned to coo to her encouragingly. She felt that some response was called for.

'Mummie,' she volunteered, 'I could sing: "The war, the war, the blooming war, Has turned my wife insane. From Kruger to Majuba, She's the Transvaal on the brain." '

There was a moment of stunned silence during which Elizabeth had her first experience of the dismay which follows a social solecism. She sought her mother's eyes and found there immediate reassurance. Mrs Inglefell was smiling in that private 'just between you and me' way that she sometimes reserved for her youngest daughter. 'That's fun to say in the nursery, darling, but perhaps not quite so suitable for drawing-rooms, do you think? Why not try "Little Bo Peep" or "Three Little Kittens".'

'I'd rather say "At Flores in the Azores". Mr O'Brien says not counting "The Wearing of the Green" it's the best poem in the language.' And without waiting for further comment, Elizabeth drew a deep breath and began in a rush:

'At Flores in the Azores Sir Richard Grenville lay,
 And a pinnace like a fluttered bird came flying from far away.'

(Here her small fat hand made appropriate wiggly movements in the air.)

'Spanish ships of war at sea! We have sighted fifty-three.
 And Sir Richard Grenville said: "We be all good Englishmen,
 Let us bang these dogs of Seville, the children of the devil,
 Because – because – er – I'm not going to turn my back on
    them.
 And the sun went down and the stars came out
 Far over the summer sea,
 But never a moment ceased the fight
 Of the one and the fifty-three.
 God of battles, there wasn't ever a battle like this one!'

(A gulping breath, then the little voice rose again imperatively, and a little foot stamped the emphasis.)

' "Sink me the ship, master gunner,
  Sink her, split her in twain!
  Fall into the hands of God,
  Not into the hands of Spain.
  I have fought for my Queen and Faith like a valiant man and
     true,

39

I have only done my duty as a man is bound to do."
After that, he fell down and died.'

There was a moment of solemn silence, then Elizabeth sat
down rather abruptly and all the ladies clapped and cried:
'Bravo!' and her mother smiled and said: 'Thank you, darling,
that was very nice. And now I'm afraid that we should be
going.' So they said good-bye to all the ladies, and Elizabeth
once again suffered herself to be kissed and called 'a clever
little pet'. Albert had been so impressed by Elizabeth's somewhat unorthodox rendering of Lord Tennyson's poem that he
forgot to put out his tongue.

They were soon bowling smartly along Moseley Street on
their way to visit Mrs Digby Faulkener. 'Beth dear,' said Mrs
Inglefell as she leaned forward to pat the satin bonnet-strings
again, 'who is Mr O'Brien?'

'Why, Mummie, he's the milkman. He comes every morning
and every afternoon with the milk in a rattly can.'

'I see. And did he teach you the poem about Sir Richard
Grenville?'

'Yes, and "Attend all ye who list to hear Our noble England's
praise", and "Captain, O my Captain, our fearful trip is done",
and he's going to teach me "St Patrick was a gentleman" and
"All in the Downs the fleet was moored". Miss Una says he's a
very decent fellow.'

'I'm sure he must be.' This was a great relief to Elizabeth as
she had had a momentary doubt about parental approval for
Mr O'Brien's histrionic talent.

As soon as the horses turned into the gateway and trotted
up the long gravelled drive-way which led to Mrs Digby
Faulkener's house, Elizabeth knew that this would be a very
different kind of visit. The winter afternoon was closing in to
twilight, but Elizabeth could see that the house they were
approaching was surrounded by spacious lawns dotted with
trees and shrubs. Beds of canna lilies and hollyhocks and

winter-flowering sweet-peas bordered the driveway. Smoothly clipped hedges and yew trees cut into the shapes of peacocks gave an air of well-kept dignity to the design of the gardens. A marble fountain gleamed whitely. A clump of tall poplars caught the glow of the sunset among their spires and cast long shadows across the grass.

The wagonette drew up before a square porch with Corinthian columns dwarfed by a gigantic magnolia tree growing out of the gravel to one side of the steps. The Florentine mosaic of the porch floor was so highly polished that to walk across it in safety required some care. The brass of the knocker and door-handle gleamed in the dim light. To Elizabeth's delight the bell was 'electric', a button in the centre of a brass plate ('Just like the one the man takes the money in, in church,' she thought to herself) set into the wall beside the doorway. As they waited for the door to be opened everything seemed to settle into a deep quiet. The magnolia tree whispered to itself. The horses crunched the gravel as they shifted their weight from hoof to hoof. Somewhere in the darkening hedge a blackbird was practising a few spring notes. But these small sounds seemed only to emphasise the silence. Elizabeth was just beginning to remember about the 'Still Magic' when the door was opened almost soundlessly by an elderly parlourmaid who immediately held wide the door and stepped aside, as though she were expecting them. Once again three cards were produced from the tortoise-shell card-case and deposited, this time on a silver tray on the hall table.

Elizabeth looked about her eagerly. The hall was as large as Mrs Robinson's drawing-room and hallway in one. It was lighted by gas globes hanging from bronze chandeliers in the ceiling and by brackets of incandescent gas burners on the side walls. Thick Brussels carpet on the floor made walking easy and soundless. The embossed and gilded frames of the many oil paintings sent back the gaslight from the walls in rich reflections. On the farther side of the hall a glowing mass of mallee roots gave off a generous warmth from the wide fireplace.

Opening a door on the right, the parlourmaid announced them by name. Elizabeth followed her mother into the drawing-room and the door was closed silently behind them.

This was the biggest room Elizabeth had ever seen, with long french windows opening on to a veranda on one side and lawn on the other. The walls were cream picked out with gold; the soft furnishings of yellow damask; the chairs and tables and cabinets of rosewood and walnut; the mantelpiece of white Carrara marble. Light danced away in a million rainbows from the central chandelier with its cascades of crystal prisms. The only pictures were two coloured prints of paintings by Marcus Stone, but the cabinets and what-nots were crowded with Dresden vases, Rockingham tea-sets, ivory temples and jade figures. Elizabeth was longing to look at every one of them, but had instead to shake hands with her hostess and say: 'Very well, thank you.' She was then seated on a low stool covered with a pattern of beads which depicted a kitten chasing a ball of wool. The picture was entertaining but rather cold and nobbly to sit on. However, the fire in its marble setting was blazing hotly and the room was cheerfully warm.

Mrs Digby Faulkener was small, grey-haired, soft-spoken. Her dress of grey French suède was plainly cut but very becoming, its simplicity relieved only by ruchings of Valenciennes lace at the neck and wrists. She wore no jewels but the broad gold wedding band on her left hand. She inquired after Mrs Inglefell's health, made some conventional comment on the weather and ventured to suggest that spring would be early this year. She was a woman who never made an original or striking remark in her life; indeed, she would have thought originality uncalled for and striking remarks in doubtful taste. Yet her gentle manner concealed a strength of character with which she ruled her large household, managed her rather domineering husband and governed her family with an effortless firmness.

Tea was brought in on a wheeled table by the elderly parlour-maid who was followed immediately by the master of the house. A large man in his early fifties, Mr Digby Faulkener made a comfortable income in the wholesale grocery trade and allied it to his wife's private fortune with profitable results.

Elizabeth was not invited to have tea. The parlourmaid handed her a silver tankard full of milk and a small square plate on which were two slices of bread and butter cut transparently thin and sprinkled with sugar.

'Oh, Prissy, tell Miss Penthorpe to bring the children down when they have finished their tea,' said Mrs Faulkener to the parlourmaid.

'Yes, ma'am,' said Prissy and left the room.

Mr Digby Faulkener stood in front of the fire with his legs apart, sipping his tea rather noisily and saying nothing in a masterly way. The ladies pursued their conversation in low voices, the blue spirit flame hissed under the silver tea-kettle, and even the tinkling of the tea-things seemed subdued as though to the house's habit of quiet.

Elizabeth had just finished her milk (and discovered that her silver mug had a gilt lining) when the door was again opened and four children came in, followed by a tall, thin woman with untidy hair.

'Ah, there you are,' said Mrs Faulkener. The children came forward and stood in front of their parents in a row, their hands behind their backs. 'This is Miss Penthorpe who supervises our lessons. James and Morley are at school now, and Sarah is staying with her grandmother at Mount Lofty. Helen and Judith, come and say "how do you do" to Mrs Inglefell.'

The two girls, aged eight and six, made curtsies and shook hands. Elizabeth was surprised to see that their dresses were plain wincey and that their hair was braided tightly back and tied with brown ribbon.

'This is Alistair,' Mrs Faulkener went on, 'he is nine years old. And Malcolm is five.' The little boys bowed solemnly.

'Your little girl must be about Malcolm's age.'

'Elizabeth is not quite five,' explained Mrs Inglefell.

Malcolm took after his mother in appearance. He was a small, thin child with a delicate face, a pointed chin and a nose too long and straight for one so young. Eyes too large in proportion to his other features gave him an air of intelligence and maturity beyond his years. His hair still had the fairness of childhood but had promise of growing darker to harmonise with his sallow complexion. His expression was as ethereal as that of a boy-martyr in some Pre-Raphaelite painting. He looked at Elizabeth with unblinking attention which made her feel self-conscious.

Throughout this exchange Mr Faulkener had continued to stand in front of the fire, looking at his children without saying a word.

'That's very nice,' said his wife, though no one could gather to what she referred. 'Thank you, Miss Penthorpe.'

This was apparently the signal for departure, for the children at once moved towards the door. As he passed, Malcolm gave Elizabeth a sharp pinch on the arm. She was so astonished that she did not even jump, and the angelic child made his way out of the room looking more like a boy-martyr than ever.

Mrs Inglefell now rose and made her adieux. In a few minutes she and Elizabeth had passed through the hall beneath the oil paintings, across the Brussels carpet, out into the polished porch and down the steps. It was quite dark though only a little after five o'clock.

'Mrs Inglefell tells me that her husband is thinking of buying a summer property in the hills,' said Mrs Faulkener to her husband. He made no reply. 'She was a Munt before her marriage. Her father was Sir Charles Maxim-Munt. They had a place near Tillie's in Somersetshire.' Her husband's only reaction to this intelligence was to pull the tasselled rope which hung beside the fireplace, to summon Prissy.

Later in the evening, when dinner and port wine and meditation had all contributed to his judgement, he roused himself from his armchair by the fire and looked across at his wife where she sat sewing. The light from the lace-shaded oil-lamp beside her fell kindly on her thin face and showed to advantage the lines of her features. Mr Faulkener cleared his throat. 'You might invite Inglefell and his wife to dine with us some evening,' he said.

Mrs Faulkener looked up from her work. 'Why, dear, that's a very good idea. Of course I will.' And the only emotion in the tones of her voice was one of satisfaction at having such an excellent and intelligent husband.

5

Spring Weather

ELEANOR and Marian went to school every morning at nine o'clock. They were proud of their new leather bags, and proud of their new dresses and coats of navy-blue serge. They found that they knew less than the other girls. Marian wept over sums that younger children found easy; Eleanor did not weep, but learnt French verbs with such a fury of concentration that she developed a crease in the middle of her forehead.

On weekdays Miss Una would take Elizabeth to meet Marian at the school gate. Eleanor had to go home to practise the piano for an hour, but the others would go down to the beach. Sometimes they would go along the road that led over the sand-hills as they had on the first day; but often Miss Una would want to go to the shops and then they could walk up the jetty and watch the fishermen casting their lines from the railings into the green water, or unpacking baskets whose original surface was embalmed in a layer of indescribable filth, the accumulation of years of fishing and manipulations of greasy, scaly and tobacco-stained hands. Elizabeth liked these baskets. She came to know just what they held. First there was the newspaper packet containing the fisherman's lunch: sandwiches and cheese, a bottle of cold tea and sometimes a boiled egg. Then the fishing impedimenta: extra reels and lines, gory remnants from the butcher for the sharks and crabs, stinking slabs of fish-carcase from a previous expedition for ground-bait; then the live-bait – jars of writhing earthworms and tobacco-tins full of maggots burrowing ceaselessly into the sawdust in a fruitless blind search for nourishment; corks and bottle-openers and knives and string and hooks and gut and cards of silk and rags and floaters painted with red or green or white enamel – all gummy with fish scales and the salt of the sea. Overhead the gulls wheeled and shrieked; or strutted bold and cautious along the sleepers of the jetty. They hopped over the railway lines and gobbled greedily any edible morsel that came their way. With head on one side they considered the fisherman's every move and watched the chance to snatch at sandwich or bait, at live fish or dead offal with dreadful indifference, delicately lifting their scarlet legs and ruffling their Quaker plumage in the wind.

The children liked walking up the jetty because there were so many things to see and do. They practised walking along the railway lines, balancing themselves with outstretched arms till, called on to admire their performance, Miss Una said they were 'real Blondins', at which Elizabeth promptly demanded an explanation and abandoned balancing until she had heard it. Sometimes they were allowed to buy a bottle of fizzy lemonade which they opened by pushing in the glass 'marble' which sealed it. There always followed the debate on whether it was worth breaking the bottle to get the 'marble' out or whether it was better to collect the half-penny which the man at the cool-drinks booth would give them if they returned the bottle intact. If they had pennies they could weigh themselves on the slot-machine. More frequently the pennies were spent at Mrs Williams's sweetshop near the railway station. Mrs Williams was a tubby little body in a tightly-fitting black dress with a high neck and puffed sleeves. She took a personal interest in her clientèle, few of whom were older than fourteen. Her little shop was so crammed with tins and jars and canisters of toffees and chocolates and lozenges that it was seldom that one could see more of Mrs Williams than a face peering out from behind the barricade of confectionery. It was a kindly, cheerful face, and the frizzy fringe that surmounted it gave it softness and charm. Marian always chose a chocolate plank with her first half-penny and an all-day sucker with her second. This combined her preference (which was for the soft, squashy sweetness of the chocolate bar) with economy, for the hard lump of toffee on its stick would last, if not all day, at any rate for half an hour. Elizabeth's choice generally lay between milk-poles, because of their length, silver-sticks because of their delicious stick-jaw qualities, and kali-suckers. These last were favourites because when you had sucked all the kali out of the little bag so that your mouth was full of prickly foam and your eyes tingled, there was still the licorice tube to be eaten. For some reason that small piece of licorice was much nicer than the licorice you bought by itself.

Sometimes the children threw pennies to the Salvation Army who played their band instruments and sang hymns on the sand, but this was only when pennies were given by grown-ups for the purpose. Elizabeth soon learnt the hymns and sang them till Miss Una found out and forbade her ever to do such a thing again.

'Why?' asked Elizabeth.

'Because well-brought-up little girls don't sing hymns on the beach,' was the answer.

'Aren't the Salvation Army well brought up?' Elizabeth wanted to know.

'It's not the same. They're very good people, but you are only a little girl, and that's quite another matter.'

'Miss Aitkin said Jesus preached on the beach, anyway,' said Elizabeth, but she couldn't remember if there had been any mention of hymns.

She and Marian learnt how to build sand castles with towers and battlements and moats. If the castle were built sufficiently near the sea and the moat dug deep enough, it would fill with water or could be fed from a scooped-out channel to the nearest pool. Ornamental gardens could be laid out with pebbles and shells and seaweeds, though seaweeds were disappointing in their limpness and in the way that they faded when they had been in the sun for a while.

The little girls learnt beach etiquette, which forbade the leaving of papers and rubbish, which taught one to fill in all deep holes before going home in case the racehorses in their early-morning exercises broke a leg; all glass must be gathered up and taken home; all live crabs restored to pools and sheltered crevices; all food scraps to be thrown to the gulls or buried. Marian and Elizabeth learnt beach manners and respected them. They were shocked at the ways of 'common' children who ran about and shouted and threw sand and pulled off the crabs' legs, or left lemonade bottles about and fought over the possession of buckets and spades.

One day they had just finished a castle, the biggest they had ever made, with two towers and a drawbridge and steps going up to the front door, when two of the 'common' children came and stood looking on as the finishing touches were added. Marian always hated to feel that the castle was finished. She liked to go on adding finer and finer rows of shells, making more and more elaborate patterns in the gardens and courtyards, sketching designs round the doors and windows, and pinching up little heaps of sand to look like people and horses and dogs. The two strange children stood in silence for some time regarding this latest creation. Their untidy hair and soiled appearance were witness to the fact that they did not belong to a family where Elsas and Miss Unas existed for the children's care and well-being. Marian pretended not to notice them. She began to feel the pride of the artist conscious that his work has evoked appreciation. Elizabeth was frankly more interested in the visitors than she was in her own work of art. She liked 'common' children, finding them much more stimulating than the well-behaved little girls who went to Eleanor's and Marian's school. She stopped work to stare back at them. One of them wriggled her feet more deeply into the sand and pronounced: 'Rotten castle!'

49

Marian glanced at Miss Una to see how this would be greeted. The shock of discovering that her creative efforts had called forth such adverse criticism was slightly deflected by the expectation of Jovian thunders about the word 'rotten'. But Miss Una, covered with a rug, seemed asleep or engrossed in her novel. At any rate, she made no sign.

'Oo, it's not!' declared Elizabeth, far more infuriated on Marian's behalf than on her own. Her interest in sand castles was perfunctory and in the ordinary way would have evaporated before the more potent attractions of two new acquaintances. But the need to defend Marian's handicraft was imperative.

'I think it's a beautiful castle,' she declared. 'I think it's the best castle on the beach,' and she looked up and down at the other groups of children digging and building and labouring.

'Gorn!' said the smaller of the two new children. 'It han't go 'ny embroidery on it.'

This was indeed news from Tartary.

'What's that?' asked Elizabeth. Marian sat dumbly before this potential menace, patting at her shells and seaweeds and wondering how a castle could be any bigger or more elaborate.

'Don't you know how to make embroidery?' asked the newcomer. Marian shook her head.

'Show us,' said Elizabeth.

The two little girls plumped down and began to scoop a hole in the wet sand until it was about a foot deep and full of slushy mud. Then with a handful of the soupy mixture, they bent to work, allowing it to trickle through their fingers in wriggling streams. The water sank and disappeared, leaving a deposit of firm sand in fine filigree patterns. It was slow work, but the result was more beautiful than anything Marian or Elizabeth had imagined possible. They dug another hole. They fell to with enthusiasm. Soon all four were hard at work, enlarging and rebuilding the castle and covering it with a myriad spires and minarets and oriel windows and moushrabir fretwork, with as many embellishments as an ormolu clock and as many superfluities as a rococo church. It was great fun. Elizabeth enjoyed it more than anything they had done on the beach before.

When Miss Una woke up and said it was time to go home, Elizabeth looked at the castle in its new splendour and knew in her heart of hearts that it was spoiled. She enjoyed it more than ever when they took running jumps on to it and broke it all down, and scattered the shells and seaweed and filled in the moat. But Marian was rather regretful.

As the days grew longer the sun brought the sour-sops into flower. They covered the paddocks with their yellow. Elizabeth found that they had a thin, astringent juice in their stems that made them delicious to nibble. However warm the sun, the sour-sops were always damp. The leaves glittered with the dewdrops of the previous night.

Elizabeth climbed the wall near the cow-byres and squelched her way through the grass of the paddocks on the other side. The paddocks were bordered with the skeletons of the almond trees and there were grass-grown mounds which indicated where rubbish and garden refuse had been thrown. Among the sour-sops were taller, thicker stems of pale green surmounted by creamy buds bursting from a transparent sheath. Thousands of snowdrops, each petal with its spot of green, spread in mad profusion over the mounds. Elizabeth gathered them in armfuls. She and Marian brought them in bunches to the house. When the narcissus and jonquil were in bloom, Mrs Inglefell put them in bowls in all the rooms, till the whole house was filled with their perfume. From the borders in front of the house came daffodils and sprays of flowering currant and ivory broom and blue periwinkles; the children learnt all their names and drew pictures of them in their drawing-books. Marian coloured hers with water-colour paints, but Elizabeth had only crayons which gave an oily unevenness of surface to the pictures unworthy of the delicacy of the subjects.

Marian was clever at painting. Her book was often shown to visitors. At Undaboo there had been few flowers for her to paint and most of her drawings were of horses and sheep and kangaroos. She was delighted with her suddenly enlarged field of observation and spent hours with her pencils and paints. Her shelf in the play-room cupboard was always littered with wilting specimens of flora and dead specimens of fauna when these took the shape of brightly-coloured butterflies and beetles found in the garden.

Elizabeth envied Marian the beauty of her exact and careful pictures. She longed to make her own painting-book worthy to be shown to visitors, but her fingers refused to guide the clumsy crayons into fine corners. With all her care the colours overran the pencil outline of the design.

On the fifth day of cloudless weather Elizabeth went on an expedition to the farther paddocks. She had purposely refrained from going near the almond trees. Even in the increasing brightness of the spring weather she could not rid herself of the forlorn feeling they gave her. Those bordering the second paddock were not as old and gnarled as those near the house and their boughs spread more widely on a lower level. Elizabeth wanted to go to a little rocky hill which looked as though it would make a splendid island for the Swiss Family Robinson, but the only way of reaching it was to break through the almond-tree hedge. She chose a spot which was fairly clear of branches and was bending down to crawl through when she was assailed by the strangest sensation. Her favourite stories were those with magic in them, and now, for one breathtaking moment, it seemed that magic was really happening. The bough in front of her, and, when she looked she found that the branches over her head too, were covered with coppery buds rimmed with pink. The almond trees were coming alive!

Elizabeth said nothing about her discovery. The next morning she could hardly wait till breakfast was over before rushing out to examine the trees near the house. Yes, it was true. They were coming to life in a million, million buds along their scarred and twisted limbs. Here and there a solitary blossom spread rose-tipped petals in the sun and before the day was over they bloomed no longer in solitude but in twos and threes together.

A dry north wind rattled the palms and set the daffodils nodding. It brought sudden memories of Undaboo.

Elsa dreamed over her housework till Miss Una scolded her and at last sent her out into the garden where she wandered in bare-footed silence, sniffing the wind and watching the sky grow dark with desert-born dust. The rain came with the sunset, at first in splashes that died in the dry wind, finally in roaring torrents.

Rain fell all the next day and the children were not allowed into the garden. Eleanor and Marian were muffled in new waterproof coats and taken to school by Miss Una. Elizabeth sat with her mother in the breakfast-room, writing in her copybook and reading out of MacMillan's *First Reader*. Her desire to be able to do things filled her with scarcely-controlled impatience. She turned back the pages she had written last year and noted with satisfaction how shaky and uncertain were the characters she had formed then compared with her present efforts. But with Elizabeth desire was always to outstrip performance. She had to pause frequently in her writing, draw in her tongue and inquire: 'When will I be able to write as quick as you, Mummie?' and 'When will I be able to write out of my head, Mummie?' She occasionally varied questions with comments and exclamations: 'There, I've smudged it with the blotter,' and 'Oh, dear, there's a hair got on it and made it all squiggly.'

Whenever she began on a new copy she read it aloud: 'Give every man his due'; 'The horse is a noble animal'; and 'Honesty is the best policy'.

'I think you'd learn to write more quickly if you didn't talk so much,' suggested her mother.

'I like talking,' said Elizabeth.

'I know you do, but you can't work so well if you talk too much.'

'Well, I think I've done enough writing. Now I'll do adding and taking.'

'Very well. Give me your book.'

Mrs Inglefell wrote out tall vertical columns of figures for Elizabeth to add up, and long horizontal rows of figures for subtraction. Counting on fingers was against the rules, but Elizabeth had early got over this difficulty by imagining all numbers from one to a hundred in a sort of landscape. One began in the south-westerly corner and ran up a fairly steep slope to ten; after a short step from ten to twelve, the path ran due north to twenty. From twenty to thirty it travelled north-west, due north again to forty and up a sharp north-easterly hill as far as sixty. From sixty to eighty was broad and flat, rising gently from eighty-seven to ninety when the slope climbed abruptly till it came out on the broad plateau of the century. Elizabeth kept this number-picture in her mind all her life, and when in later years she became an accomplished mathematician she always used it for simple arithmetical calculations.

When all the sums had been answered correctly, Elizabeth brought the Hans Andersen book and asked her mother to read the story of the Ugly Duckling.

The next morning Elizabeth was wakened early by the sun stabbing through her window in rays that sharpened the outline of everything and made the dancing dust-specks turn into burning sparks. She climbed out of bed softly and tiptoed past Marian and Eleanor where they lay asleep. Leaning out of the window she could see Tabby Tom Lickums at his morning toilet, his coat fluffy and clean after yesterday's rain. He licked carefully between the toes of a hind paw and pulled at the pad with his teeth. It was only when changing paws that he condescended to send Elizabeth a glance, a reproving glance that paid no tribute for saucers of milk received. Ordinarily she would have taken some trouble to coax him to the window, but this morning her whole mind was occupied with the one thought: What had happened to the almond trees in the rain? She had to lean as far out of the window as she could reach. The window-sill pressed her tummy and made her breathless, but she could see the first trees of the row behind the orangery. They were dowered with white and lifted blossom-packed arms to the rain-rinsed sky.

After breakfast the children ran out into the sunshine and raced down aisles of flowering splendour from which the petals showered with every breath of wind to lie in drifts among the jonquils in the grass. Only Elizabeth wandered, subdued, in a world of light and silence whose beauty had refuted all her unbelief.

6

Family Life

ELIZABETH built a house under the pepper tree. The drooping branches made a tent under which she could assemble her dolls and bricks and boxes of 'oddies' as she called them. The fallen leaves of the tree made a carpet, soft and thick, their pungency reduced by death to a sweet-scented dryness. Elsa made two mats of reeds she found on the sandhills. They were not as good as those she used to make at the Lutheran Mission, but they gave a grown-up air to the house. She also helped Elizabeth to construct a fireplace of masonry from the broken-down wall. Three kerosene cases placed on their sides, one above the other, made a tenement dwelling for the dolls, as well as a cupboard for the 'oddies'. The foliage of the pepper tree came right down to the ground, so it was necessary to break some of the branches to form a doorway, but this was done easily enough and Elizabeth soon found her hands and clothing sticky with gum from the oozing stems. She tore off the sprays of hard pink berries and put them in glass vases in the dolls' house. The skin of the berries was dry and brittle and peeled off like scales of pink celluloid. It was like Pansy's face, thought Elizabeth. Pansy was a celluloid doll given to Elizabeth by Mrs Thrace, a friend of her mother's. Elizabeth could never grow really fond of Pansy, her face was so very pink and, in spite of her obvious hollowness, she had a self-satisfied expression that resisted intimacy and made affection difficult. It was pity more than affection that moved Elizabeth to include her in the family.

Besides Pansy there were Jimmie, a worn teddy-bear of a gentle and faithful disposition who for long, and alone of all the family, had shared Elizabeth's bed; and Andalusia, a large, well-bred blonde with a blue silk dress and real underclothes that 'took off'; and then there were Mickle and Tickle and Bog, three soap-stone monkeys with paws over, respectively, eyes, ears, and mouth; Hoppy, a negro doll with shoe-button eyes and only one leg; a very small doll with a tinsel dress and a gold crown, called Princess, who had originally decorated a Christmas tree; six penny dolls of white china with black enamel hair for whom a plum-pudding fate had been intended; and finally over all, presided the sawdust, glass and china deity, Mrs Watkins.

This very large family, referred to by Elizabeth in later years as a family of true pre-Stopesian proportions, took up a good deal of her time and attention. Though they helped in whatever games were occupying her at the moment, becoming with obliging readiness Red Indians, French revolutionaries, Christian martyrs, Babes in the Wood, shipwrecked mariners or children requiring rescue from burning houses, they had, nevertheless, to be washed, fed, put to bed, sewed for and prayed for. In the house under the pepper tree they found both shelter from the distractions of a busy life and a stage on which to play whatever role had been assigned to them.

One day Eleanor brought a friend home from school. Her name was Mildred Weston and she was a year older than Eleanor. Her father kept a large drapery store on Jetty Road, and she was, in consequence, a young person of some importance. Eleanor who, both by character and age, always dominated her sisters, was now experiencing the uncertain delights of being patronised. She basked in Mildred's superior knowledge of the town, swallowed her wrath when Mildred criticised 'country people' who, in her opinion, were all 'bumpkins', and could not subdue her own satisfaction that one so versed in the ways of the world had not hesitated to bestow her attentions on Eleanor

c

Inglefell who, it seemed, would in time cease to be a country bumpkin and would, under Mildred's kindly tutelage, acquire a necessary degree of urban sophistication. She showed Mildred the house and was pleased to note that Mildred's self-confidence waned into something like awe-struck silence at the sight of the lofty rooms with their painted ceilings, rich curtains of crimson plush and crowding mahogany. Mildred, whose childhood had been spent in a stuffy little house behind her father's shop, was unprepared for such splendour and felt all the greater need to assert her own superiority.

They went out into the garden and presently came upon Elizabeth in her pepper tree tent. She was occupied with the Massacre of the First-Born. Pharaoh had already dispatched all members of the family except Pansy who, as Moses, was floating in a baking-dish filled with water. The baking-dish had been borrowed from the cook, Mrs Thompson, under a solemn promise of return. It was surrounded by sprays of bamboo leaves which made very good rushes when they were stuck upright into the firm soil of the floor. Elizabeth was annoyed that so important a role had had to be given to Pansy, but this was necessary, because, being the only member of the family to be made of celluloid she was the only one who would float. So she reposed in her cradle, a celluloid soap-dish from the bathroom, while Elizabeth dressed herself for the part of Pharaoh's daughter. She had just draped her head in an old pink gossamer veil of her mother's when Eleanor pulled aside the branches of the tent wall and said: 'This is Beth's wurly.'

'Come in at the door,' said Elizabeth in her grown-up voice. But Mildred had already pulled back more of the foliage and stepped inside.

'Only niggers have wurlies,' she said.

Elizabeth snatched off the veil.

'They don't,' she said. 'All our abos had wurlies.'

'Well, they're niggers.'

A crimson line began to mount on Elizabeth's neck.

'They're aborigines.'

'Well, they're black, aren't they? And all black people are niggers.'

'My father says only igryant people call them niggers.'

'My father says he doesn't know how your mother and father can bear to let that black gin take you about.'

Elizabeth flushed scarlet. She was stung to fury by the implied insult to her parents and the slur on her own dear Elsa who had played with her, nursed her, silently suffered for the children's pranks, told her stories and crooned her to sleep since babyhood. Even Eleanor was appalled and felt that her guest had offended against the canons of good taste. Seeing the storm about to break, she hastened to avert it.

'What are you playing at, Beth?' she asked looking down at Pansy in the baking-pan. For a moment speech was beyond Elizabeth's control, but after a moment she mumbled: 'Moses.'

'Moses? Oh, I see. In the bulrushes. Who's going to be the Princess?'

'Me,' said Elizabeth, putting rigid lips over the monosyllable. She stared at Mildred who felt it necessary to assert herself under the scrutiny.

'I don't believe those old stories,' she said.

This was declared heresy. Eleanor felt that she must protest. 'But, Mildred, it's in the Bible.'

'I know that. But every single thing in the Bible isn't true.'

'Who said so?'

'My father. He says a lot of the stories in the Bible were just made up like other stories in books are. Besides, some of them are real silly. What about Jonah and the whale? Whales can't be sick.'

'The whale wasn't sick,' said Elizabeth. 'Jonah walked out.'

'Well, all right, then, what about Moses in the bulrushes? You think a baby could have floated round by itself like that, do you? It would have died.'

'It wouldn't.' Elizabeth felt the statement a poor defence,

but this was a mode of attack entirely foreign to her and her defences were unequal to anything more than a blank denial.

'Of course it would. It would have fallen out and got drowned. Or else starved. Babies can't live without milk and how could it get milk out there on the river, I'd like to know?'

There was a momentary silence. Elizabeth fiddled with the bamboo sprays. Tears were pressing her eyes till they hurt, but pride would not let her cry before this odious iconoclast.

'Oh, come on, Eleanor,' said Mildred impatiently. 'Let's go out and I'll show you my Tobler cards. I hate dolls.'

The two older children left Elizabeth to her misery. It welled up from her stomach like a rush of pain. She snatched at the bamboos and threw them on the ground.

'I hate her, I hate her!' she stormed, sobs choking her throat and the tears pouring down her cheeks. 'Beastly mean pig.' These three words were severally and collectively forbidden. There was a furious joy in uttering them. and she repeated them with angry relish. 'Beastly mean pig, piggish mean beast.' The alternative arrangement was pleasing and she said it over and over, sobbing and choking.

Mr O'Brien came through the garden, rattling his can. He was the milkman who was bringing the milk supply until the arrival of the Jerseys. He stopped and put his head in at the door of the tent.

'And how's herself today?' said he. Elizabeth glowered at him from under swollen lids.

'Storms about but the barometer's rising,' went on Mr O'Brien without waiting for an answer to his first question. 'There's many a ship has a stiff blow this time of the year, but it's fine weather we'll be having before long.'

Elizabeth could not understand half he was talking about but she had never met a man she liked so much, and his visit to the tent had become a daily event. In his young days he had been a sailor and his speech was generally full of nautical terms and allusions to men and places he had seen in his travels.

'Many's the time I've sailed from the Gulf of Aden this time of the year, little Beth, and beating into a sou'-sou'-westerly that looked like it would blow the sea off its bed. And for every mile you sailed forward you blew back two. Many's the time coming round the Leeuwin and crossing the Bight in a monsoon I'd thought we'd fetch up on the Nullarbor Plain 'stead of the Semaphore. But the worst storms blow over. It's only a question of time.' He peered at the floating Pansy.

'Another sailor on the premises today, I see. And who might his iligance be?'

'Moses,' said Elizabeth, sniffing and wishing she hadn't used her handkerchief to make a napkin for Pansy.

'Is that so?' said Mr O'Brien in tones of intense interest. 'And a fine character of a man he must have been, keeping the Laws of God among all them pagan Egyptians.'

Elizabeth sniffed again. 'She said it isn't true,' she sobbed. 'That beastly girl who came with El-Ellie. She said the Bible isn't true.'

'Be aisy now, my girleen. There's always people to say such things of the Holy Word of God. And it's ignorance they speak from, having nothing better to do.'

'B-but she said M-Moses would have died on the river by himself.'

'Did she now? And how did she make that out?'

'She said b-babies always have to have milk to drink and Moses couldn't have milk out on the river by himself.'

Feeling that his professional status was involved, Mr O'Brien put his can down while he pondered the Higher Criticism. Elizabeth's face lightened.

'Oh, Mr O'Brien, do you think a nice, kind milkman gave him some? Did they have milkmen in those days?'

' 'Tis an idea, Beth, it is that. Some such kind of a thing may well have been. Sure, he didn't die, for how did we get the Ten Commandments? You ask your young lady friend that. We couldn't have got those from any spillikin baby, 'tis certain.'

Elizabeth did not quite follow this, but she felt that Mildred had been reduced to her proper level of unimportance and her spirits rose accordingly.

'I saved up four thistles and half my apple for Bossie,' she volunteered. Bossie was the pony that pulled Mr O'Brien's milk-cart. He nibbled the apple off Elizabeth's hand with velvety lips which tickled her palm.

'Like to come for a ride some day?' asked Mr O'Brien.

'In – in your milk-cart?' Elizabeth could scarcely believe the possibility of so exciting an invitation.

'That's right. I'll take you over to see the river and you can hold the reins while I take the milk in.'

'Oo, can I come now?'

'You cannot. You'll ask your mother, and if she says you can come, we'll fix the day.'

'Oh, thank you. Miss Una says you're a steady fellow for an Irishman.'

'Did she that? And what do you say?'

'I say you're splendid.'

7

The Dinner Party

MISS UNA was polishing the silver. The long table in the lobby was piled with entrée dishes, salvers, tea- and coffee-pots, cream-jugs, sweet-dishes and trumpet-shaped vases. When Miss Una cleaned the silver Elizabeth was always allowed to help. She enjoyed damping the pink powder and smearing it over the surface of a tray and then rubbing it off with a piece of old silk.

'Can I do the little boats? I like those best,' she asked.

'You certainly cannot,' was Miss Una's reply. 'Those are the best salt-cellars. They came from your grandmother in England.'

'P'raps my grandmother-in-England would *like* me to clean them,' said Elizabeth, breathing on the tray and rubbing very hard.

'She'd probably like you to stop talking so much.'

'Why? Doesn't she like little girls?'

'She wouldn't like little girls who asked so many questions.'

'Mummie says my grandmother-in-Heaven likes me to talk to her. Why does my grandmother-in-Heaven like me to talk to her and my grandmother-in-England not like me to talk to her?'

'For heaven's sake . . . ! Here, take this shammy and rub this lid. That ought to keep you busy for a bit. You'll have to scrub the knobs with the brush first and then polish it with the shammy.'

Elizabeth looked at herself in the lid. 'It makes me look most chekuliar,' she said. 'Like Mrs Thrace.'

'You mustn't make personal remarks,' said Miss Una severely.

'But it was you who said Mrs Thrace was chekuliar. I heard you.' Not for the first time Una Godfrey reproved her own sharp tongue.

'Well, I shouldn't have said it and you shouldn't repeat it,' she said.

'How many people are coming to the party, Miss Oonie?'

'Sixteen. That makes eighteen with your mother and father. We'll have to put all the extension leaves in the table and use the banqueting cloth.'

'The one the Queen gave my grandmother-in-England?'

'Well, the Queen didn't exactly give it to her. *Her* mother – that's your great-grandmother – had it for a dinner-party she gave to celebrate the Queen's coronation. That's a long time ago.'

'Was I born then?'

'Gracious, no. None of us were born then.'

'Then how did we have the table-cloth if we weren't born?'

'Let me see that tray. Yes, that's not bad. Would you like to help me put the epergne together?'

'Oh yes,' said Elizabeth fervently. She slid off her chair and followed Miss Una into the dining-room, where Mrs Thompson and Pearl, the house-parlourmaid, were unscrewing the table to fit in the additional panels. The room smelt of beeswax and turpentine. Elizabeth crawled under the table to see how the screw worked.

'There!' exclaimed Mrs Thompson, patting the shining wood as the last panel slid into position. 'I must get back to my kitchen.' She hurried away and Pearl fell to rubbing the table with a bright yellow duster.

'I think we'll put the cloth on straight away, Pearl,' said Miss Una. 'It's been folded so long it'll take twenty-four hours lying to get flat.'

She went out and came back with the heavy roll of white damask in her arms.

'Nine yards,' she said, and put the roll almost reverently on the table. As they smoothed the linen from its folds the light from the long windows glistened on the royal coat-of-arms and the festoons of roses, thistles and shamrocks which bordered the edge.

'Now, Beth,' said Miss Una seriously, 'you mustn't put your hands on the cloth or touch it at all. In fact, none of us must. To get a mark on it and have to wash and iron it before to-morrow night would be the death of me. Now you can fetch the epergne frame. That's right.' She placed it in the centre of the table. 'We can do the centre-piece now, but I'll have to put the flowers in tomorrow.' She added a two-tiered silver bowl to the highest bracket of the frame, and fetched a tray of fruit which she put on a chair beside her. 'You can hand me the things, if you like. First, the pineapple. We'll put that right on top, with the apples and oranges round it.' Piece by piece the fruits were arranged. Miss Una stood back to examine her handiwork, and then added several long bunches of muscatel raisins so that they hung down over the sides of the bowl. 'It's a pity that we haven't any grapes or cherries,' she said, 'they make the epergne look so pretty.'

'Why haven't we?' asked Beth.

'Because it is the wrong season of the year. They won't be ripe for another month or two. There's not much choice of dessert at this time of the year – no peaches or figs or apricots. We'll have to make up with dates and Smyrna figs and Chinese chow-chow.'

'Can I have some?'

'I expect so, when the time comes. Now the serviettes, eight each side and one each end. We'll set the dessert on this side table. Pearl will have the dinner-wagon for serving and the wine will be on the sideboard.' She was moving busily about as she talked, putting out silver and crystal dishes, nutcrackers and raisin-cutters, and plates of painted porcelain. 'Pearl, you'd better set the table in the breakfast-room for dinner tonight, and don't forget to take whatever you need from here, because when I'm finished the door of this room is going to be shut – and locked, in case a two-legged little mouse gets up to any mischief before tomorrow.'

'That means me,' explained Elizabeth to Pearl.

In the kitchen Mrs Thompson was rolling pastry dough at the central table, scooping dobs from a big bladder of lard and smoothing them over the rolled-out paste. Mrs Inglefell, looking very young and pretty in a linen apron much too large for her, was prodding with a fork at the contents of a tall jug.

'Mummie, what are you doing?' asked Elizabeth.

'I'm jugging two hares, darling. I think they are done now, Mrs Thompson. If you let them stand at the side of the stove for another three hours, in the boiler, then thicken the gravy a little and add a glass of burgundy just before serving, they should do very well. Fetch down a jar of red currant jelly the next time you go to the store-room. Have the ducks arrived?'

'Yes, 'm. Nice young birds, though the man asked a terrible price. He wanted three shillings each for them, but I wouldn't give him a penny more than five shillings the pair, and that's bad enough. I hope that was all right, mum?'

'I suppose so, Mrs Thompson. I haven't bought much poultry since we came down from the station, so I have had no opportunity of comparing prices. Are they dressed?'

'No, 'm. Finch screwed their necks not half an hour since. I'll pluck and draw them tonight. I've hung them in the larder.'

'How much does the beef weigh?'

'Twelve pounds. A beautiful sirloin with a good undercut. 'Twill take every minute of three hours roasting, even to leave it rare in the heart the way the master likes it.'

'I'll mix the batter for the Yorkshire pudding first thing after breakfast in the morning,' said Mrs Inglefell. 'Then it can have the whole day to rise. Don't forget to set aside a dozen of the warm eggs for me when Finch brings them in tomorrow. I think that's all I can do now.' She rinsed her hands under the tap over the sink and dried them on the roller towel behind the door.

Mrs Thompson slapped the last roll of raw pastry together, picked it up, board and all, and carried it to the little gate at the top of the cellar stairs.

'Why not go and have a lay down, mum?' she suggested kindly. 'You must be tired. I'll just put this down the cellar, then I'll make you a nice cup of tea.'

'Thank you, Mrs Thompson, I think I will. Come, Beth. Run and find Daddy and tell him some tea is coming. We'll have it in the sewing-room.'

The sewing-room was a small, square room opening off the breakfast-room. As it was well lit from its two wide windows and had an old-fashioned open grate which threw out a good heat, Mrs Inglefell and Miss Una had found it a convenient and pleasant place to work in while the weather was cold. Here in one corner was the sewing-machine. A large cupboard built to one side of the fireplace held the sewing-baskets, boxes of silks and cottons, piles of garments awaiting attention and all the other paraphernalia inseparable from dressmaking. A couch under the window was a favourite spot with Mrs Inglefell, for here she could rest while stitching or crocheting, and do both while supervising Elizabeth's 'lessons'.

Elizabeth and her father and Mrs Thompson with the tea-tray arrived together.

'Tired, old lady?' asked Mr Inglefell, bending down to kiss his wife.

'Just a little. Oh dear, I've spilled some into your saucer. But you joggled me. Give it back to me and I'll tidy it. The truth is, I'm rather dreading the whole thing.'

'Dreading it? Come, there's no need to feel like that, surely.'

'Oh, Alfred, it's all very well for you to say that. You know all these men and I suppose get on with them. But some of their wives I've never even met. Besides, it's positively years since I did any of this sort of entertaining.'

Alfred Inglefell threw back his head and laughed heartily. 'Well, I never thought to hear Miss Maxim-Munt of Cloverdale Park in the County of Somerset talk of being frightened of a bit of colonial hospitality.'

His wife laughed a trifle shamefacedly. 'I know it sounds silly. But remember, at home we always had Jennings and Mrs Marchant to take over the domestic end of things. It makes a good deal of difference. Poor Pearl is petrified already. I'm sure she'll drop the soup-tureen or spill gravy down the back of Captain Bossingham's uniform.'

'Oh, Mummie, is Capting Bossing coming? Will he wear his sword? Will he wear his medals?' asked Elizabeth, alight with interest.

'I don't know about medals,' replied her mother. 'But I shouldn't think he'd wear a sword. That's only at weddings, though I can't think why. He mightn't even come in uniform. In fact, he might not come at all, though he says His Excellency is very considerate about allowing him to keep his private engagements. I believe he is rather enjoying his aide-de-camp-ship, don't you?'

'Yes, I think he is,' agreed Mr Inglefell. 'A welcome change from the African veldt, I imagine.'

'What's African veldt, Mummie?' Elizabeth naturally wanted to know. Her father picked her up.

'Come along with me,' he said. 'We'll go and see if Finch has started the milking.'

Preparations for the dinner-party went on throughout the following day. Whenever Beth offered to help, she was told to 'run and play in the garden, dear'. Rooms already spotlessly clean were cleaned again; mahogany and cedar were polished and re-polished. The silver trumpets of the epergne and the silver vases down the centre of the table were filled with pink carnations and sweet-peas from the garden and sprays of trembling maidenhair from the conservatory; crystal finger-bowls half filled with water on which floated a single begonia blossom stood in a row with the dishes of preserved ginger, walnuts, bananas, raisins and blanched almonds, A melancholy waiter in shabby evening dress who had been hired to help with the serving was initiated into the mysteries of the wine cupboard by Mr Inglefell and admonished by Miss Una 'not to bump the bottles down on the rims of the glasses. These are our best Venetians'. Crisp table-napkins were folded into water-lily shapes and given each a cube of bread to hold. A moment of crisis was caused by the inexplicable disappearance of grandmother-in-Heaven's dessert knives and forks with the mother-of-pearl handles.

'We must have left them at Undaboo,' said Miss Una.

'But I remember distinctly packing them in my hat-box,' said Mrs Inglefell, 'because the packing-case had already been nailed down.'

'Perhaps they are still there,' suggested Miss Una; and there they surely were, flat on the bottom under Mrs Inglefell's old winter felt and new spring bonnet.

In the afternoon Mr Inglefell's sister, Aunt Emma, and her husband, Thomas Woodstock, arrived. They had a farm about fifty miles from the city and would sleep the night and go home next day. Elizabeth had never met Uncle Thomas before and liked him very much; he was so slow and big and red in the face.

Miss Una bustled Aunt Emma up to the spare room, 'and I'll bring you a cup of tea straight away. You must be dying for it'. Finch brought the dress-baskets in and carried them upstairs, while Elizabeth showed Uncle Thomas the little tobacco-chopping machine in the back lobby where he could make himself a cigarette if he felt inclined. But he clung to his pipe and tried not to feel in the way of the busy house staff. He was delighted when Elizabeth offered to show him the two new Jersey cows. His farm was near the famous Melrose stud at Rosebank, so he was something of an authority. He and

Elizabeth and Finch spent the rest of the afternoon counting the chickens, prodding the pigs, feeling the horses' hocks and discussing the relative merits of Jerseys and Guernseys and Friesians.

At six o'clock Mrs Inglefell came downstairs to receive her guests. She was unaccountably nervous. Absurd to feel one's heart beating so quickly at the prospect of saying 'how-do-you-do' to a dozen strangers! But she knew too well how, as a new-comer, she would be examined, criticised and discussed. No detail of her dress, the food, the furnishings of the house, and the entertainment offered to her guests would escape their appraisal. The hostess would be the last person to enjoy such an occasion! Her gown of pale pink tulle billowing softly over a lining of brown silk had been imported from Paris, but it had already brought a frown of disapproval to the face of Aunt Emma, who thought it much too frivolous for a matron of her sister-in-law's age and social position. She herself was wearing her lilac grosgrain. It was not new, but as it had been made by the city's most fashionable dressmaker and had cost five guineas, she thought it good for several years yet. She wore grandmother-in-Heaven's ear-rings and necklace of Whitby jet and looked handsome, if rather forbidding. Uncle Thomas had changed into the suit of navy blue worsted and the elastic-sided boots which he wore every Sunday to church. His wife's urgings towards black broadcloth he had resisted not by argument, but by a wordless and passive obstinacy.

Elizabeth sat on the floor of the first landing whence she could, by peeping between the banisters, watch the arrival of the guests. Each ring of the front-door bell was answered by the hired waiter, whose earlier lassitude had now given way to an air of professional sprightliness. Mr and Mrs Digby Faulkener were the first to come. Elizabeth noticed that Mrs Faulkener's dress was of the same colour and style as that which she had worn on the day they had called to see her, but now the material was a rich moiré silk. Though the

The Dinner Party

November evening was hot and all the French windows to the veranda stood open, Mr Faulkener at once took up his stand in front of the drawing-room fireplace.

Next came Mr and Mrs Goldiway. He was managing director of a pastoral company in which Mr Inglefell was interested, and therefore a person of some importance, a fact which his wife was anxious that everyone should appreciate. She fanned herself energetically and exclaimed on the warmth of the weather.

'What a way you live from town, Mrs Inglefell! I declare it took us nearly an hour to drive down, in spite of the fact that we came in the phaeton with the two new greys Mr Goldiway has just bought.'

'It is only seven miles,' said her hostess, trying not to sound like a mother tigress defending her young.

'Is it indeed? I should have thought it more. It seems quite like the country. I cannot bear to live in the country, can you?' she said, turning to Mrs Woodstock.

'I always live in the country,' said that lady firmly.

'I understand,' interposed Mrs Faulkener's gentle tones, 'that their Majesties have just returned from Sandringham. What a delightful change from London it must have been for them.' The pastoral interests were thus delicately made aware that the wholesale grocery trade could not be imposed on, and Mrs Goldiway was reminded that better people than herself chose to live in the country when they could.

This gentle exchange was interrupted by the arrival of the Misses Gladys and Dorothy Merriman, whose bouffant sleeves and lace-flounced skirts immediately effected a closure of the matronly ranks. Miss Gladys, who was tall and dark, had a manner that was animated and coy. Miss Dorothy, shorter and fairer than her sister, was coy and quiet. The older ladies privately suspected them of being 'fast'. Did they not wear their hair cut into a fringe and frizzed across the forehead? Was it possible that so delicate a flush upon the cheek owed

71

nothing to art? Could so slender a waist be achieved without the sin of 'tight-lacing'? Though not a lady present would have admitted to a waist measurement greater than twenty-four inches (except Aunt Emma, who was much too hard-working a person to bother with such niceties), they would have indignantly denied the use of anything but the most 'sensible' corsetting. Finally (and this was not suspicion, but an established fact) had not Gladys Merriman ridden astride to a meeting of the Hunt Club, instead of using the side-saddle as any well-conducted female would? Certainly the 'divided skirt' of her riding habit (the very implications of the words were slightly embarrassing!) had been several yards in width and reached right to her feet, but it was nevertheless necessary for her to throw her right leg across the animal's back and put her foot into the stirrup on the other side, a gesture quite in-compatible with lady-like behaviour. As for the physiological complications likely to arise for a woman who rode horseback astride, these could be discussed only by the married ladies and in the seclusion of their own rooms.

These thoughts had hardly had time to rise in the minds of those present before Dr Daniel O'Shawn and his wife came in. Everyone liked the doctor for his breezy manner and kindly nature. Besides, it was necessary to show the good chap that the hearty dislike one had for his religion and his country was based on the firm principles of British sportsmanship and had nothing personal about it.

The O'Shawns were followed by Colonel Patience, a retired officer of the Indian Army, and his wife, and the bank manager, Mr Pennyfarthing, and his wife, all of whom had shared a four-wheeler.

By now the drawing-room was lively with the hum of con-versation, and when the grandfather clock in the hall chimed the half-hour, Mrs Inglefell was beginning to wonder if dinner would have to be delayed. Fortunately at that moment the door-bell rang again and the hired waiter announced: 'Captain

Ross-Bossingham. Mr Harvey Wingham-Smith.' As no apéritif was to be offered, Mrs Inglefell was able to give the waiter a brief nod which was the signal for dinner to be served immediately. The double doors were rolled back and the company eddied into the dining-room.

Mr Inglefell led Mrs Goldiway and Mrs Faulkener to the head of the table and established them to right and left of his own seat. At the opposite end of the table Mrs Inglefell had Mr Goldiway on her right hand, but, in spite of her husband's demur, had insisted on seating Captain Ross-Bossingham on her left in preference to Mr Faulkener, for, as she explained, not even for the demands of good hostess-ship would she be bored on both hands at her own dinner-table. Besides, as a returned and wounded hero of the war and a defender of the Empire, Captain Bossingham deserved greater honours than his youth would otherwise have entitled him. (The discussion of these arrangements had naturally taken place earlier in the afternoon, before the arrival of the guests.)

While Mr Inglefell ladled the steaming kangaroo-tail soup from the immense tureen in front of him, and handed the plates to Pearl, the hired waiter went round the table pouring some of Uncle Het's sherry wine into each glass. (Except Mrs Pennyfarthing's. She said primly: 'You must please excuse me. I never indulge,' which had the effect of making the rest of the company feel positively Bacchanalian.) Silver baskets of toast sippets were circulated from hand to hand. Talking lulled as the business of dealing with the soup was attended to. Mr Faulkener, who had not contributed a single word to the conversation, so far forgot himself as to exclaim that the soup was as good as the turtle soup he got at his London club. At Mr Inglefell's invitation he passed his plate up for more and Mr Wingham-Smith raised a laugh by calling him 'Oliver Twist'. Dr O'Shawn told a funny story about a patient of his whom he nicknamed 'Mr Micawber' because he was always expecting something to 'turn up'.

'And did it?' asked someone.

'Lord, no,' shouted the doctor cheerfully. 'The only thing about him that ever turned up was his own toes.'

This made everyone laugh again except his wife. She was a woman of considerable beauty and fortune, but she had social ambitions and her husband's unconventional behaviour was a frequent embarrassment to her. For example, no matter how important the occasion or the company in which he found himself, the doctor always observed the precepts of the Church concerning fasting, the abstinence from flesh meat, and attendance at Mass. Mrs O'Shawn considered herself a good Catholic, but she felt that the Church was unreasonable in expecting her to flout the prevailing social codes for the sake of her soul. Eternity should really be a little more accommodating. Now she turned her lovely eyes towards Mr Wingham-Smith, who was sitting on her left. 'I have no sense of humour,' she explained. 'Fortunately Dan has enough for both of us.'

'Lucky Dan,' said her partner, with feeling. 'To have a double allotment of humour and you as well.'

Mrs O'Shawn found this compliment a little too obvious to be convincing, and as she was still deeply in love with her husband in spite of his idiosyncrasies, she had no inclination to pursue the paths of even verbal dalliance. She therefore turned to Mr Woodstock on her other hand. His conversation had a sort of bovine placidity which she found very soothing. She won his confidence and admiration at once by asking how many sheep he had. Lincolns and Corriedales and cross-bred Merinos lasted them right through the grilled whiting, the roast duckling and apple sauce, the jugged hare and red currant jelly, and the sweetbreads with sugared ham. The gentle flow of their bales and clips was interrupted at last by the advent of the sirloin. Dr O'Shawn burst into applause.

'Ar, that's what I call a noble sight,' he cried. With a spotless white apron over her best black dress and a freshly laundered cap on her grey hair, Mrs Thompson came in from the kitchen bearing the joint on the largest of the Wedgwood platters, the wells at each end of which were already filling with rich red gravy. She had cooked the meat on the bone and garnished it with the green tops of the horse-radish tied into little bunches.

Mr Inglefell gazed at the beef with pride and tapped it gently with the tip of his carving-knife before beginning to slice the undercut. 'This is one of our own beasts from Undaboo,' he explained. 'It happened that one of our mobs came in two weeks ago. They had been nearly seven months on the road, but had good feed all the way down, so they were in excellent condition. At least, I think they were. We will soon find out.'

Mrs Thompson reappeared, this time carrying the Yorkshire pudding which she put down in front of Mrs Inglefell. It had risen into a golden-brown crust, eight inches high, of biscuit crispness around the melting yellow centre. As Mrs Inglefell added a triangle of this delicacy to each slice of beef she lightly sprinkled it with castor sugar from a tall silver dredger.

The sherry-glasses had now been taken away and replaced by large goblets. The waiter began to open bottles sealed with heavy gold foil.

'I'm going to offer you some of Mr Auld's sparkling burgundy,' said Mr Inglefell. 'A red wine which sparkles may seem an oddity, but I believe that in another fifty years Australian wines will be challenging even the French. This is not a true burgundy, of course, because it was grown at Magill and not in France. However, there is a still burgundy there for anyone who prefers something more orthodox.'

Everyone (except, of course, Mrs Pennyfarthing) was eager to sample the local vintage and declared it excellent. Miss Merriman clapped her hands when her glass was filled.

'It is just what I consider wine should be,' she exclaimed. 'Crimson and foaming.'

After the beef came apple-pie, lemon snow, angel's food,

preserved peaches in jelly, cut-glass cups filled with brandied cream covered with pasty, and small mountains of strawberries each snow-capped with whipped cream.

Mrs Inglefell was finding (rather to her own surprise) that she was enjoying herself thoroughly. The duties of hospitality had proved less vexatious than she had feared. The dishes which she herself had prepared – the jugged hares, the Yorkshire pudding, and the angel's food – had been a success, and Pearl (whose first experience this was of waiting at table for so large a party) had carried out her tasks very creditably (with Mrs Thompson and Miss Una behind the scenes, of course, getting everything ready and telling her what to do next). There was one critical moment when Mrs O'Shawn, while helping herself to smothered artichokes, let fall a drop of the sauce on to her skirt. She uttered a little exclamation of annoyance.

'Don't worry, 'm,' said Pearl in a very kind way. 'I'll sponge it out for you in a jiffy after dinner.'

While this may not have been in accordance with the dictates of the best service as she remembered it in the Somersetshire home of her childhood and would certainly have shocked her father's butler, Mrs Inglefell very sensibly felt that Pearl could hardly be reproved for good nature. Mrs O'Shawn, who had been born in Australia, had had far too much experience of the servant problem to feel anything but gratitude to Pearl for her obligingness. She gave her an exquisite smile (which threw Mr Wingham-Smith into a fit of jealousy) and said: 'Oh, thank you, Pearl. I don't think it has made a mark and, in any case, it was quite my own fault.'

Dr O'Shawn demonstrated how to peel an orange with a fork, and Mr Wingham-Smith (temporarily recovered from his jealousy) took the skin off an apple all in one piece, whirled it three times and allowed it to fall upon the table-cloth, where, he claimed, it described a 'D'.

'My fate is a D!' he exclaimed, and looked across the table

at Dorothy Merriman, who responded by blushing and calling up the dimple in her right cheek. (It was a perfectly genuine dimple, but she encouraged it by poking it with a pencil-point every night and morning.) In the course of the dinner she had often glanced across at Mr Wingham-Smith to admire his waistcoat, which was of cream huckaback hand-embroidered all over in orange and yellow silk and fastened in front with buttons of purple and yellow Venetian glass kept in position by brass clips; and his collar, of double-fold linen, cut so high and starched so stiff that his chin rested on it; and his moustache, so luxuriant that it hung down over his cheeks; and his hair, fair and waving naturally from a high forehead; and his eyes, blue and bright, now expressing very plainly his admiration of all pretty women, but especially for the girl sitting opposite. No wonder Dorothy felt some little triumph, for had not her sister, far cleverer and more talkative than herself, sat next to Mr Wingham-Smith throughout the meal and yet seemed to have made little headway with him; while the beautiful Mrs O'Shawn on his other side had apparently been too engrossed in conversation with that dull Mr Woodstock to do more than exchange a few stray remarks with the younger man. The truth was that Gladys had talked too much and too gaily. Mr Wingham-Smith half suspected her of being clever and that frightened him. In any case, he preferred ladies to be fair-haired and a trifle shy.

At the conclusion of dessert only Mr Goldiway, Mr Faulkener and Colonel Patience remained to keep their host company with the decanters. The other gentlemen quickly followed the ladies into the drawing-room, preferring music to wine.

Upstairs, Miss Una had put the children to bed at the usual time, seven o'clock. Eleanor and Marian were soon asleep, but Elizabeth tossed and wriggled in the warm darkness, listening to the subdued sounds of talk and laughter, the clatter of dishes and the swing-thump, swing-thump of the servery door as

Pearl and Miss Una came and went. At last she became so very uncomfortable, so hot and thirsty, and so curious about Captain Bossingham's medals that she slid out of bed and paddled softly in her bare feet across the nursery floor, into the upstairs hall, and down the stairs to her first vantage-point on the half-way landing. Here she found that she could see only a little way in at the dining-room door. So she bumped down a few more steps. Now she could see the back of her mother's chair, the side of Captain Bossingham's shoulder, and Mrs Pennyfarthing's face every time she bent forward to put something into her mouth. She could see Pearl carrying plates and dishes backwards and forwards, and the hired waiter manipulating his decanters and bottles at the sideboard. She cuddled against the banisters and felt very wide awake and very sleepy, both at once, which was odd. She wished her mother would turn round and see her so that she could ask for a drink. She wished Captain Bossingham would turn round so that she could see if he were wearing his medals. She wished that her daddy or Miss Una would come . . .

After a long time she saw her mother rise from the table, Captain Bossingham holding back her chair. But instead of coming into the hall, all the ladies went into the drawing-room through the rolling doors, which the waiter closed after them. Elizabeth was so disappointed that she wanted to cry. Fortunately she remembered in time that she was now five years old, so she decided not to cry but just to feel miserable instead, and after a while she began quite to enjoy feeling miserable and to make up a story inside her head along the lines of the Ugly Duckling.

After what seemed a long time but was actually only ten minutes, sounds of coughing and throat-clearing and masculine talking brought her back to the present as several of the gentlemen came out of the dining-room into the hall. Captain Bossingham caught sight of her and in three strides was on the stairs at her side. He lifted her into his arms. She clasped his neck tightly and laid a hot cheek against his collar.

'I'se thirsty," she confided.

'Of course you are. We'll find Mama and get a drink of water.'

'It's not Mama,' said Elizabeth, her shyness evaporating before the need for instruction. 'It's Mummie.'

All the gentlemen laughed, though Elizabeth could not think that there was anything funny to laugh at. Mr Wingham-Smith said something about 'Bossie's way with the ladies', and all the gentlemen laughed again. She rode into the drawing-room on Captain Bossingham's shoulder. Going through the doorway he said: 'Duck,' and she clutched his hair very tightly which made him say 'Ow'and screw up his eyes.

'Darling!' exclaimed Mrs Inglefell half in laughter and half in reproof.

'I'se thirsty,' murmured Elizabeth, now quite overcome with shyness, there seemed to be so many people all laughing and talking at once and the lights were so very bright and glittering.

'Oh, the little love!' exclaimed Miss Gladys Merriman. 'Do let her stay for a while, Mrs Inglefell.' But Mummie was not to be persuaded. Elizabeth was once more hoisted to Captain Bossingham's shoulder. He said: ' 'Bout turn! Quick march!' and away they went up the stairs again. Mrs Inglefell excused herself to her guests and followed.

'Did you bring your sword?' asked Elizabeth into his left ear.

'Why, no. No sword. Did you want to see it?'

'Yes, please. And Mummie said you've got medals. Have you got medals?'

'One or two. Not very big ones.'

Mrs Inglefell came in with a glass of water and Elizabeth was tucked into bed, and the mosquito-nets drawn. 'I shall call you Bossie,' she announced. 'Mr O'Brien's horse is called Bossie. He used to eat my apple. Mr O'Brien used to bring the

79

milk in a rattly can, but he doesn't come any more because of the Jerseys.'

'I'm not sure that that is altogether polite,' said Mrs Inglefell doubtfully. 'You should call Captain Bossingham by his correct name, darling.'

'I take it as a great compliment to be called after Mr O'Brien's horse,' said the Captain. 'But only if I am allowed to call you Gloriana.'

'What name is that?' Elizabeth wanted to know.

'It is the name of a great queen who was also called Elizabeth. She, too, liked her men friends to have swords and medals. You will learn about her some day. Good night, my Gloriana. Sleep well.'

In the drawing-room the grand piano had been opened, but no one liked to begin the musical items while their hostess was absent. Mrs Patience found a congenial subject of conversation with Mrs Faulkener, who had been in India during her girlhood. They discovered mutual acquaintances whose life histories provided ample material for discussion and conjecture. Mr Wingham-Smith lost no time in approaching Miss Dorothy Merriman with an inquiry about her taste in music which naturally led on to an examination of the pieces lying on the music-stand. This move was not lost on Miss Gladys, who was not accustomed to being overlooked in her sister's favour. However, tonight she was bent on higher game. She thought it quite unnecessary of Captain Bossingham to go off like that with the Inglefell child. Mrs Inglefell should have rung for a servant to take the child to bed. She might have known that all the ladies were longing to ask him about his adventures in South Africa, to say nothing of the glimpses they hoped to catch of his present life at Government House. In the meantime, it might be profitable to make oneself agreeable to Mrs Goldiway, who was rapidly gaining an entrée if not to the most exclusive, at any rate, to the monied circles of the city's society. A little flattery judiciously applied worked wonders with that class of person. From this it may be inferred that Gladys Merriman was a woman of narrow self-interest, a view not entirely just, for she had good qualities. But she and her sister had been left orphans at an early age with resources that would do little more than prepare them for marriage, should they be fortunate enough to secure husbands, a project which Miss Gladys had every intention of forwarding to the best of her powers. Handsome, well-to-do and the son of an earl, Captain Bossingham was by far the most eligible man she had ever met. While she listened admiringly to a long description of the cleverness and good looks of Mrs Goldiway's children, one half of her mind was indulging in dreams of a début in London society, of gowns from Paris, a presentation at Court . . .

Perhaps the tender domestic scene he had lately witnessed in the nursery had softened Captain Bossingham's mood, or perhaps the more material influences of an excellent dinner were making themselves felt. Be that as it may, he was in high spirits on his return to the drawing-room and quickly gathered the younger members of the party round the piano, while at the same time he showed such charming deference to the presence of the older ladies and such a pleasing appreciation of their opinions that all thoughts of his being a young man too much concerned with his own worldly position were dismissed as unworthy.

Mrs Woodstock was easily persuaded to open the musical programme. She sang 'When the swallows homeward fly' in a deep contralto, the rich tones of which blended well with the warm moonlit night, the perfume of the stocks and oleanders which came softly in at the open windows, and the general atmosphere of the gathering which was one of well-being, contentment and relaxation. Dorothy Merriman, a pianist of some talent, accompanied the song and at the urgent pleadings of Mr Wingham-Smith went on to play a rollicking 'galop';

'rather too rowdy' in the opinion of some of the ladies, but performed with undeniable skill.

Gladys Merriman, in the meantime, had been sitting quietly beside Mrs Goldiway, giving her best presentation of the elegant, well-bred young lady that she wished to be; for her social aspirations were not such as to impel her merely to superficial good manners. She wished not only to behave as a lady, but to be one. She felt fairly confident that her air of restraint would draw to itself the notice she desired. And sure enough, when the last notes of the 'galop' had been struck, when the piano strings had quivered to silence and the acknowledgments to the pianist been paid by applause, Mrs Inglefell crossed the room and sat down on a low stool beside her.

'Dear Miss Merriman,' she said, 'I am sure you could play or sing for us. Please do.' A murmur of endorsement from the others was met by what Miss Merriman hoped was a proper degree of hesitation on her part.

'Oh, come!' exclaimed Captain Bossingham. 'We are dying to hear you. And think how tragic it would be if our desire were really to prove fatal before it could be fulfilled.' He spoke laughingly, but she seemed to hear a note of mockery in his voice. She was pricked into annoyance and was then annoyed with herself for being annoyed. She jumped up too quickly, dropped her fan, and felt herself flushing. Regaining her composure by a deliberate effort of will, she walked to the piano, comforted by the knowledge that though Mrs O'Shawn might have a more beautiful face, no woman in the room could rival Gladys Merriman for her superb figure. With the train of her gown spread fanwise across the Brussels carpet and her hands linked lightly together in front of her (for she had noticed in the illustrated journals that Madame Nellie Melba took up this posture on the concert platform) she sang 'One of those dear dreams' in a high, pure soprano. If her interpretation lacked subtlety and that degree of 'soul' considered essential to true artistic presentation, the music was performed with enough competence to make it enjoyable. The gentlemen from the dining-room came in and stood listening in the doorway till the song's conclusion. They applauded loudly and called for an encore, but Miss Merriman went back to her seat feeling that she had done what was required and had (in some obscure fashion) scored off Captain Bossingham.

Mr Wingham-Smith was now invited to sing, and as he had all along intended to do so he produced a copy of 'The Absent-minded Beggar' from his hip pocket and soon had everyone tapping their toes to his choruses and singing 'tum te tum'.

Eleanor Inglefell had been only eighteen when she had met, during her first London season, the man who within three months became her husband. Her ideas of colonial life had been nebulous. She had prepared herself for hardships greater than those she had had in fact to endure. Far more difficult than any physical discomfort to understand and become accustomed to had been the change of social habits and conventions. The Province (as the inhabitants emphatically called it, in implied distinction from the penal settlements of New South Wales and Tasmania, and in deference, too, to the powers of self-government granted by the mother country in 1856), the Province, though little more than half a century old, had already produced its own quality of life. Entertainment had for a variety of reasons found new forms, and many small customs considered *de rigueur* in the dining- and drawing-rooms of the Old Country were either lost altogether or so much changed as to be scarcely recognisable. One of these with which Mrs Inglefell had long since become familiar was the drinking of tea. After her arrival in South Australia she had continued to serve coffee after dinner in the evenings in the way to which she had been accustomed in her father's house. But so few of her new acquaintances cared for it and so many of them preferred tea that in the end she fell into the Australian way of serving tea with, or shortly after, every meal.

It was therefore no exception to the established rule of the household when Pearl appeared in the drawing-room at nine o'clock to spread the tea-table with a lace-edged cloth. She came back a few minutes later with the silver tea equipage and accompanied by the hired waiter bearing a tray of sweet cakes.

Over the tea-cups there was a change of partners and the conversation became more general. Colonel Patience discovered that the handsome Miss Merriman ('Dashed fine woman, my dear,' he told his wife later) was most sympathetic towards his views on the trend of Empire affairs; Mr Wingham-Smith seized the opportunity of improving his acquaintance with that very useful fellow Mr Pennyfarthing, the bank manager; Dr O'Shawn told Aunt Emma such a pack of non-sensical stories that she laughed more than she had done for years; while the silent Mr Faulkener, handing the cakes to Mrs O'Shawn, received a glance so breath-takingly beautiful that he became purple in the face and felt quite giddy.

After tea was finished and cleared away, Mrs Inglefell (feeling in her bones the imminence of the cribbage-board and the whist table) made a small announcement. 'We have a special treat in store for us,' she said. 'I have persuaded Mrs O'Shawn to bring her harp.'

Surprise and genuine pleasure mingled with interest as the door was again opened and Pearl and the hired waiter came in wheeling the tall gilded instrument. Mrs O'Shawn settled herself composedly and swept a long melting arpeggio from the strings while Mr Inglefell went to the gas-brackets on the side walls and pulled the little levers which extinguished all but the pilots, so that the room was lighted now only by the branches of candles on the mantelpiece and piano.

In some indefinable way the room became charged with emotion. Gladys Merriman felt rather than saw Ross-Bossing-ham as he stood behind her chair. During tea he had been most attentive, as though to make up for any shadow of teasing he may have cast on his treatment of her after dinner. She trembled a little as she thought of his almost anxious solicitude for the replenishment of her tea-cup, of his frank interest in her description of the Hunt Club meetings, of his inquiry about her favourite books and pastimes. Surely in this twilight hour the throbbing of the harp could conjure into reality feelings more tender than tea-cups, more thrilling than horses and hounds, more romantic even than mazurkas and waltzes and the novels of Ouida? She tensed herself, as though the music were a wave she must breast, a wave which would gather her up and carry her away in some delicious sweep of experience.

Mr Woodstock moved to take an empty chair near his wife. As the harp strings poured out their melody he thought her face lost its severity of expression and regained something of that youthful gentleness he had so much admired before their marriage. He sighed again for the children they had not had, and resolved that now that Eleanor and Alfred had come to live within calling distance, Emma should have more time for pleasure, more visits to town and, if the wool and wheat prices improved, some new dresses.

Colonel Patience had a rush of nostalgia for home and blew his nose very loudly. His wife suddenly remembered a boy she hadn't thought of for years – anyway, he had married that plain Philimore girl with all that money.

Alfred Inglefell was content to watch his wife as she sat with her face half turned from him, the light from the candles making a gold halo of her hair and gleaming rosily on the lovely line of her neck and shoulders. How elusive she was! he thought with a pang, as though she moved on a plane of her own, always just beyond his reach. After nine years of married life he still felt that he had not possessed her. Here was pain if he dared to let it grow.

The music changed key and fell into a minor mood of sad pleading.

Surprisingly, indeed unbelievably to most of his friends had they known of it (which they never would), the person most responsive to the heightened atmosphere was that seasoned soldier, that London clubman and man of the world, Ross-Bossingham. After listening for a few minutes, he stepped back, his footsteps soundless on the thick carpet, and slid behind the curtains, through the french windows and so on to the lawn.

The garden, sheeted in the brilliant November moonlight, was a world of its own, smelling of hot earth newly watered, the perfume of lemon trees and the heavier, warmer scent of ripening loquats. Somewhere behind the shadows of the hibiscus bushes a wagtail caught up the notes of floating music and threw them back on to the air with a poignant sweetness. 'Love me, oh love me, oh love me, Sweet pretty creature, sweet pretty creature,' he sang over and over. 'Litsen, oh listen, listen, oh listen, sweet pretty creature.'

Between the curtains Ross could see into the lighted room, the circle of listeners immobilised, wrapt and held as if Medusa-like, the harp had magicked them to stone. He could see Mrs O'Shawn's hands, as though disembodied, every time they reached for the bass strings. And just beyond the gilded upright of the instrument he could see Eleanor Inglefell, her head slightly bent, one hand touching her cheek, the other resting on the fan lying in her lap. He could see the soft tendrils of hair curling under her ears and the light touching the smooth petals of her eyelids.

Ross swung away across the lawn and there gave vent to his feelings in such a string of curses as only the men under his command in Africa had ever been privileged to hear from his lips; which was just as well, for Miss Merriman, for one, would have been horrified at such behaviour and would, indeed, have found it difficult to believe that the son of an earl could even know such words, much less express them.

The music died away to silence. The audience sat unmoving, entranced. Out in the garden, Captain Bossingham drew a deep breath and exclaimed: 'Thank God for that.' And the wagtail in the hedge warbled: 'Do it again, do it again; sweet pretty creature, do it again.'

Mrs Inglefell with an almost visible effort roused herself and went to thank the harpist. Her husband pulled down the gas-levers and flooded the room with light. The spell was broken. Captain Bossingham stepped quickly and quietly back through the window just in time to take up his host's suggestion of whist. The harp was wheeled away, the card-tables pushed forward, packs were shuffled and partners chosen.

At eleven o'clock Pearl brought in whisky for the gentlemen and a decanter of Frontignac for the ladies, and sandwiches in silver entrée dishes. Mrs Pennyfarthing did not indulge, but everyone else ate and drank cheerfully and counted their profits and losses and told each other the cards that were played and should not have been or should have been played and were not.

At a quarter to midnight Mr Faulkener took out his massive gold watch, looked across at his wife and said: 'Well, my dear . . .'

After a suitable period of protestations, Mrs Inglefell rang for Pearl and when she came said: 'Please tell the coachmen that the carriages are needed.'

Everyone shook hands with everyone else and asked Mr and Mrs Woodstock how long they intended to stay in town and 'couldn't we see something of you before you return'. In a moment of sheer reaction Captain Bossingham invited Miss Merriman to go to the polo with him the following Saturday afternoon (suitably chaperoned by her aunt, of course), and Mr Wingham-Smith held Miss Dorothy's hand longer than was strictly necessary and begged permission to call on her one evening very soon. Mrs Goldiway was complacently satisfied that she had impressed everyone with her husband's import-ance. Mr Goldiway thought that Faulkener was a useful man to know. The Colonel and Mrs Patience for the first time since they came to Australia felt that here were people to whom India was neither a joke nor a fantasy. Mr Pennyfarthing came to the conclusion that Mr Inglefell must be a pretty warm man and wondered who handled his banking. Dr O'Shawn produced a last-minute crop of jokes. The Faulkeners made their farewells in their own characteristic fashion, Mrs Faulkener murmuring something about 'your charming hospitality', Mr Faulkener bowing silently over his hostess's hand.

When the Faulkeners' victoria and the Goldiways' phaeton and the two hired cabs and Captain Bossingham's dogcart had all driven away and the clat-clat of the horses' hooves could be heard receding along the metalled road, Mr Inglefell closed the front door and returned to the drawing-room to put out the lights.

'Well, my dear, you gave us a very enjoyable evening,' he said to his wife.

Eleanor who was already feeling the premonition of reaction tried not to sound flat as she replied: 'Yes, I think it went off quite well.' She suddenly laughed. 'Did you ever see anything so funny as Miss Merriman's attacks on Ross-Bossingham? Poor Gladys and Dorothy! They are really nice girls but they will never get husbands if they try so hard. And Captain Bossingham, of all people! Mama said in her last letter that the season before last he was practically engaged to old Lord Castlecrag's daughter, the youngest one. But apparently nothing came of it.'

'Perhaps he wasn't in love with her.'

Mrs Inglefell laughed again but with a note of uncertainty. 'Darling Alfred, I love you when you are pretending to be naïve. Ross-Bossingham will probably marry for convenience one of those hideously wealthy Americans. I can't imagine him being in love with anyone.'

There was a moment's silence. Mr Inglefell turned out the last gas-jet. Then in the dimness of the room lit now only by a shaft of light from the hallway, he put an arm round his wife's waist and kissed her lightly under one ear.

'Time for bed, my love,' he said.

Out in the garden the moon was setting behind the loquat trees. In the hedge the wagtail still warbled his plaintive cry: 'Love me, oh love me, love me, oh love me. Sweet pretty creature, forlorn, forlorn.'

8

The Cauliflower

ON the Monday morning following the dinner party Elizabeth helped Mrs Thompson to do the washing. Mrs Inglefell was not well, so there were no lessons. Elizabeth was finding things rather tedious until Mrs Thompson said: 'Come along out with me to the laundry. You can hang up the dusters.'

Mrs Thompson had been up shortly after dawn. By six o'clock the fire under the big copper was lit and the nine-yard dinner cloth and all the table napkins, doilies, lace-edged tea-cloths and the antimacassars from the drawing-room chairs were bubbling merrily. The morning was bright and clear. Overhead the sky was as blue as Mrs Thompson's rinsing water. The white horizon and the bleached paleness of the distant hills presaged heat for the coming day. The laundry was already very hot. Clouds of steam rose from the tubs and mingled under the ceiling with those from the copper. The fire crackled and blazed as Mrs Thompson pushed in mallee roots and bundles of gum twigs which Finch had brought in from the paddocks. The air was full of their eucalyptus perfume and the smell of the hot suds.

Mrs Thompson moved between the tubs, her big body deal-ing easily with their great weight. Her hands, red with heat and whitish round the nails with the strong soap, beat and wrung the heavy linen with effortless competence. She set a dipper full of warm water on a low stool. She gave Elizabeth a piece of soap and put down a pile of soiled dusters beside her.

'If you could get on with these it would be a real help,' she said. 'Then later on you can give me a hand with the hanging out.'

Elizabeth rubbed all the dusters with soap and squelched them in the water. A good deal of the water went down the front of her pinafore.

'The water's all dirty now,' she said.

'That's right. We'll pour that away and have a new lot. My, there doesn't seem to be much left. Never mind, I'll take your dress and pinny off when you've finished and give them a quick wash and iron. Here you are.'

'Daddy says you can't play with water and not get wet.'

'That's a true saying. Like "You can't walk through mud without mucking your shoes". You want to remember that when you grow up.'

'There's a norful lot of things to remember when you grow up. Mummie says I mustn't say "awful" unless I mean "full of awe". What's "full-of-awe", Mrs Thompson?'

Mrs Thompson propped her scrubbing-board against the side of the tub and pushed the hair off her forehead with the back of her hand.

'That's one of those things you have to learn if you're going to talk right. I don't talk right because I never had no one to teach me. But you've got to learn to talk right because when you grow up you're going to be a lady.'

'Aren't you a lady, Mrs Thompson?'

'No, I'm not. All me life I've tried to be a good woman and do what's right. But you have to have education to be a lady and that's something I never could get.'

'Well, I don't want to get education and be a lady,' said Elizabeth earnestly. 'I want to be like you.'

'Why, you blessed pet!' exclaimed Mrs Thompson, biting her lip. 'You'll be much more than me, never fear. But don't forget, you got to be a good woman first. You can be a good woman and not a lady, but you can't be a lady – not a real lady

– without being a good woman as well. Now, bring the peg-bag and we'll get these sheets on the line.'

Under the hot sky the linen was drying so fast that it came off the lines as stiff as if it had been starched. Pearl came out to carry the first armfuls of dry clothes into the lobby where she spread them on the table, sprinkled them with water and rolled them into tight bundles ready for ironing.

Elizabeth had just gathered a load of handkerchiefs from the rosemary hedge where they had been spread to dry, when she saw a familiar figure come round the corner of the house.

'Mr O'Brien!' she shrieked, dropped all the handkerchiefs in the dust, and ran across the lawn.

Mr O'Brien tried to doff his hat, deal with the small avalanche which launched itself against his knees, and avoid, if possible, dropping an enormous cauliflower which he was carrying in the crook of his arm.

'Good morning, good morning, and how's her little ladyship this foine, bright summer day. Ah, good morning, Mrs Thompson, and the top of the morning to you.'

'If it isn't Mr O'Brien! And where did you spring from?'

'Just passing, I was, after finishing me morning round, so I thought to meself: "I'll slip in on the breath of the moment to see how it goes with them." And how's yourself?'

'Well, thanks, for me age and size.' They both laughed, Elizabeth looked from one to the other. Grown-up people, she found, often laughed at things which she could not understand at all.

'What a wopper cauli you've got there,' went on Mrs Thompson. 'Wherever did you get it? I thought it was much too late in the year for cauliflowers.'

Mr O'Brien looked a little uncomfortable and a shade of red even deeper than his usual sunburn spread over his face and neck.

'This is from my little place in the Hills. Cooler up there, of course, so I have cauliflowers right up to the New Year.' He hugged the immense vegetable more tightly against his waistcoat as though frightened that Mrs Thompson would wrest it from him.

'Come into the kitchen and have some tea. I could do with a cup myself.'

'I take that very kindly of you, ma'am,' said Mr O'Brien. Still clutching the cauliflower, he followed Mrs Thompson into the house.

'Did you bring Bossie? Are you going to come every day now? Please, can I have a lump of sugar for Bossie, please, Mrs Thompson?' Elizabeth rattled off a string of questions without waiting for an answer to the first one.

'Ee, my girleen, the ould horse is heave-to at the gate and takin' in vittles, which is to say that he's got his nose-bag on, and it's meself would be following his example, for I've been up since four bells, with a thirst like an Irishman at a Band of Hope picnic.'

Mrs Thompson cut generous slices from one of the crusty, sweet-smelling loaves which the baker had just delivered. She spread them lavishly with butter and raspberry jam, and then poured out the tea, steaming and strong, from a brown earthenware pot.

Elizabeth thought what a nice smell it all had: the perfume of the tea, rising to mingle with the yeasty newness of the bread and the fruitiness of the jam, overlaid with a faint smokiness from the stove, the distinct but by no means unpleasant effluvium given off by Mrs Thompson's soapy and steamy arms, and the smell of the kitchen itself, compounded of slate floor always vaguely damp even on a hot day, beeswax and the lingering flavours of many rich dinners.

Pearl came in to join the party. They sat round the table with propped elbows, sipping the tea loudly, biting into the warm, pulpy bread and listening to the news of the outer world which Mr O'Brien gleaned on his daily round with the milk-cans. In turn, he was told about the dinner party. Pearl became the centre of attention for she was able to describe in detail the happenings in the drawing-room, the beautiful beaded shoes worn by Mrs Digby Faulkener, 'straight from Gay Paree, is my idea of it which is funny when you think how plain dressed she is for the rest of her', and the way in which Mrs O'Shawn had played the harp, 'real romantical, Mr O'Brien, like one of they stories in *Home Chat*', and the elaborate toilettes of the Misses Merriman.

'Though, mine jew, Mr O'Brien, I don't consider that some people are real Society, not like our own lady. All very nice and lah-di-da, but not the real bong-tong, as you might say.'

'And don't you forget, my girl,' put in Mrs Thompson as she lifted the massive iron kettle off the stove and poured boiling water into the teapot, 'don't you forget that little pigs have long ears.'

Pearl tossed the strings of starched muslin which fell from her cap to below her waist at the back.

'Don't worry,' she said, 'I'm not one to say things as won't bear repeating.'

'All the same, least said soonest mended,' said Mrs Thompson, 'as the saying is.' Elizabeth was well aware that this conversation was in some way concerned with her, but she could not quite pick up the line of argument. She therefore took the offensive.

'Can't we go and look at Bossie now?' she asked, tugging at Mr O'Brien's coat sleeve.

'Sure we can that. But tell me, Mrs Thompson, how's Herself? In health and strength, I'm hoping?' Mrs Thompson understood that this was just Mr O'Brien's Irish mode of referring to the lady of the house and was intended in no way as a familiarity. She shook her head.

'We're not as well as we should be,' she pronounced. "Too much goings-on, with dinner parties and driving about to see the polo and the lawn-tennis playing. She's fair tired out, that's what I think.'

'Ah, 'tis sorry I am to hear you say it. And – er – Miss – er –

Godfrey? She's well, I trust?' Here Mr O'Brien was suddenly seized with a fit of coughing which made his face redder than ever.

'Lord love us, you'll choke if you don't mind,' exclaimed Mrs Thompson. She dealt Mr O'Brien such a resounding blow between the shoulder-blades that he nearly pitched off his chair. He snatched at the edge of the table to prevent himself from overbalancing, knocked over his teacup which tipped sideways into its saucer and sent a cascade of scalding tea on to his knees. Mr O'Brien leapt to his feet with a yell. The cauliflower, its equilibrium disturbed by all this commotion, rolled ponderously across the table to the farther edge where it remained, rocking precariously until Mr O'Brien rescued it.

When order had been restored and Mr O'Brien furnished with a fresh cup of tea, the discussion on Miss Godfrey's health was resumed. Mrs Thompson and Pearl agreed that she was much as usual, 'with a touch of pepper, like always', added Pearl. For a while Elizabeth could not puzzle out who 'Miss Godfrey' could be, until something in Pearl's tone made her realise that it was her own Miss Una they were talking about. The tea being now finished, the party sat for a few minutes in silence, till Mr O'Brien pushed back his chair, clutched his hat to his chest with one hand and the cauliflower with the other and contrived a bow over the top of both. 'Thank ye kindly, ma'am, and you, Miss Pearl. It's been a pleasure and that a real one.'

Mrs Thompson acknowledged these civilities in a manner no less becoming, and if her expression showed regret it was understood to be on account of her guest's inability further to prolong his visit, though at the time her eyes rested somewhat lingeringly on the departing cauliflower.

'Now we can go and see Bossie,' exclaimed Elizabeth, holding her sugar lump tightly in one hand while she very kindly offered the other to Mr O'Brien. As he had now put his hat on his head he was able to accept her offer. Hand in hand they walked round the side of the house and down the tradesmen's drive to the back gate. Bossie took the lump of sugar, by now rather damp and disintegrated. His soft lips tickled Elizabeth's palm and made her laugh.

Mr O'Brien seemed in no hurry to untie the horse's head or climb into the cart. He kept looking back towards the house. Once or twice he took out a large handkerchief and wiped his face and neck. Certainly, the morning became very hot. Finally, Mr O'Brien cleared his throat and said in a hoarse voice: 'Tell me, Miss Beth, Miss Una – I suppose it's terrible busy she would be at this time? It's not comin' into the garden she would be, to pick the flowers or water the pot plants or any such kind of a thing, at all?' He looked anxiously at Elizabeth.

Beth had no time for these obliquities. 'Do you want to see her?' she asked directly. 'Shall I go and tell her you want to see her?'

Mr O'Brien was in a dilemma. Inclination struggled with discretion. He cleared his throat again and mopped his perspiring brow.

'Well, yes, you may say I do,' he stammered at last, but instantly retreated. 'No, no, 'twould be no manner of good at all. Perhaps I'll come some other time. Next week . . .'

Fate had undoubtedly decided to take a hand in this affair, for at that moment a clear voice could be heard calling: 'Beth, Beth, where are you?' and Miss Una herself came across the lawn. 'Come in at once, child. You'll make yourself sick, staying out in the sun without a hat. Oh, good morning, Mr O'Brien. I didn't know you were here.'

Mr O'Brien snatched off his hat and repeated his bow over the cauliflower.

'Mr O'Brien wants to see you,' announced Elizabeth.

Mr O'Brien's complexion now gave serious indications of approaching apoplexy, but Miss Una seemed to notice nothing unusual and merely smiled pleasantly and said in her rather high-pitched voice: 'Oh, did you, Mr O'Brien? Is it about the cream? The Jerseys are proving quite a success and I don't think we will be needing any extra at present.'

'Well, no – that is, yes, ma'am,' said poor Mr O'Brien, becoming more confused than ever. 'I thought maybe – well, it was just passing the place I was and I thought to meself: "How about a nice cauli, now, that mayn't come amiss," so here it is, ma'am, asking your pardon,' and with this sudden rush of words he thrust the gigantic vegetable into Miss Una's arms and bolted through the gate. Her thanks were lost in the clatter of the cart's departure and Beth's cries of farewell.

'How very strange,' said Miss Una. But she was smiling as she carried the cauliflower up to the house.

9

Across the River, 1902

O N E day, some time after Mr O'Brien's visit, when Mrs Ingle-fell had recovered from her indisposition, she took Elizabeth to see an old friend, Madame Jalleur de Fresgne. Into a large basket with hinged lids Mrs Thompson packed some jars of jelly, custard and soup, a chicken, and a parcel of home-made cakes.

Madame de Fresgne and her husband lived in one of the 'cottage homes', a group of tiny houses erected by public charity to shelter the aged poor. The cottages were across the river, about a mile away, in an area which in the early days of the colony's settlement had been rather fashionable. But the low-lying situation, the poor soil impregnated with salt from the sea, the unsavoury little river, hardly more than a muddy tidal creek filling the air with the unwelcome odours of decay-ing seaweed and refuse, all had contributed to the unpopularity of the site which had in time become the 'poor quarter' of the town.

Madame de Fresgne was a Frenchwoman who had been lady-in-waiting to the Empress Eugénie. She had married a man much beneath her in social station. Neither friends nor fortune had been generous to them and they had come at last to Australia to seek a refuge for their old age in a land so distant from their own that poverty could be borne with some sem-blance of dignity.

Mrs Inglefell had often told Elizabeth about Madame de

Fresgne. She was old now, a roly-poly of a woman, barely five feet tall and nearly as broad, with tiny hands and feet and a face layered in fat from the folds of which peeped out two eyes of piercing green brilliance. She spent her time seated in a tall armchair, her head resting against a velvet bolster covered with a white antimacassar tied to the chair with satin ribbons. Her feet on a lofty footstool were clad in high-heeled court shoes ornamented with glittering steel beads. She sat always with her hands, as white and dimpled as a baby's, on the arms of the chair. Indeed, her arms were so very short and fat that it would have been difficult for her to fold them across the equatorial curve which would have been her lap if she had had one. The generosity of her figure and the brevity of her legs caused the embroidered shawl covering her from waist to ankle to fall in folds which gave no clue to the presence of her knees. She spoke excellent English with but little trace of French accent, but with the incisive, labial pronunciation of a person accustomed to the daily use of both languages. When she talked the intensity of a vigorous personality found expression in her speech and in the alert brilliance of her eyes, as though all the body's vitality had withdrawn itself and lay concentrated behind the massive contours of the face.

Finch drove Elizabeth and her mother in the wagonette, but Mrs Inglefell would not allow him to wait for their return. 'It's such a lovely day, it will do us both good to walk home,' she said.

Finch did not relinquish his responsibilities without a protest. 'It's the best part of a mile, 'm,' he said, 'and you not as well as could be wished for this last week or so.'

Mrs Inglefell laughed. She had long ago given up being surprised at the way her Australian servants liked to argue about her orders and give their opinions and advice on everything from the respective merits of rival brands of floor wax to the way she dressed her hair or ate her dinner. In spite of his laziness and a tendency to find urgent business requiring his presence in the chaff-shed during the hot part of the day, Mrs Inglefell knew that Finch would cheerfully fight dragons if he thought that dragons in any way menaced her convenience or security.

In response to their knock the door of the cottage was opened by Monsieur de Fresgne, a tall, cadaverous old man with rheumy eyes, trembling hands, and a high narrow skull to which some strands of scurfy reddish hair still clung. He bowed from the waist and backed with a courtly gesture to enable them to advance into the tiny room, standing then with nervous indecision until his wife's voice from the armchair bade him in sharp French to place a chair for the visitors.

Standing in one corner, squeezed among the crowded furniture were a young woman and a little boy of some eleven years of age.

'Do I know this young lady?' asked Mrs Inglefell.

'Oh, madame is too kind,' replied their hostess. 'If I have your permission it would give me great satisfaction to present to you Mrs Hardman. Come out, little one,' she added in French, 'and make your curtsy.'

The young woman came forward and bobbed modestly to Mrs Inglefell. Elizabeth could not help noticing how pale and thin she was and that her eyes were red-rimmed as though with weeping.

'Hold up your head, my child,' snapped Madame de Fresgne, 'It is necessary to have courage, is it not?' And turning to Mrs Inglefell she went on: 'This is a compatriot, Lisette Grisny, who has married a young man, an Australian, at Roubaix where I think he goes to work in the woollen mills for experience, you understand. He has died and she brings now the child to Australia, to his grandparents. They live on a farm near Mount Pleasant. Is that not so, Lisette?'

'*Oui, madame,*' replied the young woman in a low voice.

'*Eh bien,* it appears that Mr and Mrs Hardman senior are willing to adopt the child, the little Henri, but have no wish to have also the burden of the mother. It seems hard, that, but perhaps it is necessary to be practical. *Hein?*' This with a penetrating glance at the young mother who shrank back into the corner and put her handkerchief to her lips.

'Could not Madame Hardman obtain a post where she could keep the little boy with her?' suggested Mrs Inglefell kindly.

'Ah! This is what I have also said,' exclaimed Madame de Fresgne, swooping on the idea like a bird on a worm, giving it a sharp tug and then, finding it not to her taste, throwing it aside. 'But no! *C'est impossible!* Lisette, you comprehend, is a milliner by no means without talent. Of taste perhaps lacking the true Parisian *ton*, but of that I can give her some direction. She can obtain employment with the Coliseum in Rundle Street, but to have the child is not practical.'

Here the little boy in whom Elizabeth had been taking a keen interest and to whom she had already extended the hand of friendship, so far forgot his composure and his manners as to bury his face in his mother's skirt and burst into tears.

'*Oo, la, la, la!*' exclaimed Madame de Fresgne. 'This is not the way to face life.'

'Oh, the poor little boy,' said Mrs Inglefell so compassionately that Elizabeth's own lips began to tremble.

'You are more than kind, madame,' replied the boy's mother in French. 'It is not becoming that we should burden your good nature with our troubles. Madame de Fresgne, we will take our leave and with your permission will make you another visit.'

All this time old Monsieur de Fresgne had been standing motionless except for his claw-like hands which stroked each other incessantly with a sound like the rustling of dry papers. Tears dribbled from his dim eyes and fell into the hollows of his cheeks so that Elizabeth thought he was crying in sympathy with Henri until she found that he always wept, though whether from the bitterness of memory or because of some physical infirmity no one had ever bothered to discover.

When the door closed behind Mrs Hardman and her little

boy he stepped forward bowing his head like a companion bird, and placed a chair for Mrs Inglefell.

'Dear Madame de Fresgne,' said Elizabeth's mother as she seated herself, 'please allow me to ask what you think of this jelly. It is a new recipe and we have made it with white wine instead of red. I would value your ideas.' The basket with the double-hinged lids was then unpacked, the soup, the jelly, the chicken, the custard, the cakes, all were duly subjected to Madame de Fresgne's scrutiny and her opinion canvassed, that no daughter of the French Court should have her pride tarnished by any semblance of charity.

In all this ritual Madame de Fresgne did not lift a finger, her great body inert under its draperies. Only her eyes darted like arrows to each thing as it was lifted from the basket and held up by Monsieur de Fresgne for her inspection. When the basket was at last emptied and put aside, she sped her arrows at her husband and pinned him with a sharp command. 'Marcel, the keys of the cabinet! The little one will enjoy some objects of art, will she not?' The arrows were turned on Elizabeth with such piercing intensity that she felt quite confused and exclaimed: 'Oh, yes – please, I mean, thank you, madame,' without being at all clear as to what she was called on to anticipate. With the keys clinking in his trembling hands, Monsieur de Fresgne swung open the doors of a small rosewood cupboard which stood near Madame's chair. This was evidently a ceremony of practised solemnity and order, for Monsieur de Fresgne lifted each object from its place on the silk-lined shelves and put it down on a square of dark-coloured damask which he first spread on the table. Elizabeth watched these preparations with some eagerness and felt her breath catch with wonder as Monsieur de Fresgne's papery fingers set down on the silk a fan of carved ivory layered with flat diamonds of mother-of-pearl, surrounding medallions of silk painted with pastoral miniatures in exquisite colour.

'This,' announced Madame de Fresgne in a sing-song which

betrayed the reiterative character of her story, 'this fan once belonged to my glorious mistress, the Empress Eugénie, and was given to me by Her Majesty herself. This is the handkerchief I used on the first occasion on which I was presented to Their Majesties. I was then sixteen years of age.' The handkerchief lay there, a froth of unbelievably fragile lace. It brought Elizabeth's eager imagination some glimpse of a young girl, combating her shyness amid the splendours of an Imperial Court. Next came a tiny box of royal blue enamel set with a ring of brilliants edged in gold; 'the comfit box of monsieur my father, le Comte d'Estrai-Jalleur,' intoned Madame with pride. And so on until all the little treasures had been exhibited, admired, and reverently replaced, their stories told, their associations recalled.

'That was a great privilege,' said Mrs Inglefell gathering her gloves and beginning to draw on the fingers of the left hand. 'Now we must say *au revoir*, dear Madame de Fresgne. Elizabeth, thank madame for showing you these lovely things.'

'And remember,' said the old lady as she allowed the little girl to shake one of her tiny, limp hands, 'remember when you are old you will be able to say that you have spoken to the friend of a great queen.' And all her life after, Elizabeth did remember; and remembered, too, the pride that vibrated in the old voice and the dimness that for a moment hid the arrows of light in the green eyes; and sensed that here in this house of poverty and pathos were reflected the components, the greatness and the futility of that human drama we call history; that these two human beings in all the miseries of failing flesh, with their pathetic pride, their outdated courtesies, their self-importance and their senile dignity, were the symbols of an era now passing into dust as they themselves must do.

It was a subdued little girl who took her mother by the hand and swinging the empty basket on her other arm came out into the sunlight and stepped briskly along the macadam road towards the town. They had not gone many yards before the sound of horses' hooves and the crack of a whip warned them to step from the high road on to the narrow footpath.

As the vehicle approached Elizabeth saw that it was a light masher cart, painted the fashionable shade of peacock blue picked out with vermilion and drawn by a tandem pair of bays with silver-mounted harness and scarlet saddle-cloths. A groom in half-topper, a broadcloth jacket and cream breeches, black patent Wellingtons and a white piqué neck-cloth, leaped down from the cross seat and ran to take the leader's head as the driver of the cart tightened his reins with a sudden shouted: 'Whoa there, my beauties,' which threw the horses on to their haunches and jerked their heads back. The wheels had scarce ceased turning before he jumped down, threw the reins to the groom who caught them with practised ease, and, hat in hand, stood laughing and exclaiming in front of Elizabeth and her mother where they were standing, gazing at all this performance in astonishment.

'Well, bless my soul, what a lucky wretch I am! Mrs Inglefell, how do you do, dear madam, and' – here the gentleman turned to Elizabeth and with a tremendous flourish of his topper made her a deep bow '– my respects, Miss Gloriana.'

'Why, Captain Bossingham, this is indeed a surprise!' exclaimed Mrs Inglefell, who suddenly found that the bright sun and the exertion of walking had made her feel rather flushed. She put up her lace-edged sunshade and lowered her eyes to her youngest daughter. Elizabeth, however, suffered none of these embarrassments and instantly demanded to be taken up into 'Capting Bossie's' cart.

'But why not indeed,' exclaimed the Captain. 'It is hardly the vehicle I would have chosen had I known that I was to be honoured by two such lovely ladies. Nonetheless, drive you home I can and will. Your foot, dear madam,' and the Captain laughing more gaily than ever put out his hand to receive Mrs Inglefell's second-best walking boot with pearl buttons and grey

silk loops. The lady looked at the dusty road, the masher cart
rocking on its two wheels with the restless tossing of the bays,
and hesitated.

'Oh, dear, I think . . . It is very kind, but perhaps . . .'

'Jackie, drive to Mr Inglefell's and wait there for me,' ordered
the Captain, and the groom was up and into the driving seat
and away at a fast trot before Elizabeth had time to realise
that by one of those unexpectedly sudden decisions by which
grown-ups so often confused her she was after all to be deprived
of her drive.

'Oh, dear,' said Mrs Inglefell again, 'do you think you should
have done that?' And she looked doubtfully after the masher
cart which was just disappearing round the corner at the end
of the street.

'Come, now,' said the Captain easily (he had somehow
possessed himself of the empty basket which he now swung by
the handle so that the flap lids danced up and down with something of the same jauntiness as his own gait), 'come now, do
you expect me to leave you, unattended, unprotected, in a
strange and desolate region frequented by footpads, as like as
like as not, or even bush-rangers. That's it – bush-rangers, I
have not a doubt of it.'

'How absurd you are!' cried Mrs Inglefell, but she could not
help laughing too. 'But your leg, will it now be very bad for it
to be walked on for such a distance?'

'And what, pray, are legs made for but to be walked on?'

'But not, surely, when they have been injured by a wicked
Boer bullet!'

The Captain's voice held no laughter as he answered: 'Why
wicked, dear madam? An enemy becomes a friend indeed who
by his bullet could win for me such sympathy.'

The lace sunshade dipped farther. Nothing of the face beneath could be seen except lips grown tremulous.

Elizabeth, trudging along the hot pavement, wished that
the way were not quite so long or that her legs were not quite

so short or that grown-ups would not dawdle to admire the gardens or the glimpses of the sea between the sandhills or talk in low voices about things she did not understand. It seemed a long time and she was ready for her tea when at last they turned into their own street and saw Jackie walking the bays up and down in front of the gate.

'Can I go for a ride now?' demanded Elizabeth, all her tiredness forgotten.

'Yes, why not?' said Captain Bossingham and before Mummie could object he had tossed her up on to the seat and ordered: 'Off you go, Jackie. Five minutes.'

'Do you think it is safe?' asked Mrs Inglefell anxiously as she watched the cart with her ecstatic daughter sweep round the corner out of sight.

'Jackie's the best groom in the Province. I'd trust him even with my greatest treasure.' And there was that in his emphasis of the possessive pronoun which brought to Mrs Inglefell all those emotions for which she had scolded herself on more than one occasion. She bit her lip and lifted her chin determinedly.

'Captain Bossingham, will you come in and take a glass of wine with us? Mr Inglefell will be returned from town by now.' A moment's silence seemed to emphasise the coolness of the invitation. Captain Bossingham drew himself up and bowed a trifle stiffly.

'My compliments to your husband, Mrs Inglefell, and I will give myself the pleasure of sampling his wine on some later occasion. Permit me.' He swung the gate open and with no further exchange of words they walked across the lawn and just reached the porch as the masher cart with a great jingling of harness and singing of rubber tyres on the gravel swept through the gates and up to the front door.

'Oh, Mummie, isn't it wonnerful! Jackie says I can drive. Jackie says I could handle the ribbons like a champion in next to no time. Jackie is going to teach me how to run a noose and slip one over the leader. Jackie says high-steppers are the only gees for a lady. Jackie says he wouldn't be surprised if I had the wrists for the business.'

While this flood was bursting upon them, the gentleman in question was standing at the leader's head, the reins looped in his right hand, his eyes fixed at a point between the shaft horse's ears, no expression moving the black vacuity of his wizened features.

'Fickle woman,' laughed Captain Bossingham. 'Gone the glories of sword and medal. *Le roi est morte, vive le roi!*'

'Run, darling,' said Mrs Inglefell, 'go and find Miss Una. You will be late for tea. Good-bye, Captain. Thank you for being so indulgent with my small tornado.' And once again giving her gloved fingers to a brief exchange with his, Mrs Inglefell shut the lace-edged parasol with a snap and went up the steps into the house where the door presently closed behind her.

IO

Lily Lees

S HORTLY after Mrs Inglefell and Elizabeth met him at Madame de Fresgne's, Henri Hardman was put into the care of the mail man on the Mount Pleasant coach and sent to his grandparents.

Since they had come from France to this new country there had been for him and his mother nothing but insecurity, anxiety and unfriendliness. Now this parting from the only being in the world to whom he could turn in confidence and love was almost more than his childish heart could bear. Lisette had tried to cheer and encourage him, promising to write to him every day. 'Remember that your father was a brave, good man,' she told him. 'It is necessary that you grow up to be like him, a brave, good Australian. But, oh, my little one –' and here she could not prevent her voice from choking a little '– do not forget our dear France and your poor mother. Know that I will always love you and I will always be with you if you need me – in my heart and in my prayers.'

The sorrow of parting from his mother was not the only emotion that troubled the little boy. He feared the unknown road that he was now to travel. He feared the loneliness that he must face, in this strange new country which had broken the spirit of many men, strong men, a thousand times better fitted than a seven-year-old child to meet its difficulties and combat its demands. But more than this, Henri feared his grandmother. He had seen her only three times, but her forbidding countenance, her cold asperity and the undisguised antagonism which she showed towards Lisette had so impressed Henri that he dreaded being with her even for a few minutes. He looked forward to a life in her house and under her daily supervision as something frightening, a terror which had the quality of nightmare, but a nightmare without the reassuring presence of his mother to soothe and comfort him.

The coach left the city in the early morning, not long after sunrise, and the sun was still high when it drew up at the post office of the little town where Henri was to meet his grand-parents. They had driven in from the farm which lay several miles east of the town, and having bought a supply of groceries at the general store and waited at the post office counter for the mailbags to be opened and the letters sorted so that they could collect their mail, they lost no time in bundling Henri into the buggy between them and turning the horses' heads towards the country.

The colony of South Australia was of an age with the Queen's reign, for when the girlish Victoria was crowned Queen of England her faithful subjects in that far place were coming ashore with their bags and bundles, stumbling through the mangrove swamps and across the beaches of an unknown coast to build their first dwellings in a country which until then had never known a stone wall built by the hand of man, to plant the first crops before the wondering gaze of the aboriginal inhabitants who knew only how to hunt food and not how to grow it.

At first the newcomers were constrained to the narrow coastal belt of plain, for the range of hills some ten miles inland, though not mountainous, was covered with an immense forest of giant eucalypts and had many sheer and rocky gullies dense with undergrowth which offered shelter to criminals and con-victs escaped from ships and the penal settlements of the colonies to the east. But by the eighteen-forties a pass across the hills had been found and the first road built, though it was little more than a rocky track hewn through the forest across the spurs of the lower hills.

Many of the settlers found it easier to reach open country by striking northward to a place where the range was not so precipitous. Among these was Richard Hardman, who set off in the 'forties with his bullock dray to follow the tracks made by the pioneers into the rolling meadowland beyond Mount Pleasant. Here, in the days of the South Australian Company's optimistic expansion, he bought land and felled trees and cleared scrub to plant his first corn; here he married, and here his son, another Richard, was born.

Lily Lees was a farm of some two thousand acres. Now farmed by the second Richard Hardman in his quiet, rather ineffectual way, it provided him and his wife Jane with a living which yearly grew more exiguous. As he sowed his grain and herded his cattle, Richard often wondered what impulse of idealism or stress of economy had prompted his father to this tremendous adventure, to the hazards of a fourteen-thousand-mile voyage across the world in a sailing ship, to the mercies of climate in a continent as yet hardly explored, to the company of aborigines reputedly savage, undoubtedly primitive, and to a future in which danger, unceasing work and personal discomfort were almost the only certainties.

On either side of the road lay the gently undulating country, some of it still in dark chocolate slabs as the autumn ploughing had left it; some covered with the soft green of the first winter wheat. About four miles from the town the buggy turned off the highway on to a narrow rutted track which led by half a mile to the farm. The stone house was not without dignity, but its appearance was impaired by sprawling and half-dilapidated outhouses, some showing signs of amateurish efforts to keep them in repair, others fallen wholly into ruin. Even in this bright sunlight the house gave an impression of sorrow and loneliness.

Henri's thoughts, which had been raised by the adventures

of the day and by the long drive in the coach, with all the bustle of the other passengers and the unaccustomed excitement of driving behind four lively horses, might have been caught in overtones of this atmosphere had he not been jerked back to the realities of the situation by his grandmother's strident voice calling to him to climb down from the buggy and open the gate leading into the stable yard, 'and be quick about it'.

His hands trembled so much that it was as much as he could do to unlatch the fastenings and swing the heavy iron gate back to its holding post.

'Now then, Henry,' said Mrs Hardman, 'help your grand-father to carry the basket into the house. Then you had better wash your hands and face. We'll have tea as soon as I can get the kettle boiling.'

Mr Hardman unbuckled the harness straps and led the horses out of the traces into the stable where Frank, the farm boy, presently came to feed them. When Henri went forward to help with the luggage, his grandfather looked at him with a kindly twinkle in his blue eyes and said: 'You take the rugs, little chap. I can look after the baskets.' Henri felt with a rush of gladness in his heart that he had found a friend.

The exterior of the house might seem shabby and forbidding, but nothing that human effort could accomplish was missing to make the interior as shining and clean as a new pin; although, thought Henri to himself, he did not know why new pins were always supposed to be the cleanest and shiningest things people knew. He had been given a little bedroom, like an attic, in the second storey, with varnished linoleum on the floor, a bed with a white cotton counterpane, one chair and a sort of cupboard made out of three kerosene cases nailed together, one on top of the other, and covered with faded cretonne. The room looked neither warm nor comfortable, but at least it was his own and when Henri looked out of the window and saw that he commanded a view of the farmyard in which geese and chickens were running about, two cats were sitting in the shadow of the stable wall, horses standing dreamily at the railings and beyond them in the paddock a number of cows were browsing or contentedly lying, Henri felt that his lot might, after all, not be an unhappy one.

Tea was spread in the kitchen downstairs, a clean white damask cloth over the work table and blue and white cups set down with a pile of bread and butter and a plate of plain cake. Henri was hungry after his journey and did not hesitate when his grandmother told him to sit down immediately and eat his meal.

'No one could say,' she remarked, pouring tea into her husband's cup and handing it to him, 'no one could say that the young man was talkative. Upon my word, I have hardly discovered yet if he can use the King's English.'

'Come now,' replied Dick Hardman, sucking his tea noisily in through his moustache, 'no doubt it feels a bit strange to start with. We'll soon find our tongue when we have settled down a bit.'

Henri felt dimly that he should be able to contribute something to this discussion, but as both his mouth and his heart were full any words that he may have uttered were stillborn.

After tea Henri went out with his grandfather to inspect the farm and until the early darkness brought them back to the house he was as completely happy as any little boy could be who has recently said good-bye to his mother for a long time. He stood at Mr Hardman's side while the cows were brought in, stalled and milked; he watched fascinated while buckets of frothing milk were poured into the separator and was delighted when his grandfather allowed him to turn the handle which worked the machine. He soon found that turning the handle for any length of time was more than the muscles of his thin arms could support, but he watched with interest and admiration when Frank took over and whizzed the handle round at such a speed that the thick yellow cream was soon flowing into the can. If he were allowed to go on being with his grandfather and Frank, Henri felt that life on the farm would have many compensations.

After supper, which differed from tea only in that some slices of very tough and over-cooked cold meat and some very vinegary bright yellow pickles accompanied the bread and butter, Mrs Hardman took her grandson upstairs and told him to undress himself, 'and don't forget to say your prayers,' she added.

Henri obediently knelt down beside the bed, made the sign of the Cross and began: *Je vous salue, Marie, pleine de grâce, le Seigneur est avec vous.*' He had got thus far when his grand-mother's voice sharply interrupted.

'Stop that!' she exclaimed.

He looked up at her, startled. Her lips were drawn into a tight line and two bright spots of anger printed her sallow cheeks.

'I might have known it!' she snapped. 'A lot of foreign gibberish! Let me tell you that if you have come to live with us you will say your prayers properly. Now say after me: "Now I lay me down to sleep, Pray the Lord my soul to keep." '

Having thus instructed Henri in the form of prayer she con-sidered suitable, Mrs Hardman told him to get into bed and blew out the candle.

When she returned to the kitchen where her husband was reading his newspaper beside the stove, her exasperated feel-ings vented themselves, as they usually did, on his uncomplain-ing head. 'I might have known it!' she said again. 'The child has been brought up nothing but a little heathen and a Roman one at that. It is just as well we have taken him away from that woman. She would have brought him up as a papist, with his head full of superstitions and foreign nonsense, if she had had him much longer.'

'Well, my dear,' replied her husband mildly, 'don't be too hard on the youngster. Remember he is only seven years old.'

'Old enough to learn better!' was the tart retort.

Upstairs in the darkness Henri had turned again to the

Mother who, his own mother had told him, would remain with him always.. A passion of loneliness swept over him. Where was his own mother now? Would he ever see her again?

Outside, the pear tree whispered against his window in the cold wind, but it had no answer for him, and Henri slept his first night at Lily Lees farm as he was to sleep many others, with the tears of loneliness on his cheeks.

The Moreton Bay Fig Tree

THE State School was half a mile up the road. Before nine in the morning and after three in the afternoon the street was noisy with children who chased one another, climbed on the fences to pull at the fruit trees, tore branches from the hedges, fought, scrambled on the road, or strolled, arms entwined, along the footpaths. They drew hopscotch games on the asphalt, satchels left lying and hats flung down. The older ones bought lolly sticks at the grocery store on the corner and the little ones hung beggingly about till given a share.

Elizabeth knew, of course, that these were 'common' children like those on the beach. The children from Miss Liddier's school where Eleanor and Marian went did not play hopscotch in the street or fight and yell. They walked sedately two by two or were driven in governess carts. Only in the absence of nurse-maids or parents did they venture to climb fences or pull at the sprays that hung over garden walls.

Elizabeth liked the 'common' children from the public school. She used to go across the paddocks towards the school in the middle of the afternoon and wait for the bell to ring. Then she could hear the whoops and yells as the human cataract launched itself into the school yard and out into the road.

One afternoon she crossed the paddocks and climbed a Moreton Bay fig tree the arms of which stretched over the fence and across the pathway. The foliage formed an effective screen from behind which she could peer into the school yard. She was feeling depressed. Her mother was ill again, so she had had no lessons, and the day had dragged its hours with wearisome monotony. Miss Una said 'Shish' when she crept up to her mother's closed door; and the house took on a hushed secretiveness which weighed on her spirits. Eleanor and Marian had stayed at school for lunch, so that there was not even their chatter about the morning's events to bring variety to the day. Elizabeth ate a meal of Irish stew and rice pudding in solitude. She tried to play in the wurly, but the pre-Stopesian family for once refused to enter into their allotted parts with any zest, and when Andalusia fell off the dolls' house roof and broke her nose, Elizabeth despaired of the game and wandered moodily out into the paddocks in search of adventure.

The sun was hidden behind an even grey sky, pale and remote and silent. The air was warm and the day seemed wrapped in some mystery of its own making. Far away the murmur of the sea was but an echo of itself, as though heard from the heart of a shell. In the paddocks the grass was long and green. The almond trees formed green barriers and Elizabeth wondered how she could ever have thought them dead. Where the grass was short and sparse near the hedges, she found some trapdoor spiders and annoyed them by pulling open their little doors to say 'how do you do'. They pulled the doors shut again with a tug on the silken cord but not before she had seen the silk-lined tunnel with its irritable occupant at the bottom.

The Moreton Bay fig tree was easy to climb. About three feet from the ground its trunk divided into several boughs so broad that any one of them made a comfortable seat. The upper branches gave a choice of views across the country beyond the houses and were a grandstand seat for events in the school yard and the street. Elizabeth would have liked to build a house in this tree but she knew that it would never be free of the depredations of the school children, so she gave up the idea.

She had not long to wait before the ringing of the bell brought the children racing into the yard. They streamed through gateways and out on to the road. The air rang with the cacophony of five hundred voices raised in the clamorous irrelevancies of childhood.

Elizabeth wriggled along the bough belly-wise, with her arms and legs clutching its bulk and her cheek resting on the bark. Now she was over the top of the boundary fence and could look down on the heads of the children as they milled about on the footpath outside.

Some bigger boys were advancing from the nearest gate. They threw their caps into the air and pulled each other's bags in a surge which carried the group from one side of the pavement to the other. As they came under the Moreton Bay one threw a cap into the branches and there it stuck. Elizabeth's hiding-place was now discovered, for they began to pull at the boughs and shake them in an effort to dislodge the cap which fell and was pounced on.

Elizabeth clung to her support, though not without trepidation, for the onslaught from below had redoubled. Three of the boys climbed on the fence and tried to reach the bough from below, but they had no means of hauling themselves upwards. They hesitated about venturing into the paddock as 'trespassing on private property' had more than once in their young lives carried with it dire penalties. Finally, one took his courage or his bravado in both hands, jumped down from the fence and ran to the base of the tree which he then began to climb. The others renewed their attack on the leafage and by jumping up and down had set up a pendulum movement of the boughs that threatened to dislodge Elizabeth from her perch. She hung on stubbornly, but the rear-guard had advanced while the enemy in front were now on the top of the fence, demanding surrender. She could neither advance nor retreat. There was only one thing to do. She fell off.

Fortunately, there was a strip of soft soil between the fence and the asphalt, and she broke her fall by clutching at the thick leaves of the lower branches. Bruised and dishevelled,

Elizabeth picked herself up and launched herself without an instant's hesitation at the nearest of her tormentors. He was a boy of about ten years old and twice her size. Quite unprepared for the silent fury of the attack he went over in a tumble against the fence, bringing down on himself the three of his companions who had climbed on the railing.

Elizabeth was crying, but more with rage than pain. She fought on blindly. With fine disregard for the rules of sportsmanship, to say nothing of the standards of lady-like behaviour enjoined on her by a careful upbringing, she kicked and beat her adversaries as they lay struggling before her. It was not to be expected, however, that the advantages of the battle would long be with her and it was only a few minutes before Elizabeth knew that she was beaten.

Although there had been a good deal of noise, very few words had been used in the course of the engagement; but now one of the boys, perceiving the origin of his wounds, exclaimed: 'It's that kid from the monkey-tree house!' and made a thrust at her. This marked a general move to re-open hostilities. Elizabeth did her best to take up a position of defence, but her first fury had died and she began to feel herself unable to carry on so unequal a contest. Her tears flowed faster than ever and one of the boys began to shout: 'Cry, baby, cry,' so that humiliation followed rage and pain. The battle had become a teasing match. Elizabeth put her arms over her face and began to cry in earnest. The biggest of the boys, he who had received the brunt of Elizabeth's first attack, pushed away the other and shouted: 'Leave her alone, can't you? She's only a little kid.' The others, who had begun to tire of the situation, now looked rather ashamed of themselves. They started a last-touch game across the road and had soon forgotten Elizabeth and her woes. The big boy and Elizabeth were left together. 'Here, don't cry any more,' he said and held out his handkerchief. It was rather grubby, but Elizabeth gratefully blew her nose and wiped her face.

'What's your name?' he asked.

'Elizabeth Inglefell, and it was m-my tree, anyway. Those other p-pigs didn't have any right to climb up my tree.'

The boy was pulling up his socks. 'All right. You needn't be wild any more. My name is Luke – Luke Stevens. If you're one of those Inglefell kids you must live in the house with the monkey-puzzler. I'll walk home with you if you like.' He picked up his cap and school bag and they set out together.

It was a fairly long walk, for they had to follow the fence along the paddocks and turn at right angles into the next street to reach the front gate. There was little conversation. Elizabeth sobbed and blew her nose at intervals, and Luke whistled to hide the embarrassment he felt at his own chivalry. He was relieved when they reached the tall iron gates and he was able to say a gruff good-bye.

'Good-bye, Luke,' said Elizabeth moistly. 'You've been very kind to me. One of these days I'll be kind to you.'

Luke kicked the toe of his boot against the gate and said: 'That's all right, kid. Sorry you fell off and all that. Good-bye.'

12

Come Winter

THE summer was ending and Eleanor and Marian were back at school. The days were turning cold and the nights frosty. In the mornings Elizabeth sometimes found little slivers of ice on the trough near the stables. Mr Inglefell said good-bye to his family and went away to the north to inspect his stations and talk to his managers. Elsa went with him.

She and the children had a tearful parting. Her chocolate eyes were spilling tears for days before she left, but the call of her own place was too strong to be denied. She longed to 'go walkabout' among the salt bush and to sit down among the lubras in the outer ring round the fire. During the summer she had taken to sleeping in the garden. When the nights grew cold she moved into Beth's wurly, but never again did she sleep under a roof. When Mr Inglefell returned to Undaboo, he took her back to her tribe.

Mr O'Brien had fallen into the habit of calling every Sunday afternoon (for Sunday was the only day in the week in which his clients were constrained to forgo their second delivery of fresh milk for the day) and he came always carrying a vegetable of some kind, either the largest cabbage or cauliflower or pumpkin his garden could supply, or a basket of peas, beans, sweet turnips, sprouts or asparagus. Sometimes it was a head of celery three feet long and as thick as one of his own brawny arms. At other times it was a brace of crisp lettuces or a cut-down kerosene tin filled with raspberries. It was now accepted in the household that these offerings were tribute to Miss Una.

Come Winter

Before the winter was out, the milk-cart was replaced on Sundays by a smart sulky. Bossie was given a half-holiday while the sulky was drawn by a fast-stepping trotter. Elizabeth and Miss Una were invited to take an airing. These drives along the foreshore and home by the road around the race-course became a regular feature of the Sunday routine.

As the winter advanced there inevitably came a Sunday when the rain poured down with a persistence that made a drive unacceptable. After dinner, when the children had eaten their dessert and swallowed the last mouthful of fizzy lemonade, a glassful of which they were always allowed to have with their midday meal on Sundays, Mrs Inglefell was about to go upstairs for her afternoon rest when Miss Una went to the window, pulled aside the velvet drapes with a noisy rattling of wooden rings and looked out at the weather. Then in a voice even more high-pitched than usual, she exclaimed: 'Goodness, it's still raining! It will be much too wet to go driving.'

Mrs Inglefell, fully alive to the implications of this observation, smiled gently.

'You don't think that Mr O'Brien will find it too wet to come? The rain must be even heavier in the hills.'

Miss Una's plain, sunburnt face flushed an ugly red and her big, bony fingers interlaced each other nervously.

'You must think me an awful fool,' she said suddenly.

'Dear Una!' replied Mrs Inglefell, laughing softly, 'I was only teasing you a little. Indeed, I think you are a wise, wise woman. He is a good man. But be sure of what you are doing. If today, instead of driving, you invite him in to have tea, you have as good as committed yourself. You know that.'

Una gulped. 'Yes, I know . . . I mean, that's why I wondered . . .' She paused awkwardly before adding with a rush: 'We could have tea in the nursery. The fire's alight there already.'

Mrs Inglefell laughed outright. 'You have decided! Well, I am sure Beth makes an excellent chaperone if only for the reason that she never stops talking.'

After that, if the weather were wet, Mr O'Brien would be invited in to sit by the fire, but as social convention prevented Miss Una from taking tea in the kitchen with Mrs Thompson and Pearl, Mr O'Brien joined the nursery party and drank his tea with Eleanor, Marian and Elizabeth to the accompaniment of stories of seafaring life and Elizabeth's opinions, conjectures and speculations about storms, shipwrecks, cannibals, desert islands, and the possibilities of a girl ever being allowed to join the Royal Navy.

One day towards the end of the winter, Elizabeth was scrambling through the fence between the garden and the paddocks. She was on her way to the sties to see how the young pigs were getting on. As she made her way through the thicket she had that strange sensation that most of us have at some time in our lives – of having done this before or of having some fore-knowledge that we would do it. There were the orange trees, well pruned now, their fruit less numerous than last year, but larger and cleaner. There on the other side of the paddock were the almond trees. Of course, she remembered now – that very first day at the new house when her father and Finch had told her that the trees were alive. Now, once again, the first blossoms were appearing on the bare branches. It seemed such a short time ago, but Elizabeth realised, with a little shock, that a whole year had passed since they had left Undaboo and come to live at the seaside.

When she got back to the house, she found her mother reading a letter from Madame de Fresgne. Monsieur de Fresgne had brought it, walking all the way from the 'cottage homes'. Now he was sitting on a chair in the hall, thinner than ever, and so still and pale that, had it not been for the trembling of his hands, Elizabeth could have believed him already dead. Pearl brought him a glass of port wine and a piece of butter cake which he drank and ate with enjoyment as soon as the screw of his extreme courtesy was sufficiently loosened to enable him to accept them. In the meantime, Mrs Inglefell had gone to her desk and written a short letter which she gave him.

'Tell dear Madame de Fresgne,' she said, 'that I will do everything in my power to help this poor young woman. And now I am going to send you home in the wagonette. It is much too far for you to walk again.'

When the old gentleman had been persuaded to enter the wagonette and had been driven away, Mrs Inglefell sat down at her desk again and wrote to her sister-in-law, Emma Woodstock: 'This young Mrs Hardman, of whom I told you before, is a Frenchwoman by birth and was married to the son of Richard Hardman, your neighbour at Lily Lees Farm. It seems that the grandparents have undertaken to care for the child now that their daughter-in-law has been left a widow, but they feel that they cannot afford to support the mother, which is, perhaps, reasonable enough, as I imagine that they are by no means well-to-do. The girl has been working as a milliner in a city emporium, but has lately fallen ill of a galloping consumption and is lying at the Public Hospital. My old friend, Madame de Fresgne, writes to me in grave concern, asking me to do what I can to influence Mr and Mrs Hardman to bring the child to see her, which she seems to think they are unwilling to do. This I find difficult to credit, but perhaps they are not aware of the seriousness of the illness. There seems little doubt that young Mrs Hardman is going to die and that within a week or so. Alfred is not yet returned from Undaboo and I can do little more than go to the hospital and find out for myself whether there is anything to be done in the way of relief or cure. But I am wondering whether you and Thomas could approach the Hardmans and persuade them to bring the boy to town. If this is not possible, you could assure them that if he is sent in the care of the coachman we will meet him and look after him during his visit. There is no one I could more confidently count on in such a mission, dear Emma, than you and our good Thomas . . .'

When, two days later, the mailbag was opened at Rose Lees

and this letter was read, Emma Woodstock handed it across
to her husband and remarked with even more than her usual
asperity: 'We know quite well why Jane Hardman won't let
that boy see his mother. She's consumed with jealousy. She's
never forgiven the girl for marrying her precious son and
blames her for his death. She's a wicked woman.'

Thomas read the letter without verbal comment, but finished
his dinner, lit his pipe and then pulled on his riding-boots.

'I'll be a couple of hours,' he said as he went through the
door. Emma thrust a parcel into his hands. 'Here, it's a jar of
my new plum pickle. I grudge it to her, dear knows, but it'll
give you an excuse for turning in.' Thomas pushed the parcel
into the wide pocket of his old jacket, pulled his hat more
firmly over his eyes and went to saddle his horse. Half an hour
later he rode up the clay track to the Lily Lees homestead.

Thomas Woodstock was a good farmer, a good friend and a
respected neighbour. Richard Hardman was glad to see him.
He recognised in the other man those qualities of ability,
application and strength of will which he himself lacked. They
leaned over the yard railings together and discussed the weather
and the crops and the price levels of wheat and barley and wool
and livestock. Presently they sauntered up to the kitchen where
Mrs Hardman gave them tea. Emma's jar of plum pickle was
handed over and was accepted with some semblance of grace.

It was not until he was taking his leave that Thomas said
casually: 'Sorry to hear about young Mrs Hardman. The
missus has had a letter from Mrs Inglefell, that's Alfred's wife,
you know. Seems she's going to see the young lady in hospital.
Suppose you'll be taking the little chap down to see his mother.'

Jane's thin face drew itself into sharper lines and her eyes
glinted dangerously under their wrinkled lids.

'If young Mrs Hardman is in trouble it's nothing but what
she's brought on herself,' she said. 'As for going to town,
Richard and I have more to do with our time and money than
to go flying off to the city every time she makes a fuss. In any

case, it's better for the child not to have anything to do with her. It's only unsettling for him.'

'Well, I dare say you know best,' said Thomas in a deceptively easy-going tone which nevertheless managed to convey that he held her entirely responsible for this decision. ''S matter of fact, Emmie and I were thinking of going to the city for a couple of days next week. We could take him along with us and bring him back, if you like. Think it over. So long.'

In the meantime, Elizabeth had been taken by her mother to see Lisette Hardman at the Public Hospital. She was of the generation which considered that a child should be taught the duty of visiting the poor and the sick. If the poor were at times unappreciative of this patronage and the sights presented by the sick somewhat unsuitable for childish eyes, it was none the less a duty to be done, and part of the child's moral training.

It was a cold and showery day when Elizabeth and her mother went to catch the train from Miller's Corner. This was only the third time that Elizabeth had been in the train, and she was still excited at the novelty. She had often stood to watch it arrive at the pier, steaming down Jetty Road, the guard standing on the platform ringing a large hand-bell to warn all citizens in this busy street that the monster was approaching. But of course it was much more important to climb up the ladder at the side and take one's place in the long, open compartment on a basketwork seat with a string bag at one side for holding one's parcels. Each pair of seats was separated by a handsome mirror with bevelled edges, set in a frame of ornamental brass and surmounted by an enlarged photograph of Australian scenery, generally a gully of densely overgrown ti-tree, very gloomy, or a view of waves dashing over the rocks at Victor Harbour, very dramatic. As the train drew away from the streets and houses of the town and began to travel through open fields, Elizabeth pressed her nose and both her hands against the window-pane to watch its progress. The next town was Morphettville, and Mrs Inglefell, in a mood of instruction, pointed out the ordered fences and buildings of the race-course and, on the other side, the old stone mansion of Mr Morphett, surrounded by gardens of hibiscus and oleander and wider parkland where cattle and horses rested beneath giant white gum trees, survivors of the original trees which had once covered the savannah of the Adelaide plain. Farther on, at Black Forest, the trees were thicker, though the gum trees and wattle groves were already being replaced with olives and vines.

'This used to be a real forest,' explained Mrs Inglefell. 'It is not so many years ago that bush-rangers lived here and made it dangerous for travellers to ride through the forest. Though,' she added reflectively, 'I don't think they were real bush-rangers, mostly escaped convicts from the Victorian settlements, or drunken sailors from the ships at Hobson's Bay.'

'Mr O'Brien says,' instantly volunteered Elizabeth, 'that sailors ought to be allowed to get drunk sometimes, because life at sea is very hard, and after a few months of it a man needs a blow, even if he does create shenanigans.'

Mrs Inglefell gave this view the serious consideration it deserved, for she would not for a moment under-rate the importance of Mr O'Brien's contribution to her daughter's education. After a pause for thought she concluded: 'Mr O'Brien is probably right as long as the sailors have someone to look after them and see they don't get into trouble. But I'm glad we don't have bush-rangers in the Black Forest any more, because we couldn't get to town so quickly and easily, could we?'

The train took only half an hour on its journey from the seaside to the city. At Victoria Square, as the rain was still falling and a very cold wind blowing, they took a four-wheeled cab. The Public Hospital was a tall, deep-gabled building of dark-red brick situated on the North Terrace of the city, at its eastern end, and so a considerable distance from the railway station. As the cab turned in at the gateway and clobbed its way up the avenue of pine trees from which the rain dripped drearily, Elizabeth clutched her mother's hand and tried to feel brave. Narrow, stone-framed windows with diamond panes were impeded in their function of lighting the interior of the building by the proximity of the trees which came up to the walls of the hospital, sighing and creaking in the wind as though to join their lamentations with the sufferings of the unfortunate inmates. Even the kindly-faced nurses, dressed in long, freshly-starched dresses and tall caps with stiff muslin bows tied under their chins, could not altogether dispel the gloomy atmosphere nor Elizabeth's nervous fears. Here in a sepulchral gloom were things she did not understand, but sensed dimly in the choking sounds, the hoarse breathings, and in the elusive, fetid stench which clung to the air of corridors and dormitories with a sickening persistence.

They walked between the rows of beds and paused before one in which lay a young woman who stared at the ceiling with unseeing eyes. In her wasted countenance Elizabeth could find no trace of the pretty French girl she had seen so short a time before at Madame de Fresgne's cottage. The cheeks were patched with colour which flamed on a dead-white skin stretched to the bones with hideous tautness, the lips drawn back over the teeth in a grimace like that of an animal, the nostrils pinched by the fingers of death, flaring out and in with every tortured breath.

The nurse bent over the bed. 'Here is a lady to visit you,' she said, and placed a spoonful of water in the gasping mouth.

'I have a message from your little boy,' said Mrs Inglefell, with more pity than truth. 'He sends you his love and hopes to come soon to see you.'

The agonising eyes rolled sideways and the lips drew together in an effort at speech. '*Sainte Marie, mère de Dieu, protégez-le, je vous implore.*' Mrs Inglefell could barely discern the breathless words. A wave of compassion rushed into her heart. She bent over the dying woman.

'Be comforted, my dear,' she said, slowly and distinctly in French. 'We will look after your little Henri and see that he is cared for.'

A spark of recognition seemed to light for an instant in Lisette's eyes and a pathetic attempt at courtesy made her exclaim: 'Madame . . .' But the effort was too much and she sank back into her feverish stupor.

Henri Hardman never saw his mother again, for she died that night. A notice sent by the hospital authorities to inform Richard Hardman of his daughter-in-law's death lay for nearly a day in the post office at Mount Pleasant before being carried out with the other mail by the lorry from the butter factory which drove out to Lily Lees every morning to collect the cream-cans.

'Well, it's just as well we didn't rush off on the first coach,' said Mrs Hardman; 'nothing but a waste of money, it would have been.'

Richard looked up at the wooden clock ticking loudly on the kitchen mantel. 'You have good time to get the boy washed and dressed and be ready to catch the afternoon coach,' he said. 'I'll get the horses in from the paddock straight away.'

'Richard Hardman, you must be mad if you think I am going off to town today. The girl's dead, isn't she? And just as well, too, is my idea of it. She was never much good when she was alive, nothing but a burden and worry to everyone.'

Richard Hardman was a quiet man, and like many people of weak character he did not often argue, preferring to leave decisions to his dominant partner. But occasionally he could be obstinate.

'She was my son's wife,' he said now. 'Henry is going to his mother's funeral. It's not easy for me to leave the farm, but I dare say Frank could manage for a couple of days.'

'Oh, well, if that's the stand you're going to take!' exclaimed Jane, planking down the saucepan she was holding with a vicious thump on the table, 'I suppose you'll have to have your own way, as usual. Dear knows, the farm work's behind enough as it is. If you ask me, the whole place is running to rack and ruin. If you'd had your son here to help you, as you should have, instead of sending him off on that fool idea to France and letting him marry this wretched woman . . .'

Richard did not wait to hear the end of this familiar harangue. He had heard it so often over the years that he had come now to close down the curtain of his own sorrow and retreat alone into his house of mourning. As he went out to the home paddock to bridle the horses he asked himself how he could find courage enough to tell Henri of his mother's death, for he could not face the thought of him learning the news from Jane. Leaning on the post-and-rail fence, he let his head drop into his hands. Why did he have to lose his only son? For the thousandth time he cried out to himself the un-answered question. He was tired now, sick at heart and weary of body, and what lay before him but the continuing round of hopeless work, the ploughing, the sowing, and a harvest which grew less with every year of work, as though to mock his efforts. And for what? Dear God, was there to be no end to it? No respite from the heat and the cold and the weariness of it, from the worry about money, from Jane's venom which seemed to increase and grow more bitter with the years.

In the cow-shed he could hear Henri's treble as he talked to Frank. Suddenly a resolution formed in Richard's mind. This was his son's son, blood and bone of his body. When he drove Jane and Henri into the township that afternoon to catch the coach he would call and see Mr Deed, the lawyer. He had meant the farm to belong to his son. Well, he would bequeath it to his grandson. Perhaps in watching the boy grow up he would regain something of the sense of purpose with which he had started his life. With new animation amounting almost to hope in his mind, he cried out with sudden resolution: 'Henri! Come here, my boy. I have something to tell you.'

13

The Coach Journey

'WOULD you like to go and stay with your Aunt Emma Woodstock and Uncle Thomas for a week or two?' asked Mrs Inglefell one morning, looking up from a letter she was reading.

Elizabeth put her head on one side. 'Could I take Pussy Lickums?' she asked. 'And Pansy and Jimmie and Mrs Watkins?'

'Perhaps Jimmie and Mrs Watkins, but I really don't think Pussy Lickums would enjoy it. Besides, there are quite a number of cats on the farm, as well as dogs and ponies and chickens and ducks and geese. I believe Uncle Thomas even has some deer.'

Elizabeth was still undecided. 'Would I go in the train?' she wanted to know.

'Part of the way. You would go from here to Adelaide by train and then go in one of Hill and Co.'s coaches with four horses. If you are good, Daddy could arrange for you to sit on the box seat next to the driver.'

Elizabeth instantly decided that nothing must prevent her from enjoying this experience.

And so it came about that the dress-basket was packed and strapped, and Jimmie and Mrs Watkins provided with new winter coats very obligingly made for them by Pearl, and all the other members of the pre-Stopesian family were carefully put away in the nursery cupboard and admonished to 'be good till we got home again'. A last and tearful farewell was said out

130

of the window to Pussy Lickums, who was indifferent to the whole affair; and at five o'clock on a dark winter morning Elizabeth was buttoned into her warmest coat – the one with the fur collar and the muff which hung by a cord round her neck – and taken downstairs to eat her breakfast by gas-light. At six o'clock Finch brought the wagonette to the door and Elizabeth and Miss Una embarked, Elizabeth silent and keeping back the tears only by remembering about the coach and four, Miss Una talking a little more loudly and cheerfully than usual. Finch drove them to the station, and when they heard the mournful 'ding-dong' of the bell as the train puffed its way along Jetty Road and came tiredly to a standstill, Elizabeth would have cried openly had not Finch put the dress-basket in the guard's van and then raised his hat and said to her as though she were a real grown-up: 'Well, good-bye, Miss Beth, and a good journey.' This made her feel very important, and the tears were wiped away with the hankie she kept inside her muff where she also had two large silver pennies which her Daddy had given her as an advance, so to speak, against her sixth birthday, which would occur while she was at Rose Lees.

When the train arrived in the city half an hour later, the day was lighter, though still grey and cold. As the distance was short between the station and the place from which the coach was to take its departure, Miss Una decided that a cab was an unnecessary expense. After giving minute and repeated instructions to the railway porter to bring the dress-basket and the parcels across the square to the coach office without delay, Miss Una gathered up her handbag, a jar of Mrs Thompson's last batch of currant jelly which she was anxious for Aunt Emma Woodstock to pass an opinion on and which could not be entrusted to the railway porter, and a small basket containing Elizabeth's 'night things' in case the dress-basket went astray, for it was axiomatic that no railway or coach company could be trusted to deliver one's luggage on time.

They walked across the square where Queen Victoria looked

down from her new stone pedestal through the mist of the morning. The four-wheeled cabs were taking up their stand in rows under the Moreton Bay fig trees. The trams rumbled clumsily along their rails, the horses straining under the momentum of their double-decked burdens, wearily, as though at the end instead of at the beginning of another day. A lamp-lighter on a bicycle was riding slowly and wobblingly from lamp-post to lamp-post, pulling the little chains with his long hook to extinguish the gas lamps.

A crowd of some thirty or forty persons was gathered under the veranda of a building on the north side of the square. From the piles of bags and baskets which strewed the pavement, from the rugged and muffled and top-coated garb of the men who stood about it, chafing their hands and stamping their feet against the cold, it was evident that these were Elizabeth's fellow-passengers and the friends and relations who had come to see them off. She and Miss Una had no sooner made themselves part of this gathering and Miss Una had assured herself that the railway porter had indeed carried Elizabeth's dress-basket safely across the square, and had inspected its position among the other baggage and the security of its straps and buckles and labels, and had rewarded the porter with a new threepenny piece, when a stir and an exclamation and a general air of expectancy made itself evident among the assemblage. Cries of 'Here she comes', and 'At last!' proclaimed that the coach had rounded the corner from Light Square and was now coming along Franklin Street at a spanking pace. As Elizabeth saw the top-heavy vehicle with its huge wheels and unwieldy body, painted a bright canary yellow, swaying along in fine style behind six bay horses, the coachman wheeling an immensely long whip over their backs, she felt her heart jump with excitement.

'Oo, Miss Oonie, look, look, there's six horses! You said there would only be four.'

One of the gentlemen standing near-by turned to her with

a smile. 'Extra lot of passengers today, so they're sending one of the big coaches.'

With a crashing of hooves and a ringing of harness and a shout of 'Whoa, whoa, there!' from the driver, the coach drew up before the veranda. At once all was confusion. Two men jumped down from the box seat and pushed their way through the crowd. Everyone was clutching at coats and rugs and bags and bandboxes, shouting instructions, embracing, calling good-bye, weeping, or elbowing their way impatiently through the throng. A man in a scarlet coat elbowed his way across the pavement, crying: 'Make way for the mails! Make way, there, for His Majesty's mails!' He was carrying several canvas bags which he flung up to the coachman who stowed them away into a deep, dark cupboard under his feet, a cavity which Elizabeth soon learnt was called the 'boot'.

Most of the ladies took their seats inside the coach. A number of the men climbed up the ladder and on to the tiers of seats on the roof, a position which seemed to Elizabeth precarious in the extreme.

'Where am I going to sit, Miss Oonie?' she asked.

'In a minute, dear. Don't be impatient,' was the answer. They had drawn to the edge of the crowd. While waiting for the other passengers to settle themselves, Miss Una satisfied her-self that the important dress-basket was safely stowed. Another lady was evidently of the same mind, for she, too, was standing to one side, making no move to present her ticket. Dressed entirely in black, her figure was severe, even forbidding. She was tall and thin, her face of sallow complexion, roughened and lined as though she were accustomed to be much in the open air, the lips compressed to a thin line, the nostrils pinched, the eyes coldly grey under grizzled brows. For a moment they turned down to meet the childish gaze of the little girl. Elizabelt felt suddenly cold. The sun, now risen and casting its first pale beams across the street, seemed momentarily obscured as though the chill mists of night were not yet dispelled. The woman was accompanied by a little boy and, as he peeped shyly from behind her, Elizabeth saw to her delight that it was Henri Hardman. She tugged at Miss Una's hand. 'Look, look, Miss Oonie,' once again came the familiar exclamation, 'it's Henri Hardman, the little French boy I met when Mummie took me to Madame de Fresgne's.'

The dark lady stared at Elizabeth with frowning brows. 'I do not know who you are, little girl,' she said in a hard and bitter voice, 'but my grandson is not French and his name is Henry, not Ong-ree,' and the inflexion she used was filled with scorn. Henri's pale face, which for the moment had looked almost happy as he recognised Elizabeth's friendly greeting, now turned away, his lips trembling and his eyes dark with tears.

Miss Una, to whom Mrs Inglefell had recounted the meeting with young Mrs Hardman, now saw that with the exercise of a little tact, the situation might with advantage be improved. She turned to the older woman and introduced herself.

'And this is Elizabeth Inglefell,' she explained. 'She is going to Mount Pleasant to stay with her aunt, Mrs Thomas Woodstock, with whom you are perhaps acquainted.'

Mrs Hardman acknowledged the introduction very coolly and made no advance which might encourage Miss Godfrey to place Elizabeth in her care during the journey. As the ticket-collector now called to them to take their places on the coach, there was no further opportunity of improving the acquaintance, but Elizabeth did manage to give Henri a cheerful smile which reassured him a little when his grandmother gave him a merciless prod towards the ladder leading to the second row of seats on top of the coach.

Elizabeth did not have to climb the ladder. No sooner had Miss Una begun her explanation to the ticket-collector than he held up a large hand. 'Not a word, miss,' he exclaimed. 'The Boss has had a letter from the young lady's pa, and the pleasure's ours.' He turned his cheerful, shining countenance to the coachman, who all this time had been sitting immobile

on his box, his form enveloped in coats and capes and his huge
left hand with its bunch of 'ribbons' resting lightly on his left
knee.

'Here you are, Bill,' cried the ticket-collector, 'here's your
little bundle of nonsense,' and, before Elizabeth could grasp
what he was about to do, he put his strong hands under her
armpits and swung her high into the air. There was a shout
of laughter from the men in the crowd. Two gentlemen on
the box seat seemed likely to have their hats knocked off by
Elizabeth's boots, but they good-humouredly passed her along
to her seat beside the coachman. When she was settled in a
position under his left elbow and the immense leather covering-
rug had been fastened by brass hooks to the railing in front,
she found that she could see over the top of it very well. The
driver looked down at her over the curve of his great-capes.
Two red-rimmed eyes gazed fiercely into hers and a hoarse
voice growled: 'Na, then, you stays there and no hankie-panky.
Your pa's put you in my charge, and if you don't behave it's in
the boot you go. Have you got a label arahnd your neck?'

Elizabeth looked up bravely. 'I've got a ticket,' she replied,
'but it's not around my neck. Are you Mr Hill?'

'Yo, ho,' roared the coachman, as if this gave him great
satisfaction. 'Mr Hill, indeed! No, Bill's the name, Billiam it is
and always was.'

At that moment the clock on the post office tower chimed
the first of the Big Ben cadence for seven o'clock. Without so
much as a glance behind him to see that his passengers were
prepared for the start, Bill instantly tightened his handful of
reins, the long lash snaked out to catch the left-hand leader a
flicker on the ear and returned in loops to the driver's hand.
The horses plunged forward, the coach heaved and swayed
behind them, the wheels turned. The journey had begun.

Elizabeth waved to Miss Una, and her little voice crying:
'Good-bye, good-bye' was lost in the noise of the coach gathering speed. As the clock struck the seven strokes, the coach

rounded the Post Office corner, the man in the red coat who had taken the highest seat on the back of the coach blew three blasts on his horn. His Majesty's mails were on their way.

At first Elizabeth was rather nervous and a little sad at leaving Miss Una behind, but the bugle-music had cheered her with its thrilling notes. As the six horses raced along, their brass trimmings winking in the sunlight, the heavy wheels of the coach making an echoing thunder in the city streets, almost empty of traffic at this early hour, windows were flung up and heads popped out, and the milkmen on their carts stopped to wave their hats and cheer. Once out of the city and on to the Walkerville Road the horses seemed to change the rhythm of their pace. Before, it had been all plunging and high-stepping and showing-off; now it settled down to a long, steady, fast trot, so evenly matched that all six horses sometimes kept perfect step. The coach, too, fell into a comfortable, easy swing which could make one very sleepy if it went on for long, thought Elizabeth. But at present she was much too interested in everything to feel sleepy. Whenever they overhauled a tram-car with its slow, plodding horses, they rattled past with a cheer and a great show of pace. All the tram passengers looked out of the windows, which made Elizabeth feel very important. But she was sorry for the tram horses; they were so faithful and so patient.

The tram-lines soon came to an end. The houses set in pretty gardens gave way to farm-yards and open fields, newly-springing with young wheat. It seemed no time at all before they were swinging to a standstill at the O.G. Inn on Gilles Plains.

The stop was only for a few minutes, to leave a passenger, drop a mail-bag and change horses.

'How's my little bit o' nuisance getting on?' asked Bill, squinting down at her from under his broad-brimmed hat. His voice was deep and gruff enough to frighten anyone and was no less terrifying than his eyes, which because of their blood-shot condition and the fact of their having no eyelashes, gave him the appearance of being constantly in a choler. Elizabeth felt an inevitable timidity, but she spoke up resolutely.

'My Daddy said I wasn't to be a nuisance to you,' she replied. 'Perhaps,' she offered politely, 'I could help you. Hold the reins or something. Jackie, who drives Capting Bossie's cobs, said I've got the makings, given the chance.'

'There's an idea!' bellowed Bill, and without more ado put the bundle of leathers into her hands. Elizabeth could hardly hold them all, even with both paws. But she remembered what Mr O'Brien and Captain Bossingham's groom had taught her about holding her left hand palm upwards with the ribbons for the leader between her little and third fingers and those for the shaft horses between her thumb and the index and second fingers. The leaders had been taken away by the ostler to be changed and the four shaft horses were standing patiently enough, but Elizabeth could not help but feel a trifle anxious as, tongue between lips, she sorted out the reins and arranged them between her fingers. Bill said not a word, but sat watching her struggle. When the leathers were all in their correct positions, it was quite impossible for her to close her hand on them, but she looked hopefully up at Bill and asked: 'Is that right?'

'Not bad for an amachoor,' Bill answered, with a fearful glare, 'but I don't hold with no women drivin' my coach.' And he took back the reins with one sweep of his left hand. 'Hen-ery!' This last in an ear-shattering roar. 'Where the blinkety-blink-blink blazes have you got to with them ponies?'

'Coming, Mr William, sir,' called the ostler as he came round from the stables leading two piebald colts which pranced and jerked, full of corn-fed energy. He backed them into the traces and had barely fastened the last buckle when they leaped forward with such a plunge that the coach started like a tramcar and Elizabeth was only prevented from falling headlong on to the floor by the barrier of the leather rug. Her instability was partly due to having just turned round to glance back at

Henri, who was sitting immediately behind her. The coachman's cry of 'Hen-nery' having reminded her of her little friend.

Henri was sitting pale and cold with his legs dangling from the high seat. He had neither overcoat nor rug, and the cold morning air had made his knees purple and his hands numb. The misery in his heart had given to his childish face an expression too tragic for its years, accentuated now by fatigue and hunger, for it was many hours since he had eaten. Beside him sat his grandmother, upright and apparently unmoved by the frostiness of the weather or the activities of Mr Billiam's mettlesome colts. Elizabeth's friendly advances, abruptly interrupted by the horses, met no response from either of them, though for different reasons: Henri because all warmth of feeling, either physical or emotional, had left him, and Mrs Hardman because she thought Elizabeth merely an impertinent child who needed discouragement. Elizabeth longed to ask Mr Billiam if Henri could come and sit beside her on the box seat, but even Mr Billiam's masterly skill was now fully occupied with the pair of leaders under his hands. Elizabeth had all she could do to hang on to the edge of the leather rug with both hands while the coach heaved and plunged along the sloping road, took the corners with a sickening swing and raced along the level stretches at almost a gallop.

The way now left the open farmland and led into the hills, where the road was closed in on either hand by tall gum trees and masses of uncleared bush. The grades grew steeper. The gullies, shadowed where the early sun had not yet reached them, echoed to the sound of running water and the laughter of kookaburras. At the end of an hour Elizabeth began to feel the tiredness of the journey and the fresh air on her eyelids. She had just begun to nod, suspiciously near the borders of sleep, when with a ringing shout and a swerve to the right the team pulled into a gravelled space in front of the Chain of Ponds Hotel.

Ostlers ran forward to the horses' heads. Parties of lounging idlers, intending passengers and postmen waiting for the mail-bags sprang to life as Mr Billiam put his great boot on the rung of the brake, pulled in his reins and brought his team to a standstill. He roared out at the top of his voice: 'All down for breakfast.'

There was an instant scramble from the seats on the top of the coach. Some of the younger gentlemen did not wait for the ladder to be put up, but took flying leaps on to the macadam. Mrs Hardman gathered up her long skirts and carefully descended the steps, saying to Henri as she did so: 'Mind you stay there and do not leave until I get back.'

In the meantime, ostlers were taking the shaft horses away while the leaders were tied to the hitching-posts. 'Now then, my hearty,' said Mr Billiam, turning to Elizabeth, 'time some people had their breakfast,' and he lifted her down on to the roadway where, her feet being as cold as they were and her head rather giddy from the recent careering of the coach, she promptly fell over in a heap.

'Yo, ho,' shouted Mr Billiam, 'that is no way for a young lady to enter an hotel,' and then roared with merriment at his own crude joke. 'Hot tea and porridge is what you want, my beauty.'

From her undignified position on the gravel, Elizabeth could see Henri still sitting pathetically all by himself on top of the coach. 'Oh, dear Mr Billiam,' she cried, 'cannot Henri come too? Look, he is all by himself, and I am sure he is very cold and hungry.'

The coachman rolled an eye towards his little passenger. 'Come on, young gentleman! All down for breakfast.'

The little boy was almost too cold to speak, but in a trembling tone he managed to say: 'My grand'mère told me I was not to move.' This seemed to rouse Mr Billiam to choleric fury. He reached forward and snatched Henri from the seat before the child had time to protest. 'All down for breakfast,' he repeated at the top of his voice. 'I will have no passengers on my coach who do not eat their breakfast.'

The entrance to the hotel was crowded with men where the bar was doing a brisk trade. Tankards of beer were being handed over the counter, or passed over the heads of the crowd to those in the rear ranks. German farmers were standing about drinking wine out of red and gold glass cups.

Mr Billiam shepherded the two children through this hub-bub and into the dining-room which was full to overflowing with passengers from the coach. The maid-servants were flying about between the tables bringing dishes of hot porridge and eggs and chops and steaks and cups of coffee and mugs of cocoa. Over everything was an air of great bustle and excite-ment, for the arrival of the coach was the event of the day.

In spite of all this occupation, the entrance of Mr Billiam produced an immediate effect upon the assemblage which re-sulted in a place nearest the fire being instantly cleared for him and three seats at a table made vacant. He ordered the waitress to bring three plates of porridge and milk. Elizabeth piped up: 'I am not very fond of porridge and milk, Mr Billiam, thank you.' A mighty fist smote the table so that all the knives and forks jumped, the plates and cups rattled, and the glasses nearly fell off on to the floor.

'Yo, ho,' came the now-familiar roar, 'I will have no passengers on my coach who do not eat their porridge.'

Elizabeth felt that she did not dare to go against such an edict or she might be left behind and the coach go on to Mount Pleasant without her.

At that moment the door of the dining-room was again opened and the formidable figure of Mrs Hardman entered. She swept the company with a cold eye and advanced towards the table where Mr Billiam and his charges were sitting.

'Henry,' she said sharply, 'did I not tell you to remain on the coach? Go back this instant, and you, sir' – turning to Mr Billiam – 'how dare you bring the child into the unsuitable atmosphere of this public house! I will report your conduct to your company.'

Mr Billiam rose to his feet, the capes of his greatcoat heaving about his shoulders like the sails of a ship in a heavy sea. 'Ma'am,' said he, and as he spoke he seemed to tower above her, not only by his physical height, but by the authority of his bearing, 'no passenger stays on my coach cold and hungry when it is my dooty to carry him on his journey safe and comfortable. So says my contract and so does Mr Hill say the same.' He turned to Henri, who had risen and was standing shaken with cold and fear beside his grandmother. 'You sit right down and eat your breakfast, young feller-me-lad.'

Happily at that moment the waitress put down on the table three large basins of steaming porridge and a jug of hot milk.

Feeling herself no doubt routed by the course of circumstance, Mrs Hardman withdrew from the dining-room with what dignity she could muster, while Henri gathered courage from the fierce eye of his protector and was soon eagerly eating up his breakfast and enjoying the warmth which was beginning to creep into his toes from the red-hot mass of mallee roots burning in the fireplace. To her astonishment Elizabeth found the porridge very good indeed. She not only finished her basinful, but went on to scrambled eggs garnished with bacon followed by new crusty bread spread with salted butter and plum jam, washed down with a large mug of sweet chocolate.

'My!' she exclaimed, looking up at Mr Billiam at last while her tongue tried to reach the rim of chocolate round her lips. 'My! Miss Oonie will have to let out all my buttons when I get home.'

'Nothing like it!' was the opinion of Mr Billiam, who had himself done full justice to the generous bill of fare. 'Nothin' like good vittles for man and beast. Never saw a pony any good as didn't take his oats.' He heaved himself back comfortably in his chair and patted his belly with affection.

The rest of the journey passed for Elizabeth in a kind of

dream. Mr Billiam had conjured up a rug from somewhere in which he wrapped Henri when lifting him back on to the top of the coach and which, with exaggerated courtesy, he extended to the service of Mrs Hardman, who could hardly refuse this attention without entering into an undignified altercation with someone she considered much below her in social position.

Of the last stage of the drive, when the shadows were shortening under the noonday sun, Elizabeth could afterwards remember very little, and it was a sleepy little girl who was finally handed down to the care of her Uncle Thomas. She was delighted to see his cheerful face. The excitement of arrival, the locating of the dress-basket and the safe handing over of Mrs Thompson's bottle of jelly soon brought her wide awake again. She noticed that Mrs Hardman and Henri had been met by an elderly gentleman with a broad beard and gentle blue eyes. She was glad for Henri's sake that he looked so kind. She saw them get into a sulky and drive away.

Uncle Thomas gathered up all her baskets and packages and put them into the trap and was about to lift her in after them when she cried to him reproachfully: 'But I haven't said good-bye to Mr Billiam!'

'Why, now,' said Uncle Thomas, taking off his hat and scratching his head as he always seemed to do in moments of perplexity, 'now who might Mr Billiam be?'

'Why, there he is!' cried Elizabeth, pointing to where the coachman was sitting, lordly and motionless on his box, as though above the paltry distractions of disembarkation. When he saw Elizabeth's face below him and her childish voice crying: 'Good-bye, Mr Billiam, good-bye, dear Mr Billiam!' he wound the reins firmly round the brake handle and clambered down over the side of the coach. 'Well, my little bundle of nuisance, all present and correct?' he bellowed gently, like a thunderstorm rolling away when the sun comes out. 'All signed, sealed and delivered as per invoice?'

'Oh, good-bye, dear Mr Billiam,' cried Elizabeth again. 'Now

I shall eat my porridge every day and when I come back I can help you hold the reins again.' She tiptoed up to offer her lips. This caused Mr Billiam acute embarrassment. Puffing and blowing and yo-hoing in a subterranean sort of way, he glanced to right and left, drew the cuff of his greatcoat across his mouth in a mighty sweep and bent to take the offered tribute. Then, redder than ever, and with all his capes plunging and lumping, he climbed back on to the box and resumed his granite pose.

Elizabeth and her Uncle Thomas got into the trap and were soon driving across the countryside to Rose Lees.

14

The Picnic

F o r Elizabeth life at Rose Lees was a round of joyous adventure. She got up at dawn to watch Uncle Thomas and Oscar do the milking. Oscar was the rouseabout, a large German youth from Nuriootpa who spoke little English and went through his day's work almost as dumb as the beasts he tended. When the new milk had been poured from the buckets into the separators and the skim had been carried away to the bran-house to be mixed with the pigs' food, Elizabeth was allowed to collect some cream in a jug and take it up to the house for breakfast. They did not make butter at Rose Lees any more. Aunt Emma said it was too much work and not worth it. When the lorry from the butter factory called every forenoon for the cans of cream, the man left three pounds of factory-made butter in part-payment for the raw cream.

Elizabeth learnt how to scour and scald the milk-buckets, the cream-cans and the separators; how to mix the bran and pollard for the chickens; how to fill the feeding bottles for the baby calves; how long to leave the pans of milk on the stove to clot the cream. (Uncle Thomas was partial to a Devonshire tea, with new-made scones and scalded cream and strawberry jam, or perhaps honey if Oscar had found a comb near the creek when the white gums were blossoming and the honey sweet, for the wild honey from the stringy-bark scrub was too dark and tasted of eucalyptus). She learnt how to hang up the skim milk in muslin bags to make cream cheese and how to put the oatmeal to soak in the evening and stir the saucepan to prevent the porridge from burning. Although she still did not like porridge very much, she ate it every morning in honour of Mr Billiam.

Oscar taught her to ride Puddles, the farm pony. Soon she was able to follow Uncle Thomas when he went riding on Tall Timber as long as he did not canter too fast. They rode out in the paddocks together to look at the sheep or down the road to inspect the crops in the Far Paddocks.

Every week she measured her waist with Aunt Emma's tape measure to see how much fatter she had become, and stood still with her back to the wall while Uncle Thomas put the carving knife flat on the top of her head so that a mark could be made on the wall to show how tall she had grown. These statistics were carefully recorded in laboriously pot-hooked letters to her mother. In the evenings she was so sleepy that more than once Uncle Thomas had to carry her up to bed. When she said her prayers she was urgent in her requests for Heaven's choicest benedictions on Uncle Thomas and Aunt Emma for being such kind relations. The first time that they heard these recommendations Emma's eyes filled with tears and Thomas swore with unaccustomed vigour as he knocked out the dottle of his pipe red-hot into the palm of his hand.

In accordance with their promise to Mrs Inglefell to 'keep an eye' on Henri, they made several attempts to bring the two children together, sometimes stopping at Lily Lees on their way in to town, to invite Henri to join the party or to be brought back to Rose Lees for tea. Henri had only twice been permitted to accept these invitations, but Thomas and Emma, in no way weakened in their determination by Jane Hardman's inhospitality, did not hesitate to leave Elizabeth at Lily Lees for two or three hours at a time while they drove to Mount Pleasant for their marketing or banking, confident that her cheerful disposition would not be affected by Jane's lack of cordiality.

To Henri these first encounters with Elizabeth were bewildering. But his shyness and the citadel of grief which he had built within himself had no defence against her vitality, her inventiveness, and the happiness which snatched at each day's events with an eager joy incapable of timidity or satiety. She lived her life like a greedy child pulling cherries off a tree, grabbing with both hands at all it offered and swallowing down the fruit of experience with so avid an appetite that the occasional bitterness only served to enhance her enjoyment of the sweets.

Henri was now going to the public school in the town. He had to walk four miles every morning which any normal child of his age would have found no great hardship, for children have astonishing powers of physical endurance. But Henri was not very strong and the strains to which he had been subjected in the last year had made him physically weak as well as emotionally timid. After school every afternoon he came home with the lorry from the butter factory, sitting up with the driver who soon became a good friend. He even overcame some of his nervousness with the horses, two giant greys bred by Stan Williams at Frummocks, a stud some ten miles away on the Onkaparinga side, acquiring a shy, proprietary pride in their strength and pace which rolled the big truck laden with cans across the countryside twice a day, summer and winter, wind or weather, fire or flood: literally meant, too, as the driver unfolded tales of storms that brought down great gum trees across the road, or bush fires that swept across twenty miles of country in a night, to say nothing of the time the creek flooded and the horses pulled the lorry across the creek-bed with the floodwaters up to their bellies. The drive home in the afternoons made up a good deal for many miserable hours of fright and loneliness. In the twilight of the winter mornings the walk along the deserted country road became for him a kind of nightmare. He who had known only the close intimacies of family life, mostly lived in one room, was cowed by the vast stretches of country that rolled emptily away for miles on either side of the road. At one place a patch of bush where the gum trees grew in a dark archway and the wattle and ti-tree clustered thick along the banks formed a tunnel through which he must walk.

Even with the brighter days of spring Henri's fears were not stilled. To walk along that road in the bright sunshine was to move under the witch's spell in a fairy-story. Here the quiet was something to be felt, as though the whole world were in the grip of enchantment, like the castle of the Sleeping Beauty where the pageboys were magic-motionless in the act of putting food into their mouths and the water of the fountains was suspended in mid-air, condemned to a frozen stillness by a power stronger than the laws of nature. In this world of suspended life the warble-music of the morning magpies fell as a series of little shocks, their flutes like the pipes of the Pied Piper of Hamelin at once terrifying and irresistible. Henri would hurry along the road, frightened without knowing what he was frightened of; or he would dawdle, putting off as long as possible his entry into the dark tree-tunnel where the rain dripped from the boughs overhead and the wind made squarking noises in the eucalyptus trees, the long strips of bleached bark hanging and banging in the restless air. Sometimes he dawdled for so long that all the other children had gone in to school by the time he arrived, so that he did not have their company even from the outskirts of the town.

Fortunately the school discipline was sensibly elastic, the schoolmaster having long since adapted himself and his methods to the vagaries of scholars who had, many of them, to get up at dawn and milk cows and make butter before setting off on a five- or six-mile walk to school, or had to ride in from outlying villages and farms across the paddocks and creeks and, before leaving for home again in the afternoon, had to pack on to their ponies parcels from the general store and perhaps a mail-bag or two. A good teacher, Mr Patchly managed to knock a surprising amount of knowledge into the minds and some discipline into the bodies of his pupils, though they varied in age from five years to sixteen: the State system of education at that time provided only for children to the age of thirteen in this type of school, but Mr Patchly continued to teach privately those scholars who wished to compete in the public examinations for entrance to the university. He knew the family histories of most of his charges. The apparent stupidity of the new boy from Lily Lees he diagnosed at once as due to physical weakness and emotional tension. And so for the first few weeks Henri was not asked to make any more effort than was required to overcome his shyness in the presence of more children than he had ever met in his life before.

He might more easily have adjusted himself to this new life if each day had not begun in the shadow of the road, for the walk in from the farm had now become personified in his mind as a waiting presence: the ribbon of white macadam rising and falling under the enormous arch of sky which touched down on horizons lost in the haze of distance or of mist or dust; the long, low hillsides moving and receding, were like the limbs of some animate presence, surrounding, enveloping, pressing in on him, the small and shrunken pivot on which, as he walked, this whole gigantic organism revolved.

When the spring holidays began during the first week of September, he felt a sense of relief that he had no longer to face this daily ordeal, even at the cost of being now, more than ever, vulnerable to the flagellations of his grandmother's irritability and sharp temper.

One morning Mr Hardman came up to the house carrying a letter which he had found tied to the handle of one of the empty milk-cans at the gate. The factory lorry had brought it from Rose Lees on its way to pick up the full cans and leave the empty ones.

Mr Hardman brought the letter into the kitchen, took his steel-rimmed spectacles from behind the clock where he always kept them, and read it aloud to his wife who was ironing.

'It's from Rose Lees,' he announced. 'It says, "Dear Mrs Hardman," so it's really for you, my dear.'

'Well, for goodness' sake, read it out and don't be all day about it,' was Jane's impatient comment as she took a flat-iron off the stove, spat on her finger to test the heat of the iron and then wiped it with a beeswax cloth.

Her husband cleared his throat, adjusted his glasses and went on: 'It's from Mrs Woodstock. It says, "Next Saturday will be Elizabeth Inglefell's sixth birthday and we are inviting our friends to a picnic at the Fern Creek Pool. We hope you and your husband will come and bring Henry to meet us at the Pool in time for dinner at midday. If the weather is wet we will come to Rose Lees instead and have our party in the barn." Hm-m,' said Mr Hardman thoughtfully as he put the letter down on a pile of freshly-ironed linen whence Jane instantly snatched it, 'next Saturday, that'll be the eleventh, I think.' He crossed the room to consult a large, brightly-coloured calender hanging on the wall which, besides the days and seasons, announced that 'Gordon and Cedric Bluddenbone, Butchers, Meat Vendors and Purveyors, of Mount Pleasant, would wait upon Families with Courtesy and Despatch. Our Motto being Highest Quality only at Lowest Prices', which Jane was wont to declare a worthless claim, seeing that Gordon Bluddenbone always did tell lies, even at school, and the last lot of beef he sent out was nothing but a piece of one of Hurtle Johnson's old cows that he bought at the Gumeracha sale and, when told so, not showing any of this courtesy he blathers so much about, to say nothing of his prices, which is downright silly to talk about, as everyone in the district knows what he pays for every beast he buys.

At the moment, however, Richard was not concerned with the quality either of Mr Bluddenbone's manners or his meat. He ran his finger down the list of September Saturdays.

'That's right. Next Saturday is the eleventh. I've an idea that's our own little chap's birthday too.' He left the kitchen, crossed the passage and entered the parlour where he groped about (for the window-blinds were drawn down) among the mahogany and plush, until he found the Family Bible which he carried back to the kitchen. He clumped the heavy volume down on top of the clean shirts.

'For crying's sake, Richard Hardman, take that thing off the table. If it isn't enough for me to have all these shirts to wash and iron every week without you messing them up before they're even worn.'

'Sorry, my dear.' Richard picked up the offending scriptures and retreated to his comfortable old chair near the stove. He opened the rear cover of the Bible where, to his great satisfaction, he found an entry in his own handwriting: 'September 11, 1894. On this day Lisette, wife of Richard Hardman, gave birth to a son, Henry, at Roubaix, France.'

'There we are, my dear. Henry will be eight years old next Saturday. Fancy the two youngsters being born on the same day.'

Jane gave vent to her characteristic sound which can only be described as a snort. 'Of course they weren't! Henry is two years older than Elizabeth. Well, I suppose we have to go to this picnic, though what sort of pleasure people get out of this sort of thing I never can understand – sitting about on the damp grass and eating a lot of unsuitable food when they'd be better off in their own homes. As for Henry and the birthday side of it, there's to be no nonsense about presents or anything of that sort. First and last, that young man and his worthless mother have cost us more than enough. And if Emma Woodstock thinks we have money to waste buying presents for that spoilt Inglefell brat, she is much mistaken.' And Jane thumped the iron down on the towel she was ironing to emphasise her word, but Richard was listening with only half his mind, the other half already engaged with a plan to saddle up and ride in to the township where he remembered having seen some picture books and boxes of coloured chalks in old Ebenezer Skethaway's store. They wouldn't be very expensive; in any case, he could give up smoking for a few weeks. This was always Richard's private resolution in times of financial stress. He had never actually carried it into effect, but it was always there, a means of reassurance, a bulwark against bankruptcy. He had only to tell himself that if things got worse he would give up smoking, and his financial worries, if not dispersed, at least lost most of their terrors.

Saturday when it came was one of those perfect days that spring sometimes gives us between the icy blasts of the south-westerly monsoons and the first heat of summer. The sky was cloudless and as blue as a starling's egg, the air sweet with the perfumes of spring flowers and the new green and the scent of the sun on the ploughed earth.

Henri had never been to a picnic, indeed he had only the vaguest idea of what a picnic was. His feelings, therefore, were not entirely pleasurable, but rather a mixture of pleasure at the idea of seeing Elizabeth again, shyness at the prospect of meeting a lot of people and dread that his grandmother's anger – that unpredictable, terrifying force which dominated his life – would in some way use the occasion to punish him.

Fern Creek Pool was a favourite picnic ground, some two miles from Rose Lees. In the rocky little creek, dry all the summer, the water was now bubbling happily over the pebbles, making small falls between the rocks before spilling over, in a fit of the giggles, to form a wide pool from the banks of which ferns hung down to give shade and protection to the frogs, tadpoles, minnows and yabbies that lived under the banks. The grass under the gum trees, green and long, was starred with buttercups and bachelors' buttons. Overhead, the kookaburras watched the picnickers arrive and went into roars of laughter at the sight of so many human beings invading their private territory.

People came in wagonettes and buggies and sulkies and on horseback. The horses were unharnessed and turned into a

near-by field, the owner of which, Mr Rosenthorn, told everyone that he would charge them rent at the rate of a gallon a
year, a joke he made every time a picnic was held, which was
several times a year, and as he had a very red face, a purple
nose and a bibulous manner and was a strict teetotaller, everyone agreed that it was a very good joke indeed. Henry was surprised to find that all the boys and girls of his own age from
the school had been invited as well as their mothers and fathers
and uncles and aunts and cousins.

Mrs Woodstock said that as it was her invitation which had
brought them to the picnic, she should provide all the food and
drink. She made Oscar unpack several hampers from which she
drew prodigious quantities of roast turkeys, pork pies, cold
boiled fowls, a whole milk-can full of fruit salad and a smaller
one of cream.

But the established community custom on this sort of
occasion was too strong to be overcome by these tactics, and
the other ladies brought out baskets and bags the contents of
which soon rivalled hers in quantity and variety. Mrs Braddock
from Pine Trees had brought a ham; Mr Jessopy who lived by
himself at Polly's Corner had driven the Murphy children over
because their father was away at Kapunda getting super-
phosphate because the local agent had run out of supplies and
he wanted it quick and their mother was having another baby,
the eighth; but she sent a leg of lamb because she had roasted
a whole side to see the family through her confinement, and Mr
Jessopy being a bachelor didn't have anything cooked but
brought two pounds of chocolates and a dozen bottles of beer;
and the Partridge children rode across on their ponies and were
sorry their mother couldn't come because of Aunt Ellen's
rheumatics but she sent a lovely cake with pink icing to wish
Elizabeth and Henry many happy returns of the day and please
could she have the tin back as she couldn't seem to make cakes
except in this particular tin, they never seemed the same
like.

The Picnic

By the time the Hardmans drove up, the fires had been lit and chops and steaks and sausages were sizzling on the gridirons. The scent of the burning gum sticks mingled with flavours of the grilling meat to give everyone a sharp appetite. Billies filled with water from the brook were slung on hooks of fencing wire over the flames to boil for tea. Rugs were spread and leather cushions from the traps were put on the grass for the ladies to sit on, while the men sat on logs or among the granite rocks scattered through the grass.

After more food had been eaten and more mugs of tea and glasses of beer had been drunk than anyone would have believed possible, Uncle Thomas proposed the health of the two guests of honour, whereupon everyone began to sing 'For they are jolly good fellows' and Elizabeth was so surprised and excited when she found that it was for her that she sat down suddenly on the remains of Mrs Partridge's cake with the pink icing and Henri burst into tears and had to be led away to be nose-blown.

After that the grown-ups dozed a little or lit their pipes and argued sleepily about the wool-market and the rainfall until it was time to shake the crumbs out of the tablecloths, scrape the plates, pack the remains of hams and sausages and chops away from the ants, and refill the billies and stir up the fires to make more tea.

The children ran away to play along the creek where the golden wattle was in flower. Elizabeth and Henri were initiated into a great secret, a place where the white gums gave way to stringybark and ti-tree. Here in the damp of a deep leaf-mould grew spider orchids, tall, elegant green stems on which balanced delicate, top-heavy heads with red velvet hoods and hairy lips, surrounded by six green and brown 'legs', each two inches long. Elizabeth was enchanted, but a tiny bit repelled: the orchids looked so exactly like real and very large spiders. Because it was her birthday the other children allowed her to pick several, showing her how to do it without pulling the root up from the loose mould and enjoining on her the strict rule that never, never must wild flowers be pulled up by the roots.

Henri, recovered from his brief tears of excitement, entered into this with bewilderment. The bush, then, with its lofty trees and dark groves, its strange silences and sudden inexplicable noises, could be something one loved and understood; it had secrets to share with its friends, and its harshness and eeriness held soft beauty and intimacy that could be explored and, once discovered, reverenced. When Elizabeth allowed him to carry half her orchids because it was his birthday too, he was so happy that he could not understand what was happening to him and felt very sick.

All too soon Aunt Emma called them back to the camp by banging on a tin tray with an iron ladle. They drank their tea and ate another slice of the birthday cake rather hurriedly, for the men had already brought in the horses from the paddock and harnessed them. Though it was only four o'clock, they all had cows to milk before sunset.

For Jane Hardman the day had been far from happy. Her opposition to the picnic had not prevented her from rising early to bake cakes and pies and to pack the baskets with cups and plates and bottles of home-made raspberry vinegar. All this activity was prompted less by a desire to celebrate Henri's birthday than by the determination that Emma Woodstock would not outdo her in housewifely display. She was therefore tired and cross by the time they left for the picnic ground and not in the mood to share the exchanges of neighbourly gossip and light-hearted banter which characterised these occasions. Richard and Henri had to suffer a good many complaints about life in general, with particular reference to Richard's inability to keep his collars from looking as though he had slept in them and repeated injunctions to Henri not to get his clothes dirty in the course of the day and not to sit on the wet grass and not to drink too much of that fizzy ginger-beer Emma Woodstock made which in Jane's opinion was downright immoral and should be stopped by law, containing as she was sure it did a perceptible percentage of alcohol.

Throughout the day she watched Henri constantly, correcting his manners and telling him what to eat and what not to drink and what to say. Her neighbours were used to her lack of cordiality and took it good-humouredly, forgiving her for the sake of her husband whom they all liked. None of them realised, she herself least of all, that she was a woman on the defensive against the desperate sorrow and loneliness in her own heart. Her unkindness to Henri was revenge against him for not being Richard, her son. The frustration of her own affections, robbed of the only object towards which they yearned, made her emotions a cage from which there was no escape, no outlet, no relief.

She made no objection when Henri went with the other children to play in the scrub, but busied herself with gathering up the food scraps, repacking the baskets and tidying the plates and dishes. If spoken to, she answered shortly, taking no part in the general conversation and laughter. Emma tried to break down her reserve but realised after one or two attempts that Jane was in a particularly difficult mood and was better left alone.

On the drive back to Rose Lees she spoke about it to her husband.

'Jane Hardman's getting downright queer. Hardly a civil word to anyone the livelong day.'

Thomas slapped the reins meditatively against the horses' rumps. He had noticed Jane's bad temper but was more concerned with what he had sensed during his recent visits to Lily Lees. He was not a talkative man and had kept his opinions to himself, but in truth he had feared for some time that things were far from well with his neighbours.

'My idea is she's never got over losing that boy. Can't seem to get it out of her mind. I thought she might take some comfort from the little chap, but it almost seems he has made things worse, as if she thought it was all his fault, like. I don't like it, Emma, and that's a fact. I don't like it at all.'

'Well, I think she ought to go and see Dr Templeton. First chance I get I'll tell her so. She works too hard – run herself to skin and bone, she has, this last few months. She needs a good tonic and a good talking to.'

Thomas chuckled as he guided the horses into the yard and pulled up at the kitchen door.

'You'll be the one'll get the good talking to,' he said. 'All the same, I think you're right. You don't like to see your neighbours driving into the bog without a tow-rope. We must do what we can to help. Richard Hardman is a good chap.'

15

The Storm

O n the day after the picnic, Henri was awakened before dawn by the wind blowing warm and dry from the north. The pear tree outside his window wrestled with the stormy gusts, its branches beat against the panes with animate urgency. The early sunlight was sulphur-yellow, the sky obscured not with clouds but with dust that made for the parched earth an ominous pall, which presaged an end to the calm spring weather. By breakfast-time the wind had worked up to half a gale, deepening the darkness of the northern sky and bringing an electrical tension to the air.

'Terrible dry season they're having in the Centre, by the look of this dust,' said Richard, as they drove towards Mount Pleasant on their way to 'church'. The inverted commas are justified by the fact that the members of the religious group to which the Hardmans belonged would have repudiated any description of themselves as being associated with a church. They called themselves the 'Sons of God'. Once a month an earnest bespectacled young man came from Adelaide to lead the group in prayer and scriptural discussion.

The meetings of the Sons of God were held in the committee room at the rear of the Institute building, a bare and comfortless place perhaps not inappropriate to the austerity of doctrine taught there. Here some twenty adults and as many children spent two hours on the morning of each fourth Sunday to re-assure themselves of their own eternal salvation and to pray earnestly (but not hopefully) for the miserable sinners in the world outside. Not entirely guiltless of spiritual pride, the Sons of God derived a certain measure of comfort from their own predestined security, enhanced (though not with any conscious lack of charity) by their conviction of the terrible doom which awaited their sinful neighbours. Their own position, however, was not without danger, for if once shaken by any loss of faith or consciousness of sin, they had no protection against the logical conclusion of their own doctrines. There was nowhere to fall but down. And the converse of spiritual pride being despair, such an unhappy soul could find neither hope nor comfort in the Mercy of God. Already their small number had been depleted by two suicides whose epitaphs the Leader had pronounced when he exclaimed solemnly: 'Let their name be erased for evermore. Let it be as though they had never been.' To fail was the greatest sin of all, the sin for which there could be no forgiveness, no mercy.

Richard was not an enthusiastic Son of God. He was much too kind-hearted and easy-going to agree with the peculiar theology of the group, but he went to the meetings because Jane liked to go and because he still accepted the old-fashioned convention that it was 'right' to attend a place of worship from time to time. And so once a month he harnessed the horses into the trap and he and Jane drove the four or five miles into the town. At least (he told himself) it made a change from the farm and was good for Jane, who so seldom got away from the house. Not that the Sons of God were exactly cheerful company, but once away from the meeting the Sons quickly reverted to their more natural characters as good farmers and amiable neighbours, good for a yarn about the weather and crops and the likely winners at the next Show.

By the time the sermon had been preached, the scripture-reading completed, the (rather reluctant) testimony of faith pronounced by each of the Sons of God in turn, and the little congregation gathered in the Institute porch for a friendly exchange before scattering to their farms and shops, it was past mid-day.

The Hardmans had an uncomfortable drive home, though fortunately with their backs to the wind. The sky was dark. The sand blew in almost horizontal streaks that whipped and stung the exposed flesh like needles. In the farmyard everything movable was blowing about. Barn doors and windows swung to the danger of hinges and panes. Bundles of hay and sacks and drifting newspapers had been caught in the gale and blown tight against walls and fences. By now the whole firmament was obscured and the colour of the yellow desert sand by which it was burdened, except where the storm clouds drew their purple curtains.

Richard had barely unharnessed the horses and firmly bolted the barn doors when the first crack of lightning split the sky down with a white-hot knife. Big raindrops fell, splashing flat on the paving-stones like thrown pancakes on Shrove Tuesday. Half an hour later it was raining hard, with the wind steady and cool from the west.

The rain fell all night and by the following day the landscape was as cold and grey as an English spring. Henri stayed indoors for most of the day, drawing pictures with the coloured pencils his grandfather had given him and turning over in his memory the events of the picnic. For the first time in his short life the realisation had come to him that other people, other children, could be friends instead of enemies, and that life was not a progression from one fear to another but could have times of enjoyment and, especially, could provide things of interest to occupy the mind and hands. His grandfather's little birthday gift had brought him a wondering awakening of love. Elizabeth's vitality and, above all, her acceptance of him as a friend, had stirred him to the beginnings of self-confidence, strengthened now by having seen his school-fellows as other children like himself, beyond the restriction of school and the restraining influence of parents and guardians.

Jane was kneading dough for the weekly batch of bread. She had been unusually silent all day and, if not cheerful company for Henri, he had at least been free of her sarcasm and impatience. When she had rolled the bread-dough into big lumps and put it aside to wait for the yeast to do its work, she went on to mix dough for scones which she cut out into shapes with a cutter she had made from an empty cocoa tin. She put them in neat rows on an iron tray lightly sprinkled with flour. Then she rinsed her hands under the tap over the sink, took off her apron, wiped her hands on it and threw it into the dirty-clothes basket in the scullery.

'Now I'm going up to change my dress,' she said to Henri. 'I'll put this tray of scones in the oven. They'll take quarter of an hour to bake.' She glanced at the clock. 'It's a quarter to, now. When the clock strikes five, take this cloth, open the oven door and lift out the tray. Put it down on the table. Look, I'll spread a newspaper because it will be pretty hot. Now you are eight years old it's time you learned to give me a hand in the kitchen.' As she spoke she opened the oven door, put in the tray of scones, closed the oven door, and then went upstairs.

Henri received these instructions with nervous attention. He stood in front of the stove watching the clock anxiously. He waited for several minutes but the clock seemed to move hardly at all, so he went back to the picture he had been drawing. This represented Elizabeth, in a guise that her friends and relations might not easily have recognised, handing him half her orchids. As he was very anxious to do justice to the orchids he drew them life-size which gave them, in proportion to the figures of Elizabeth and himself, the stature of trees. This composition required a good deal of tongue-out concentration and pencil-point licking in order to satisfy the artist, concentration presently rudely interrupted by the ominous odour of burning scones. With frightened dismay and a glance at the clock which now showed ten minutes past the hour, Henri jumped to his feet (for he had been sitting on the floor with his drawing-book), snatched up the cloth and opened the oven door. A cloud of blue smoke billowed out into the room accompanied by a rush of heat. Henri could scarcely bear the heat of the tray, but he pulled at it bravely. Several blackened scones rolled off on to the floor. He had the tray half-way out of the oven when the sound of his grandmother's voice gave him such a fright that he dropped it. The tray slid on to the flagstones. Burnt scones rolled merrily in all directions.

'I might have known it!' stormed Jane. 'I should have had more sense than to leave you to look after them, useless brat that you are!' She leaned over and gave him a box on the ears with both hands. In a half-kneeling position as he was, the violence of the blow knocked him sideways among the scones. With his head ringing and dizzy, he screamed with pain as his bare knees came in contact with the hot oven tray. Jane put out a hand and pulled him to his feet by the collar of his jacket. She was beside herself with rage.

'Stop that noise, you little pest!' she shouted. 'Isn't it enough that I have to work my fingers to the bone to feed and clothe you, without you spoiling good food by your disobedience. Stop that noise instantly, do you hear?'

Poor Henri could no more have ceased to cry than he could stop the sickening pain in his knees, but his screams were modified to gulping sobs and moans, which, try as he would, he could not subdue. And somewhere behind the physical pain was the shock of disillusion, of finding that the glimpse of happiness and beauty he had had could be dissolved and shattered by hatred in an instant.

'Very well, young man,' Jane was saying, her eyes glittering with anger, 'if you can't do what you're told, you'll have to be taught.'

When in the early years of the colony's settlement, Richard Hardman's father had cleared the native scrub and begun to plough the acres that were to become Lily Lees farm, he had built for his family a sturdy stone cottage with a storage cellar.

The cottage had long since fallen into ruin and been replaced by the house in which Jane and Richard now lived. But the cellar for many years had been used as a dairy and kept in fairly good repair. It was some distance from the house, a large square room with massive walls half submerged in the earth, the door, some six feet below ground-level, approached by a downward flight of brick steps. The only light came through a square window in the ceiling, the glass panes of which had been broken and replaced by a heavy iron grid.

The rain had ceased but the sky was still cloudy and an early twilight was darkening the landscape as Jane marched the sobbing child across the farmyard, through the patch of neglected orchard that lay on that side of the homestead, and down the steps to the door of the old dairy.

'In you go,' she snapped as she gave him a push. 'In you go and there you stay till you learn to do as you're told,' and she slammed the door and shot the bolt. Then she strode back to the house to vent her feelings on the mess of scones and cinders on the kitchen floor.

Half an hour later Richard came in from the milking sheds. After the usual evening ritual of washing his face, arms and hands under the tap in the scullery and combing his grey hair in front of the piece of cracked mirror on the wall, he sat down to his tea.

'Where's the young'un?' he asked, as he saw that the table was set with only two places.

'I've sent him to bed,' Jane replied, shortly.

'Oh, come now,' protested her husband, 'don't be too hard on the boy. Remember he's still only a nipper.'

'He's old enough to know right from wrong. I'm sick and tired of his disobedience.'

'I don't think he means to be disobedient, you know, my dear. It's just that he's sort of nervous still. A bit frightened, like.' It was a lame defence, not strengthened by Richard's apologetic tone.

'Well, I'm sure I don't know what he has to be frightened about,' said Jane bitingly. Richard was silent. He could not explain, but he knew only too well that feeling of nervous dread which assailed him when Jane was in one of her bad moods. After a moment he said: Well, I'll just go up and see if he's all right.'

'You'll do nothing of the sort!' said Jane sharply. 'A lot of good it is if I punish the child and then you go making a fuss of him. Besides, he's probably asleep by now and you'll only go upsetting him.'

'Well, if you say so, my dear,' said Richard sadly, 'but try not to be too severe with the boy. He's not yet got over his mother's death, I dare say.'

'Then the sooner he does the better,' snapped Jane. 'Here's your tea.'

'As a matter of fact,' Richard went on, as he stirred the sugar in his tea-cup, 'I'm going to bed myself soon's I've eaten my supper and had a glance at the paper. I want to take the grey plough-horse in to the sale tomorrow morning. If I get a decent price for him I'd like to try for one of Stan Williams's. I hear he's bringing in a couple of pair. He's got wonderful blood out there at Frummocks. Trouble is, he'll probably want a terrible price for them.'

'Well, don't go thinking we're made of money the way you generally do when you go to a sale,' was Jane's acid comment.

'We'll leave early. Frank can lead Primrose. Poor old girl! I hate to sell her but she's nearly past milking. So breakfast at five and we'll get away by six. I want to be back by mid-morning. If it doesn't rain tonight we can get the ploughing finished by tomorrow night, long as we get started by noon.'

Now Jane had fully intended to bring Henri back to the house after tea, but the lie she had told about him being sent to bed seemed to harden her resentment within its sheath of anger, besides making it difficult for her to know how she could smuggle the boy into the house and up the stairs without her husband's knowledge. She waited until Richard had stumped up to his room, fussed about the kitchen pretending to find more tasks needing her attention, until her husband's voice calling: 'Aren't you coming to bed?' impelled her to go upstairs.

At four o'clock the next morning, after a night of restless sleeplessness, she got up, crept down in the bitter darkness before dawn to light the kitchen fire and cook Richard's breakfast. When he had eaten it and left for the market, driving the buggy to which the grey plough-horse was tied, followed slowly by Frank on horseback leading the cow, she sat motionless and cold at the kitchen table, feeling as though some malignant hand had squeezed away her heart and left only a fearful pain which threatened to rise and engulf her whole being.

At Rose Lees that morning Thomas Woodstock had also decided to go to the sale, but as the beasts in which was interested were not to be offered until later in the morning, he did not leave the farm until after eight o'clock.

'Why not take Elizabeth with you,' suggested Emma. 'You could leave her at Lily Lees as you go past and call for her on the way home. Or maybe I'll put Puddles in the pony cart and go over later this morning myself. I might try and bring Jane back here for tea. Do her the world of good to get out a bit more.'

So Elizabeth went off with her Uncle Thomas and was set down at the corner where the highway ran along the Lily Lees paddocks. From here she could take a short-cut to the house instead of going half a mile farther on to where the lane turned off the main road towards the homestead.

She did not hurry. The morning was sunny and fresh after the rain and in the grass along the fence she found buttercups and a clump of forget-me-nots which must have sprung from an errant seed brought by bird or wind from a distant garden. Then she found daisies and after picking several handfuls she sat down to make a daisy-chain, a laborious process which took her nearly an hour. It was after ten o'clock, then, by the time she reached the ruins of the old cottage. Here she paused again, this time to hop from stone to stone among the mossy ruins and to invent a make-believe that she was Pharaoh's army crossing the Red Sea. Suddenly she heard a voice crying and calling, a voice that seemed to come from nowhere.

'*Maman*, oh, *Maman!*'

At first she was frightened. In that wide, wide country under that wide, wide sky in which billowy cloud-masses were moving silently and majestically in the wake of last night's storm and the cool sunlight was making rainbows of every raindrop suspended from the grass-stems, in the silence of that landscape not broken even by the cattle grazing on the far slopes it was strange to hear a human voice crying, '*Maman*, oh, *Maman!*' But as she heard it the second time she realised that it was unmistakably Henri's voice and therefore that he must be near at hand, though where, she asked herself, looking at the paddocks, the apple trees of the old orchard and the scattered stones of the derelict cottage, where he could be she could not imagine. The voice, calling again, seemed to come from under her feet. Pushing aside the elderberry bushes and the bracken fern which here grew tall and rank, she found an iron grating in what seemed to be a cement floor, very mossy and grass-grown, but which, she found on further exploration, was the roof of the old cellar. She tried to peer through the grating but it was too dark to see far into the cellar and she got cobwebs across her face and entangled in her hair.

'Is that you, Henri?' she called. 'Where are you?'

His voice answered but only by crying again: '*Maman, Maman, viens vite! Aide-moi, écoute-moi, je t'en prie!*'

'Oh, dear,' thought Elizabeth to herself in her practical way, 'I suppose he has fallen in and hurt himself. He never talks French now except when he's frightened.'

She went to the other side of the ruin and found the steps

leading down to the door. She banged on the door with both fists.

'Henri! Are you in there? It's me, Beth. Can you hear me?'

After a moment's silence Henri cried in English: 'Beth, oh dear Beth, please come. Please come quickly!'

'All right. Wait a minute till I get the door open.' But the bolts were too high for her, and pull and tug with her finger-tips as hard as she could, she could not shift their rusty grip on the iron staples.

'I can't open the door,' she cried to Henri. 'I'll have to get a stone to stand on.' She spent some time hunting about for something she could use as a step, but the stones lying in the wet grass were too heavy for her to lift, much less to carry down to the cellar door. She was just thinking: 'I'll have to go up to the house,' when she saw, across the paddocks, the buggy with Richard returning from the market. He was driving the two bays.

She waved and shouted and began to run across the ploughed field, but found herself bogged in the wet earth and had to go back to the grass verge.

Mr Hardman had seen her and, sensing some urgency in her signals, he reined in the bays and waited for her coming. She was just climbing breathless through the wire fence bordering the lane, when Frank rode up behind the trap on a heavy plough-horse with what Elizabeth called 'whiskers round his hooves'.

'That's little Beth Inglefell from Rose Lees,' said Mr Hardman. 'Seems like something's the matter. Hope there's no trouble over at the Woodstocks' place. Saw Thomas driving in and he seemed all right.'

Before Frank could make any comment of his own on this, Elizabeth had reached them and, gulping for breath, was pouring out her story.

'Oh, do come, Mr Hardman, please. Henri has fallen down some steps where all those old stones are, but the door's bolted and I can't open it, but I don't think he's hurt much, only crying like anything.'

Mr Hardman got out of the buggy and tied the reins to the fencing post. 'Take the grey to the stable and then come over to the old dairy,' he ordered Frank. Taking Elizabeth's hand he went with her towards the ruins. Some instinct of which he was unconscious prompted him to avoid the shorter way which would have led them near the house.

When they reached the cellar steps, he put Elizabeth to one side and bade her stay at the top while he went down. He picked up a small stone, hammered the bolts back without much difficulty, and opened the door. Henri was crouching on the brick floor. His face was dreadfully pale and streaked with dirt and tears, his clothes and legs were covered with cobwebs and mud which mingled with the blood and lymph oozing from the broken blisters on his knees. Mr Hardman, with a terrible expression twisting his gentle face, picked him up in his arms and held him close.

'It's all right now,' he said in a choking voice. 'You're quite safe now.' The little body shivered and clung. 'It's all my fault, Henry-boy, I should have found you last night. I should have guessed. But it's all over now, all safe with Grandpa now.' For several minutes they stood, the old man soothing and comforting, the boy gradually becoming less convulsive. 'Just one thing, Henry-boy,' said Richard at last when the child had become calmer. 'Tell me just this. Did your grandmother put you in here and have you been here all night?' A violent nodding of the head and a renewed outburst of sobbing were the answer.

'Well, it's all over now, my boy. Never again, Henry-boy. It will never happen again.' And repeating these assurances over and over, he carried the hysterical child to where the horses were tethered.

Frank had arrived after stabling the new plough-horse and Elizabeth was glad of his supporting hand on the way back to the lane, for she felt rather tearful herself without quite knowing why.

'Get in, Frank,' said Mr Hardman, with an unaccustomed tone of authority in his voice, 'get in and drive them both over to the Woodstocks. The missus will be there, won't she?' he asked, turning to Elizabeth. She nodded. Henri clung to his grandfather who explained very gently and patiently that he would come as soon as he could, but it was only when Elizabeth said stoutly: 'I'm going with Frank and if you come with me I will show you my new pony that I got for my birthday, and I will let you paint a picture with my new box of paints,' that he was reassured by this tone of normal cheerfulness in what had become for him a nightmare world. Frank took him on his knee and put one arm round him with the reins in his other hand, while Mr Hardman unhitched the bays and turned them round by the head.

'Tell Mrs Woodstock the boy's had an accident,' he said to Frank, without meeting his eye. 'Tell her I'll take it kindly of her to look after him till I get there. Then you'd best drive in to the Mount and get Doctor Templeton. I don't think the boy's badly hurt, though his knees look nasty, but we'd better be sure. He might have caught cold lying on that damp ground.'

After the buggy had driven slowly away, it was with a feeling of dread that Richard went to the house. He realised now that this was more than an act of cruelty to a child and that his own feelings were more than anger or sorrow. This was a crisis in all their lives towards which events of the past few weeks had been mounting with a horrid inevitability.

When he reached the kitchen he found Jane moving slowly about in an aimless way, as though her feet were too heavy to lift. He closed the door and stood with his back to it.

'I've found Henry,' he said.

Jane stood motionless, perhaps waiting for him to go on but more as if she lacked the willpower to make any movement.

'I've sent him over to Rose Lees,' continued Richard. 'He's

not coming back. I don't know yet what I can do with him, but he's not coming here any more.'

Still Jane stood without moving or speaking. Richard felt all at once so tired that it was as though every weariness he had ever experienced in his sixty years of life had returned to him in this moment. All he could say was: 'You shouldn't have done it. Not that, Jane.'

'Why not? Why shouldn't I do it?' Jane suddenly spoke in a cracked whisper that was more like the snarl of a tormented animal than a human voice. 'Didn't he and that wretched girl take away my boy? Why shouldn't he suffer? I have suffered – for years I have suffered – and slaved and worked and broken my heart, and who cared for me?' Her voice rose harshly. 'You make a great deal of fuss about him, petting him and cuddling him. What about my boy? Where is he now? What did you ever do for him but send him away where I'll never see him again. Can I go to him? Here I stay till I'm in my grave, for all you cared or gave me a thought.'

'Why, Jane,' said Richard, and his voice shook with pity. 'I didn't understand all that much. I know I haven't been much of a husband to you – never made money like I hoped to when we started, but I never knew you were all that unhappy . . ' He took a step towards her and put out a trembling hand.

'Get away! Don't come near me!' Jane screamed and stepped back into the corner of the room. 'Don't come near me! I've had enough of you. I'm sick of it, do you hear? Sick of the very sight and sound and smell of you. Get out of here! Let me alone, can't you?'

Richard was appalled at the violence of this outburst. Seeing her distraught manner and wild gestures he realised that, for the moment at any rate, Jane was on the verge of madness.

'Now, look here, old girl, steady on there. You're not well. Let me get you a cup of tea or something. You better go and lie down for a bit. You've been overdoing it and got yourself all worked up.'

Jane burst out laughing in a shrill discord that was horrible to hear. Richard stepped quickly forward. She screamed again. 'Get back, get away! Leave me alone, I tell you!'

In the corner behind her, leaning against the wall as it always did, held by the wooden rack he had built for it, was Richard's gun. Jane put up a hand and grasped it.

'For God's sake, what are you doing, Jane!' exclaimed her husband. 'Put that thing down or you'll be having an accident.'

'An accident!' she shouted. 'Accident! That's a joke. An accident! It was no accident when you took my boy away from me to his death. Dead, that's what he is, did you know? Dead! Dead. . . !'

The noise of the explosion hit the confined space of the kitchen with a ferocity that seemed to shatter the very air. Richard put his hand to his heart where the blood was running red over his fingers. The little room was still pulsating with sound and the air was thick with the smell of the burned gun-powder, and yet between the two there was a silence in which all the years of their two lives, so closely associated and yet lived so dreadfully apart, had now met at this point to confront each other.

'Why, Janie-girl,' said Richard in a gently surprised voice as he sank slowly forward on to the floor. 'Janie-girl, you shouldn't have done that.'

When they found her, Jane was lying with her head on his shoulder and her arms flung about him as though to protect him. The gun lay on the floor where it had fallen.

Thomas Woodstock, riding hard along the lane, was just in time to hear the second shot.

Book Two

Book Two

16

Defence of the Weak, 1904

WHEN Elizabeth was seven she went to Miss Liddier's school
with Marian and Eleanor. Here she met again Judith and
Malcolm, the youngest of the Faulkener children. Malcolm
was still thin and pale, as Elizabeth remembered him three
years before, when she and her mother had had tea in the cream
and gold drawing-room. When he met her in the playground
on her first day at school he promptly pinched her. But Elizabeth was no longer the rather shy little girl he had seen then:
she had learnt to ride a horse and climb trees and had held the
reins for the driver of a six-horse team. She not only pinched
him in return but buffeted him about the head with both fists.

There was immediate uproar in the playground. The other
children crowded round to encourage or deter the combatants.
One of the teachers came hurrying up to restore order.

'Why, Elizabeth Inglefell,' she exclaimed, 'and your first day
at school! I am surprised at you. We can't have fighting in the
playground, you know.'

'He pinched me,' said Elizabeth bluntly. Malcolm stood with
his hands in his pockets, saying nothing and looking the picture
of innocence.

'Go straight into the schoolroom, Malcolm,' said the teacher,
'and write out ten times on your slate, "I must not fight." '

'Thank you, Miss Jones,' said Malcolm with perfect polite-
ness and turned at once to the schoolroom as though writing
on his slate was of all things the one he most desired to do.

'As for you, Elizabeth,' went on Miss Jones, 'as it is your

173

first day you need not do an imposition. But this must never happen again, you understand.'

Elizabeth did not in the least understand. For her the essence of defence was the principle of an eye for an eye and a tooth for a tooth and, if possible, two. From then on, she and Malcolm went through their schooldays together in a sort of uneasy truce which flared into active hostility whenever they were alone together with any chance of being uninterrupted by grown-up people. As for Judith, Elizabeth thought her most uninteresting – a fat, placid child who did nothing but play with dolls in that dressing-up and putting-to-sleep way that Elizabeth thought exceedingly unenterprising, with none of the excitement and inventiveness of Moses in the Bulrushes or Assyrians coming down like a wolf on the fold. She herself still played under the pepper tree with the pre-Stopesian family, though the games now were more of Ned Kelly or King Henry the Eighth.

On Saturday mornings all the children had piano lessons from Herr Hermanschreimer, a fat little German with hands scarcely larger than Eleanor's. Eleanor was the star pupil, for she had genuine talent. As Herr Hermanschreimer listened, he would urge her on to greater and greater speed in her scales, watching her with a shining enthusiasm in his eyes. With Marian he was the patient instructor, beating time with his pencil and saying: '*Ein, zwei, drei.*' With Elizabeth he was fatherly and gentle until he found that she could play 'Chants sans paroles' without the book, and Chopin valses with verve and progression. After that he treated her as an equal and, forgetting the limitations of her years, shouted excitedly when she stumbled in the Schumann 'Klavierwerke' and told her that she played the Clementi sonatinas like a stuffed pig.

'Well, I don't like Schumann,' said Elizabeth.

'So! This little girl, this little baby, she is so clever. She does not the great master like,' he rejoined, bubbles of saliva appearing at the corners of his mouth and his pointed moustaches quivering to the extremities of their waxed ends. He wore a black silk watch ribbon across his rather greasy waistcoat, and when he was agitated the numerous gold seals that were suspended from its length bobbed and jingled with the hollow rattle of dog chains.

Elizabeth sat still, her legs hanging down from the too-tall piano-stool.

'Why do you not like Schumann?' demanded Herr Hermanschreimer. 'Eh?' The last interrogatory syllable was like a projectile. Elizabeth was silent. How could one explain things like music? Why did she dislike Schumann? It was something – a little – to do with the two hands. Schumann made her two hands antagonise each other, so that she felt that she was playing two different pieces of music, one with the right hand and one with the left, and when the right hand was dominant the left had to be dragged weakly and protestingly after it instead of playing an indispensable part of the musical design. She could not have explained all this in so many words; and there was more, too.

Her mother had once had a visitor called Mrs Thrace, who wore sweeping dresses of pale-coloured silk, quantities of necklaces and chains and dangling ear-rings and jingling bangles. She used some faint perfume and her sleeves dipped with flounces of lace. She kissed the children and called them endearing names and was altogether gracious and charming and detestable. Elizabeth had just the same feeling for Schumann's music as she had for Mrs Thrace. Years later, when she had learnt more of life and of Schumann, she was ashamed of this prejudice, but she never entirely overcame it, and she needed always a distinct effort of will to sit and listen to Schumann music. But when she was eight years old she could not explain any of this to Herr Hermanschreimer. The little man glared at her through his spectacles and rapped on the keyboard with his pencil.

'Now then,' he would say, curling out his lips and tucking

the corners of his mouth into tight involutions, 'this lovely melody from the gommencement we will play. *Ein, zwei, drei. . . .* Perhaps one day you a little more sense will learn.'

Miss Liddier's school broke up for the May holidays a few days earlier than the State school, so Elizabeth was still able occasionally to indulge her favourite occupation of sitting in the Moreton Bay fig tree to watch the children.

Luke Stevens was now thirteen years old, but she remained on friendly terms with him and with several of the others. She had not, in the three years since her battle-royal, had another encounter in direct action with them, until one day when Mr Chin Ling Su came to call.

Chin Ling Su was of honourable if humble lineage. His father had come to Australia as a free migrant, though he travelled in a ship with several hundreds of his Chinese compatriots who, under contract for work on the gold-fields, were landed at Robe in South Australia and driven like cattle across the inhospitable and scarcely-explored region of the Murray Valley into the mountain gullies of the Victorian bush. If the hardships they suffered can be assessed by the graves that mark the route of their journeying, they were hardships no less severe than those of their European masters who died with monotonous frequency of drought and typhoid and colonial alcohol.

Chin Ling Su was born in Australia, in a mining camp. He spoke no language during his childhood but his parents' native dialect. When in the course of years and nature Chin the Elder was gathered to his ancestors, it was found that his mining and his trading had left him a moderately well-to-do man with fortune enough to ensure that his sons took his body to China for burial and found themselves, on their return to Australia, the inheritors of a prosperous business. Leaving the youngest in charge of their store in Bendigo, the two elder boys went, one to Melbourne and one to Adelaide, to expand the family interests.

Chin Ling Su acquired a dingy little building in Hindley

Street, a narrow, dark shop-front from which a rickety stair led to three tiny rooms above, where the windows were darkened by half a century of dust and the grime from the railway yards which descended in sulphurous clouds whenever the wind blew from the north. The rooms were suffocatingly hot in summer and always their atmosphere was thick with the odours of frying fish from the Greek eating-house next door. Here Chin Ling Su established himself and his wife and their three boy-children. The little shop, crammed with merchandise, was presided over by Mrs Chin while the babies played among the tea-chests and the dusty bins of rice and cashew nuts with the grave concentration of all Chinese children from time immemorial.

Each morning, Chin, clad in black cotton trousers and neck-buttoned jacket of butcher-blue twill, left the shop at seven o'clock and, slipping his thin shoulders under the flexible bamboo yoke, lifted the two immense wooden packs which contained his wares and made his rhythmic, jog-trot way from house to house to offer for sale cottons and needles and crochet-hooks and hairpins, packets of cloves and nutmeg, dried ginger and figs and nuts and rice and tea, to housewives willing enough to spend quarter of an hour and a shilling or two to save themselves a walk along the hot and dusty streets of the town to the shops.

Every five or six weeks Chin Ling Su turned into the little lane which led to the back door of Mr Inglefell's house, for though of honourable lineage he never presumed to think of himself as worthy to approach the doorway guarded by the tall iron gates and the monkey-puzzle tree.

Everyone enjoyed his visits. Even Finch would come up from the stables or the garden to buy a plug of tobacco or a bag of peanuts, and sometimes Mrs Thompson would carry an armful of silks and embroidered linens into the morning-room to show Mrs Inglefell.

'Good morning, evlybody,' Chin would say, for although

born in Australia, his tongue had spoken too long the language of the family to overcome entirely its difficulty with the English 'r', while his voice had retained the lilting quality of his father's race.

'Good morning, evlybody,' he would chant, smiling in his gentle, friendly way as he let down his burden and slipped out from under the shoulder-pole. The cords released would slide to the floor of the veranda; Chin would begin to take down the boxes which were made up of layers, each consisting of a shallow wooden tray, the grooved edges of which slid into the grooves of those above and below. Then would be displayed the packets of sweet-scented tea: Orange Pekoe in basket-work packets lined with filmy rice-paper and Lapsang in pale yellow paper that looked like silk; apple-blossom jars of ginger and chow-chow in syrup; bamboo fans with red and green silk tassels; dry roots, silk handkerchiefs, bone skewers, *cloisonné* ash-trays, phials of perfume and incense sticks, cards of mending wool, embroidery silks and cheap laces. The children would crow with delight as they explored the treasures, and as they pulled his stock into disorder and scattered the contents of the trays over the kitchen table, Chin would only smile amiably and bow with his hands in his sleeves in a way that would have graced a mandarin.

Always when the purchases were completed, when Pearl and Miss Una had chosen the threads and ribbons they wanted, and Eleanor had urged with Marian about the merits of Brazil nuts in preference to Turkish delight, and Mrs Thompson had solemnly handed over the larger sums required for a renewal of the household supplies of tea and spices, Chin would give Elizabeth his blessing gift, generally a minute bag of sweets scented with rose-water, sometimes a ribbon or what she called a 'pudding doll' of white china which could be baked in a Christmas pudding as a surprise.

'Mr Chin is my special friend,' she explained; 'nearly as special as Mr O'Brien.'

Pearl sniffed. 'I wouldn't go making a heathen Chinee my special friend,' was her unsympathetic comment. 'And them Boxers murdering the white people this very instant minute, as like as not. It's my idea they should never of been let to come to Australia in the first place.'

Mrs Thompson's motherly heart having no place for such politico-social considerations, she never failed to offer Mr Chin a cup of tea which he, with exquisite courtesy, never failed to decline.

At this time Chin Ling Su was a man in his mid-fifties, but his stature was so slight and his face so wrinkled that he looked more like a man of seventy. It was not difficult to see, therefore, how he came to be defenceless in the face of attacks from hooligans and larrikins who took advantage of the public antagonism to the Chinese aroused by the cruelties of the Boxer rebels, to let off their youthful high spirits whenever they met a Chinaman.

> 'Ching, chong, Chinaman,
> Born in a bar,
> Christened in a tea-pot,
> Ha, ha, ha!'

This jingle was the song of the moment, not infrequently accompanied by thrown stones and jeering cat-calls.

One day Elizabeth was playing by herself in the pepper tree house, when she heard the familiar sound. School was just out and she could hear the shouts and yells of the children as they raced down the street from the school gates. As she often did, she ran down the garden and across the paddock to a place where she could watch them through a gap in the fence. She had regained her courage since her battle with the boys, and besides, now she was seven she felt herself equal in combat with anyone up to the age of twelve.

'Ching, chong, Chinaman,
Born in a bar . . .'

The chant grew louder and was mingled with a deeper note, uglier than the customary noisy cheerfulness of childish voices.

Elizabeth saw Chin Ling Su in the roadway surrounded by excited schoolboys. They had knocked off his hat, pushed him over into the gutter and were dancing round him, Red Indian fashion, war-whoops mingled with the derisive 'Ha, ha' of the song. Elizabeth was through the fence in a flash and once again entered into combat with her enemies. Her fighting method of kick and scratch would have horrified Miss Una, who (had she seen her) would instantly have sent her to bed without any tea; but it was not without effect on her opponents and at least provided a diversion. But she was hopelessly out-numbered. Within a minute the boys had closed in on her, rejoicing that they had a new object of attack. Fortunately at that moment she saw Luke Stevens and several of the bigger boys leaving the school gate. The noise was deafening, but Elizabeth had an excellent pair of lungs, and she used them to their fullest capacity.

'Luke! Luke! Come quickly!' she shrieked with all her strength. The boys came, rejoicing.

When they found that they were expected to defend the minority rather than attack with the majority, they hesitated for only an instant and then, like good mercenaries, fell to with zest, by no means unwilling to knock a few heads and push a few shoulders in the cause of down-trodden humanity.

Elizabeth flew to where Mr Chin lay.

'Oh, darling Mr Chin, are you dead?' she sobbed, tears running down her cheeks. She flung her arms round him and tried to lift him up, but of course he was much too heavy, thin though he was. He was only momentarily dazed, however, and soon roused himself to a sitting posture.

As the crowd drifted in its noisy way down the street, Luke and his friends were left to survey the battle-ground. The boxes had been too solid for the children to overturn, but two of the trays had been dislodged and cards of pins and reels of cotton lay scattered about in the dust. The boys clumsily began picking them up and putting them back in the trays. Luke picked up the broad-brimmed straw hat and handed it to Chin, while Elizabeth went on dabbing at the cuts on his face with a corner of her pinafore (which she had lavishly dampened with lick) and asking him if he was dead or feeling better.

'Better now, missie,' he said. 'Klite well now.' Chin got to his feet rather shakily.

'You must come home at once. Oh, Luke, couldn't you run and tell Finch to bring the wagonette?'

'No, no,' protested Chin. 'I orl-lite now.' But he looked so frail and his colour was so ghastly yellow and the cut on his forehead was bleeding so freely that the boys began to feel uneasy. Even Chinamen might call down the wrath of parents or, even – dreaded thought! – the police constable.

'It might be a good idea to get Finch,' said Luke. 'You chaps stay here while I cut across the paddock and see if I can find him.'

Finch, always willing to lend a hand with anything that necessitated an interruption in the digging of potatoes, the mowing of lawns or the chopping of wood, was soon back to take charge of the situation.

'Now, John,' he said to Mr Chin, 'you and Miss Beth had better get on up to the house and let Mrs Thompson put something on that cut. You kids get on home before there's any more trouble.'

'What about Mr Chin's boxes?' asked Elizabeth, with an eye to the practical, as usual. 'Couldn't you carry them up to the house?'

'Lor' lumme, who, me?' asked Finch rhetorically. He put a tentative hand on one wooden tier. 'Cor, Miss Beth, I couldn't so much as lift one of them boxes off the ground, let alone two. And as for carrying them to the house, it couldn't be done in a month of Sundays.'

'But someone might steal them,' wailed Beth.

'Well, don't worry,' said Finch, taking out his pipe, 'I'll just keep an eye on them for a bit. Perhaps by the time old Ching-Chong has had a wash and a cuppa tea, he'll feel well enough to carry them himself. Though how he does it is a bloomin' mystery, and no mistake.' With which comfortable reflection Finch settled himself in the shade for a leisurely smoke.

In the kitchen Mr Chin allowed himself to be fussed over and sponged and dried and dabbed with arnica and his clothes brushed and his hands washed, while Elizabeth, grubby and tear-stained, lingered at his knee, crooning like an anxious mother-cat hovering over an injured kitten. Mr Chin even accepted a cup of tea, to which he added a great deal of water, and drank without milk or sugar.

Half an hour later, looking somewhat restored, he took his departure, after bowing himself out of the kitchen with a dignity which made them all slightly uncomfortable. Elizabeth went with him. 'Lean on my shoulder if you feel faint again,' she advised earnestly, which had the effect of halting Mr Chin in the driveway so that he could bow to her several times.

They found Finch, rather sleepy, sitting where they had left him, in a street deserted by school-children. He replied to Chin Ling Su's grave courtesy by tipping his hat forward over his eyes and scratching his chin.

'Now don't you go a-bustin' yourself along o' those boxes,' he advised. 'If you take my tip, you'll get the train at Miller's Corner and get a ride into town. You look fair knocked up. Those young devils want their hides tannin'. Give 'em wot-for, I will, if I catch them.'

Mr Chin slipped the cords round the packs and with an easy movement shrugged himself under the yoke. Up came the boxes about six inches off the ground and he was soon making his way down the street with his customary swinging gait.

Finch stood looking after him. 'Fair got me beat,' he murmured. 'It's all in the knack, o' course, all in the knack. But it's got me beat, just the same.'

17

The Goddess of Fortune

ABOUT a fortnight later Mr and Mrs Inglefell were lingering over their evening meal, enjoying each other's company in
the way that married people do when they are fond of their
children, but are glad when they have been sent to bed. This
was the only time in which they had leisure to exchange news
of the day and to discuss plans and people of mutual interest,
or in which they could indulge themselves in the luxury of
not talking at all.

Pearl had just cleared the table and folded the table-cloth
and put it away in the sideboard drawer when the front door-
bell rang.

'Well I never;' exclaimed Pearl to herself. 'Whoever can that
be at this time of night?' A question which, as the hour was
only eight o'clock on a fine spring evening, was entirely
rhetorical and framed rather to express her own annoyance
at the possible arrival of visitors than any desire to know their
identity which, in any case, would be revealed to her in another
two minutes if only she could get this dratted chain off the
hook, and if she'd told Finch once to oil it she'd told him
twenty times.

Mr and Mrs Inglefell, in the meantime, had settled themselves in the morning room where a small fire in the grate was
just enough to create an atmosphere of cosiness without un-
duly increasing the mildness of the evening.

For Alfred this was the moment of greatest content. He went

every day to the city, where for the past two years he had had an office in which he attended to the affairs of his sheep and cattle properties and the business in which he was now associated with Mr Goldiway.

Mr Goldiway was a large, florid man with a hearty manner with which he strove to assure his fellow-citizens and all prospective customers of his good will and excellent intentions. He was in various lines of business. The brass plate on the door of his office described him simply as 'agent', and perhaps that does describe more than any other single word his position in the various business 'deals' in which he was involved. He bought a large quantity of merchandise which he sold profitably in a number of stores he owned in several of the larger country towns; he bought and sold land and stock and crops, standing or bagged; he financed mining ventures and the building of factories for making rope and twine. When several of the bolder spirits among his friends brought back from Europe a horseless carriage, he undertook to supply them with the petroleum, oil and rubber tyres of which these new machines seemed to require an inexhaustible supply. In short, he was enterprising and capable.

Mrs Inglefell did not like him at all. She knew that in a new country where the inhabitants had still to develop their own form of economy and way of life it was absurd to have prejudices based on the customs of an older, more stable and more mature civilisation. When she found uncongenial Mr Goldiway's loud voice and obvious enjoyment of his own success, and when her sense of good taste was outraged by Mrs Goldiway's elaborate satin dresses and too-plentiful jewellery, she called herself a snob and roused up her own generosity and kindness of heart. All the same, she knew very well that in all countries and in all societies there are certain standards of behaviour, of integrity or character, virtues of honesty and modesty and consideration for the welfare of others. These qualities she knew that the Goldiways did not possess and she wished fervently that her husband need not be so closely associated with them. Alfred was less sensitive in the matter. He said Goldiway was a good fellow, a rough diamond, with a gift for money-making that amounted almost to genius. He profited considerably by the deals they undertook together and was no more than mildly amused when he realised that the Goldiways were socially ambitious, willing to trade their business ability for the opportunities for social advancement afforded by their connection with the Inglefells.

On this particular evening Alfred was more than usually glad to relax. He and George Goldiway had been to Gawler to inspect a property they were thinking of buying. Though they had made the journey from the city comfortably enough by train, they had also ridden and walked a good many miles to inspect fences, count stock, examine water supplies, and view the house and outbuildings. He had hardly flung himself down in his arm-chair in front of the fire and spread open the pages of the *Morning Register,* which his trip to the country had prevented him from reading earlier in the day, when Pearl came into the room and exclaimed excitedly: 'Please, 'm, sir, there's four Chinamen at the door, asking to see you.'

'Dear me, that's rather unusual,' said Mr Inglefell. 'Chinamen, did you say? What have you done with them?'

'Left them on the porch and shut the door quick, sir. Fair gave me a turn, it did, sir, to see them murderous-looking cut-throats standing there.'

'Oh, come, I don't suppose it's as bad as all that,' said Mr Inglefell, amused by Pearl's agitation. 'I'd better go and see what they want. Take them into the dining-room, Pearl.'

'What, are you going to let them come into the house, sir?' exclaimed Pearl. 'I don't think it's hardly safe, sir. Real wicked they looked.'

'Come, come, my girl. Show them into the dining-room, and if they murder you, come and tell me.'

Pearl sniffed to show that she quite understood that the master liked to have his little joke, but that if her dead body was found treacherously cut to pieces and scattered about on the front door-mat by yellow devils, she would have died in the true British way, a martyr to duty, such as England Expects this Day that every man, and in her case woman, shall do. She flung open the front door with an enjoyably heightened sense of the dramatic. It was something of an anti-climax to realise that the murderous villains were only old John Chin from whom she bought her needles and thread every so often and his three sons who were standing patiently on the porch, looking exceedingly respectable, innocuous and law-abiding.

'The master will see you in the dining-room,' said Pearl, loftily pretending that she had never met Mr Chin Ling Su before and composing in her mind delightfully blood-curdling phrases in which to describe to Cook how her blood ran cold having to conduct these four dangerous ruffians across the hall and into the dining-room. They were carrying a wooden box, some three feet long by half as wide, covered by a piece of dark yellow silk embroidered with faded gold dragons. They placed the box on the dining-room table, after spreading the silk cloth to protect the mahogany. Then they stood like a receiving committee, Mr Chin with his hands in the cuffs of his best European-style suit, his three sons ranged in a respectful semi-circle (if such a thing is possible) behind him.

When Mr Inglefell came in they all bowed deeply and Mr Chin said: 'I am Chin Ling Su, who wish that your honourable sir will excuse me. I am plesenting my thlee sons, Albert, Edward and Clarence, sir.'

Mr Inglefell shook hands very cordially with the bearers of these royal appellations and lingered for a moment with Clarence, the youngest.

'Haven't I met you somewhere before?' he asked.

'Yes, sir,' said Clarence, smiling cheerfully. 'I work for Mr

Goldiway. I'm accountant at the Quorn store and often see you when you come in with the boss.'

'Of course. I remember now. I was sure I knew your face. Sit down, gentlemen, and tell me what I can do for you.'

The three young men looked at their father, who, however, did not accept the invitation to be seated. He bowed again, and in some indefinable manner conveyed that he wished this occasion to be ceremonious rather than informal, deeply honoured though he was by Mr Inglefell's condescension to one of low degree.

'Your honourable sir's young and beautiful daughter, Miss Elizabeth, has placed upon my head a burden such as will be callied by my humble self and family for ever,' began Mr Chin.

('Oh, Lord,' thought Mr Inglefell to himself, 'what the dickens has Beth been up to this time?')

'When I am overthrown in the road by bad boys and my valuable stock of trading is scattered in the dust, she has come to save me and fights velly stlongly against the bad boys.'

'Yes, she's certainly a pretty good fighter,' acknowledged Mr Inglefell, and now that he came to think of it he recalled having been told something about the matter. 'I hope you were not hurt, Mr Chin.'

Mr Chin bowed gravely. 'Thank you. I am now recovered flom my injuries. Your daughter's velly kind help gives me and family much glatitude to cally for ever. If I have your honourable sir's permission, I wish to give small humble gift to missie.'

'What? You want Elizabeth? I think she's in bed, but we'll soon find out. Excuse me for a moment.' Mr Inglefell went back to the morning-room and briefly explained to his wife the reason for this unusual visit. Mrs Inglefell rang for Pearl to wake Beth up and bring her downstairs, 'and mind she puts on her warmest dressing-gown and slippers'.

Elizabeth looked rather sleepy and bewildered when she came into the dining-room wearing a cherry-coloured woollen gown and a pair of Indian moccasins. But when she saw Mr

Chin she uttered a little cry of welcome and ran across the room to take his hand.

'Hullo, dear Mr Chin! Are you feeling quite well now? Did you put more arnica on your cut when you got home, like we told you to?' she wanted to know.

'Yes, thank you, missie. Velly well now.' The three young men were introduced and shook hands solemnly.

Then Mr Chin placed his hand on the top of the box and, taking Elizabeth's right hand in his left, he placed it beside his own.

'Please to accept this plesent from all Chin family, to say thank you to missie for ever and ever.'

'Oh,' was all Elizabeth could find to say in a blank tone.

'Say thank you very much for this very kind gift,' admonished her father.

'Oh, thank you very much indeed,' said Elizabeth readily, looking at the box and wondering what was inside it and hoping that it was an enormous jar of chow-chow which she loved and was never allowed to eat enough of.

Mr Chin then bowed deeply again several times. The four shook hands with Mr Inglefell and Elizabeth, bowed again and departed, escorted across the hall and to the front door by Pearl, who suspected hidden knives.

Mr Inglefell and Elizabeth remained gazing at the box.

'Well, that's all very strange,' said Mr Inglefell.

'What do you think it is, Daddy?'

'We'll soon know.' He ran his hand over the box to find a hinge or lock. He found that the box was fastened by a bamboo rod which slid smoothly into a groove along the entire length of one side. When the rod was withdrawn, one side of the box opened on a hidden hinge to reveal a cavity lined with silk across which vermilion and gold dragons sprawled in a dazzling splendour of scales and talons and tongues. In the deeper section of the box, set into the cushioned silk, was another box, exquisitely carved in ebony, ivory and mother-of-pearl,

189

with little doors meeting in the centre and fastened by mother-of-pearl buttons linked with emerald green cord.

'Perhaps it's a doll's house,' said Elizabeth expectantly, having by now given up hope of chow-chow.

'No,' said her father thoughtfully, 'it's not a doll's house, at least, not exactly.' With a slight feeling of excitement he untied the emerald green cords and swung open the doors of the inner cabinet. They revealed a figure of white, semi-translucent porcelain. The woman, for the figure seemed to be that of a woman, was seated on a pedestal of porcelain, in itself a sort of box, surmounted by a lotus flower. Above the head of the figure was a spray of flowers and leaves in white and green jade which made a fan-shaped canopy.

'Is it a doll?' asked Elizabeth doubtfully. 'Is it a Chinese doll?'

'N – no, old lady. It's not a doll. I don't know much about these things, but I think it's a goddess.'

'What's a goddess, Daddy?'

'Something to do with religion. Something that heathen people worship and believe in to bring them good luck or punishment, as the case may be.'

'Will it bring us good fortune?'

'I rather think that's the idea. She's by way of being an expression of gratitude, so she's probably got something to do with good fortune, or protection from evil, or something of that nature.'

'Let's take her to show Mummie,' suggested Elizabeth, but when she tried to lift the box off the table it was too heavy for her to carry.

'Astonishingly heavy,' agreed her father, who found that he had to make a considerable effort to bear the goddess to the morning-room. Mrs Inglefell looked at the gift appreciatively.

'It's really rather lovely,' she said. 'The silk is glorious and the work on the little inner cabinet is charming.'

'Yes,' agreed her husband, thankfully relaxing once more in

his chair. 'It wouldn't surprise me to discover that it was quite valuable. I hardly knew whether to let Elizabeth accept it, but probably old John would have been offended after carrying it all the way down here – and it's a frightful weight, I may tell you – he'd have probably been offended if I hadn't let her keep it.' His wife agreed that he had taken the right course.

'But what in the world are we going to do with it?' she asked. 'It's not exactly something one can put on the drawing-room mantelpiece. I suppose Beth will want to look at it, seeing that it belongs to her. In the morning I will get Finch to put it away on the top of the nursery cupboard. It will be safe enough there and out of the way.'

And so the Goddess of Fortune was put into the nursery cupboard, where she was shut up and, like the princess in the fairy-tale, forgotten for seven years.

18

The Continental

THAT year Mrs Goldiway gave an evening garden-party in November. She called it a 'Continental', and sent out large numbers of pale pink cards printed in Gothic gold lettering (very difficult to read) to all her friends and acquaintances and even to persons who would have counted themselves as neither but who accepted the invitation in spite of this, partly because everyone likes a party, and this party promised to be unusually large and lavish. It was planned for the night of the full moon, the November moon being, as everyone knows, the most splendid of the year.

First the children were invited to high tea, preceded by Rouse's One and Only Original Gipsy Roundabout, erected on the side lawn and resplendent in a new coat of orange and blue paint ready for its annual appearance on the twenty-eighth (which it should be explained for the benefit of those whose knowledge of British history does not extend to these finer points) is the date, three days after Christmas, when the anniversary of Captain Hindmarsh's arrival at Hobson's Bay in the good ship *Buffalo*, year 1836, and the proclamation of the foundation of the colony in the name of King William the Fourth, is celebrated with a good deal of energy by the citizens of that worthy community. Rouse's One and Only Original had been a component of the day's celebrations for longer than anyone could remember, and three generations of children had become familiar with its dappled grey ponies which rose and fell with majestic if monotonous regularity on their shining brass poles and with the carriage drawn by two white swans into which the younger children could be safely strapped by scarlet leather belts with brass bells.

By half-past three large parties of children had gathered on the lawn: the girls looked self-conscious and excited as they pointed their new shoes and twitched their muslin frills; the boys, surly in their best suits, thumbs in trouser pockets, dug divots out of the well-rolled turf with the toes of their boots and wondered miserably when the eating would begin; the nannies in their grey alpaca coats and grey pointed caps with long silk pleats stood about carefully ignoring each other while they 'kept an eye on' their young charges. The general air of discomfort was partly due to their hostess who had greeted them with an air of bustle and exaggerated 'brightness' which, she imagined, was the way to make children 'feel at home'. She had thereby antagonised them instantly and made herself despised by the nannies.

Presently Miss Manning appeared and began quietly to move the group away to the side lawns where Johnson, the head gardener, had arranged a cricket match for the boys and some swings for the girls. Miss Manning was governess to Cecilia and Nancy, Mrs Goldiway's two girls, who, though not twins, were so much alike that no one (except, perhaps, their own family) could tell them apart: a shy pair, overshadowed by the dominating personalities of their parents.

When Miss Penthorpe arrived with the Digby Faulkener children she and Miss Manning formed a natural alliance against the nannies. Elizabeth, with neither nurse nor governess, felt rather superior, for Miss Una, after escorting her as far as the gate, had then gone away to meet Eleanor and Marian at school and bring them in time for tea at five o'clock.

Elizabeth was always bored with parties. The races were insipid affairs, not nearly as exciting as those she ran by herself across the paddocks; the games were artificial and less interesting than those she had invented to play with Henri in the holidays. At Christmas Henri would be coming to stay and school would be finished and they would be able to spend all day on the beach (and perhaps part of the night, too, if it was a heat-wave like the Parsee with the hat from which the sun was reflected in more-than-Oriental splendour on the beaches of Socotra and Daddy read out of the newspaper at breakfast that the temperature was over a hundred yesterday and was expected to be at least a hundred and five today, and what about supper on the beach tonight, as he could just do with a swim after all day in that 'infernal office') and she would be able to teach Henri to swim.

The little boys were playing cricket in a rather languid manner because Malcolm Faulkener was batting and no one would ever get him out. Elizabeth asked if she could bowl. Her intervention was not looked on with any favour until she sent down one of the evil 'googlies' that Finch had taught her, spreading the wicket neatly and bringing down the bails and Malcolm Faulkener's pride, all in one stroke. That lordly young gentleman, overcome by mortification which was not lessened by the evident pleasure of the others at his downfall, went into the sulks. Elizabeth's popularity further increased when she announced that she didn't want to bat, thanks, as she didn't like batting and, anyway, she wanted to go and ask Johnson if he had a doctor for his orange trees. As it was plain that the little boys had no idea what she was talking about, this further enhanced her feeling of superiority. With a good deal of pleasure she noticed that the girls were now playing 'Last Touch', a game she heartily despised. She crossed the lawn and looked about for Johnson. He was on the farther side where, helped by the Faulkeners' groom (who had driven the children over in the wagonette which he had left in the yard in the care of Mr Goldiway's stable-man), he was carrying a barrel which, set upon an upturned box, soon revealed itself to be an ice-cream tub (or receptacle of Ambrosial Nectar according to taste). Two maids carrying large trays stacked with saucers and spoons now came across the lawn from the house, and soon the whole party were enjoying that degree of bliss only to be attained by limitless ice-cream (free) on a roasting hot day in mid-November when one is any age between two years and . . . well, the age at which one suddenly discovers that one is enjoying, not the thing itself, but the memory of how one used to enjoy it years ago.

Scarcely had the last dollops been sadly spooned and licked up and the saucers put down on the grass, their final unspoonable and unlickable remnants now reduced, under the still fierce heat of the late afternoon sun, to their original yellow custardness, than the sound of music, instantly recognisable as that of Rouse's One and Only Original Gipsy Roundabout, brought the company whooping across the lawns to the other side of the garden where the tall hedges had so far hidden this beloved and faithful friend from view.

Even the nannies were caught up in the whirl of pleasure and so far unbent as to be gracious to Miss Manning and Miss Penthorpe and help them on and off the dappled ponies and give it as their opinion that Mr Rouse was a very decent man as could be trusted with the children at any time, as Madam and the Master had often remarked, which was more than could be said of most.

Marian and Eleanor had now arrived and were in time to have two rides on the roundabout before tea was announced and everybody trooped to the side veranda where a long table had been set up with every delicacy that imagination of childhood could conjure and more, even, than the capacities of the children could compass. But they fainted not nor flinched before what now confronted them. Even the mountainous piles of jellies and trifles and cream cakes and strawberries were soon to present a depleted and reduced aspect in face of this determined locust-horde.

It was six o'clock. Some of the smallest children were sleepy and cross. There were signs of party tantrums, firmly quelled by nursely voices saying: 'That will do. Come along, Miss Charlotte. Say "Thank you very much for having me." '

In no time at all the party was over and the maids were clearing away the remains of the feast. In the garden Johnson and his men were gathering up stray balloons and paper caps and streamers, while on the big front lawn, where the children had not been allowed to go, carpenters were still hammering at the dancing floor which Mr Goldiway had had built for the occasion, tacking up strips of bunting along the sides and setting banks of potted palms around the stage where the band would play. Bamboo chairs were placed here and there about the garden and what had been the children's tea-table was converted into a buffet with dozens and dozens of glasses, upside down, and a row of tubs for the ice. A proper sit-down supper, with hot roast turkeys, and cold chickens and iced champagne, would be served inside, the ballroom converted into a supper-room, Mr Goldiway having decided that the weather was too hot for dancing in the house.

Elizabeth watched these activities with a good deal of interest. Her mother and father were dining with Mr and Mrs Pennyfarthing and would afterwards come with them to the ball. Miss Una had gone to stay with Mrs Pennyfarthing's two little boys during the evening while their parents were away. Eleanor and Marian went back with the Faulkener children and would spend the night with them and be brought to school with the Faulkener contingent in the morning.

By one of those mysterious misunderstandings which can sometimes happen in human affairs, no one knows why, Miss Penthorpe clearly understood that only the two elder Inglefell children were to be in her charge for the night, while Miss Una was equally certain that Elizabeth was to accompany Eleanor and Marian on their visit to 'Kirkwall'. These two worthy women therefore both left the Goldiway's house, each taking it for granted that Elizabeth had already departed in the care of the other and happily unaware of having left her behind.

Elizabeth did rather wonder why Miss Oonie was so long in coming to fetch her, but, as by that time Mr Rouse had begun to dismantle the One and Only and she was engrossed in the technique of taking the dappled ponies off their brass poles and unscrewing the swans from their position on the circular platform, she gave it only a passing thought. Elizabeth was not a nervous or worrying child. When the lengthening shadows finally brought her to the realisation that it was now getting really late, she thought it rather a lark. Perhaps if she could keep out of the way of the grown-ups for long enough, she might be able to see the beginning of the ball.

The last of the sunlight was gilding the poplar trees, the carpenters had finished their hammering and gone away, and the garden was gently settling into the twilight hush, when Mr Rouse finished the last of his packing and unscrewing. He went round pulling big sheets of canvas over everything until the One and Only was neatly and safely tucked up for the night. 'Got to move her down to the sea wall in the morning,' he volunteered. 'This is our busy season. Don't generally take on private jobs at this time of the year, but Mr Goldiway he made a special offer, like, and I couldn't refuse, times being what they are, besides not wanting to disappoint all you young ladies and gentlemen. I must say as I like to see young people enjoy theirselves.'

'Thank you very much,' said Elizabeth sincerely. 'I'll come and see you on the sea wall, if you like. Henri is coming to spend the Christmas holidays with me. He lives with my Uncle Thomas and my Aunt Emma now, at Rose Lees, and he's never seen the One and Only and he doesn't know how to swim, and he's never been in a boat except when he was a baby, and he doesn't remember. So we'll have a busy season too.'

'Well, every little helps, as they say,' said Mr Rouse. 'Good night now, and if I don't see you before, a merry Christmas and my best respects to your pa and your lady mother.'

Elizabeth was fascinated by this mode of speech, but felt

that she should explain. 'My mother isn't Lady Inglefell. She's only plain Mrs Inglefell. It's my grandmother-in-England who is lady because her husband was a baronet, but there weren't any sons so there was no successor. Though,' she added, feeling that truth must be served, 'I'm not sure what that last bit means.'

Mr Rouse listened attentively and pondered a moment before replying. Then with a little shake, as though the solution were beyond him and could therefore be discounted, he said:

'Well, no doubt it's all for the best, and now I'll be off.'

After he had gone Elizabeth felt just a little bit lonely, so she wandered along the hedge and talked to the blackbirds. They were singing their evening song with all their best notes. The wives were much too busy looking after the young chicks to listen properly, but probably enjoyed it just the same, as so often is the case when husbands are trying to please.

By now the garden was quite dark and quiet except near the house where every gas jet was lit and strings of Japanese lanterns had turned the verandas into magic grottoes of light. Elizabeth found a hammock slung between two walnut trees and curled herself up on its cushions. She did not feel exactly sick (she told herself this indignantly; she was long past the age at which she got sick after a party), but the large quantities of cake and strawberries and cream which she had superimposed on a not inconsiderable layer of vanilla ice-cream, to say nothing of ice-cold Hall's stone ginger-beer and three rides on the One and Only, had certainly left her inside in a disturbed and uncertain condition, sufficiently so as to make the cushions of this hammock doubly acceptable, now that the excitement was over and the garden quiet. She fell into a pleasant dream. It was still suffocatingly hot. In the west a huge star hung like a lantern against the fading sunset.

Beyond the farthest hedge on the other side of the garden a crimson glow began to spread into the green of the sky. 'Bush fires in the hills,' thought Elizabeth sleepily. But ten minutes later, as the rim of its enormous yellow globe appeared above the trees, she realised that here was the full moon, punctually keeping his appointment with the ball. By the time the first guests arrived he would be well along on his skyward journey.

About then Elizabeth must have fallen asleep, because one minute she was reciting the bit about 'now doth the moon her glorious veil unfold', and the next minute (or so it seemed) she heard her mother's voice saying: 'I believe it is cooler here,' and the sounds of someone moving across the grass.

Elizabeth was still very sleepy and not at all sure where she was. She felt comfortable on her hammock. The garden and the moonlight and her mother's voice were all part of a pleasant dream. She snuggled into the cushions again, drowsily aware that the dream was going on. A man's voice was saying: 'You know, don't you, that I am going home. I've been here for over three years, a year longer than usual. You can't have been unaware of the reason I stayed.'

A rustling as of someone making a gesture of protest was followed by the man's voice again: 'No, let me say it. A week today I shall be homeward bound and all this can be part of a dream that can never come true, part of the garden and the moonlight and the whole sweet-bitter fantasy I have been living for these three years. It all began, you know, that night you gave your first dinner-party and Mrs O'Shawn played the harp. It was a night like this. I believe . . . yes, it was, the November full moon. I went out into the garden and watched you through the window. One of those damned wagtails kept saying: "Love me, love me, sweet, pretty creature", until I could have murdered it. And all the time, there you were, so beautiful . . . Oh, my dear, my dearest dear . . .' There was a sort of choking sound which made Elizabeth come nearly awake, but the silence was so profound and went on for so long, and the strains of the Blue Danube Waltz came so liltingly across the moonlight air from the dance floor, that she fell quite to sleep and did not wake up at all even when someone found her and told Mr Inglefell, who, torn between exasperation at his youngest daughter's capacity for getting into the most unaccountable scrapes, and relief that she was safe and sound, not unmixed (it must be confessed) with satisfaction at the good excuse this afforded him for leaving the party early, carried her to the wagonette and told Finch to drive them home, after making his excuses to Mrs Goldiway and arranging for Captain Ross-Bossingham to escort Mrs Inglefell home at the end of the ball. He was not to know that Jackie was given urgent orders to drive the dog-cart back at top speed, leave the unharnessing to Thomas, and return post-haste with the phaeton and a pair of fresh horses, the dog-cart being no vehicle in which to drive a lady home from a ball, to say nothing of the twenty-eight yards of satin and lace that swirled about her lovely feet. Good God, what a fool a man can be! But who would ever have imagined such a stroke of luck?

And so it was that not for a good many years did Elizabeth remember her dream as anything but a dream. But every evening the wagtails in the garden continued to call to each other in their musical, stupid way:

> 'Love me, oh love me,
> 'Love me, oh love me,
> Sweet, pretty creature, forlorn, forlorn.'

19

The Ogre, 1910

WHEN Eleanor was seventeen Mrs Inglefell took her to England, where she was to go to school and spend the between-term holidays with her grandmother, Lady Maxim-Munt, in Somersetshire.

Elizabeth still went to Miss Liddier's school in the High Street, but Marian was now a weekly boarder at the Church of England College for Young Ladies in the city.

Even at thirteen years of age, Elizabeth's ideas of geography were vague in the extreme, and only when she saw the big trunks being brought down from the attic and a 'daily' dress-maker installed in the sewing-room did it dawn on her that 'going to England' was a rather more serious undertaking than going to Mount Pleasant for the school holidays. When she learnt that Eleanor would be more than four weeks on the ship before arriving in London, and would be away for at least two years, she looked on her elder sister with a new aspect.

Eleanor seemed in no way excited or disturbed by the experience now opening before her. Rather unimaginative, she was what people generally describe as 'a fine girl'. She would in-evitably end up as head prefect of any school she was sent to, and could be relied on to do her duty, if in rather a pedestrian way. Though her musical talent was exceptional, it was execu-tive rather than creative or interpretative. Her large capable hands dealt firmly and delicately with the intricacies of Brahms concertos and Beethoven sonatas, without her mind being in any way stimulated or aroused by the beauty or significance of the music. The technical excellence of her performance would always deceive unknowledgeable people into believing her to be a fine musician. She had promise of handsome looks, and Mrs Inglefell felt that with a little European polish her eldest daughter could be relied on to carry off a presentation at Court and a London season with reasonable credit.

She herself was anticipating this voyage with mixed feelings. It was now ten years since she had been home. A little uncertainly she looked at herself in the glass and saw there a face, still youthful certainly, but finer drawn in its lines than it should be at her age, her hair not quite as shining as her London maid would have approved. ('It's all this dreadful sun,' she thought to herself, 'it withers one up to a husk.') But these things could be corrected with a few weeks of moist English air and some London grooming. It was the deeper changes that she feared. Inevitable that one should be 'out of the swim'. There would be people she didn't know, stories she hadn't heard; there would be allusions that would elude her, books she couldn't discuss, plays she hadn't seen; she would miss all those little nuances that mean one is firmly established in one's 'milieu'. 'The truth is,' she said to the face in the mirror, 'you've become a provincial. Neither one thing nor the other. You aren't an Australian, but you've ceased to be English. Like a newt, neither a tadpole nor a frog. How horrid!'

Of meeting Ross-Bossingham again she hardly dared to think. It was now nearly six years since he had returned to his regiment, four years since he had inherited his title on the death of a worthy if undistinguished father and, retiring from the army, had settled down as Lord Ross, Viscount Bossingham and Braith, to the management of his estates. So far he had not married, his sister's three young sons providing him with an assurance of family survival, not only because his title was one of those which can, if necessary, descend through the female line, but made doubly sure by the fact that his sister had married a cousin who would have been the next heir if she had predeceased Ross (as the lawyers say) without children.

'Perhaps I won't see him at all,' said Mrs Inglefell to the face in the mirror. 'He is probably completely Scottish by now and all bogged down with porridge and mist. Anyway, it was all a long time ago and rather silly, really.' And very sensibly putting aside memories of moonlit gardens and the Blue Danube Waltz, she went to see how Miss Stitchaway was getting on with Eleanor's velveteen dress and whether Marshall's had delivered the piece of cream serge that was to be her new skirt for the ship. 'How heavenly it will be to get some things really well tailored again,' she thought.

For part of the time that Mrs Inglefell was to be away, Uncle Thomas Woodstock and Aunt Emma were to come and stay at Sandridge. After the death of Mr and Mrs Hardman, Thomas, as one of Henri's trustees under Richard Hardman's will, had taken over the farm at Lily Lees and had put Frank in to manage it. Frank was a good farmer and had married, shortly after, one of the daughters of a thrifty, hard-working German settler in the district. Within a year or two the farm had that prosperous well-cared-for appearance which poor Richard Hardman had dreamed about but never achieved.

Henri, at the age of fifteen, was a quiet slender boy, serious beyond his years, but doing well at school and devoted to his foster-parents, who lavished on him all the affection they would have given those longed-for children who had never materialised, with a little extra for the stroke of fate, at once tragic and fortunate, which had brought him into their care. As for Elizabeth, in spite of his two years seniority, she treated him as she always had, as a devoted slave, to be ordered about, led into mischief, teased, and relegated to whatever rôle the exigencies of the moment required. In other words, he was what the pre-Stopesian family had been years ago, friend, playmate, foil, audience and confidant. She taught him how to climb trees, where to find the best birds' nests, and how to find the places on the beach where the cockles buried themselves. She taught him to swim and derided his nervousness until he could dive, if not with fearlessness, at least with determination. She dragged him on long expeditions through the sand-hills in forays against the Faulkener children ('Cowboys and Indians'), and in the evenings and on wet Sunday afternoons read aloud to him out of Mr Henty and Walter Scott, that his education should, in all important respects, not be neglected. But this year he had been entered as a boarder in one of the city's colleges, and holidays were now three months apart.

When the big P. & O. ship had sailed away from the Outer Harbour and Elizabeth on the wharf had continued to wave her handkerchief long after she had ceased to distinguish her mother and Eleanor from the other fluttering figures crowded along the promenade deck because she had a horrid feeling that if she once stopped waving she would begin to cry in a babyish boo-hooing way which would be ridiculous; when Marian and Henri, who had been allowed to come from school for the day of the departure, had gone back to school; when Daddy and Miss Una had talked in a falsely cheerful way all the way home in the train and cab; when they came in at the front gates and past the monkey-puzzle tree to a house strangely quiet and empty now of the big trunks which had stood about the passages for weeks so that one had become used to them; and when Mrs Thompson had put down on the dinner-table all their favourite dishes in the manner of one offering funeral bake-meats, Elizabeth felt that something had happened to her life, that Nothing Would Ever Be the Same Again. And whereas this can be truthfully said of any moment of our lives, there are some times when it seems to be truer than others.

Miss Una was, of course, now Mrs Patrick O'Brien, but everyone still thought of her as Miss Una. She and her husband lived at Ti-Tree Gully. Mr O'Brien did not drive to town every day as he used to do. He now sold his milk in bulk to a butter factory only a few miles away, and once a week he sent two lorry-loads of vegetables to the East End Market. As he had recently bought more land and doubled the size of his dairy herd, he and his wife were comfortably off in a hard-working way.

Miss Una stayed for a week, which comforted Elizabeth a good deal. She was puzzled by her own feelings. She was devoted to her mother, but only in the way that one becomes attached to something or someone because it or they are always there. This sudden uprooting of the accustomed order of life left her bewildered and vaguely resentful. 'I hate things changing,' she suddenly discovered to herself. 'I want everything to go on *exactly* the same, always.' After this brief rebellion against destiny, she put her head under the bedclothes and cried herself to sleep.

Next morning she felt much better and when the time came for Miss Una to say good-bye and go back to Ti-Tree Gully, she was comparatively cheerful. 'Do tell Mr O'Brien to come next time,' she called. 'I haven't see him for ages.'

That was in March. A month later Thomas and Emma arrived from from Rose Lees and at the beginning of May Henri came for the first term's holidays. If Elizabeth had half-expected a change in him after his week with all those boys, her fears proved groundless. He had grown an inch and looked paler and lankier than ever, but he resumed at once his relationship with her as brother, friend and faithful lieutenant.

Elizabeth was more than usually glad to see him. The truth was that she was growing a little too old for Miss Liddier's school and was becoming bored with it. The Faulkener family were still useful as natural enemies, but James and Morley were now young gentlemen at Oxford and she had nearly forgotten what they looked like; Sarah was at school in Paris which (in Elizabeth's opinion) would probably result in the loss of what little intelligence she had ever possessed; Helen was at the Young Ladies' Church of England College in Adelaide where (much to Elizabeth's disgust) Marian had formed a friendship with her ('But Marrie is always so beastly good-natured, she makes friends with *anyone*,' was Elizabeth's inward and unspoken defence of her sister). There remained only Judith, a placid, amiable child, a year older than Elizabeth but in the same class at Miss Liddier's, and Alistair and Malcolm at Prince Albert House, the boys' college rival to Saint George's where Henri went. Alistair and Malcolm were now allowed to drive the pony cart by themselves, and, though despising it as 'kid stuff' unsuitable for men of fourteen and sixteen, were glad enough to use it as a means of transport for picnic baskets and cricket bats and the other impedimenta necessary to a day on the beach. 'Cowboys and Indians' had given place, with the years, to 'Exploring'. They would call for Elizabeth in the morning, pack her and Henri and their gear for swimming, fishing and eating, into the pony cart and drive two miles down the coast to where Mr Faulkener kept his boat, a fourteen-footer neatly housed in a trim shed on the sandhills. Here they would tie up the pony with a nose-bag in the shade of the shed where he would doze happily for hours, occasionally snuffling into the chaff but for the most part content to sleep and dream of green pastures. As he was the oldest member of the party this was considered to be his privilege. The others would then adjourn to undress, the boys to the shelter of the sandhills, delicately conceding to Elizabeth the privacy of the bathing-house.

Elizabeth's bathing-costume was always of bright red 'turkey twill', which, made by Miss Una for Eleanor, had already over several summers justified its reputation for being practically unwearoutable. It reached from her neck to her knees and was finished very becomingly with a Peter Pan collar edged with zigzag braid. Its brilliant scarlet was chosen purposely, as it was supposed to frighten the sharks and to be of assistance to the rescuers on any occasion when the owner was in danger of drowning. Elizabeth was never in danger of drowning. She could race Malcolm in any test at the big swimming-baths at the Jetty, and she had already graduated to the highest of the three diving platforms.

March that year had really excelled itself in the matter of heat. The drought broke with a thunderstorm in mid-April, but after three days of rain, the sun came out, the sky cleared, and the thermometer went on its cheerful way towards the century as though a season called autumn had never been heard of. By the first week in May the weather was still hot enough to make the beach in one's swimming-togs a most acceptable place to spend the day. They swam, they ran, they wrestled, swam again, and then played French cricket. This was always unsatisfactory as Henri was now such a good batsman that no one could get him out.

On one of these days they had eaten their lunch (Mrs Thompson had put a whole roast chicken into the basket and a stone flagon of home-made ginger-beer, icy cold from the cellar and kept at this temperature by a kind of eiderdown filled with straw and specially invented for the purpose), and they lay on the warm sand in a mood of lazy argumentativeness or of drowsy silence.

Elizabeth suddenly giggled. 'Do you remember when I bowled you out at that Goldiway party, Malcolm? You were as wild as a Hottentot.'

'You were pretty heathenish yourself – on the whole, one of the most revolting of my childhood acquaintances.'

Elizabeth was lying on her back with her eyes closed, seeing everything red because the sun was so strong on her eyelids.

'It's my idea that you Faulkeners weren't Scots at all. I think you were Picts, part of the barbaric hordes that forayed against the outposts of civilisation. Our history book says they were small hairy people of low intelligence.'

This challenge would duly be dealt with later in the day, but at the moment everyone was too full of chicken and ginger-beer to do more than roll over on the sand so that their sunburn would cook evenly. Elizabeth sifted the hot, pure white sand through her fingers. The seagulls waited in a circle, boldly advancing to snatch a piece of discarded food, and then retiring to watch for the next chance.

'That house up there,' she went on, gesturing towards a white and green bungalow beyond the sandhills, 'is where we met the Ogre that time. Queer old bird. I wonder if he still lives there.'

This reference was to a time when Elizabeth, aged eight, had tried to cultivate the acquaintance of the gentleman who lived in the green and white bungalow. Mr Clifford Breve was a pianist of international reputation, now retired from the professional demands of the concert platform to a life of carefully guarded seclusion. With his garden, to which he was devoted, his musical instruments, his library, and his cats, he resented any intrusion on his privacy or interruptions in the work of writing his memoirs with which he was now engaged.

Elizabeth had spied him in the garden one day when she was passing the house and had lingered to say: 'How do you do.'

'Go away, little girl,' said Mr Breve.

'Yes, I'm going to Mr Faulkener's. But you might say "How do you do". My mother says we should always answer when spoken to.'

'Don't be impertinent.'

This injustice was really more than Elizabeth could endure

'But I wasn't,' she protested. 'It was me being polite and you being impertinent when you wouldn't say, "How do you do".'

Mr Breve was neither of the fibre nor of the inclination to counter this sally. He took refuge in flight and disappeared into the house.

'I've a jolly good mind,' said Elizabeth five years later, as she looked ruminatively towards the green and white bungalow, 'to go up and see if I could smoke him out.' She raised herself and lazily watched the sand sliding in white cascades from the creases of her red costume.

'Oh, Beth, don't be so energetic,' moaned Alistair. 'Energetic women are the curse of civilisation. Women should be "gracious, pale, of gentle voice".'

'Rot,' was Elizabeth's brief reply. 'That's only you trying to be grown-up. Besides, it's "modest", not "gracious", and Tennyson was saying that Maud was, not that she ought to be.'

This snub, for once, silenced Alistair. Somehow one always thought of Elizabeth as the energetic, practical type, incapable of appreciating the finer intellectual pursuits. He was just entering a phase of intense devotion to the Victorian poets and was no little dismayed to find that young Beth, three years his junior, could out-quote him. Henri could have told him differently. Elizabeth did not have a profound or reflective mind, but she was possessed of an insatiable greed for knowledge, a retentive memory and a brain which worked at lightning speed, gifts which were inclined to make her impatient with others whose reactions were slower.

She jumped to her feet, shook herself like a spaniel, and went up through the sandhills.

Mr Breve was working in his garden, where behind the shelter of tall fences of ti-tree brush, he was cultivating prize carnations and other well-loved plant specimens. He was now engaged in arranging a twig-barrier to protect the young sprouts of the winter sweet peas from the depredations of the starlings.

With a sense of mischief for which she cannot be excused, Elizabeth stood in the gateway and called, in a voice honey sweet with courtesy: 'How do you do.'

Mr Breve looked up. The reel of black cotton in his left hand fell on to the cement pathway and rolled under the straw mat on which he was kneeling. He made a sketchy, reluctant movement towards his straw hat.

'Good afternoon. Oh, it's you again. Go away, little girl.'

'Oh no, I'm not little *now*,' said Elizabeth. 'That was five years ago.'

'Well, go away, in any case,' said Mr Breve, looking vainly

for the cotton-reel. He had a nervous dread of dogs and children, being convinced, probably justifiably, that music and a garden were impossible with either.

Elizabeth went along the fence to be nearer him and climbed on the first strand of wire so that she could lean comfortably on the cushions of brush that, bound with wire, made an ornamental top to the fence, like the velvet-covered railing of the dress-circle at the theatre. Mr Breve, still groping short-sightedly for the cotton-reel, was irritable. The sun was hot on his back. The birds had already attacked these precious green shoots. If the crop of winter sweet-peas was to be saved it was essential that the work be finished this afternoon. Schreimann should have sent that score from New York by the last mail. How could he possibly go on with his new chapter without it? By all infernal discords, the wretched thing was here in his hand not two minutes ago; where could it have gone to? All children should be kept in cages till they reached the age at which they could be tolerated.

'Your sweet-peas are higher than ours,' volunteered Elizabeth. 'But Finch didn't plant them till after the rain, because he said they would only hang fire in any case till the break in the season. Last year ours grew nine feet high. We picked *millions*. This fence won't be nearly tall enough if yours grow as high as that. You'll have to get bamboos and they'll probably all blow over with the south-westerlies.'

Mr Breve, who had, to his own annoyance, already realised this, was stung to action.

'Will you go away!' he shouted, getting to his feet. 'No one wants you here, and you are nothing but an interfering, bothersome child.' (At least he didn't call her 'little girl' again.)

He was a tall man, now nearly seventy years of age. Long white hair hung down behind his ears, and long white eyebrows hung down over his eyes. His cadaverous face at this moment was red with exertion and exasperation, his blue eyes angry and red-rimmed. Elizabeth was enchanted. He was living up so well to his soubriquet of 'the Ogre'. She danced away across the sandhills singing at the top of her voice, 'The lass with the delicate air', in a very high key, with all the embellishments and twiddly bits and a few trills and runs put in out of sheer exuberance of animal spirits. When she got to the top of the sandhill and looked down on the three boys, still lying among the picnic baskets on the beach, she was astonished to hear a voice behind her, shouting: 'Come back, you! Confound it, can't you hear me? Come back at once!'

The Ogre was standing on his tool-box brandishing a trowel. Just for a second Elizabeth hesitated. He looked so truly ferocious. But, after all, she could always run quicker than he could, if necessary, and now that Alistair had taught her those new ju-jutsu grips, she felt equal to wrestling anyone. She went half-way down the sandhill.

'Come back!' repeated Mr Breve in an almost normal voice. 'I want to ask you something.'

Prompted by curiosity, Elizabeth went the rest of the way down the sandhill and up to the ti-tree fence.

'Where did you learn to sing like that?' asked Mr Breve.

'Oh, I never have. I mean, except class-singing at school.'

'Can you play the piano?'

'Yes, of course. We've all had lessons from Herr Hermanschreimer for *years*.'

'Hermanschreimer, eh? Then you probably use that disastrous Clementi method?'

'Oh, yes, aren't they awful! I simply hate them. They make your fingers all stick up. I like the Kuhlau 'Klavierwerke' much better. Some of them are quite exciting.'

Mr Breve pointed with his tool. 'Go along the fence and come in at the gate,' he ordered.

Wonderingly, Elizabeth obeyed. The Ogre had somehow disappeared and been replaced by a kind old gentleman interested in sweet-peas who agreed with her about Clementi.

She followed him up the path, across the porch and into an

enormous room with wide windows looking towards the sea on one side and the far-away blue hills on the other. The walls were lined with bookshelves and cupboards. The only other furniture was a kitchen table placed between the westerly windows and covered with writing materials and sheets of music manuscript, a few chairs, and two grand pianos side by side.

'Oh, you've got two pianos too,' she exclaimed. 'So have we, but they're both uprights. Only one is in the nursery and one is in the drawing-room, so we can't play concertos. But Daddy says if I practise hard he will get another one so that I can play the Mozart Number Seventeen with Eleanor. Mummie says that two pianos in the drawing-room would look silly. The trouble is, Ellie plays much better than any of us, but she never sticks *up* for anything. I *know* Daddy would do it if we made him.'

She was examining the Bechstein with interest. 'The Faulkeners have got a Bechstein,' she went on, 'but they never play it. It is covered with a silk shawl and has photographs and flower-vases all over the top. I don't think the Scots are musical people, do you?'

Mr Breve was taking no notice of her chatter, or seemed to be taking no notice of it. He was lifting the lid of the second piano which turned out to be a Steinway. Suddenly, without striking a note, he turned to her and said: 'Sing the C major scale.'

Not at all discommoded by this abrupt command (because, all at once, she had stepped into the world of music and was quite at home), Elizabeth did so.

Muttering to himself something about 'absolute pitch', Mr Breve struck a few chords.

'Now sing "The lass with the delicate air".'

'It's better in A natural,' suggested Elizabeth.

'Quite right, quite right,' agreed Mr Breve as to an equal, and slid his improvisation up a tone. Then he passed into the opening bars and Elizabeth sang, a trifle timidly at first but then, remembering the incident in the garden, she put a little amusement into her voice and ended the song with some of the mocking trills she had made on the sandhills.

'Why do you end it like that?' asked Mr Breve.

'Oh, just for fun,' said Elizabeth. 'I know it isn't right really. Herr Hermanschreimer says that half the time I am playing Elizabeth Inglefell instead of Chopin and Beethoven.'

'Impertinence, eh?'

'Oh, yes,' exclaimed Elizabeth, realising with delicious quivers of excitement that she had found a kindred spirit who would be a friend for ever.

'So you play Beethoven, eh? Ridiculous!'

'That's what Daddy says. He says no one can play Beethoven till they are over thirty. But you can *learn* him.'

'Perhaps, perhaps. Now sing a scale upwards in B and do a trill at the top,' which she did, of course, quite easily.

'My child,' said Mr Breve shutting the piano decisively, 'you have a remarkable voice, truly remarkable. You have been blessed with absolute pitch and a perfectly balanced natural trill. But there must be no more class-singing in school. I must go and see your father. What did you say your name is?'

On the beach the boys had begun an earnest conversation about the future.

'What are you going to do after you leave school?' asked Henri of Alistair.

'Oh, I dare say I'll go up to Oxford,' said that young man with an air of careless unconcern.

'You mean you wouldn't *mind* going?' Henri asked, and the undisguised astonishment in his voice was more salutary than any snub he could consciously have administered.

Alistair ceased to be the lordly undergraduate and became his usual, rather pleasant human self again. 'Oh, well,' he admitted, making geometric patterns on the sand with his toes, 'some of the chaps seem to think it isn't bad.'

'I think it's tripe,' said Malcolm. Even at fourteen he still had that deceptively angelic appearance, reflective of his mother's fragility. But like her, he possessed a clear, logical mind and a will of tempered steel. 'I shall be an engineer and make masses of money. You see, in a new country like Australia, engineering will be the thing. Like America. What are you going to be, Frog?'

'Oh, nothing much, I dare say,' said Henri, feeling a rush of that insecurity which had shaken his childhood and which would always be waiting to engulf him in moments of his own weakness or the onslaught of circumstance. 'There's the farm. I'll have to look after that, I suppose.'

'Why? Frank Coppins is making it a darn sight better farm than you ever could,' pronounced Malcolm with the uncompromising truthfulness of youth.

'I say,' said Alistair suddenly, 'I wonder where Beth is. She said she was going to find the Ogre, but she's been gone for ages. I suppose she's all right.'

Henri got up. 'I'll go and look.' He turned towards the sandhills. When he reached the ti-tree fence of the green and white bungalow, an extraordinary sight met his eyes. Beth, on her knees, was rapidly winding black cotton backwards and forwards between the twigs stuck into the ground along the rows of young sweet-peas in the garden bed. An elderly man in a tattered, wide-brimmed straw hat was watching her intently.

'You see,' she was explaining, 'if you do it this way the thrushes can't get in by walking underneath. They come after the snails, and that's useful, of course, but they're so strong and heavy that they break everything down. These ti-tree fences harbour the snails, Finch says, and he won't let Daddy have one. Or rather, it's Mummie really who wants them because she says iron is hideous. But if you put a layer of Solomon's Sluggo between the fence and the seedlings, that ought to finish the pests.' She tied the last of the cotton and jumped to her feet.

214

'Oh, hullo, Henri. Mr Breve, this is my friend Henri Hardman, who is staying with us for the holidays. Mr Breve has two grand pianos and is coming to see us and I am to learn concertos and he promised to show me some real photos of Madame Melba and says she is the Divine Nellie. Good-bye, Mr Breve. Thank you very much for having me. Don't forget the Sluggo.'

Looking slightly dazed, Mr Breve raised his hat in return to Henri's polite salute, and they said good-bye.

As the party drove back to Sandridge, they could hear the sound of church bells mournfully tolling.

'Sounds as though someone had died,' said Alistair.

'Then lots of people must have,' said Elizabeth, 'because that tenor bell that has just started is the Baptist one, and the mezzo one with the crack is the Congregational, and that sweet thin one a long way away is St Augustine's.'

They listened to the slow call of the bells while the pony trotted patiently along the macadam road.

'I say, something must have happened,' said Elizabeth. 'That new one is the Town Hall and they practically never ring those, and the little one you can hear quite near is the Roman Catholic church school behind the paddock.'

'P'raps the mayor is dead,' suggested Malcolm hopefully.

'He's a Congregationalist, so the Catholics wouldn't toll for him,' answered Elizabeth.

'Ding, dong, bell, Pussy's in the well,' quoted Alistair (and wished afterwards that he hadn't).

Elizabeth and Henri got down at the gate and carried their things, all rather sandy and salty, into the back veranda.

'Bags first shower,' cried Elizabeth, running into the outside bathroom at the end of the veranda where Household Law decreed that everyone who had been on the beach must first wash and shake the sand out of their clothes before coming into the house.

It was heavenly to come in from the beach on these warm, golden evenings; to watch the long shadows on the lawn, to smell the perfume of the newly-watered earth, and hear the sleepy half-songs of the birds going to bed. In the middle of pegging up the wet towels and the nearly-dry bathing-gowns on the line, Henri fell into a dream of such profound happiness that he could almost feel himself palpably part of some celestial reality. There are times when to be too happy is almost as painful as sorrow.

When Henri had showered and dressed and combed his hair, he went into the dining-room where he found Elizabeth and her father with Thomas and Emma Woodstock. There was a general air of solemnity about the gathering which as sensibly as words conveyed the atmosphere of News.

'My boy,' said Alfred rather sententiously, 'we have just received the news that His Majesty the King is dead.'

No one who has not experienced it can understand the sense of loss suffered by loyal subjects on the death of a beloved sovereign. Even the humblest, the poorest and the least important feels that he has lost a personal friend; more, a personal friend so powerful, so just, so benign, that to live within the sphere of his influence is to feel strengthened against the stroke of misfortune and fortified against the malice of enemies. When we ask God to save the King, and to confound the knavish tricks of his enemies, we are asking Heaven not for an extra division of soldiers but for that steadfastness of purpose which, united with that of our Sovereign, will triumph in the everlasting struggle against evil.

Next day, Aunt Emma and Pearl were busy cutting down an old black dress of Eleanor's to fit Elizabeth, and stitching *crêpe* arm-bands on all Mr Inglefell's suits. Henri had a loose one he could move from one coat to another. In the afternoon Pearl and Elizabeth went down to the shops to buy purple ribbon, but the shops had sold every yard of such material they had had in stock. Thousands of yards of light-coloured stuff had been sent away to the factories to be dyed. All the houses and shops were hung with black and purple. Flags were at half-mast. Portraits and photographs of the late King were displayed everywhere draped in black.

But far more expressive than these outward signs of national mourning were the emotions of the people. They stood silently in groups outside the newspaper offices waiting to read the latest cable messages from London posted from time to time on the hoardings. Some openly wept. A feeling of common calamity drew everyone together so that strangers in the streets and trains talked to each other and exchanged views in hushed voices.

'Who will be King now?' asked Elizabeth of her father. 'Oh, of course, the Prince of Wales. It will be queer to have a new King.'

'Do you remember him and Princess Mary when they were here in Australia? But perhaps you were too little, though it seems only a short time ago.'

Elizabeth wrinkled her brows in the effort of memory. 'I sort of remember you and Mummie going to a party, though I don't know if I really remember it or if you told me about it afterwards. Somehow it is all mixed up with the smell of ostrich feathers and a lot of shiny things.'

'Well, that shows what a queer thing memory is. Because your recollection of the ostrich feathers is quite right. She was wearing a very beautiful ostrich feather cape that night, and you were allowed to be in the room while she dressed. No doubt you played with the jewel-case. You always used to like that. It is now eight weeks since your mother and Eleanor left. Next week's mail-boat should bring their first letter from London.'

The expected letter, written by Eleanor, duly arived a week later. It was addressed to Elizabeth. It made no mention of the King's death, of course, as it had been written five weeks before, but it gave an account of their arrival, of their reception at Grandmother-in-England's London house, and of the new suit which had already been ordered for Eleanor at Bradley's.

'Listen, Daddy,' said Elizabeth importantly. She had never

received any letters with foreign stamps before and had greatly enjoyed the arrival of those from Colombo and Bombay and Marseilles. 'Listen, Daddy. Eleanor says that Grandmother-in-England has given her a pearl necklace but she is not going to be allowed to wear it until she goes to Court. Oh,' she exclaimed, looking up from the letter, 'will she be able to go now? Go to Court, I mean. Will King George and Queen Mary have presentations and garden parties and things?'

'Not until after the Coronation is over, of course, which will be next year, I suppose. In any case, we did not intend Eleanor to be presented until the Season after next. She has to be over a year at school and perhaps some time in Paris, if your mother can find someone suitable to take her.'

Reassured, Elizabeth went back to the letter.

'"Who do you think was here to meet us?"' she read out. '"Captain Ross-Bossingham, only he's a lord now and has got rather fat. He brought me an enormous box of chocolates and Mummy some lovely flowers all done up with silver lace, and is going to take us to the opera next week. He brought Grandmother Munt a huge piece of Scotch beef from his farm in Scotland. We had it for dinner last night and it was wonderful but he said the best beef he ever tasted was some of ours from Undaboo. Tell Daddy."'

Something in her father's stillness and unresponsiveness made Elizabeth hurry on with the rest of the letter almost nervously. A heightened sensitivity, part of the mysterious process of growing up, had warned her that here was a thin patch in the emotional ice. Afterwards, when she was by herself, she puzzled over it. Unbidden, elusively, out of the mists of memory, came a dream she had once had, of a moonlit garden with far-away music and her mother's voice saying: 'I think it is cooler here.' Could it have been Ross-Bossingham's voice which had exclaimed with such passionate tenderness: 'Oh, my dear, my dearest dear!' Was it a dream or had it really happened?

Mrs Inglefell, looking younger and happier, came back from England in September. Wonderful presents were unpacked from the trunks: Liberty silk dresses for Elizabeth and Marian, tortoise-shell brushes and combs and a Japanese silk dressing-gown from Ceylon for Mrs Thompson and Pearl, a truly magnificent set of pipes for Uncle Thomas and a tailored over-coat for Aunt Emma with elaborate braidings across the front, the very pink of fashion. Fine cambric shirts, silk pyjamas, and a twilled silk dressing-gown were Alfred's portion. But perhaps more exciting than all these were the things sent by Grand-mother Munt. Three great packing-cases full of linen, heavily embroidered with the family initials and coats of arms, of a quality to make Miss Una say: 'I've never seen anything like it,' and Mrs Thompson exclaim: 'The responsibility of washing it would be the death of me.'

Mrs Inglefell was amused. 'My mother says that I have three daughters and this must be part of their wedding linen.'

Two more boxes contained family silver, also initialled and crested, and yet another two with a magnificent Sèvres dessert service and two tea-sets of old Staffordshire.

Alfred looked at all these treasures as they came to light from their straw and tissues.

'Well, my love, you seem to have carried out a fairly success-ful expedition.' His wife laughed happily, in itself so rare a happening as to make him feel that six months' absence was almost worth it.

'This time I took everything that Mother offered me,' she admitted, 'and even made a few suggestions myself. After all, she is right. The three girls will soon be growing up and needing such things. It was a good opportunity to bring them.'

The following year Marian went to England to join her sister at school, but Mrs Inglefell did not accompany her. In June, 1912, Eleanor was presented at Court by Lady Munt and after-wards went to Scotland for a month to stay with Ross-Bossingham's sister, the Hon. Mrs Ross Graver. In October she came back to Australia.

At first Elizabeth scarcely recognised this elegant young woman as her sister Eleanor. She was thinner and bore herself with a graceful assurance that showed to advantage the simple and well-designed clothes she was wearing. When she began to speak, Elizabeth went into peals of laughter.

'Oh, Ellie, what a lark! You've learnt to speak all Englishy and what Pearl would call "la-di-da".'

Eleanor was not in the least dismayed. 'And you, my dear Beth, talk with a truly atrocious Australian accent,' a remark which did no more than express the truth. For however we may wish to dissociate ourselves from the controversy that rages round the question of the King's (and in our case, Queen's) English as it is spoken in these our two beloved countries, it cannot be denied that a young lady who has just returned from more than two years in an exclusive English boarding-school and one who has lived all her life in Australia will speak with widely differing intonations.

Elizabeth had followed her two sisters to the Young Ladies' Church of England College, but only for part of the week. On the other days she attended the Conservatorium of Music where she was studying voice production, the theory of music, French and Italian, musical composition and the history of the opera, as well as having piano lessons. Mr Breve had been as good as his word and had arrived one evening, unannounced, to call on Mr Inglefell who was not a little astonished and perhaps not entirely pleased to learn from a renowned authority that his youngest daughter had a singing voice of unusual quality. His attitude, if not his spoken words, could be summarised by the query: 'Well, what in the world can we do about it?'

'I assure you, sir,' Mr Breve had continued emphatically, 'that to allow such a voice to remain untrained or to be ruined in the training would be a tragedy. Yes, sir, a tragedy, I repeat.'

As Alfred Inglefell was a man who never despised dis-

interested advice offered to him on a subject by someone who
knew more about it than he did, and as in any case he disliked
tragedies, he agreed to the necessary modifications in Elizabeth's education and reinforced with parental authority the
injunction uttered by Mr Breve forbidding her to sing. 'Above
all,' urged that gentleman, 'don't let her take singing lessons
from that Madame Catterwaul, as I call her, who has to my
knowledge ruined more good voices than enough. Yes, sir, I
repeat, ruined.'

Elizabeth enjoyed it all and more especially the unofficial
lessons she received from Mr Breve himself when she went to
see him on Saturdays or Sunday afternoons or during the
holidays. At first he was in despair at her piano-playing and
threatened to tie up her wrists to strings suspended from the
ceiling. More than once he resorted to a ruler brought with
painful force under the forearm. 'Keep those elbows and wrists
up,' he would shout, glaring at her from under the overhanging
brush of his eyebrows. 'Weight from the shoulders and back,
speed from the fingers, lightness from the wrists. Watch the
pipers running across the sand. Their feet scarcely touch the
ground and they move like lightning because they suspend the
weight of their bodies from their wings. Use your wrists and
arms to lift all the weight of your hands. Then your fingers
will be free to run like lightning over the keys. When you want
weight for the big chords *fortissimo*, it should come from the
whole length of your arm with the strength of your back and
shoulders behind it. Playing the piano is very like golf. Do you
play that repulsive game?'

In the cool of the late afternoon after the lessons and the
arguments were over, they would go into the garden where
Elizabeth with considerable skill would manœuvre Mr Breve
into a basket chair while she dragged the hoses round and set
the sprinklers to work on the lawns, fitting the watering-cans
with hair-sprays for the seedlings still too young and tender for
the hose, and doing any jobs that required the stooping that

Mr Breve's ageing back was now beginning to protest about.

Sometimes, if the weather were hot, Mr Breve's housekeeper, Mrs Porter, would bring a big jug of lemonade and put it on the table under the loquat tree; sometimes, if the weather were cold and wet, Elizabeth would stay to tea which they would have by the open fire, toasting their bread on long wire forks held out to the glowing coals while Mr Breve would recount endless stories of the older Rubinstein, of Kubelik, of Clara Butt and Adelina Patti, great gala nights at the Scala and seasons at Bayreuth and Salzburg.

But generally, when the garden work was done, Elizabeth would ride home on her bicycle with nothing more in her head than a desire for the biggest possible tea that Mrs Thompson could provide.

20

The Ball, 1913

ELIZABETH was singing at the top of her voice: 'Bee-*coz* God made thee mine, I'll cherish *thee-ee.*'

Mrs Inglefell came into the nursery schoolroom which Elizabeth now used as her workshop. She had covered the table with books and papers and was copying something into a large black exercise book.

'Ought you to be doing that?' asked her mother.

'No,' said Elizabeth. She threw down her pencil. 'But, oh Mums, sometimes I feel that if I don't sing I shall burst. All those voice production exercises we do at the Conserv. are all very well, but they don't let off any steam. Brevie says it's not my voice he's frightened of, it's the teachers. He thinks they'll get me into bad habits and get my voice wrongly placed. He says yelling on the beach and cheering at football matches is all right because it's just using the voice naturally. So I thought singing "Because" is pretty much the same as barracking for Saints to win the football.'

Mrs Inglefell laughed. 'It was certainly loud enough. And no doubt the team would be much encouraged to know that you cherished them.'

'Henri says that St George's have a jolly good chance of winning this year. Mummie, do you think I could have a proper evening dress for Sarah's party? I'm sick of that old muslin of Ellie's.'

With a faint sigh, Mrs Inglefell paid involuntary tribute to the passing years. To hear her youngest daughter, aged sixteen, asking for a grown-up evening dress was to realise that in another year all her chicks would be flown and youth would have said good-bye to the family until brought back by the first grandchildren. She hesitated. 'It's the penalty for being the youngest, Beth. You can't help coming in for Ellie's and Marian's left-overs. And I didn't want to buy you a new one because of having to get so many new things for next year – if you really are going to Italy. I can't help wishing you were going to Paris. Marian and Sarah both say that school is excellent. You could stay at the school and have your music lessons from there, couldn't you?'

Over Elizabeth's face swept that expression of patient suffering which parents so often bring to the faces of the younger and wiser generation. How could she explain to this dearest but stupidest of mothers that here was no question of 'music lessons', but rather of living a passionately dedicated life to a Great Cause.

'Well, you see, Mummie,' she explained patiently, 'Brevie says that only the Italian method will do my voice justice. I think he would have liked to send me to Germany because he has so many friends there. But he says no, it must be Milan. And if I had a new evening dress now –' reverting firmly to the subject in hand '– I could save it up for next year. We could leave the seams wide so that it could be let out. I dare say I'll expand a bit.' Elizabeth drew a mighty breath and smote herself violently on the chest. As generally happened, Mrs Inglefell felt herself defeated – not convinced – merely defeated, by Elizabeth's physical vitality.

'I can't think how I came to have such a daughter,' she lamented to herself. 'She is so dreadfully energetic. She flings herself so whole-heartedly into whatever captures her interest or loyalty. Her life will be one long procession of burnt boats.'

These thoughts came to her with troubling frequency now

that her youngest daughter was pluming her wings for flight into the world. The world could be very cruel to a spirit so eager, so unrestrained. Broken wings could result from so swift a flight, a broken heart from feelings so ardent and unbounded. Mrs Inglefell was not a particularly religious woman but she found herself praying often these days for the safety of this young life and the promise of its brilliant, uncertain future.

The party for which Elizabeth wanted her dress was being given by Mr and Mrs Faulkener for their eldest daughter, Sarah, who had returned from her finishing school in Paris. On the voyage back to Australia she had met a man named Charles McGallun and had fallen in love with him. Mr and Mrs Faulkener had approved of their daughter's wish to accept his proposal of marriage. He owned a station called Paraparlinga, the homestead of which was only a hundred and fifty miles from Undaboo. He could therefore be thought of as a near neighbour of good friends. Moreover, he was of solid Scottish stock, well-to-do in that unobtrusive way which believes in plain living, detests ostentation, has a good opinion of itself and no debts. Sarah would spend her life in a ramshackle house, in a climate which froze the water-pipes in winter and climbed to summer temperatures of 120 degrees Fahrenheit in the shade. She would see no white women for months at a time. She would cook for thirty or forty men in the shearing season. She would ride with her husband to inspect dams and fences. Her nearest white neighbour would be sixty miles away; her Paris dresses would lie in their boxes till eaten by cockroaches and silverfish; her fine complexion would grow tan red and leathery with the fierce winds and sun; her soft hands would be chapped and calloused with hard work; but she would be a happy wife, a good mother, a fine woman. Yes, Mr and Mrs Faulkener approved her choice.

Generally, the parties given for the young people took place in the summer so that lawns and verandas could be used for dancing and games. But this was to be a proper ball, in the middle of the winter season. The ballroom had been extended by the erection of a large marquee and one of the big verandas had been entirely enclosed by canvas curtains and banks of ferns to make a 'sitting-out' place.

Elizabeth's new dress was of very pale blue silk with a bouffant skirt reaching to her calves, what a later generation would describe as 'long ballerina'. She had begged to be allowed to go into really long skirts and to 'put up her hair'. But Mrs Inglefell had demurred. 'You are not really "out" yet, my darling. It wouldn't be suitable. Next year, before you leave for Italy, we will give a dance specially for your début, and perhaps as a welcome-home for Marian. Then you can have a real ball-gown and put your hair up. But this time you can plait it and pin it up on top, and I'll fix a bow of satin ribbon at the back.'

Actually, when it was finished, the dress was nearly ankle-length, owing to the kindly co-operation of the dressmaker who, in response to hideous grimaces from Elizabeth, the purposes of which were unmistakable, had turned up the hem an inch less than the length indicated by Mrs Inglefell. With the same kind-heartedness (or perhaps weakness in the face of forces stronger than herself: 'Don't you dare leave it like that or I shall call down upon you the Curse of the Inglefells which causes you to come out in a rash of pins and needles every third Sunday after Whitsun') Miss Stitchaway, in imminent danger of being choked by pins and needles even before the third Sunday after Whitsun, had cut out the necklines of the dress just a little more than Mrs Inglefell would have approved and, instead of the usual Peter Pan collar, had embroidered it with tiny pink silk rose-buds. Altogether, it was a very pretty dress, but not in accordance with Elizabeth's present mood of sophistication.

Eleanor was to wear one of the gowns she had brought back from London. It would be quite in the latest fashion, for the winter modes which prevailed in Paris and London must wait six months before being displayed in Adelaide and Melbourne, an unexpected result of the earth being global in shape and travelling round the sun and turning on its axis and performing those other rituals of cosmic behaviour which provide a common ground of discussion between the astronomers and the designers of the *haute couture*.

Eleanor had become a handsome woman, with a self-assurance and composure which Elizabeth envied but could not emulate. Young men were admiring but somewhat in awe, and so far had been content to worship from afar.

The evening of the ball came, cold and clear. When she saw herself in the long mirror in her mother's room, Elizabeth was quite astonished at her own appearance. Between them, she and Miss Stitchaway had converted her tall figure, inclined to be angular, with movements more impetuous than graceful, into something approaching elegance. Mrs Inglefell came into the room while she was twisting and turning in front of the glass.

'Really, I believe you have grown another inch since I saw you last,' she exclaimed with her 'private' laugh which Elizabeth always loved. 'Look, I have brought you something for your neck,' and she slipped over Elizabeth's head a long string of moonstones. 'We bought them in Colombo on our way out, and I've been saving them for you.'

The little drops of blue moonlight glistened against the blue of the silk and Elizabeth was so enchanted by them that she did not envy even Eleanor, who was wearing Grandmother-in-England's pearls.

Finch, too, had done justice to the evening's importance by brushing his half-topper and putting on the most sporting of his jackets. After all, he was going to spend the evening with Cox, Mrs Faulkener's coachman, who wore patent-leather half-Wellingtons with cream breeches, and had brass buttons on his jacket. Mrs Faulkener always drove in an open victoria with two horses. This carriage had little steps that folded up at the sides and had to be opened out like a concertina when she wished to alight. It was lined with grey felt and had a silver trumpet vase above the seat into which Cox always put two carnations whenever he was driving his lady abroad. As an ambassador's flag signifies the presence of the nation's envoy, so the two carnations were the sign that Mrs Faulkener and none other was using the victoria.

Finch could not rise to these august heights, but he gave his horses an extra grooming and washed and polished the wagonette till he felt himself to be reasonably safe from any criticism of a professional nature that Cox might be constrained to express.

When the wagonette drew up at the front door, Pearl came out of the house with an armful of rugs which she placed on the seats. At last the great moment had arrived. Mrs Inglefell, her gown covered by a fur cloak, entered the vehicle, followed by Eleanor and her father. Elizabeth found herself to be so nervously excited that she dropped one of her gloves on the gravel whence it was retrieved by Pearl who carried it back to the hall to examine it under the lamp for dirt marks before she would allow Elizabeth to have it.

'I feel very peculiar,' said Elizabeth suddenly, as they were driving through the quiet streets of the town.

'I hope you aren't going to be sick,' rejoined Eleanor, with elder-sisterly lack of sympathy.

'No, I don't think so, although I have got a squeezed-up feeling in my tummy. It's an important sort of feeling.'

'This is an important occasion,' said her mother. 'It is your first grown-up dance.'

When the wagonette came up to the porch with the Corinthian columns, Elizabeth remembered the first time that she had paid a visit to this house with her mother, how quiet it had been and how they had waited for the door to be opened. Tonight they did not wait at all, for the door stood open and the front hall was crowded with people in evening dress, taking off coats and furs and saying 'How do you do' to each other. Prissy took them upstairs to one of the bedrooms which had been transformed into a ladies' cloakroom.

'I wonder who sleeps in here,' Elizabeth remarked, peeping into a wardrobe to see if she could find any clothes she recognised.

'Don't be inquisitive, dear,' said her mother. 'Take off your coat, put on your gloves and come here while I fix your hair. I think the bow would look nicer if it were a little higher.'

Elizabeth waited impatiently, wriggling about under her mother's ministering hands. She was longing to go downstairs to see the ballroom.

Mr and Mrs Faulkener were receiving their guests in the drawing-room, with Sarah and Charles (because the party was to celebrate their engagement) and Malcolm (because the party was also a farewell to him before he left for Oxford). From the drawing-room the guests went on to the ballroom, a room which reflected the social ambitions of an earlier generation, with its gilded archways, crystal chandeliers and miniature stage. A waiter was standing at the door holding a tray on which were piles of little pink and blue cards, each with a tiny blue or pink pencil tied to it by a silk cord. Elizabeth accepted one of the pink programmes and looked doubtfully at the gold printing on it. Eleanor had a whole bunch of these trifles hanging from the mantelpiece in her bedroom at home, representing the dances she had been to that season.

When Elizabeth looked about her at the groups of young people laughing and talking in the ballroom, she found that she knew hardly anyone there. She was sure that no one would want to dance with her. None of those young gentlemen in black broadcloth and butterfly white ties would want to write his name in her programme. Suddenly all her eager anticipation turned to misery. She could play better cricket than Malcolm. She could swim better than Henri. She could sing better than Eleanor and quote Browning much better than

Alistair. But these accomplishments were all at once of no importance at all, compared with that social grace which enabled Eleanor and Sarah and Cecilia and Nancy and their friends to laugh and chatter together, to share jokes, and to hand their programmes over with just the right mixture of readiness and indifference for the young men to write their names against the dances they wished to claim. Elizabeth looked at the girls in their lovely ball-gowns and felt herself nothing but an awkward schoolgirl in a home-made dress. She wished she could sink through the floor. She wished the roof would fall in. She wished some cosmic calamity would happen so that she need no longer stand here by herself feeling a positive fool. (Whatever had made her look forward to this beastly dance?) This mood of gloom was interrupted by her father, who, taking her programme out of her limp hand, wrote his name on the line which said: 'Third Dance. The Lancers.'

'I must dance the first one with your mother and the second one with our hostess. But you must save me the Lancers, my dear. You mustn't allow the young men to rob me of my daughter at her very first ball.'

Elizabeth smiled feebly and thought what a darling Daddy was, but she went on feeling miserable. A few minutes later Mr Inglefell brought up a young man whom he introduced as Robert Placker, a clerk in Mr Inglefell's city office. He asked Elizabeth for the pleasure of a dance in a rather dutiful voice and when she handed him her programme and he wrote his name in it, Elizabeth was sure he did it only because Mr Inglefell had threatened him with instant dismissal from his position in the office if he didn't. It may be added at once that when he found that the boss's schoolgirl daughter was a very good dancer, and when she found that he was an enthusiastic fisherman, they got on very well.

Elizabeth looked at her programme. Certainly the two entries had done something to make it less forlornly empty. But now the ballroom was rapidly filling up with people and the band had begun to tune its violins and prop up its music on the spindly brass music-stands. Elizabeth in her corner found herself hemmed in by the crowd, surrounded by people whom she did not know. She was just deciding desperately that it would be much better to go home (she could pretend to be ill. How lucky that she had mentioned that queer feeling her tummy on the way here!) when someone took the programme out of her hand. It was Henri. He had just left school, having stayed over the summer term to play cricket for his school. He was now working in Mr Faulkener's office.

'Cheer up, Beth. You promised to save me at least two dances and a third if you can spare it –' he wrote them in '– and here's Kevin Lang; he's just left school too, and was Captain of the School Eleven. I promised him a dance with you.'

Elizabeth's programme was now beginning to look quite respectably filled and she cheered up a little. Kevin was pleased when she burst out with an obviously sincere and well-informed speech about the innings he had played against Prince Albert House in the last cricket match. He wrote his name in her programme once and then asked, almost shyly, if he could have a second dance. Elizabeth began to feel quite grown-up as she graciously conceded him this favour.

Now the orchestra struck up the first dance. People moved away from the dance-floor to the edges of the room to make way for the host and hostess to open the ball. There were hurried claimings of partners and last-minute programme adjustments. Elizabeth could see Cecilia Goldiway, who had become a very pretty girl, looking on in a laughingly indifferent manner while three young men argued heatedly as to who had the prior right to put his name against the fifth, sixth and seventh 'extras' at the end of her over-full programme.

No one had asked Elizabeth for the first dance, so she could only stand against the wall and watch, as Mr Faulkener led his wife on to the dance-floor and the ball began. She felt herself seized by the arms and pulled on to the dance-floor. Malcolm's voice said: 'Sorry I'm late. Had to welcome the last guest even though I could hear the loud bassoon.' Elizabeth giggled. She was no longer in the least miserable. It did not matter that her dress was rather schoolgirlish and that her hair was not really 'up'. She was dancing at a real ball and her programme was more than half full. She was only thankful that Providence, wiser that she, had ignored her prayers for the earth to open and swallow her up, and for the roof to fall in. Malcolm had guided her skilfully on the polished floor, (much slipperier than that of the Institute hall where they had all had dancing lessons every winter). When the dance was over, he led her to a corner of the room and tugged at the programme which dangled from her little finger. She surrendered it with a return of her self-conscious shyness.

'Tut, tut, you've left practically nothing for me,' said Malcolm, rapidly writing his name in several places. Elizabeth looked over his shoulder.

'But, Malcolm,' she protested, a little breathless, 'that's the supper dance.'

'Certainly. Must see that you don't make a pig of yourself, or alternatively, starve to death on the door-mat.'

Elizabeth blushed, a most unusual experience for her. Everyone knew that people danced the supper dance only with other people they were in love with, or engaged to, or had other very special and serious obligations to. Of course, she and Malcolm weren't in love with each other and would never be engaged or anything like that, so she could only imagine that he was asking for the supper dance because he was sorry for her and was trying to be a considerate host, because Malcolm was very gentlemanly in his behaviour, one had to admit, even though he could be so horrible and she hated him. Perhaps it was just as well that this confused train of thought was interrupted by a newcomer, a tall man, some years older than Malcolm, who now addressed her.

'I say, aren't you Elizabeth Inglefell?'

Elizabeth looked at this athletic stranger and recognised her past ally and champion, Luke Stevens. Quite forgetting her newly-acquired status as a grown-up young lady, she let a little shriek escape her.

'Luke! Wherever have you been? I'd quite forgotten you . . . at least . . . I'm sorry, but I mean I haven't seen you for ages.'

Luke laughed. 'No. My people moved away to another suburb about four years ago, and I've been doing an engineering course at the university.'

They exchanged hurried items of news until the music for the second dance began. Luke then asked for her programme, saying: 'I don't suppose you've anything left by now,' but found an empty place and wrote in his name. Then Charles McGallun came to ask for a dance and had to be content with an 'extra', written after the last of the numbered dances printed on the card. Elizabeth was certain then that her first ball was going to be a success. Every girl who had to write 'extras' at the end of her card was a social success.

Charles was accompanied by an elderly gentleman whom he introduced as his father, a tall, broad-shouldered, weather-beaten man with a heavy cavalry moustache and small, shrewd, bright eyes. Though he was wearing evening dress clothes of old-fashioned style that were much too small for him and decidedly shabby, he managed to be impressive and, to Elizabeth, rather frightening. He ignored the young man who had come to claim Elizabeth for the dance, and kept her in conversation.

'They tell me you sing very well, young lady.'

'Oh, not yet. But I'm going to Italy next year to study.'

'That's right. Delighted to hear it. Nothing I enjoy more than a woman singing well. Most of 'em out here don't know the rudiments. Can't stand this drivelling nonsense half of 'em sing. Give me a good operatic soprano every time. But you don't get good opera in Adelaide, more's the pity. Tell you what, young lady, when you make your debut at the Scala, I'll come to hear you. That's a promise.'

Elizabeth laughed. She felt that it was a fairly safe promise to make, but she was flattered, all the same.

'Gosh,' said her youthful escort, as they finally began the one-step, which was already half over, 'you must be able to sing jolly well if old Mr McGallun says so. He's a tartar. My dad says he's the toughest business-man in the State and the richest. Is that his son who is engaged to Sarah Faulkener?'

Sitting on the narrow gilded chairs along the walls of the ball-room were a number of elderly ladies who had come to the ball as chaperones to the girls. Among them Elizabeth noticed Mrs Wingham-Smith and her sister, Miss Gladys Merriman. Poor Miss Merriman! Her dreams of making an advantageous marriage, of living in England, of bearing a title and of a pre-sentation at Court had proved to be dreams and nothing more. The passing years had left her as handsome as ever, though her figure was perhaps a trifle more unyielding, her facial ex-pression more severe and her complexion a little more deter-minedly bright than when last we met her. Her younger sister, Dorothy, had married that cheerful Mr Wingham-Smith and had presented him with two little girls. She had lost her looks and was now of comfortable figure and uncomfortable temper, with a tendency to complaints and self-pity which made her husband a good deal more cheerful abroad than he was at home.

In the smoking-room, the elderly gentlemen had settled down to whist and cribbage. A pleasant aroma of expensive cigar smoke filled the air. Mr Goldiway was at his most expansive. He won several games, so increasing his self-importance. When the rubbers were completed, he threw himself back in his leather chair and patted his white, stiffly-starched waistcoat with its mother-of-pearl buttons, rather too large for good taste. He had an air of condescending satisfaction, as much as to say: 'There, I have amused the children and shown them how to play this game.'

'Nice house you have here, Faulkener,' he said, looking round at the solid furnishings, the thick Turkey rugs, the gilded pictures, the bronze statuettes on the mantelpiece. 'Must have cost you a pretty penny.'

'As a matter of fact, I inherited it from my uncle,' replied his host, in a brusque tone. He was not accustomed to having his guests remark on what he had paid for his possessions. What an odious bounder this Goldiway was! Mr Inglefell was annoyed with his business partner. An amiable man himself, he had never objected to Goldiway's ignorance of the finer forms of social good manners, and had, to his satisfaction, noticed that he had improved in the last few years. No fool, he had realised that if his social ambitions were to be realised, he must learn, at any rate superficially, the ways of polite society. But tonight he had dined very well, he had won several card games, he had drunk several glasses of his host's excellent port wine, and now was in the mood to patronise the world.

'I see you are still keeping up your horses,' he went on, turning again to Mr Faulkener. 'I have just bought a Vauxhall motor-car. In my opinion it's only a matter of two or three years and there won't be a horse left on the roads. These new motors will be all the thing, mark my words.'

'Nasty, vulgar things,' growled Mr Faulkener. 'Wouldn't have one at any price.'

Mr Goldiway was in no way cast down. 'What sort of season have you had?' he asked next of Mr McGallun. The older man glared at him.

'No doubt the weather reports would provide you with this information,' he replied cuttingly. Mr Faulkener stirred uneasily and cleared his throat. Heaven knew, the man was a bounder, but he was a guest in the house and if old McGallun really took him up, there might be an unpleasant situation. But he need not have worried. Mr Goldiway was impervious to any implied snub.

'We've had a very good offer for Station Downs,' he said. 'I tell Inglefell we oughtn't to sell. If the drought continues it will be invaluable for stock coming down from the north. You'll all be coming to us for accommodation.' He laughed contentedly and patted his waistcoat again. Every pastoralist in the room silently vowed that his stock could die of thirst before he asked agistment from Goldiway.

Mr Faulkener rose. 'Supper must be about ready,' he said. 'No doubt you gentlemen would like something to eat. I must find my wife.'

The smoking-room party broke up. When Malcolm was taking Elizabeth into supper, they passed Mr McGallun standing, a solitary figure, in the hall. He beckoned Malcolm.

'Tell me, my boy,' he said, in what he imagined to be a confidential tone of voice, which boomed through the hall like a fog-horn, 'tell me, my boy, who is that lady standing on the other side of the ballroom talking to the short lady in the blue dress?'

Following his glance through the gilded archway, Malcolm replied that he thought it was Miss Gladys Merriman. 'Isn't it, Beth? You know her better than I do. Or is that Mrs Wingham-Smith?'

'No, the lady in the blue dress is Mrs Wingham-Smith. The tall, dark one is her sister, Gladys.'

'Dashed fine figger of a woman,' boomed Mr McGallun. 'Like you to present me, my boy. Excuse us, m' dear,' he added, turning to Elizabeth, 'won't keep your young man more than a couple of minutes.'

He and Malcolm turned back to the ballroom, and Elizabeth watched through the gilded archway while the introduction was made. Ten minutes later, when Malcolm had rejoined her and they were drinking hot soup out of cups and deciding whether they would have roast turkey or cold galantine of chicken to follow, she saw Mr McGallun escorting Mrs Wingham-Smith and her sister to the supper-room and bow-

ing them to their seats with old-fashioned ceremony. Presently
they were joined by Mr Wingham-Smith (who had been lavish-
ing some of his cheerfulness on the other gentlemen in the
smoking-room) and a further introduction took place. The little
group settled down to a convivial supper at which the formidable Mr McGallun was evidently setting out to make himself
agreeable, for there were bursts of laughter from time to time,
Mrs Wingham-Smith forgot to make acid remarks to her husband, Mr Wingham-Smith became more cheerful than ever,
and Miss Gladys Merriman looked younger and younger, her
colour, heightened above even its usual fixity, giving evidence
of her enjoyment of the stories and anecdotes provided by this
new and unexpected acquaintance.

Malcolm was much too polite to make any remark to Elizabeth about the part he had been asked to play in this little
comedy, but catching her glance as it strayed to the group at
the other table, he began to laugh, and in a few seconds they
were choking in the grip of one of those giggling fits which are
more likely to afflict one in church at the age of ten. This quite
destroyed, for the time being, Elizabeth's vision of herself as an
experienced, rather blasé woman of the world, and she and
Malcolm resumed their more usual conversational method of
thrust and parry.

'When you are at that dull Oxford place, I shall be in
wonderful Milan, singing all day and going to the opera every
night.'

'That'll be nice for Milan,' retorted Malcolm. 'More likely to
be eating spaghetti in some third-rate pensione that reeks of
garlic,' he added unromantically.

'Oh,' exclaimed Elizabeth, suddenly deflated, 'I forgot about
garlic. Is it so awful?'

'Frightful. And they eat it with every meal and extra on
Sundays.'

'Oh, Malcolm, you are a hound! You're only trailing bait, I
know you are.'

'Hounds don't trail bait. They follow scent – in this case, jolly strong scent, believe me.'

'Well, I don't believe you. You're only pulling my leg, you deceiver.'

Malcolm stabbed delicately at a piece of turkey with his fork.

'I was going to suggest that I could come and visit you in the vacations, but the thought of garlic puts me off. You'd better come to England, instead, but don't forget to go into quarantine for a couple of weeks' thorough de-garlicising. I can't have the pure atmosphere of Oxford sullied by the effluvia of low acquaintances . . .'

Elizabeth looked helplessly at the crowded room, at the evening dress, the banks of flowers, the glittering chandeliers, the tables sparkling with candles and the rich profusion of food, and she felt herself strategically outwitted. On the beach she would long ago have settled this argument by mortal combat; in this splendid supper-room the restraints of civilisation were too much for her. There were evidently some drawbacks to growing up, after all.

After supper she had engaged to dance with Luke Stevens. Perhaps it was only because she had not seen him for several years that he seemed to have changed so much. He appeared older than his twenty-one years, though whether because he had become so tall and broadshouldered or because he had worked so hard – for his family were poor and he had had to spend his vacations and his leisure hours in earning enough money to supplement his university scholarship funds – she did not know. She only knew that while this was undoubtedly the Luke who had fought so valiantly on her behalf and had lent her his handkerchief, he was also a stranger, not a boy, but a man, older, more experienced, a part of that adult world outside her own life that she had yet to enter.

While they were dancing, Malcolm had kept up an uninterrupted stream of nonsensical conversation addressed in a murmuring voice to her right ear. Luke danced in silence, and as they swung together in the rhythm of the waltz, Elizabeth was, for the first time, caught by the enchantment of dancing with someone whose steps were so perfectly matched with her own that she lost all sense of her own identity; she and Luke were one, with no other existence or being beyond the beat of the music and the rhythmic movement of their own bodies.

When the dance was over, it was as though she had to return from a distant place. Luke slipped a hand under her elbow and led her to the marquee which had been erected over the lawn beyond the french windows of the ballroom. He collected some glasses of lemonade from a buffet near at hand, and they settled themselves on a sofa partly screened by a row of palms and ferns.

Luke stretched out his long legs and said decisively: 'Now, tell me everything that has happened since I last saw you. Have you been having any more fights?'

'Oh yes,' said Elizabeth, and told him about Mr Breve and her plans for Italy.

'Well, you are an extraordinary kid. I might have known by the way you fell out of that tree that day that you wouldn't do anything like anyone else.'

'Oh, I don't know. No one does anything like anyone else. When you come to think of it, everyone is different from everyone else.'

Luke didn't agree, but, as she discovered later, he generally argued in silence.

'Now you tell me what you have been doing.'

So Luke spoke a little about his life at the university and of his hopes for qualifying as an engineer after another year of study and then joining a well-known firm of engineers.

The music for the next dance was beginning, so they left their chairs and strolled back to the ballroom.

'I say,' exclaimed Luke, 'who is that stunning girl standing over there? Do you know her?'

Elizabeth looked in the direction he indicated. She laughed.

'Goodness, yes. That's my sister Eleanor. Do you want to meet her?'

At two o'clock in the morning, when the last of the 'extras' had been danced and a final polka had been romped round the room, and the band had played 'God Save the King' and everyone had said 'Good night, but it's really good morning' to everyone else, and thanked their host and hostess for a wonderful evening; when the carriages and wagonettes and one or two motor-cars had driven up to the Corinthian porch and coats and furs had been donned and rugs had been spread (for the night had become very cold and a misty rain had begun to fall), Elizabeth did not feel at all tired and would have been willing to go on dancing until the dawn. But no sooner had the rugs been tucked in and the little door of the wagonette been slammed and the horses had begun to trot briskly and willingly homeward, then she fell asleep on her father's shoulder and had to be well shaken before she could be induced to get out of the cab at her own front door.

21

The Return of the Goddess, 1914

T H A T summer everyone played tennis. Mr Inglefell had had a court built in the field behind the shrubbery, and here, every Saturday and Sunday, the young people gathered to play in singles and doubles, drink quantities of iced lemon squash, and engage in those mild flirtations which make life so interesting between the ages of sixteen and sixty.

Luke had formed the habit of coming on Saturdays to play tennis. He had invited Eleanor to the university ball in August, to the Tennis Club ball in September, and to an afternoon performance by Ada Reeve at the Theatre Royal in October. When the heat began in November, everyone was too busy with end-of-year examinations to have parties, but after the New Year he invited Eleanor to go to a river picnic. Mrs. Inglefell gave her permission when Luke explained that there would be ten or twelve young people in the party and they would be chaperoned by the mother of 'one of the other chaps', a lady with whom Mrs Inglefell was acquainted.

Elizabeth, of course, was used to Eleanor receiving invitations in which she was not included. But as she watched them drive away together in Luke's little motor-car, she could not help feeling envious. A river picnic sounded so very romantic, and, after all, it was not Eleanor who had fallen out of the Moreton Bay fig tree that time. Eleanor had never climbed a tree in her life. When on her return Elizabeth asked her how she had enjoyed the picnic, she sounded rather unenthusiastic.

'The mosquitoes were awful,' she said, 'and Luke does nothing but talk about machinery.'

The next day, Sunday, Luke came again, bringing his tennis racquet. It was a gruelling day and Eleanor refused to play tennis, saying that it was much too hot. So he played two sets with Elizabeth before admitting that perhaps it really was too hot. They lay on the lawn in the shade of the little summer-house, sipping their lemon squash.

'I'm afraid your sister doesn't like me much,' said Luke rue-fully. 'I asked her to a tango tea and she wouldn't come. Doesn't she approve of the tango?'

'Oh, I expect she does. It's just that she's been away for so long that she's out of touch with our crowd.'

'Yes, I suppose so. She's been used to mixing with all those important people in England. Gosh, Beth, she's wonderful. I've never met a girl like her. She sort of makes the rest of us look second-rate, doesn't she?'

Elizabeth considered this carefully. It was a new view of her sister Ellie, but she had to admit that it had something apt about it. It was not only all those London clothes she had brought back with her, it was something cool and self-possessed in her own personality that set her apart from the other young people of their circle.

'I tell you what,' said Elizabeth, sitting up abruptly, 'it's no good you expecting Ellie to like talking about things as we do.'

Luke accepted this advice with grateful humility. 'But what can I talk to her about? I don't know any of the things she likes.'

'You let her do the talking,' was Elizabeth's good counsel.

But even this was unfruitful. Saturday after Saturday came and went, but, except for a few games of tennis, Eleanor showed no disposition to spend her time in Luke's company.

February and March brought no change from the heat. Week followed week without rain. The gardens lay parched and shrivelled. April came with cloudy weather and a few showers. Everyone looked hopefully at the sky, but the clouds were high and pale. And so autumn came and winter, with no real relief from the drought.

Coming into the house one evening in June, Elizabeth found her parents deep in conversation together, or rather her father was talking while Mrs Inglefell listened in silence. He was looking worried, thinner and older.

'I don't like it,' he was saying. 'Undaboo is nothing but a dust-heap. Our position with the bank is fairly sound at present. But it's next year I am worried about. We'll get nothing off the place, not a penny.' He was walking restlessly about the room as he spoke. 'Tatiara we'll have to let go. I'll concentrate everything on saving Undaboo. Station Downs is a help. Thank goodness we brought a lot of stock down three months ago. It's too late to move them now. Even those that are still alive are too weak to travel. Goldiway had some idea of selling Station Downs a few months back. It's just as well we didn't. If this goes on much longer it might be the only thing we can save out of the wreck.'

'Do you mean,' asked Elizabeth, 'that we're going to lose all our money?'

'Oh, hullo, Beth. I didn't know you'd come in. No, not all, my dear. But that for a few years everyone in South Australia is going to be much poorer than they have been, I think there is no doubt. This is the worst drought the State has ever experienced.'

Mrs Inglefell still sat in silence. She, too, was looking paler and thinner. The fine sewing she was generally busy with lay neglected on the table beside her. Now she spoke with some decision.

'Well, Alfred, I have an idea. You say you have done everything possible, and if you stay on, you will only worry yourself half to death with affairs you can do nothing to cure. I think that you should come to Europe with us in September. I dare say you could get a cabin, as it is out of season. You haven't been abroad for nearly twenty years. It is time you had a holiday.'

'Oh, Daddy, do come. It would be wonderful.' Elizabeth was delighted with the idea.

'Impossible, my dears, quite impossible, much as I should enjoy it. As it is, we must do what we can to keep down expenses. As things are going, there can be no question of an extra passage to Europe.'

'But, Daddy,' a dreadful possibility had suddenly presented itself to Elizabeth, 'surely you don't mean that I can't . . . that you can't afford . . . that I oughtn't to go to Italy.'

'No, no, my dear, nothing of the sort,' her father said irritably. 'Of course you can go. Your steamer tickets are bought and paid for and I have already arranged a credit for you with Lloyd's Bank in London and Milan. But it is certainly not possible for me to come with you.'

Elizabeth went slowly up to her room. It was in some disorder, as she had been pulling her books off the shelves, trying to decide which she could endure to be parted from for three years and which she would take with her. The contents of the big cupboard in the nursery were spread over the work-table. The box containing the Goddess of Fortune had been lifted down from the top shelf and was standing on the floor. It was covered with dust and Elizabeth decided to leave it till the morning. She had not looked at it for years and had almost forgotten it. She certainly could not take it to Italy, it was much too big and heavy. She would give it a good dusting and put it back in the cupboard.

But the next morning she went to see Mr Breve. The old gentleman had lost much of his ferocity these days. He could no longer work in the garden and spent most of the day seated in his basket chair, sharing a rug with the cats, and gazing into the fire or out of the windows across the sand-hills to the sea, grey-green under the wintry, rainless sky. Elizabeth felt sad when she saw him there, so old, so shrunken, his white hair

244

that had been so long and glossy when she first knew him, now yellow and dry, and on the arms of his chair, bony, misshapen and feeble, lay the fine, powerful hands that had once governed the big Steinway with a mastery of skill.

She sat down on a little stool by his side. One of the cats nosed against her, climbed into her lap and curled up.

'I shall miss you, my dear,' said the old man, after a long silence.

Elizabeth roused herself from some rather tearful depths she had been wandering in.

'Brevie, would it matter very much . . . Is going to Italy so very important? I mean, couldn't I stay in Australia and study just the same? Isn't there a wonderful teacher in Melbourne or Sydney I could go to who would be just . . . or nearly as good as the ones in Italy?'

Something of the old fire returned to Mr Breve's sunken eyes, and for a moment he looked almost like the Ogre.

'What's this you are trying to tell me? Not go to Italy, after all our work, after all I've taught you? There's gratitude for you! Losing your nerve, are you? Getting home-sick, like some silly, sentimental servant-girl. Then I give you up! Let me tell you, it takes more than a good voice and a fine figure to be a professional singer. Beautiful voices! Chah! Europe is stinking with them. Two a penny. Anyone can have a good voice. But brains, personality, application, musical knowledge, health, and above all, nerve, courage – call it what you like – those are what make a singer. But give it up, if you like. Throw it away, don't mind me. I'm only an old dotard . . . finished . . . one foot in the grave. But don't come here again. If you don't go to Italy, you needn't come here again. I've finished with you. Get out! . . .'

Elizabeth was nearly in tears and kept trying to interrupt him. But only when the storm had somewhat blown itself out was she able to make herself heard.

'Oh, darling Brevie, it isn't like that at all. Do listen to me.'

'What, what? Then what's it all about? Speak up, girl. Fallen in love, have you? Some young fool wants to marry you. Well, take your choice. But I tell you this – music and matrimony don't mix, especially for women. Have a few love affairs, if you want to – no harm in that, deepens your understanding of life – but nothing serious, nothing lasting, or your career's finished. Give you fair warning . . . wash my hands of you.'

'Yes, yes. I mean no, no. I'm not in love and I don't want to marry anyone. Except you, and you wouldn't have me.' (Whenever Mr Breve became the Ogre, Elizabeth could never resist teasing him.)

'Vixen!' exclaimed Mr Breve, but he sounded less ferocious. 'Then what is all this?'

'It's money,' said Elizabeth bluntly. 'Daddy says the drought in the north is awful and we're nearly ruined – I mean, not just us, but everyone. He says he has sent money to England and Milan for me, and he says I must go. But I feel mean, spending all that money if the others are going to be poor. Are you sure I couldn't do my training in Australia?'

'Sure? Of course I'm sure. It isn't just the lack of good teachers. It's the lack of a musical world in which to live and gain your experience. But if it's money you're worrying about, that's a different matter. Let me tell you, if you work hard and don't let any of this sentimental nonsense turn you aside from your career, in five years you'll be able to repay your father everything he's spent on you. And in ten years' time you'll be richer than he is now.'

Greatly cheered up, Elizabeth rode home on her bicycle full of determination to work as no one had ever worked before. Whenever she felt like reading a book instead of doing her French and German exercises, she would think of Nellie Melba and darling Mr Breve and, thus fortified, would renew her strength of will.

She found Mrs Inglefell and Pearl surrounded by luggage. 'These will have to go to the saddler to be mended,' her mother was saying. 'That one is too old to stand another voyage. I told Marian to buy some good English luggage in London. When she gets here next week we will decide which are the best pieces for you to have.'

'Oh, and Mummie, what will I do with the Goddess of Fortune? We got her down from the cupboard last night and she's covered with dust.'

Mrs Inglefell looked puzzled. 'The goddess . . . ? I don't understand. Oh, the Chinese idol that old Mr Chin gave you. I wonder what happened to him. He hasn't been here for a long time.'

'Neither he has,' said Elizabeth, and felt faintly guilty, as she had when meeting Luke Stevens again, that a friend could be so little missed amidst the crowding events of one's own life.

'That old John Chinaman who used to come here selling things?' contributed Pearl, an older and drier version of herself in earlier years, but with the same prejudice against foreigners. 'He died three or four years back. My gentleman friend has a friend works near them in Hindley Street and he told my gentleman friend that Chin dropped dead in the shop, he did, one morning, sudden. Terrible wailings and goings-on there were, my gentleman friend's friend said there was – regular commotion, and a policeman had to come and there was a post-morting. But the doctors said it was a heart attack which no one would be surprised at seeing as how he used to lug those great boxes about, in summer and winter, made no difference, so it's no wonder.'

'Poor Mr Chin,' said Mrs Inglefell gently. 'Take the box into the dining-room, Beth, I'd like to see the figure again.' But Pearl had to bring Finch to help with the box, it was so very heavy. They had just placed it on the dining-room table, and Elizabeth had taken out the long bamboo rod to release the lid, when a ring at the front-door bell summoned Pearl away. She returned escorting Mr Breve, a frail, shaky Mr Breve, who had roused himself to take a cab and be driven to Sandridge, the first time for months that he had left the security and seclusion of the green and white bungalow.

'Darling Brevie,' said Elizabeth, divided between joy and anxiety. The old man was helped to a chair and as soon as he had regained his breath, he gasped: 'My apologies, madam,' bowing sketchily towards Mrs Inglefell. 'Come to see your husband. Hope he's at home.'

Pearl went to find Mr Inglefell and, in response to low-voiced instructions from her mistress, to bring a tray with glasses, brandy, madeira wine and shortbread biscuits.

Mr Breve, white and exhausted, was leaning back in his chair with his eyes closed, when Mr Inglefell came into the room.

'Don't get up, don't get up,' Alfred hastened to restrain the old man from rising. 'Good of you to come. Delighted to see you.'

The Ogre opened his eyes and poked a finger at Elizabeth. 'Silly girl doesn't want to go to Italy. Thinks it will cost too much.'

'Dear me,' said Mr Inglefell mildly. He was rather annoyed with her, but touched, too, by her impulsive unselfishness. 'The trouble with Beth,' he had often thought to himself, 'is that she is always trying to kill someone with kindness, and one of these days she's going to succeed.' Now he laughed a trifle apologetically and went on: 'You haven't known my youngest daughter for several years, Mr Breve, without becoming aware of her powers of exaggeration. Yes, her three years in Italy will no doubt cost quite a large sum of money, but no more than I am very willing and able to provide.'

'Ah, that's what I wanted to know. Thought this drought might have put you in a bad place. Many people ruined – well-known fact. Pity if it prevented Elizabeth from entering her career. Had intended to present the Conservatorium with a sum of money for an overseas scholarship, but I'd prefer to give it to Elizabeth. She'd win it, anyway. Comes to the same thing. No offence, I trust.'

'Certainly not,' Mr Inglefell replied warmly. 'It's very good of you. Seeing all that you have done for Beth and the interest you have in her success, I would certainly not have stood in the way of her accepting this practical help had she been in need of it. Happily that is not the case. I have arranged for her to draw regular sums from a fund I have establised for her with Lloyds Bank. However, we are both grateful for your generosity and for the trouble it has cost you to come here.'

Elizabeth was looking a little uncomfortable. She was sensitive to her father's disapproval. Grown-up people were so queer about money. It was as though they were ashamed of it, yet they thought it very important. Her mother had said to her, not long ago: 'Now that you are nearly ready to go out into the world, Beth, you must remember that there are three things that are never discussed in polite society – religion, politics and money. And there are three things you must never accept from a man unless you are married to him – jewels or money, clothes, and physical attentions.'

Elizabeth hadn't been quite sure what her mother meant by the last one, but she supposed it was kissing and letting a boy put his arm round your waist and things like that. Of course she knew that having babies was part of it, somehow, but that sort of thing only happened to people after they got married, and she was much too intent on music and Italy to bother about it now.

She stood at the table fiddling nervously with the silken cords of the little cabinet which held the Goddess of Fortune. Pearl came in with a tray. The wine was poured. Mr Breve preferred brandy, and after he had drunk a glass and eaten a shortbread biscuit he looked much better and even mildly Ogre-ish.

'What have you here, Elizabeth? Something to take on your travels? Handsome box.'

Elizabeth told the story of Mr Chin. 'It's been up in the cupboard ever since,' she added. 'We were going to clean it and put it away again, but Mummie wanted to look at it.' She opened the little ebony doors as she spoke, and there was the Goddess of Fortune, as inscrutable, as beautiful as she had been years ago, the rich silk a trifle dusty, but as brilliant as ever, the white and green jade and the mother-of-pearl as softly gleaming as the evening Chin Ling Su and his sons had carried her to this room.

Mr Breve drew in a hissing breath, hitched his chair closer to the table and fumbled in his waistcoat pocket for his eye-glasses.

'But this is incredible!' he exclaimed, as if to himself. 'Amazing!'

'Yes, she's really quite lovely, isn't she?' said Mrs Inglefell, putting out a delicate finger to stroke the silk.

'Lovely? She's . . . magnificent. I congratulate you.'

'We didn't know what to do with her,' Beth explained. 'It seems a pity to leave her in that cupboard, but what else can we do?'

'If she belonged to me,' said Mr Breve, 'she should occupy the place of honour in my house, in a special cabinet.'

'You think she is of some value, then?' asked Alfred. 'I know very little about such things, myself.'

'Value? My dear sir, this is Kwan-Yin, the Queen of Heaven. I should hazard a guess, of the Ming period. As to her value, I would say certainly several hundreds, possibly as much as ten thousand. I doubt if there is another in Australia. She is a treasure, sir, a great treasure.'

There was a moment's startled silence. Then Elizabeth exclaimed excitedly: 'Oh, do let's take her out of the box. We never have, you know.' She put both hands on the figure of the goddess and gently lifted her. The porcelain box-like throne on which she was seated came up with her, all in one piece. Elizabeth put her carefully down on the piece of silk which Mrs Inglefell spread to receive her, and for a few minutes they all stood in silence, worshipping at this unorthodox shrine. Then Elizabeth went back to the box.

'Look,' she exclaimed, 'you can lift the little inside cabinet right out.' She lifted it out. 'It fits into grooves on the top of this box thing underneath. It's like a drawer.' She tugged at it. The drawer slid forward with silky smoothness. Inside it, completely filling the inner space, were little cylinders covered with white paper. Elizabeth picked one up. It was very heavy. She unfolded the paper. A shower of gold pieces fell on to the table and rolled on the floor.

For seven years the Goddess of Fortune had been enthroned above her hidden store of five hundred English sovereigns.

22

The Goddess Looks On

O N 29 June the *Morning Register* expanded its decorous headlines (its type generally being so small that only persons of robust eyesight could ever read what it printed) to announce the assassination of the heir to the Austrian throne.

Everyone felt very sorry for the Austrians and said how barbaric those dreadful Serbians were, and then forgot about it. The newspapers discussed the event for three or four days and then gave their major headlines to the death of Mr Joseph Chamberlain.

At the beginning of July Marian came home from England. Her schooling had changed her less than it had Eleanor. She was more like Mrs Inglefell than the other two girls. Elizabeth had always generously maintained that Marian was the best-looking of the family. During her absence she had become prettier than ever. Otherwise, she was just the same Marian, gentle, sweet-tempered, soft-voiced and not at all clever.

The household was now in a turmoil of unpackings and packings-up. Marian's luggage had to be emptied and turned over to Elizabeth. Once again the big trunks stood about in the passages, while Miss Stitchaway worked from morning to night in the sewing-room and Finch drove hat-boxes and cabin trunks down to the town to have straps and locks repaired.

Preparations were begun, too, for the dance which Mrs Inglefell had promised Elizabeth a year ago. It would be her début dance, but with no social season to follow, for it would be held on 12 August, and they would sail for Naples on 5 September. Mrs Inglefell would see Elizabeth safely installed in her *pensione* in Milan, satisfy herself that all was well ordered for her stay of three years, and then go on to London to see her own mother, now growing old and frail. She hoped to be back in Australia by February of the New Year.

The Goddess of Fortune had been returned to her box and Mr Inglefell had carried the five hundred sovereigns to the bank to deposit them in Elizabeth's account. He was disturbed about them, uneasy that Mr Chin's gift had proved so much more valuable than they had realised. He had insured the Goddess for five hundred pounds and resolved that the next time he was in the city he would go and see Clarence Chin, who was now chief accountant at Mr Goldiway's warehouse. Had he known at the time of the gift that this large sum of money was concealed in the cabinet, he would never have consented to Elizabeth accepting it.

But the Goddess, silent and hidden in her ivory and ebony shrine, smiled her inscrutable smile. She had not finished with the Inglefell family yet.

One morning Mr Inglefell was reading his newspaper in front of the fire. He noticed that His Majesty the King had been reviewing the Fleets at Spithead. 'One of the greatest assemblages of warships the world has ever seen,' declared the *Register*. 'Eleven lines of warships commanded by twenty-five admirals.'

In another small paragraph the German newspapers were accusing Russia of warlike intentions, and troops were reported to be massing along the Austrian frontiers. Pearl came into the morning-room.

'There's one of those Chinamen here to see you, sir,' she announced, as one bearing tidings of doom. For once her gloomy prognostications were to be substantiated.

'Bring him in here,' ordered Mr Inglefell, 'this room is warmer than the dining-room.'

When Clarence Chin came in he welcomed him cordially. 'Good morning, my dear chap. Come up to the fire. A nasty bleak morning it is. What brings you here? But I'm glad you've come. There's a little matter I want to discuss with you, as it happens. Sit down, sit down.'

'Thank you, sir.' Clarence Chin sat down in an arm-chair to one side of the fireplace. He was a good-looking young man in his early thirties. Born and brought up in Australia, his Chinese appearance had become so modified that only his eyes betrayed his Asian origin. He looked uncomfortable and ill at ease.

'I must not lose time,' he said, as though forcing himself to overcome some natural reluctance. 'You know, sir, that Mr Goldiway is leaving this afternoon by the mail-boat for Western Australia?'

'Yes,' said Mr Inglefell. 'Mrs Goldiway is taking her two daughters for a trip to Europe, and Mr Goldiway told me that he would go with them as far as Fremantle and return on the next boat. He wants to look at some business prospects over there, I understand.'

'No, sir,' said Clarence. 'That is only an excuse. He has no intention of returning. He intends to stay on the ship and go to London, or perhaps leave at some intermediate port.'

'What are you implying?' Mr Inglefell's tone was sharp. 'Are you trying to tell me that my partner is running away?'

Clarence bowed his head. 'Yes, sir. He is running away and taking with him the whole cash proceeds of the sale of Station Downs and the chain of Northern Trading Stores.'

'Be careful of what you are saying, young man. This is a very serious accusation. How do you know this?'

'As you know, sir, I have for some time now been in charge of the warehouse books. That does not include the station books or those of the Trading Stores. But much of the stock for both passes through the warehouse, and during the past few months I have been puzzled by certain discrepancies I have noticed in the accounts which I have drawn to Mr Goldiway's notice. In each case he has promised to give the matter his personal attention. But I have not been satisfied. These matters do not affect you directly, as your partnership with Mr Goldiway does not include either the warehouse or the Trading Stores. But when, a few days ago, I was told to finalise to date the accounts of Station Downs, I made some investigations of my own. I find that Station Downs was sold a week ago to the Redman interests, and that the sum of sixty-five thousand pounds was paid into Mr Goldiway's London bank. I then inquired at the shipping office, and find that Mr Goldiway has booked a passage on the mail-steamer for London, not only for as far as Fremantle, as he had told us.'

Mr Inglefell was gripping his chair with both hands in the effort to control himself.

'But Station Downs . . . it's impossible. He can't sell without my signature.'

'No, sir. That is what I thought myself. But if you examine the deed of partnership covering your joint ownership of this property, you will find that each partner has the right of sale if he notifies the other partner in writing of his intention to dispose of his share in the station seven days before the date of actual disposal.'

Mr Inglefell sprang to his feet. 'But he has never given me that notification. I must see him at once. He must be stopped.'

'Yes, sir. That is the reason for my visit. I felt you would excuse my coming to your house.'

'Yes, yes, of course. Tell Finch' – Mr Inglefell turned to Pearl, who had come in answer to his ring – 'to put the horses into the dog-cart immediately. I have urgent business which takes me to the city. And tell your mistress that I will not be in to luncheon, and may be delayed for dinner. Come, Clarence. We will catch the next train without delay.'

He found George Goldiway at his house, surrounded by the disorder of a household on the eve of departure.

'My dear fellow,' was his hearty greeting, 'this is very good of you to come and wish us good-bye. My wife will be delighted.'

Mr Inglefell did not offer to shake hands.

'I have not come to say good-bye. I have come to talk business.'

'Well, well, it's rather a last-minute decision, isn't it? After all, I'll be away only for two or three weeks, and as far as I know we have nothing outstanding that cannot wait until I get back.'

'Are you coming back, Goldiway? Or are you absconding? Absconding! Yes, it's an ugly word, isn't it? But tell me at once. Is it true that you have sold Station Downs without telling me?'

'My dear chap, don't get so excited. Dear me, I don't think I have ever seen you excited before.'

'Is it true? Have you sold Station Downs?' shouted Alfred.

Mr Goldiway shrugged his shoulders. 'Well, I suppose I may as well admit that I have. It was a good offer – too good, I felt, to refuse. You were mistaken – forgive me, my dear fellow – but, yes, I couldn't help feeling that you were mistaken to hang on to that property just now when things are so difficult in the pastoral business.'

'But, good God, man, Station Downs was our one chance of pulling through. That's why the Redman interests wanted it. It's almost the only property in the country with any water.'

'Now look here, Inglefell,' Goldiway's tone had lost its jocularity, 'we haven't a hope of pulling through, and you should have seen it. Redman's gave me a hundred and ten thousand for the Downs, sixty-five thousand in cash payable in London, the balance in twelve months. I may say that I have already transferred the sixty-five thousand to an account in a Swiss bank under a name which I will not divulge even to you, my dear fellow.'

'But that means you've sold the whole property. I don't know how you did it, but it certainly means that somewhere along the line you've forged my signature. I can repudiate the sale and sue you for my share of the money. And what's more, I'll not hesitate to do it.'

'Now, look here, Inglefell, play this right and you'll collect your just share of the hundred and ten thousand . . .'

'You're a cad, sir,' shouted Alfred, striking the table with his fist. 'You know as well as I do that if you leave the country now, every cent of that money will be absorbed by your creditors, or rather the creditors of our partnership. And if our debts are to be honoured, I will be ruined, while you . . . you will be enjoying a Swiss holiday.'

Goldiway laughed. It was an ugly laugh, but had in it a tone of self-congratulation.

'I don't say you're wrong, my dear chap. But I assure you that my Swiss account holds a good deal more than the sixty-five thousand.'

'That I can well believe, and a fair slice of it at my expense, no doubt.'

'Come now, be reasonable. I'll tell you what I'll do. I'll give you half . . .' A swift glance at Alfred's stern expression, and he corrected himself. 'No, I'll be generous. We've been friends, I'll be generous. I'll pay forty thousand pounds into any foreign bank you care to name against your credit. When this end of the affair blows over . . . because it will, you know, my dear chap . . . nine days' wonder . . . you will have a nice little nest-egg waiting for you.'

Alfred got to his feet, an expression of disgust on his face.

'You are not catching this ship this afternoon, Goldiway,' he said. 'You can do one of two things: you can come to the office with me now to work over our accounts and see what we can do to straighten out this mess – for I have little doubt that this fund you have established for yourself overseas has been at the expense of our mutual interests – or you can refuse. In the latter case, I warn you, I shall inform the police and you can face prosecution. I may as well tell you that I have already seen my solicitors, and they are even now engaging a firm of auditors to examine our books.'

Mr Goldiway pursed his lips in thought, his shrewd eyes watching his partner under lowered lids. Finally he shrugged and made a conciliatory gesture with his heavy hand.

'A pity, my dear Inglefell. You're making another mistake. Take my advice and a great deal of this trouble would be avoided. As it is, you are running us both into ruin and scandal.'

'This is no mistake,' replied Mr Inglefell, with a grimness in which anger was mixed with determination. 'Ruin we almost certainly face, and probably scandal as well. But let me tell you this, Goldiway. Face the music now, honestly and courageously, and no business man will accuse you. There are going to be a good many bankruptcies in the next year or two, if this drought continues. But leave the country as you intended to do, with your affairs in disorder behind you, and never again in any community where British business is done could you hold up your head.'

In the end, Mr Inglefell agreed that Mrs Goldiway, with Cecilia and Nancy, should be allowed to catch the ship without being told of the sudden crisis in their affairs. Mr Goldiway would excuse himself from accompanying them on the grounds of important business, but he would hope to come on a later ship. Even this concession troubled Alfred's conscience, for he felt it very probable that his unscrupulous partner would take advantage of his wife's departure to send with her as many valuables and negotiable securities as possible.

During the following week investigations by auditors and solicitors showed that Goldiway had liquidated every asset (in some cases forging Mr Inglefell's signature for the purpose). Alfred sat grimly silent while these researches were in progress, listening to his partner's plausible explanations and never once repudiating his signature, even when he knew that in certain cases it must have been written by a hand other than his own.

It was finally evident that by selling almost all his own invest-
ments, adding them to what could be extracted from Goldiway, the debts of the partnership could be paid and defalca-
tions made good. Although nothing was said in front of the
auditors about the secret fund in Switzerland, Mr Inglefell was
adamant that the cash for the sale of Station Downs should be
placed at the disposal of the partnership to help with the clear-
ance of debts. He could prove easily enough that this money
had been paid to Goldiway's London bank. If necessary, he
was prepared to repudiate his signature on the documents of
sale and accuse Goldiway of forgery.

Actual bankruptcy was avoided, but by so narrow a margin
that Alfred was left with little more than his house and
Undaboo, the latter mortgaged to the maximum with the
bank. Goldiway owed him nearly a hundred thousand pounds,
a fact which seemed to worry that gentleman not in the least.
In fact, as the investigations continued, he grew more cheerful,
more optimistic. He continued to smoke his expensive cigars,
his appetite was hearty, his manner confident.

'Depend upon it, my good chap,' he said to Alfred in the
patronising tone he had always adopted when talking to his
partner and which, until now, had only amused Alfred,
'depend upon it, we'll make a bigger recovery than ever. I have
some ideas on the overseas markets that would astonish you.'

'On the contrary, they wouldn't astonish me in the least,'
Alfred answered dryly.

He had said nothing of all this to his wife. She had not failed
to notice his preoccupation, his loss of appetite, and his pallor,
but attributed it to his anxiety about the drought. It pained
her to leave him at such a time, but she felt that Elizabeth
could not begin her new life without some help and supervision. She made another attempt to persuade him to go to
Europe with them, and was rather hurt and astonished at the
abruptness of his refusal. He was a man of even temper broken
very occasionally by irritability (which she had always privately

called 'a touch of liver'), but in all their years together, she had never seen him in this mood of angry taciturnity.

Alfred had been so preoccupied with his own affairs that it was with a shock of incredulity that he opened his newspaper on the morning of 28 July to read that 'Europe is on the brink of war'. Some startled exclamation which escaped him made his wife look up from her letters. He tapped the newspaper with his forefinger.

'This European situation is beginning to look very serious,' he said. 'If there's going to be a war, I wouldn't like you and Elizabeth to catch that ship.'

'But, Alfred, those Balkan countries are always having wars. Bertie Desmond – you remember, he was at our Embassy in Bucharest – said to me last time I was home that it's a sort of national pastime. And those horrible Albanians are always killing people.'

'All the same, my dear, it's too near Italy for my liking.' He did not add that it was less the cautious and brief reports from Paris and Vienna which disturbed him than the paragraphs he had read about the movements of the British Fleets. He sat frowning over his newspaper for longer than usual, and finally went to the city with a mind distracted from his own affairs for the first time since the morning Clarence Chin had called on him.

He found his partner sitting at his office desk in a state of unconcealed jubilation. He had a number of international cable forms spread out in front of him.

'Alfred, my boy,' he exclaimed, 'things are going splendidly, magnificently. Before the end of the year we'll be millionaires.'

'You may be,' said Alfred. 'I don't know what you're up to. But remembering certain wise words about the green bay tree, I wouldn't be surprised if you end up as rich as Croesus.'

'Ah, hah, always trying to pull my leg. No, no, my boy, this is really something big. I've been watching these moves in the Balkans for a long time. If things go as I suspect they might,

I'll clean up enough to make this little set-back we've had a mere flea-bite. We'll be rich yet my boy.'

'You may be,' repeated Alfred, 'but you can count me out. I've already told you that as soon as the auditors have finished and our business is more or less straight, I'm asking for a termination of partnership. Your business methods are not mine, Goldiway. I'm no gambler. I like my business to be quiet and steady.'

Goldiway laughed with great good humour. He seemed to take this aspersion on his business methods as a compliment. 'Of course, my dear old chap,' he replied heartily. 'It's just because you are the quiet and steady type that our partnership has been so successful.'

Mr Inglefell winced.

'Successful? I know that it has cost me nearly a hundred thousand pounds to keep us out of the courts, if you call that successful. If we get good rains on Undaboo I may just make a living. Otherwise, I'm ruined.'

'Nonsense, my boy. If these deals come off' – Goldiway made an expansive gesture towards the cables lying on his desk – 'I'll pay you back the hundred thou. with interest at ten per cent and never miss it.'

Alfred could not respond. He was sickened by his partner's vulgarity and lack of feeling, and yet he reproached himself bitterly for not having realised before that the man was a gambler who loved the risk of the game for its own sake. After all, Alfred told himself angrily, he had been willing enough to benefit by Goldiway's undoubted business ability to advance his own interests, and he had been content to leave his partner too free a hand in things over which he should have exerted himself to keep a close control.

Alfred sat down at his desk. His clerk brought him letters requiring attention and placed his appointment list in front of him. But Alfred could do nothing but sit with his head in his hands, lacking now the fierce anger and determination which had carried him through the first days of this critical time. He was bowed down by a fearful depression of spirit, which was partly emotional reaction from the fight he had waged against a will stronger, a personality more overbearing, a mind more agile and less scrupulous than his own. He was drained of strength, and could see nothing before him but the failure of his work and comparative poverty for his family.

After a little while he roused himself and began, with an effort of will, to attend to the papers his clerk had brought him.

Half an hour later he was interrupted by Goldiway, who came bursting into his room with even more noise and less ceremony than usual. He was waving a cable form in the air.

'Well, there you are!' he shouted, flinging down the sheet of paper on Alfred's desk. 'It's war! Austria-Hungary has declared war on Serbia. My agent in Berne has wired me this message. It is an agreed wording. You see, it will be in all the newspapers tonight, or tomorrow morning at the latest. Now, listen, Inglefell. I must go to Melbourne on this afternoon's train.' He took his watch out of his waistcoat pocket. 'Yes, there's ample time. The train doesn't leave till four. I'm not running away, never fear, my dear fellow. It's a thousand pities you stopped me from taking that boat. I could have managed this all much better from London. But everything is going splendidly, splendidly. You'll have your hundred thousand by Christmas, and more to follow.'

'But, Goldiway,' protested Mr Inglefell, bewildered by his partner's exuberance, 'this is appalling news. This may mean a general European war. It's too horrible to contemplate.'

'Well, well, I suppose it is, if you look at it from one point of view. But I thought it would come. I gambled on it coming. The friction between Greece and Turkey, and the trouble in Albania during this past year were sure to lead to something bigger sooner or later. As for us, my boy, it is our opportunity.'

'Now wait a bit, Goldiway,' said Alfred, getting out of his chair. 'Pay me back what I have put in to save the business from collapse, that's all I want. I'll have no dealings in war stock or armaments, or whatever you are dabbling in. Pay that debt, if you can, and I'll be satisfied.'

'Still the conservative! Well, I won't argue about it. I must catch that train and I've a dozen telegrams to send before doing it. I should be back within the week, but in any case you can find me at Menzies' if you want me.'

As Goldiway had predicted, the declaration of war between Austria-Hungary and Serbia was announced by the newspapers the following morning. Public sympathy with the Austrians, which had been strong after the assassination of the Grand Duke and the Grand Duchess, began to veer. It was felt that the diplomatic moves had been high-handed. *The Register* quoted the London *Daily Telegraph* in its criticism of the Austrian Note to Serbia, 'which,' it declared, 'goes far beyond international usage.'

That evening Mr Inglefell called his wife and Elizabeth into the morning room.

'Now, my dears,' he said firmly, 'you won't like what I am going to say, so the sooner it's said the better. Beth, my child, there can be no going to Italy while this war is on.'

Beth looked rather white. 'You mean, we can't catch the ship? I – I can't go to Milan?'

'Well, my dear, look at it for yourself. You know how the Italians have always hated the Austrians. Do you think they will be content to look on at what is happening across the Adriatic and not join in, sooner or later? It may not last long, pray God it doesn't. But I can't let you go, you must see that, Beth, while there is any danger. When the situation clears you shall go, I promise you.'

Beth did not protest or cry or argue. She went to her room, where the luggage was standing about. She kicked idly at the corner of a cabin trunk, then picked up a stack of books and threw them violently into a corner.

In the days that followed she made no sign of disappointment. Only her mother noticed that, for the first time for years, she did no singing practice, she did not play the piano or go near the work-room. She made no move to open the luggage which had been packed, to put her books back on the shelves or take any interest in the completion of the new clothes that kept Miss Stitchaway so busy in the sewing-room. She did not go even to see Mr Breve, but went for solitary walks along the beach or across the paddocks, making her body tired to draw out the sting of her thoughts.

Mrs Inglefell and Pearl went quietly to work in her absence. Piece by piece the luggage disappeared, the clothes and books were put tidily away into their shelves and drawers.

Coming home late in the afternoon of 5 August, when the winter sunshine had already disappeared behind the westerly clouds and a bleak flurry of rain blew against the windows, Elizabeth found her mother sitting, white and trembling, at the table in the hall where the telephone was kept. Tears were running down her cheeks. Elizabeth was shocked. How selfish she had been, to be so wrapped up in her own unhappiness that she had given no thought to the sorrow that her mother must have at not seeing her own mother again. She ran across the hall and put her arms round her mother's thin figure.

'Darling Mummie, don't cry, please don't.'

Mrs Inglefell stroked Beth's hair and drew a long, shuddering breath.

'That was your father, Beth dear. He just telephoned from town to say . . . to tell us . . . oh, Beth dearest, England and Germany are at war. We are at war.'

23

Ebb-Tide

'K N I T one, slip one, knit one, slip one, pull the slipped stitch over, turn.'

Beth counted laboriously. She was learning to knit, and so far had not progressed beyond the stage of looping the wool round one needle while all the other needles stuck out like porcupine quills, dropping their stitches and finally sliding away altogether. But King and Country demanded that she learn to knit, so she persevered, and with such a fury of concentration that at times she felt that the whole German Army was being held from the Channel ports entirely by the strength of her knitting-needles and skein of wool.

The dining-room was full of ladies knitting and sewing. The table was covered with material which was being cut into long narrow strips which Red Cross workers were teaching them how to roll tightly into bandage packs.

Pearl had left suddenly, tearful and rather defiant, saying that she was going to marry the gentleman friend she had been 'walking out' with for eight years, as he intended to volunteer for the Light Horse. Mr Inglefell put up the dog-cart and sold one pair of horses because Finch offered himself for the Expeditionary Force as soon as it was announced in the newspapers that the Australian Government would place the Royal Australian Navy at the disposition of the Admiralty and would provide a force of twenty thousand men for the army.

Eleanor, in her capable way, had taken over the management of the household, and no housemaid was engaged to take Pearl's place, Marian and Elizabeth sharing the work of bed-making and dusting and carpet-sweeping. Elizabeth also looked after the chickens and the stables, with the help of an old man who came morning and evening to milk the two cows.

By the end of the spring it was as though they had known no other kind of life. The pre-war world slid away into the past, never to return. The young men still came every Saturday and Sunday to play tennis, but now many of them were in khaki uniform. The side veranda became a depository for Sam Browne belts, kit-bags, army boots and tunics, while the owners disported themselves in cream flannels on the lawns. In the evenings they danced or sang patriotic songs round the school-room piano. The cult of the tango was intensified. Dancing became a craze rather than a pastime.

Every man between the ages of nineteen and forty fell into one or other of two classifications: if he volunteered for service with one of the fighting forces, he became a hero, to be deferred to, waited on, and idolised; if he did not, he was cold-shouldered, snubbed and even actively persecuted. Citizens of German name whose families had been in Australia for two or three generations were suspected of disloyalty and looked on with suspicion. The towns in the Barossa Valley where many German families had settled sixty or seventy years before, were reputed to be full of enemy spies. Dark stories were told of hidden stores of arms and ammunition and mysterious lights and movements of men. No one had ever actually seen these things, but he always knew someone else who had.

Poor Herr Hermanschreimer came to Sandridge in great distress. Larrikins had thrown stones and broken the windows of his house and more than half his pupils had suddenly decided that they no longer wished to study music. He protested, with tears in his eyes, his loyalty to King George. He was no longer young. How could he now earn a living? And it was also necessary to report to the police because in Germany he had been born, and could Mrs Inglefell tell what was to become of him? They comforted him as well as they could, but what could they do to help him? The Liedertafel was disbanded. The Bavarian band that played every evening on the sea-wall in the summer months had been forced to discontinue their performances. Many German families changed their names or conveniently discovered that they were of Swiss origin.

One day in December Luke Steven came bounding up the front path to ring the door-bell. Elizabeth went to open the door. Years afterwards, it seemed to her that history was divided into two eras: that period when you never answered a door-bell because there was always a parlour-maid to answer it for you; and that period when parlour-maids had ceased to exist and had been replaced by kindly, amiable and generally inefficient 'helps' who came by the hour or the day 'to oblige' and who did not consider that answering bells was part of that obligation. The long brocaded ribbon that hung from the ceiling beside the fire-place in the drawing-room, and the little brass buttons in the walls of dining-rooms, smoking-rooms, breakfast-rooms, bedrooms and nurseries became obsolete, outmoded curiosities surviving from a vanished age.

Luke was in high spirits. The results of his examinations had just been announced. He had passed, high up on the list, and he was now a qualified engineer and a graduate of the university. He seized Elizabeth by the waist and whirled her across the hall. Elizabeth's own hopes and ambitions had received such a set-down that she had felt no spontaneous enjoyment since the day she had learned that she could not go to Italy. But now her spirits responded to Luke's with a rush of joy.

'Oh, Luke, how thrilling! I am pleased. A thousand congratulations!'

'Thanks, Beth. But where's Eleanor? I must tell her.'

'She's out on the tennis-court, trying to put the lines down for play on Saturday.'

Luke jumped the steps and ran across the garden. All Elizabeth's joy evaporated. Tears stung her eyelids. Couldn't he have stayed one minute to talk to her? Ellie wouldn't even care whether he passed his exams or not. And now he was qualified they could get engaged, and she hated both of them, and she was making a fool of herself, and why, oh why, was everything so horrid now, when it used to be so lovely? Those b-beastly Germans!'

She rubbed her eyes vigorously with her handkerchief, looked with loathing at her latest piece of knitting (certainly slightly less amorphous than her earlier attempts) where she had thrown it when the door-bell rang, and decided that nothing would induce her to stay in the house to see Eleanor and Luke come back from the tennis-court. She got out her bicycle and rode at high speed to the green and white bungalow, arriving hot and dishevelled and in a very bad temper, but somewhat. drained of her misery.

Mrs Porter opened the door to her, and putting her finger to her lips, shook her head portentously.

'I'm glad you've come, miss, or I'd have been telephoning for you. The master's very low. It's my idea he's sinking fast. Never been the same since the war started. Does nothing but talk about his friends in Salzburg and how the military have spoiled his beautiful Germany. It's downright pathetic, miss. But come in out of the heat. The master's in the music-room. I'll bring you something cool to drink.'

The old man was lying in his chair, staring vacantly at the sea, the dark blue sea of midsummer. Outside the windows his garden lay in ruins, for the winter and spring had passed without rain, and now even the trees had begun to droop. But of that he was no longer conscious. His failing mind dwelt only upon the country he had loved, which was to be destroyed by men whose crime it was to bring ruin and desolation not only to their enemies, but to their own people, perverting and de-grading the highest and best of their own national genius.

Elizabeth sat down on her little stool and leaned her cheek against his hand. For a moment it seemed that he recognised her. He seemed about to speak, putting out his hand to touch her hair, as he used to do. Then his eyes closed again and his pallid lips mumbled: 'Villains, villains.'

And Elizabeth cried, because she was still too young to have any other way of meeting sorrow and death. She cried because the sun was setting in a blaze of torrid splendour; because of the solitude of the wide sea; because time passes and cannot be held; because of the loneliness of her own heart.

Mr Breve died that night, and two days later a long, official-looking letter arrived for Elizabeth to inform her that he had bequeathed to her, Elizabeth Inglefell, all whatsoever he had died possessed of, for her exclusive use, benefit and enjoyment, and that awaiting her esteemed instructions were faithfully hers, X, X, X, W, Y and Z, solicitors, barristers and attorneys-at-law.

Mr Breve's fortune was not a large one, but it would provide Elizabeth with a comfortable income for the rest of her life, together with the green and white bungalow, two grand pianos and three cats.

Elizabeth was puzzled what to do with these possessions. Mrs Porter agreed to stay on for the time being, to feed the cats and look after the house. For a long time Elizabeth could not go back to the house. In her present mood of heightened sensitivity, the sense of loss was too acute to be borne.

The bequest was a great relief to Mr Inglefell. One of the gravest results of his business losses was his anxiety about the future of his three daughters. His wife would have her own, not inconsiderable, fortune when her mother died and, with Elizabeth provided for, he felt less fearful for Eleanor and Marian. The promised repayment from George Goldiway had never been made. That gentleman, had, in fact, not returned to

Adelaide, but had remained in Melbourne where he was reported to be making a great deal of money by providing, in the most patriotic way imaginable, for the material needs of His Majesty's gallant soldiers and sailors.

With that lack of consideration which is the distraction of busy housewives, Christmas and the plums and apricots all arrived together. Mrs Thompson sat up late at night in the hot kitchen, stoning the fruit and stirring the pans of boiling jam. The house was full of the perfume of ripe fruits and hot sugar. Elizabeth liked to help her cover the earthenware jars. She spread the white paper flat on the kitchen table and cut out circles wide enough to fit over the jars, then made a big pot of paste with flour and boiling water and pasted the circles of paper over the pots. In spite of the dry season, the trees in the orchard were laden with fruit, and no matter how much jam they made every evening, every morning would see another harvest being carried in from the garden.

Henri arrived to stay for Christmas, and for a brief while he and Elizabeth renewed the comradeship of their childhood. They went to the beach with packets of food and bundles of towels and bathing-gowns tied to the carrier-grids of their bicycles. The fat pony had long since departed to those pastures where good ponies go when they die. Alistair Faulkener had gone to the most distant of his father's cattle stations, after a medical examination had pronounced him unfit for military service owing to a heart condition of which until that moment he had been completely unaware. Here he worked harder and lived in conditions as severe as those of the Libyan Desert, but at least he escaped the ignominy of receiving a white feather from someone, which he undoubtedly would have, had he remained in the city. Malcolm kept sending frantic and expensive cables from Oxford begging his father's permission to join the army. Mr. Faulkener replied by letter that the Military Command had made nineteen the age limit for service in the army, and he was not prepared to disagree with them.

'Do you remember that day you went up and bearded the Ogre?' said Henri. 'Golly! Malcolm and I thought he'd eaten you.'

Elizabeth rolled over and buried her face in the warm sand.

'Don't let's do any remembering,' she said in a muffled voice. 'I can't bear it.'

'Sorry, Beth. I forgot for the moment. I say, I wanted to tell you something. I haven't told anyone else yet.'

Beth sat up and pulled off her bathing-cap.

'Don't tell me yet. I know what it's going to be, and I don't want to hear it. Let's go in just once more. I'll race you to the first breaker.'

She swept her hair tightly up on to the top of her head and put her cap on again. The westering sun was making the sand so hot under their feet that it was a relief to reach the hard wet sand below the tide-mark. 'Beat you,' cried Beth, as she took a running dive into the first line of surf. They swam and splashed each other and raced along the shallows till they were breathless, and when at last they returned to their picnic spot to find towels and shoes, the sun was touching the horizon. Then the sky became malachite green and Venus hung her lamp in the glow of the sunset.

'You must let me tell you,' said Henri. 'There's not much time.' He put out a hand to touch her, and at his touch a strange fear put its finger on Beth's heart. It was the fear of hurting him. Dear Henri! She loved him so much, and yet some instinct warned her that the kind of love she had to give him, had always given him, would not be the love he wanted. Henri would be always one of those to be hurt.

'You know I've always loved you, always you, Beth. You've been the whole of my life from the very first day I ever saw you at Madame de Fresgne's when we were both little.'

Beth let down her hair. It fell over her shoulders and hid her face. Why was she frightened of Henri, who had been a brother and a comrade for so long? And the answer was being given her – for this was not the brother and comrade she had known almost all her life. This was a new Henri, not a man who was giving himself to her, but a man who was denying himself the thing he most desired in order to give himself to something greater than them both.

'. . . catching a ship in about a fortnight's time,' he was saying. 'I must get to France. I've had a thorough medical and Dr O'Shawn says I'm absolutely fit, so that part of it ought to be all right. But I wanted you to know before anyone else. Uncle Thomas and Aunt Emma will be coming down tomorrow, and I'll have to tell them then. That'll be the hardest part of all, to leave them after all they've done for me.'

They rode home in the early evening, and two weeks later Henri sailed away to give back to his mother's country the life she had given him.

24

High Tide, 1915

THE New Year brought news of Ross-Bossingham. He wrote to Mrs Inglefell to tell her that he had rejoined his regiment and hoped soon to be sent to the Front. He sent his love to Gloriana, which, when her mother gave Elizabeth the message, puzzled her. 'When you were very little he used to call you that,' explained Mrs Inglefell. 'I don't remember him very well,' said Elizabeth.

On Tuesdays, before the war, Elizabeth used to like going to the beach to watch the mail-boat arrive from England. The big ship made a stately progress up the Gulf to discharge passengers and mails at the Outer Harbour. On Wednesdays the postman would bring the letters and newspapers from home. There were always six copies of *The Times* (six weeks old) and letters from Grandmother-in-England and cousins and friends. Mrs Inglefell would spend every Wednesday in a small confusion of her own, surrounded by sheets of note-paper, opened envelopes, scattered newspapers, piles of new books, and perhaps one or two parcels containing silks and muslins from Harrods or confections from Gumpers'.

But since the war began, the regularity of this routine had been somewhat disturbed, and although the mails came and went every week, their arrival and departure continuing to be advertised in every newspaper (the *Emden* having been sunk, to the pride of every Australian, by the gallant ship H.M.A.S. *Sydney*), the exact hour and day could no longer be foretold with certainty.

The first Australian troops had sailed in October and early in December it was announced that the First Australian and New Zealand Imperial Expeditionary Force had landed in Egypt. To her astonishment Elizabeth began to receive letters from Robert Placker, who had joined the Tenth Infantry Battalion at the beginning of the war and, now in Egypt, felt the need for news of the fish in South Australian waters. He sent her a scarf covered with silver embroidery, rather tarnished by its long sea voyage, and an enamelled pencil with the Sphinx's head. 'We're not supposed to say where we are,' he wrote, 'but this will give you an idea.' The scarf and the pencil, though unusable, immediately became Elizabeth's most treasured possessions.

It now became a patriotic duty to write to as many soldiers as possible. Elizabeth posted a letter to Henri every week, addressing some to his London bank and some care of Lloyds Bank in Paris, as she said, 'in case'.

The war began to assume a new character. From being a disagreeable something that interfered with one's own plans and ambitions, it became an exciting pageant of dramatic events and heightened emotions. If, in later years, it seemed to this generation that their attitude at this time had been one of almost unbelievable blindness and selfishness, it must be said in explanation, if not extenuation, that they had had no experience of war, the men who had fought in the Boer War being so small a proportion of the population that their exploits in South Africa had made very little mark on the national consciousness. Australia had had no direct contact with armed conflict; no alien shot had ever been fired, no foreign blow had ever been struck, no enemy foot had ever been set, upon her soil. If Australians at first seemed strangely indifferent to the cataclysmic events in Europe, it was the indifference of ignorance, like that of children who do not fear evil because they have never encountered it and therefore cannot imagine it. The newspapers every day carried reports of battles, of massacres, of horrors on a scale unprecedented, but it was all unreal, far away and of little direct concern to Australia.

The disastrous drought in South Australia continued, but the eastern part of the continent was enjoying a rising prosperity, and this, with a growing mood of patriotism, made for a very comfortable feeling of self-satisfaction. The mails from home were rather irregular, but the weekly movements of ships could still be followed from the newspapers. Cargoes of wheat and wool could still be lifted and prices remained firm and even rose. Britain undoubtedly continued to rule the waves. These Germans were a barbaric lot (we began to call them the 'Huns'), and the sooner we beat them the better, so that the empire on which the sun never set could continue to bask in its eternal sunshine.

It was a mood of false values, but false only because the people, faced with a situation for which they had been unprepared, had not yet found the principles by which to guide their actions when at last they were to meet the realities of history.

Since Mr Breve's death and the cancellation of her passage to Italy, Elizabeth had discontinued her music. She no longer went to the Conservatorium for lessons in method and composition. She did not sing or practise on the schoolroom piano, and her French and Italian exercise books lay neglected on the shelves. It was as though some mechanism inside her had run down and stopped, and nothing came to give it new life and vigour.

January was so hot that even swimming was hardly worth the effort required to walk to the beach. Tennis had become impossible. The lawn was brown and dry. Every drop of water that could be spared from the house was needed to keep the grass alive. The garden, dusty and neglected, shrivelled under the merciless sun. Even the monkey-puzzle tree seemed spikier and drier in the withering air.

Mrs Inglefell, white and exhausted, spent the days in her room, with the windows shut against the heat and the blinds lowered. Elizabeth crept in and out at intervals to bathe her forehead with eau-de-Cologne and fan her with a broad palm-leaf fan.

In the kitchen Mrs Thompson cooked over the big wood-burning range, her only concession to the heat-wave being to ask Elizabeth to carry the food up and down the cellar steps. 'It's me legs, Miss Beth. There's nothing the matter with me, but me legs is not as young as they were.'

Elizabeth had not seen Luke since the day of Mr Breve's death. The Christmas and New Year holidays passed without a visit from him. As Eleanor did not speak of him and went her own way about the house, self-possessed and unruffled, even by the heat, Elizabeth could only conclude that any hopes Luke had had of making Eleanor responsive to his devotion had remained unfulfilled. Well, she told herself angrily, people who could not even come and wish their friends a happy New Year and who could ignore the bonds that existed between them and people who fell out of trees deserved to be ignored, especially when other people who were wearing khaki uniform of a most hideous but heart-thrilling style and going to fight for King and Country required to be played tennis with and danced with and written to and have their buttons polished with Brasso and their Sam Browne belts anointed with father's best tan shoe-cream, and their puttees rolled into tight cylinders like the bandages they rolled at the Red Cross meetings, and knitted for (scarves and Balaclava helmets and mittens – very difficult – and waistcoats) in the thickest possible wool which, as everyone knew, were invaluable when going to one of the hottest climates in the world because of the nights in the desert being bitterly cold.

She was therefore quite unprepared to receive with appropriate indifference the large khaki-clad figure which presented itself at the front door one day in January. At first she did not recognise him. The tunic of the uniform, with its box-pleated pockets, made him look broader, the wide hat with its upturned brim and cockade of emu feathers made him seem taller even than his six feet and two inches.

Luke saluted and said: 'Hullo, Beth,' but in a tone that made it sound more like 'How do you do, Miss Inglefell', so politely formal was it. Elizabeth felt shy and excited and cross and bursting with pride, in a whirlpool of conflicting thoughts. This man, so big, so handsome, was Luke the despicable, who was unworthy to be thought of at all and whom she hated, and he was wearing the King's uniform and the cockade of the famous Ninth, the picked Regiment of Horse, in which (so it was said) every man had to be six feet tall. It was quite the most exciting event in her whole life, so exciting that rushing rivers of joy were carrying her heart away and the stars were streaming across the firmament of her mind.

'Hullo,' she said.

The hall was dim and cool after the heat of the afternoon sun on the porch.

'I'll tell Eleanor,' said Elizabeth, and went away, leaving Luke standing in the hall.

Half an hour later Eleanor came into the school-room where Elizabeth was lying on the floor reading *La Dame aux Camélias,* and wondering why her elders were so shocked by it.

'Luke wants to see you,' said her sister. 'He's in the morning room.' Elizabeth looked at her sharply, but Eleanor seemed no different, no light of great events illumined her brow or sparkled in her level eyes.

Elizabeth scrambled rather untidily to her feet. Her dress was crumpled and she spent a moment trying to smooth it down. She now wore her hair with the plaits pinned up in a coronet round her head, and as she crossed the hall she nervously pushed the hairpins more firmly into place.

Luke was standing by the fireplace, looking grim.

'Will you come out with me?' he asked, without preamble. 'I want to go for a long walk.'

'All right.' All Elizabeth's nervousness suddenly vanished.

'But we'll die of heat.'

'I don't think so. I think the wind's going round to the west. The cool change will be here in an hour.'

'Wait a minute till I tell Mummie.'

They walked without speaking through the streets of the town and then to the end of the long jetty. The height of the holiday season was past, but the heat-wave had brought many thousands of people from the city to the beach. Children in bathing-suits were playing on the sands and splashing in the shallows. Elizabeth and Luke bought ice-creams at the little kiosk at the end of the jetty and then sat dangling their legs over the wooden piles. Below their feet the water was deep and darkly green, sucking at the piers to make mysterious patterns in the shadowy depths under the jetty where water-ferns swayed and tiny fish darted in silver streaks. The sun set stormily. The wind, crossing the sea, began to blow coolly, with a promise of rain.

'I told you it was coming,' said Luke.

In the twilight they walked back to the esplanade and along the beach.

'I wish we'd brought bathers,' said Elizabeth. 'It would have been lovely to swim.'

The cold wind and the stormy, threatening sky had quickly dispersed the crowds, and the beach was almost deserted as they made their way at a brisk pace towards the southern curve of the bay. They walked hard for an hour. The twilight deepened under a starless sky, but no rain fell. At last Elizabeth, breathless, flung herself down on the sand.

'I give up,' she laughed. 'I'm not as young as I was, you know.'

Luke was contrite. 'Gosh, Beth, I am sorry. I set much too hot a pace.' He sat down beside her. 'Better not catch a chill. The temperature's dropped at least twenty degrees, I bet.' He pulled off his tunic and put it round her shoulders.

They sat, silent again, while the lightning played in vast sheets of sudden glare along the horizon, throwing the storm-clouds into relief and lighting up the sea, whipped into tossing white plumes by the breeze.

'I asked Eleanor to marry me, and she wouldn't,' said Luke abruptly, at last.

'I know. I mean, she didn't tell me or anything, but I thought you must have.'

Luke picked up a pebble and threw it as hard as he could into the sea. It caught the inland-swirling line of water, skipped several times, flipping up spurts of foam, and then sank.

'I haven't much money, but I'm qualified now, and the firm say they'll reserve my job for me till I get back from the war, which ought to be in a year, say two years at the longest. I know I'm not good enough for her, Beth, but gosh, if she'd only be human, if she'd only let me – well, take her out sometimes, if she'd even be wild with me, it would be something I could grasp. But she's so damnably polite and cool. I just don't know how to tackle it.'

'Poor Luke,' said Elizabeth gently, and in that brief exclamation expressed a new lesson in the realm of experience, for when love is broadened and deepened by pity it begins to learn a little of its own strength.

Luke was leaning forward with his arms on his knees.

'I don't know why I'm telling you all this,' he said apologetically. 'You're a funny kid. I seem to be able to tell you anything.'

Beth shivered suddenly. Luke jumped up. 'You're cold too, and the tide's coming in fast. We'd better move or we'll be caught. What a selfish hound I am. Come on.' He put out his hands and grasped hers to pull her to her feet, then picked up the jacket and held it out.

'Put it on properly with your arms in the sleeves,' he commanded.

She slid her arms into the rough serge and smelt the odour of it as he hooked the collar under her chin.

'There, my soldier-girl,' he said, putting a hand on each of her shoulders. She moved closer to him, leaned her forehead against the thick woollen shirt he was wearing, his arms slid across her back, tightened, drawing her body against him, and so they stood, folded in a timeless unity, the bleak wind beating unheeded against them, the sea surging and crying in the darkness and trying with every wave to reach them where they stood above the tide's rim.

Luke was the first to break away. But he kept an arm about her as he hurried her, breathless and half-weeping, to the sandhills. Here in a hollow deep enough to be sheltered from the wind, where the white sand was soft and warm from the day's heat, they clung together as though obsessed by a desperate fear of separation.

At last Luke said: 'Oh, God, Beth, what must you think of me? It must have been you all the time. Ellie was right. She knew I wasn't in love with her, not really, not like this. Darling Beth, my girl, my girl.' He buried his face in her hair and began pulling at the braids until they were loosened and free.

Then he kissed her and Beth for the first time knew the fierce pain of mature passion.

25

Shadow of the Goddess

T H E Ninth Regiment of Light Horse sailed for Egypt with the Second Expeditionary Force in March. Elizabeth's joy in her love for Luke was so complete that it was unclouded even by this physical separation. There had been no engagement between them. But it had come to be accepted in the family circle that when Luke came to the house he came to see Elizabeth. If Eleanor had any feelings of injury or jealousy or even amusement at this, she gave no sign.

It was a golden autumn. Day succeeded day of calm sunshine, followed by nights of translucent beauty. Adelaide has one of the loveliest autumn climates in the world, and this year was a benediction of colour and light. Perugino never painted skies more placidly clear, Turner never imagined sunsets of more gorgeous radiance. It was as though an enchantment had been laid upon the place, a moment given of peace that could be remembered in the days of storm to come.

Every hour of his leave, Luke spent with Elizabeth. After that first wild moment of discovery, their love ran a gentle, untroubled course. They walked on the beach or across the paddocks, spent absurd, argumentative hours polishing his accoutrements, guessing where the regiment would be sent for service, making imaginary, extravagant plans for the future which always included a brilliant engineering career for Luke, punctuated with bridges and railways and harbours and hydroelectric stations, and for Elizabeth world-shaking appearances as prima donna at the Scala or the Metropolitan. They wanted only to be together, to touch hands, to exchange glances, to have private jokes and understandings unshared by others.

When the regiment sailed, she wrote him long letters, full of inconsequential nonsense and detailed descriptions of her everyday doings. After a lapse of some weeks, his first letters arrived from Egypt, thin, tattered and worn, as though handled by many, not very clean, hands. They had a characteristic odour of dust and close confinement in canvas bags. Elizabeth said that they smelt 'like the insides of ships'. As sentimental as any girl-heroine in a novel, she kept them tied up in blue ribbon, but repudiated the almost inevitable accompaniment of sweet perfume. The redolence of the army in Egypt was much more romantic than lavender or rosemary.

She began to work at her music again, for next year, when the war was over and Luke had come home, she must be ready to convert their dreams into reality. Every morning saw her at the piano doing her sol-fa exercises. She was tempted to begin singing the operatic parts she had studied, but she remembered Mr Breve and remained obedient to his commands, knowing that she lacked the knowledge of singing technique necessary for the big arias. She confined herself to the Marchesi and Concone exercises and the simple songs she had learned at the Conservatorium. After Luke's departure for the Front, she began to accept invitations to sing at patriotic concerts and the necessity of preparing a repertoire of songs gave an incentive to her work.

The possibility of attacking Turkey by forcing an entrance through the narrows of the Dardanelles had been discussed for some time, and on 23 April the newspapers reported that 20,000 British and French troops had landed at Enos, sixty miles from Gallipoli. When, therefore, on the thirtieth, the news reached Australia of the attack on the Gallipoli beaches by the First Australian and New Zealand Imperial Expeditionary Forces, it was not entirely unexpected. The casualty lists published day after day initiated that tragic procession of names that was to cut deep into the national life. From this time the war took on a different aspect, as seen from the antipodean side of the world. The public mood became harder, more determined, more cohesive. It is sometimes said that such-and-such a date or event marks a 'turning-point' in a situation. The landing of our troops on Gallipoli can truly be so described, for this young nation, lacking self-consciousness, concerned chiefly with the simple business of breaking new soil, making a livelihood, fighting the elementary dangers of climate and terrain, was until then of a malleable, unformed character. In April, 1915, it found itself suddenly in the world's limelight, fighting a desperate and bloody battle against a brave and resourceful enemy. In the hell of the Gallipoli beaches, Australia's nationhood was born.

About this time Mr Inglefell went away to inspect his properties in the north. When he returned he had a terrible story to tell of cattle dying by thousands, of tracts of country, barren, waterless, strewn with the skeletons of sheep and horses, cattle and wild animals. The water-holes, patches of sunken mud under the pitiless sky, were banked high with the withering bodies of the creatures which had struggled to find there the water which had long since disappeared. Hundreds of property-owners left their land and retreated to the city to wait for rain. There was nothing they could do to save their cattle or their crops. Many were ruined. The banks and pastoral companies had extended credit as far as possible, but the drought was so extensive in area and had lasted for such a long time that in the end there was nothing left to mortgage. Men who had worked for years to pioneer and establish their stations and farms now saw the banks foreclosing and counted themselves lucky if they were put back at a modest salary to manage a property that they had once owned.

Mr Inglefell still owned Undaboo, though he had lost almost

к*

everything else. But it was now only a question of months before Undaboo would fall into the hands of his creditors. The drought had reached the stage at which human effort could do no more.

By June the war, too, had entered a grimmer phase. Ypres for months had been the centre of fierce battles. The confident opinion that 'the war will be over by Christmas' was no longer heard.

Mr Inglefell still read the *Morning Register* at the breakfast-table, throwing items of news to his family as crumbs to starving sparrows. But when one morning he emitted a choking exclamation and hurriedly put his tea-cup down on the edge of its saucer, causing Elizabeth to make a running dive to retrieve both from disaster, they knew that something had attracted his attention with more than usual importunity.

He poked at the newsheet with his finger.

'Extraordinary! Fantastic! Can't think what the Government is up to. Suppose I'll have to write to the fellow.'

His family sat round the table, respectfully silent while waiting for enlightenment. Mr Inglefell was not disposed to share his morsel, but sat growling over it to himself like a cat with a mouse.

'Bad policy! Brings the whole thing into disrepute.'

Mrs Inglefell had long ago learned the art of reading her husband's moods. She waited without speaking, and even contrived to look interested in these incoherent fragments. Her daughters were less patient.

'Have you found an important item of war news, Father?' asked Eleanor. Mr Inglefell glanced round the side of the newspaper.

'War news? Who said anything about war news?'

'You didn't, Pa dear,' said Elizabeth naughtily. 'You made lovely volcanic sounds and got us all curious and then didn't tell us what it was about.'

'You know I like to read my paper in peace without irrelevant interruptions,' said Alfred, the martyr. 'Eleanor, pour me some fresh tea. How often have I told you I like my tea very hot.'

Elizabeth got up purposefully, leaned over the table and took the newspaper away from her father's hands.

'Now, you jolly well don't get it back till you've told us what it was you were boiling about,' she said firmly.

'Beth dear, I wish you wouldn't use these slang expressions,' murmured her mother, England's last stand against the rising tide of Australianism. Everyone (except Beth) looked anxiously at the master of the house, expecting the storm to break. But Mr Inglefell secretly enjoyed being bullied by his youngest daughter, and now seemed only mildly surprised that his family had not understood him.

'George Goldiway has been knighted in the King's Birthday Honours,' he said. 'Beth, bring my tea. I'll finish my newspaper in the morning-room.' As this was his invariable habit, the request was complied with as part of the morning's domestic routine, only varied by Beth's loud and unladylike guffaw.

'Oh, glory, glory be!' she sang. 'Think of our Lady Goldiway! There'll be no holding her. Rings on her fingers and, I wouldn't mind betting, bells on her toes.'

'Beth, don't be vulgar,' said her mother, quite sharply, and then had to endure a suffocating embrace.

'Darlingest Mums, you're only jealous. You know you couldn't be a *nouveau riche* if you tried – or should it be *nouvelle* for you?'

In his city office, Clarence Chin sat looking thoughtfully at the newspaper. He decided that it was time he took a holiday and went to see his brother Albert who had a shop in Swanston Street, Melbourne. By midday the next day the brothers were sitting together in the dark little room above the stores of rice and ginger and dried bamboo shoots.

'Everyone should pay his debts,' Clarence was saying. 'Our father left this debt for us to pay. I am receiving every month this man's money. How can I continue to accept his money

when I know that he has never paid his debts – dishonourable
debts – and that it is only the honourable conduct of his creditor
that has kept him out of prison?'

'We must attend to it,' said Albert.

'Yes,' agreed Clarence, 'we must attend to it. I will write to
Edward and tell him to come from Bendigo.'

Three days later Edward arrived from Bendigo and the
brothers had another conference. Clarence and Albert had
used the interval of three days with profit. Albert had many
business acquaintances in the city, not only among the Chinese
colony, but also among the clerks in the banks, among ware-
housemen, importers, Customs officials and wholesale and retail
salesmen. By the time that Edward reached Melbourne there
was little about the financial resources of George Goldiway unknown to the three brothers.

What more natural than that Clarence, on the fourth day,
should call on his employer at the expensive hotel suite where
he was living during his wife's absence, to pay his respects, to
report on the state of his business affairs in Adelaide, to inquire
after his health, to congratulate him on the honour he had just
received from the King, to wish him long life, good health,
and prosperity, but especially prosperity? And what more
natural than that he should be accompanied by his two brothers,
who wished to take this opportunity of being presented to a
man of such importance in their world of trade and
finance?

As Clarence had said, to pay one's debts is an honourable
custom. We will not mention, therefore, the ugly word 'com-
pulsion', much less the even more sinister word 'blackmail'.
We will add simply that a few days later Alfred Inglefell
received a most cordial letter from his old friend, George Goldiway, who explained that, his business affairs having prospered
greatly ('as I told you they would, my dear boy'), he proposed
to recognise his indebtedness to their late partnership by
dispatching a sum of money from time to time until his obliga-

tions had been fulfilled, in accordance with which he enclosed a cheque for ten thousand pounds and remained Alfred's sincere and obliging.

Alfred was agreeably and genuinely surprised, not only because the money was welcome but because the bitterest part of their business failure had been his own misjudgement of his partner's character, and this partial repayment seemed to vindicate his earlier opinion that George was a rough diamond but a good fellow at heart. He became quite cheerful and was able to sign a letter of acknowledgement and congratulation with comparative truth, 'sincerely yours'.

With the coming of the winter, rain began to fall and the crisis of the drought in the southern areas of the State was past. But it would be a long time before its ravages in the north could be repaired, where for years the landscape would be dotted with skeletons, bleak reminders of, or rather witnesses to, this time of ruin and despair. Reminders were not required, for the memories of this drought would be still lively three generations later.

Elizabeth, who of the three girls was closest to their father in affection and understanding, did not fail to notice, even in the midst of her own happiness, how much better he looked, younger and more easily amused. With the coming of the rain they worked in the garden together, rooting out dead shrubs, cutting back those that were burdened with dead wood but showed still some signs of life, and attacking the weeds which had grown with wild abandon in the new moisture. This seemed to both of them one of the happiest periods of their lives. Their days were full of useful and healthful work, and if news from the battle-fronts was constantly graver and more terrible, its harshness was softened by distance and, for Elizabeth, by the blessed ignorance of youth to which suffering is alien and death unfeared because unknown.

Every week the Red Cross sewing circle met in the dining-room. Mr Inglefell always on that day discovered that a vast amount of business required his attention in the city, where he lunched at his club and met his friends of the financial and pastoral world, as an antidote to the somewhat oppressively feminine atmosphere in which he lived at home.

Elizabeth was by this time fairly proficient at knitting, but she and Marian gave most of their attention on these occasions to the preparation of an ample tea for the ladies who came to work. She was therefore free, on an afternoon in July, to open the front door in response to the postman's ring. He handed her a large assortment of mail, and glancing at the envelopes she saw that an English mail must have arrived. There were no letters with Egyptian stamps, so her interest was not as keen as it would otherwise have been. She put the letters and packages down on the hall-table and went into the dining-room to tell her mother.

The room was crowded with some twenty or thirty ladies, all sewing or knitting, and all talking. At the table, Eleanor was cutting out flannelette to a pattern for pyjamas, while in one corner of the room two sewing-machines contributed their own clatter and hum to the general noise.

Among the company, thus so pleasantly and usefully occupied, we recognise without difficulty several old friends. Mrs Robinson, as effusive as ever, was an assiduous attendant at these meetings, which gave her access to the houses, not of her social superiors (that she would not concede, for the late Mr Robinson was of a family whose social eminence she was fond of emphasising), but to houses where fortune had smiled a little more generously than it had on the (alas!) humble establishment that she was able to maintain since Mr Robinson had departed for realms happier and, we hope, more appropriate to his social distinction.

Little Mrs Pennyfarthing, more shrivelled than we remember her thirteen years ago, was however still devoted to the ideals of temperance and never tired, though the same could not, perhaps, be said of her listeners, of extolling the example of

His Majesty who had given up all alcoholic beverages for the duration of the war and who had publicly expressed the hope that the whole Empire would do the same, as a means to personal and national salvation. Listening to her, one was left with the inescapable inference that the Germans were a degraded and barbaric people principally because they drank so much beer and grew some of the best wine in the world. One felt that, according to Mrs Pennyfarthing, '*Hoch, der Kaiser!*' should really be spelt '*Hock, der Kaiser!*'

Mrs Faulkener no longer drove about in her carriage. Cox was growing old and had been pensioned off. Mr F. could not yet quite bring himself to buy a motor-car, so, with the drought and the war as an excuse for economy, the governess-cart, driven by the stable-boy, was used for excursions into the town and to the railway station. Every week the little equipage would turn in at the iron gates and past the monkey-puzzle tree to deposit Mrs Faulkener at the Inglefells' front door. It was a modest arrival, consonant with her quiet, mouse-like appearance which seemed never to change with the passage of years.

In contrast is this splendid Vauxhall motor-car, driven by a uniformed chauffeur, with its high-set seat and glittering brass-work. The lady who emerges is wearing one of the fashionable ankle-length tube skirts, very narrow, its high waist setting off her figure to perfection. A wide-brimmed hat crowned with sweeping ostrich plumes might not seem altogether suitable for a wintry afternoon, but is undoubtedly impressive, especially when accompanied by a long stole of expensive fur. With this evidence of wealth, even of opulence, can we associate the talented Miss Gladys Merriman? Happily the answer is in the affirmative, though she must now be introduced as Mrs Charles McGallun Senior. We refuse to join Elizabeth's amusement at the idea of Gladys Merriman being Sarah Faulkener's step-mother-in-law. She was a good wife to her husband and made him happy in his old age, and if in so doing she became a very

wealthy woman who enjoyed her wealth a trifle too ostenta-
tiously for good taste, can we be sure that our criticism of her
is entirely guiltless of envy?

In the Red Cross working-bee, Mrs Patience came into her
own. As the wife of a colonel in the British Army of India
(retired, it is true, but nonetheless a man of military experience)
she was able to speak with the voice of authority. She was so
very militant, indeed, that only the good manners and the good
nature of the other ladies prevented them from reminding her
that they, too, were British and just as devoted to the Mother
Country as she was.

Elizabeth leaned over her mother's shoulder and said in a
confidential voice: 'The postie's just brought a big mail from
home. I've left it on the hall-table.'

Mrs Inglefell looked about her. All the ladies seemed busily
occupied with their several tasks. Surely she would not be
missed if she went away for just ten minutes to glance at her
letters? She slipped quietly from the room, gathered up the
mail and carried it into the morning-room. Picking out the
envelope which bore her mother's writing, she quickly opened
it and read the contents. Thank goodness, she was safely in her
country house, away from London and in the care of faithful
old servants. Mrs Inglefell smiled as she read her mother's
spirited comments on the conduct of the war. The Germans
seemed almost civilised compared, in her opinion, to several
British generals of her acquaintance.

The next letter that attracted Mrs Inglefell's attention bore
a Scottish postmark. 'That'll be from Clarrie Ross Graver,' she
thought, as she opened it. 'She will have news of Ross.'

Twenty minutes later, her husband, coming in from the city,
found her still sitting with the letter in her hand.

'Eleanor, my dear, are you unwell? You look very pale.'

She turned to him a face on which grief had etched its lines
so deeply that it had become a piteous mask of its gentle self.

Alfred took the letter from her limp hand. As he read it, all the love that had lain for so many years quietly in his heart went out to her in tenderness.

'My love, this is a great sorrow for you. He was a gallant soldier who died doing his duty. It was what he wanted, remember that. He would have wanted no other kind of death.'

They sat together in silence for a long time. At last, more composed, Mrs Inglefell roused herself and turning to her husband, said: 'There is something I want to say, dear Alfred. Ross . . . Ross was such a good man, such a dear friend . . . but Alfred, I do want you to know that I never loved . . . never wanted to marry anyone else but you, my dear.'

When he bent to kiss the hand he was holding, Alfred, with great happiness, thought with gratitude of the man who had valued his love too highly to do other than preserve it honourably.

26

September Comes In

T H E telephone rang.

Elizabeth answered it and remained talking for several minutes. When she came back to the dining-room where the family was at luncheon, her cheeks were flushed and her eyes bright with excitement.

'What do you think?' she exclaimed. 'You'll never guess.' Everyone agreed with her and made no attempt to do so.

'That was the secretary of the committee which is organising the big concert at the Town Hall on the first of September, in aid of the Belgian Relief Fund. And they've asked me to sing. Think of it! In the Town Hall! The Governor and the Lord Mayor and everyone important will be there. Oh Mummie, isn't it wonderful!'

The family were suitably awe-stricken. No matter how much we admire and encourage our loved ones, there is no doubt that we have a tendency to take their talents for granted until the world outside the family circle endorses their claims to achievement.

During the following weeks, Elizabeth spent a good deal of time at the Conservatorium, where her teachers gave her sound advice about a choice of songs for public presentation, as well as some instruction in stage deportment.

At home the discussions raged back and forth on the vexed question of clothes. Marian offered to lend a ravishing dress from Paris, of lilac gauze covered with sequins. Eleanor offered a ball-gown of rose-pink satin. Being a wise mother, as mothers so often are, Mrs Inglefell let the girls enjoy their arguments and their tryings-on in front of the long mirror. Then she quietly brought out a simple dress of white silk which had been made for Elizabeth to take to Italy. It set off her thin figure admirably and suited the colour of her hair which had become darker as she grew older.

When her daughters questioned her choice, Mrs Inglefell explained: 'You see, my dears, Beth will be the youngest performer. I have read the list of people taking part in this concert and they are all well-known, established musicians. Beth will be the only newcomer. She will be given the least important place in the programme. And it will be a sort of début for her. It would be quite unsuitable for her to wear anything elaborate. She should have something that, if anything, makes her look even younger than she is.'

The white dress was decided on, thought not before Beth had cast more than one longing glance at the lilac gauze.

She had been excited but not at all nervous at the prospect of her first public appearance of any consequence. But on the afternoon before the date of the concert, Mrs Inglefell, coming into the schoolroom, found her pacing up and down, weeping uncontrollably. She was, indeed, bordering on hysteria.

'I'll never do it! I'll forget the words, I know I will. I'll die, up there in front of all those people. Oh, Mummie, whatever made me say I'd do it. I'll only make a ghastly fool of myself and you'll all be ashamed of me.'

'Nonsense, you'll do it perfectly well,' said her mother in a matter-of-fact tone. Half an hour later, Elizabeth had been tucked firmly into bed, with an egg-flip laced with brandy and two aspirins. She slept for twelve hours and her attack of stage-fright was over.

The occasion was sufficiently impressive to make even an experienced performer nervous. The Town Hall was so crowded that several rows of chairs had had to be placed on the stage to accommodate members of the audience. The auditorium was draped with the flags of the Allied nations and banked with flowers and greenery. Red velvet chairs were provided for the Governor and his lady and for members of the State and city governments. Moreover, the emotional tension was high, a reflection of the war atmosphere, accentuated by public sympathy for the Belgians who had withstood with such heroism the violation of their country by the Germans. When the Belgian Consul entered to take his seat, the audience rose to its feet and cheered with a fervour second only to that with which the National Anthem was sung on the arrival of the Queen's representative.

Beth made her appearance at the end of the first part of the programme, just before the interval. Although she had recovered from her attack of nerves, she felt, as she looked out across the hundreds of faces in front of her, at the galleries which reached nearly to the ceiling at the back of the hall and on either side of the stage, alone and strange, as though it were not Elizabeth Inglefell who stood there, but someone other than herself. She made her curtsy to the Governor with composure and acknowledged the tentative applause which greeted her entrance on to the stage. She sang correctly and pleasingly, but her voice lacked warmth. The applause was generous rather than spontaneous, appreciative of a lovely voice, and, while kindly encouraging to an obviously young and inexperienced singer, it was not enthusiastic.

Half-way through the second part of the programme, Elizabeth sang again. She had chosen a bracket of three Brahms songs. While she was singing the second, 'Der Schmied', the music, with its emphatic, demanding beat, suddenly took charge of her. Her voice, responding, increased in tone and brilliance. And then she experienced that intoxicating sense of power which comes to a performer, whether orator, actor, or musician, when he knows that he has won control of an audience and can make it laugh or cry, applaud or be silent at his bidding. This time the applause was warm and prolonged. There were cries of 'Encore, encore'.

Elizabeth was now completely in command of herself and her listeners. A second and a third encore were demanded and given. Then she turned to her accompanist and said: 'I will sing "The Lass with the Delicate Air".' When she reached the end of the song she closed it with that cadenza of runs and trills which she had invented for Mr Breve, so long ago. For a moment the pianist was a trifle disconcerted at this unexpected variation, but adapted his rendition after only an instant's hesitation. Elizabeth sang that song for Mr Breve, with all the mischief and the teasing of the first time he had heard her. And there was now an added expression of sadness, almost of irony, that made the interpretation more mature than the thoughtless trilling of a mischievous schoolgirl on the sand-hills. This was her memory of him, her gratitude, her love. This was her tribute to him.

And it was her triumph. The audience was completely under her spell, and they refused to let her leave the stage until she had made many curtsys and showed unmistakably that she would not sing again.

Next morning the newspapers were eloquent in their praise of her performance. The *Morning Register* called her a 'promising young singer'; the *Advertiser* asked rhetorically: 'Have we discovered a new Melba?'

Marian came to her room to ask, quite respectfully, whether she would like breakfast in bed.

'Good Lord,' answered Elizabeth, 'whatever for?' and bounced out of bed with her usual energy.

'We're really proud of you,' said her mother at the breakfast-table. 'The *Register* has given you a paragraph all to yourself.'

Alfred emerged from behind his newspaper long enough to say: 'Well done, my dear,' but the glance he directed towards her from over his glasses did not betray his feeling of intense satisfaction. Apparently that queer old chap, Clifford Breve, had really known what he was talking about. When the war was over he would see that Beth went to Europe and pursued her career.

Elizabeth felt only a sense of relief. She had at last faced an audience of discernment and had acquitted herself, if not brilliantly, at least creditably. She must go on now with steady work.

She went as usual to the schoolroom for her customary hour of practice, and then helped Marian with the housework.

'Ellie has gone to the village,' said Marian. 'She said if you could, would you meet her at twelve o'clock at the Institute to help with the flowers for the Red Cross bridge party tonight. If you do, tell her we'll have lunch at one-thirty in case you are late.'

When Elizabeth returned to the house an hour and a half later, she was carrying an armful of golden wattle. Its heavy, honey-sweet perfume filled the hall as she came in. Mrs Thompson met her at the foot of the stairs. She seemed flustered and upset, as though she had been working over a hot stove.

'Oh, hullo, Mrs Tom,' said Elizabeth. 'Be a dear and put this in water. It was so lovely, I couldn't bear to throw it away, but we had far too much for the Institute, so I brought this lot home.'

Mrs Thompson took the branches from her. 'And your mother says would you go and see her. She's in her room.'

'Right you are. Oh, and Mrs Tom, do hurry up with lunch. I'm starving.'

Elizabeth sprang up the stairs two at a time and left Mrs Thompson staring after her. The heavy branches with their balls of yellow fluff fell unheeded from her grasp as her hands sought the steadying support of the stair-rail.

Elizabeth could hear her mother's voice calling: 'Is that you, Beth?'

'Yes, Mums.'

'Come here for a moment, dear.'

Mrs Inglefell was sitting in a low chair, her hands idle in her lap.

'Come near me, dear.'

The unusual request brought a momentary anxiety. Elizabeth bent over and kissed her cheek. 'We got some gorgeous wattle for the hall. You look a bit peaked, Mummie. Are you all right?'

Her mother reached out and took her hand. 'Beth, I've some bad news for you. Oh, my darling, try not to grieve too much.'

Elizabeth snatched her hand away. 'Tell me,' she said. 'Is it Daddy?'

'No, Beth. It's Luke – Luke Stevens. He's been killed.'

'But that's impossible!'

'I know it seems so, but it is true, my dearest. His father telephoned just now. They knew yesterday, but did not want you to know because of the concert last night.'

The concert last night – all their plans together for the future – Elizabeth felt as though the world had suddenly come to a standstill. Anger, incredulity, and even impatience, swept over her in waves. Grief, not yet.

She turned and went downstairs and out into the garden, past the pepper-tree house, deserted now by the pre-Stopesian family, past the pig-sties and the stables, empty and grass-grown, and so into the paddocks to where the broken-down wall still displayed its gaps in the fallen masonry and the jonquils once again bloomed under the almond trees.

'Dead? How could Luke be dead? People don't just cease to exist, not people as alive as Luke, not people you love.' She flung herself down on the wet grass and fought something within herself that was threatening to strangle her. 'Luke, Luke, where are you? You must be alive, you must be. People can't stop being alive.'

Somewhere out of the echoes of memory a voice said: 'They're not really dead.' It was her mother's voice telling her about the almond trees. They seem dead. But they are only sleeping.'

Elizabeth opened her eyes and looked at the branches over her head. They had shed their blossom. All about her the fallen petals lay in the grass. And now under the tender blue of the September sky, all the branches were clothed in their new green.

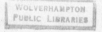